DAMAGED

SOUL SEER CHRONICLES, BOOK 8

S. J. CAIRNS

This is a work of fiction. Names, characters, places, and incidents either are the product of the author's imagination or are used fictitiously. Any resemblance to actual persons, living or dead, events, or locales is entirely coincidental.

No part of this product was generated by the use of artificial intelligence (AI).

Cover design by Getcovers
Logo created by S.J. Cairns
Logo image by CNuisin depositphotos.com ID 265803116
Tree vector by Volykievgenil depositphotos.com ID 184180340

ISBN 978-1-998875-01-6 (Ebook)
ISBN 978-1-998875-02-3 (Paperback)
ISBN 978-1-998875-03-0 (Hardcover)

Black Thumb Publishing
Ontario, Canada
www.sjcairns.com

 Formatted with Vellum

Homeschoolers: For making your journeys known so others like me could do our best to provide meaningful knowledge to growing young minds in loving environments.

Public Schools: For offering a nurturing space for the future brains in charge of our planet and giving this grieving homeschool mom the freedom to delve into fantastical worlds with undivided attention.

ACKNOWLEDGMENTS

I want to acknowledge those who took this ride with me and made any efforts to encourage me through the trying times of an author journey while parenting a little one, including focusing me in my lack of time to create, and providing knowledge of the ever-changing writerly world.

This series is a labour of love and would be nowhere without the attentions of those who owe me nothing and freely gave everything.

1

MERCILESS CREATIVITY

Donovan

The sick fuck was finally dead. Not dead by someone else's rumoured account or a sketchy disappearance scheme. Sophie obliterated Brandon into nothing more than a skid mark of what our father molded into my replacement when I turned down his gift of ruling at his side time and time again.

Not that Brandon was my true brother outside of sharing Tobias Sorrel's DNA, but still...dead? Brandon was dead.

Tobias must be fuming about losing his right-hand psychopath. A grave inconvenience instead of true grief over losing a child.

Who was next in line for the Sorrel throne? Jesse? No, he died in the first fight at Diluculo. I think. Too easy a death for such a pri—

Pain exploded in my shin. "Ow! What the fuck?"

Hall sat across from me at a Prison Creation cafeteria table and pointed at my plate. "I said, you gonna eat that or turn it into art?"

I rubbed my leg to dull the throbbing. "My shin's not made of steel, y'know? Unlike your boot."

Hall scoffed and snatched my plate. "Don't be dramatic."

Kim sipped on some kind of herbal mixture from a mug next to the big guy. "Plus, Sophie felt that."

"Good," Hall spoke around a mouthful of my cold fries. "She could use the reality check, too."

I snatched the plate back from Hall.

"For real?"

"For real my fries. Stand your Viking ass in line for more." Once the Prison Creation bloated with Magics, food scarcity was erased and magically formulated to serve an endless array of food options day and night. And right now, tragic deaths from Loring hitting the Niagara Falls tourist area was cause for people stuffing their faces like they were choosing their death row last meals. Or celebrating the fact they were among the breathing.

"How're things with Sophie?" Kim slid her plate over to Hall with half her fries and some strawberries left. She missed Hall's expression of adoration while waiting for my response. You'd think she delivered a platter of gold coins in a bikini.

"Right, 'cuz that's a better subject." I twisted my neck to the side, the movement doing nothing to release my tense muscles. "The Ballards lost people in the Niagara Falls attack. Olive's devastated. The family's lost enough, including killing their homicidal ancestor and the collapse of their family estate. None of that equals happiness for Sophie, even if she was herself."

And she sure as fuck wasn't. Nothing about her was right.

"Has the Soul Magic re-connection changed anything? It seemed like it did."

I leaned back into my chair and rubbed my hands across my face, the pressure not enough to relax the strain in Sophie's features as she was upset about something somewhere else.

Kim always had questions I couldn't answer.

"Who knows. If it's not her problematic attitude, it's mine. Antagonistic at best. Could be the Soul Magic needs more healing or maybe she just hates me. She's not actively trying to slit my throat, so that's something."

Kim scowled. "Low bar, buddy. Don't give up. Feeling all the little bits of love from you and whatever else you two feel through the connection will help."

"*Pfft.*" Hall telekinetically snatched back my plate, having polished off Kim's. He popped a forgotten pickle into his mouth and devoured the fries. "Short of delivering Vincent to her cell door, nothing will turn the woman's head around."

I leaned forward, elbows on the table. "You think?"

Hall stopped chomping and then pointed at me with a fry. "No."

"Hmmm." I looked up at the ceiling as if thinking something over.

"Donovan. No." The growl in Hall's tone was one you used to order around a dog.

"What?" Kim missed the twinkle in my eye Hall caught when the 'ah-ha' moment hit me.

I hurried from the cafeteria, ignoring Hall's protests and Kim's confused questioning.

A shitload of muscle blocked my way, dragged me into the nearest office by my shirtfront, and shoved me into the wall. Hall stepped nose-to-nose, the Viking in him visible behind a thin film of restraint as he pressed a strong arm across my collarbones to lock me in place. The issue with the tactic was that Hall was one of countless who opted to drive their brand of common sense into me through intimidation.

I was not scared.

A click was Kim shutting the office door. "Someone start talking. What'd I miss?"

I focused on Hall's unblinking icy blue eyes. "Gotta be done anyway."

Hall exhaled through his nostrils, his breath smelling of my stolen pickle. "Not so you can win your girl's favour. Try flowers and a cock ring. Or, I don't know, engaging in an adult conversation."

"A cock ring? Gross." Kim stood at Hall's shoulder, eyes narrowed at me. "What exactly are you trying to do?"

Hall shook the arm digging into my collarbones. "This moronic masochist wants to bust into the Sovereignty and sashay through the front doors with the son of one of the most prominent figure heads of our system of law tucked under his arm like he's on a bagel run."

It took Kim a moment to process what Hall meant. "You wanna break Vincent out of a Sovereignty prison cell?"

Hall growled with frustration. "You'll kill yourself and Sophie in the process and Vincent will still rot. If not his body, he'll lose his mind in there. Not to mention when Vincent learns of your deaths, which I'm sure his daddy or brother would be much obliged to relay, then Vincent will blame himself. Again. You two may not be around to see the devastation Vincent endures every time he loses you both, but I have been too many times whether I knew of your Soul Magic or his role as Overseer or not. After you're buried alive, burned, run off a cliff, shot, or killed in any number of ways Fate decides to punch your card, things turn really ugly. Vincent doesn't move on. Maybe the first couple of times he did. By now, he's learned how pointless it is when you'll eventually show up again. He holds his breath until the next time either of you trips into his path, and then he gets the pleasure of deciding if enough years have passed for him to endure another smashing heartbreak when you're inevitably ripped from his life again."

Kim mumbled something and shifted in my periphery, clearly uneasy with the reality of the impact of Sophie and my Soul Magic glitch.

Questions buzzed in my brain about all of the things Hall mentioned since I certainly didn't remember being forced off of a cliff and Sophie hasn't read into our past lives. Though, I'm not sure why. If I had the capability to do so I'd have already done it and taken notes.

"Come with me."

Creases in Hall's forehead deepened. "This is not the time for a recruitment speech."

Kim laid a hand on Hall's muscled arm holding me captive. "I bet we could do it."

He straightened, releasing me to stare at her, his jaw slack, brow furrowed in search of whatever punchline she must be getting to.

To her credit, Kim was never visibly put off by the big guy. "We have internal contacts in place, weapons on top of many fighters with an array of abilities, intimate knowledge of the Sovereignty, and a deeply safeguarded place to retreat to regardless of success. You've said it before, it's time for fence-sitters to jump to a side. We need a workable plan, obviously, but insiders know schematics, schedules, what type of Magics we'll encounter—"

"Ones who will slice through your irresistible throat to convey a message to all others to quash their audacious vendettas so they don't end up in the same feckless bloodshed. Or worse, they'll imprison you. You'll remain subject to the Llewellyns' merciless creativity until they grow bored, or any others still alive who remember your rebellion are long dead, and you're forgotten in their system. I will damn every soul to a gory and painful end, including my own, before I allow the Sovereignty to place a hand on you."

A softness overtook Kim as her crossed-armed step brought her closer to an impassioned Hall, a wordless plea in a lingering outward silence between them.

I recognized the look in their eyes. Sophie and I shared many of the same, and I watched something non-magic work on Hall as the big guy's tense shoulders fell. Whatever passed between them was enough to get Hall on board. He hadn't said anything, he still focused on Kim, but those few relenting moments told me I wasn't alone in this.

I swallowed through the awkwardness since my presence was clearly forgotten. "Who else can we trust?"

My question went unanswered as Hall absorbed the gravity of our mission or whatever he felt for Kim in their brief telepathic exchange. If the big guy's feelings ran anywhere as hot or as deep as what spilled from him a moment ago, he would cross an ocean in a

Solo cup raft if it meant Kim was encouraging him to reach the other side.

Kim recovered faster than Hall. "Sophie has to come. Even if she's half her normal self, leaving her behind is absurd. Caine's persuasion is super useful, though he hasn't been in the field much since the Creation escape. Maybe he'll talk Ness into joining. Her illusion skills are prime, and she wouldn't rat us out to Ranlyn. Neither would Derek, though I don't know much about his skills beyond his ability to survive. Ranlyn has immense skills all his own, but he's a Mother Coven Elder. No way he's up for that kind of a political warfare. Same with Veata."

Understatement. Ranlyn was Sophie's first bodyguard, but once the guy became an Elder, he weighed every action so thoroughly the rest of us waited too long for him to act. Veata was aloof but calculated and a bit of a wildcard.

"What about the other Tactical Team members?" Kim glanced between us.

Hall lifted his bowed head looking to me as if to ask the same. Maybe he couldn't speak yet.

With Jessabelle bled dry by a devotee during Loring's attack in Niagara Falls, the remaining Team's mindset could go one of two ways. Bent on revenge and ready to rescue their leader at all costs or sunk in despair at the loss of their comrade and refusing to forge a mission which could result in further losses. The pinch was without asking, there was no telling which side they would land, and once they were questioned, we risked them going to the Elders.

"I think our best bet is going straight to Lincoln."

I couldn't help but laugh at Kim's suggestion. "Lincoln'll crawl straight to Ranlyn."

"Think about it, Jessabelle would've been perfect, but she's gone. Bronya is, well, we all know what Bronya is, and she won't help us."

Hall gave me a pointed stare. "Give her fifteen minutes of your time and she would comply to your every desire."

Guess Hall found his voice.

I returned his glare. “Not even with a hazmat suit, man.”

Kim ignored our commentary. “Gregor, Ismail, Arden... They’re soldiers and will adhere to the chain of command. Whatever Lincoln says, goes. Why not start at the top?”

Hall ran a hand over his stubbled jaw. “The guy does have the contacts we need. We can’t move in without those names. I have my own contacts, but we don’t want to use them only to be accidently blocked by Lincoln’s in some state of confusion.”

I scoffed. “Have fun convincing him to give them up.”

Hall shot me a questioning brow.

I scoffed again. “You think Lincoln’s all about pleasing me? He may not be your karaoke buddy, but he likes you more than me. I may as well be Sophie, and everyone knows what he thinks of her.”

The argument was made that Lincoln’s opinions of Hall were neutral enough to slide a word in without Lincoln dropping dead from laughter or locking Hall up in a cell. Hall has known Vincent longer than anyone. If he played up the sympathy bargaining chip, it may work.

“What about Caine?” Hall asked.

My laugh was sharp. “You’re really that freaked to talk to Lincoln?”

“Freaked?” Hall pointed at his chest. “I don’t freak. Furthermore, I see failure days ahead of destruction.”

“You mean you want Caine to persuade the info we need from Lincoln?” Kim pinpointed the gist.

Hall gave an affirmative head tilt at her. “Would be cleaner. Caine can gather the info and erase the conversation. Result without consequence.”

“If Caine goes the shady way, but can’t erase Lincoln’s memories of it or if it’s only temporary memory loss, Lincoln will never trust us again.” Kim stated this like it was some great tragedy. “I’m not sure how strong he is without Gareth’s magic attached to him.”

Without Aunt Lacey’s piggy-backing son funnelling his after-life power through Caine’s vessel, results could be unpredictable. What I saw of them as a team while trapped inside Diluculo while protecting the other survivors from Evaristus and Loring's daily attacks was impressive. We could use some teamwork now. If only I hadn't disintegrated Gareth's ancient ass and ended his slow takeover of Caine's body.

"Asking Caine first is still safer than asking Lincoln. Wait here," I told them. "You two can chat freely about whatever sweet nothings you telepathically exchanged while I find Caine. Spell lock the door if things get sweaty."

"Come on, man." Hall's complaint was weak.

Kim tried calling after me, the door closing them and their soon-to-be intimate and awkward conversation in.

I spotted Caine playing cards with Jet and Andy at a cafeteria table. The kid was clearly having trouble sleeping since it was late at night, and he was in racecar pajamas. Not that he needed an excuse to stay comfy since he never went anywhere.

I plonked into a seat next to Caine and across from Andy who I hadn't spent much time with since his mother returned. "Hey, kid. Any money riding on a win?"

Andy flashed a huge smile, devoid of any fear, so I guess I didn't have any telltale death spots on me. "Three new spells and a trip to Canada's Wonderland."

"Keepin' it diverse. Nice!" We exchanged a hearty high-five.

Jet placed down a card. "Thanks for teaching him how to gamble, by the way."

"Yyeaahh. Sorry, I wasn't raised around kid's games and there's not much to do when you're in hiding. Everything from extra snacks to your wildest dream is on the table."

"Don't I know it." Jet's exhausted smile was a testament to the dedicated effort of entertaining a kid in the least enjoyable place ever.

Playing Evaristus's captive and literal flying assassin did a number on her. She wore it on her skin like a lengthy illness and still wasn't quite herself. Guaranteed she woke Andy up from a healthy dose of post-traumatic night terrors.

I pointed at Caine and motioned to a table in the corner. He excused himself and followed, probably thinking it was about Sophie. Who would have thought my relationship with Caine would be less arduous than with her.

Weird fucking times.

I dove into our plan to break out Vincent, and the role Caine would play in the initial stages and inside the Sovereignty if he chose to join the rescue party.

Caine shrugged. "Sure."

"Really?"

"Sure," he repeated.

I searched his face for any indication of him screwing with me. "I expected to slam nose first into a wall."

Caine half-smiled. "Don't get me wrong, I know your true motivations lie with Sophie's happiness and have little to do with Vincent himself."

Damn. I hadn't even mentioned Sophie. "They can't be both?"

"They can, but they're not. Regardless of how it impacts anyone else, getting him from behind enemy lines is a no-brainer. We aren't a military, but even the Blind don't leave their soldiers behind."

"Even if Vincent put himself in there?" I wasn't arguing, simply poking holes in Caine's resolve now instead of risking him ducking out later.

"A greater purpose lands most of us in hot water. He needed to find Cora-Lynn's soul and fumbled. Doesn't mean we forget about him."

"And you're agreeing to our method of info retrieval knowing full well the other Elders will be pissed, Lincoln might murder you afterwards, and we may get dusted or stuck in the Sovereignty cells ourselves? They'd sure love to get a hold of you."

The edges of Caine's lips downturned. "I'll have a few conversations with some people first, but like I said...sure."

"Okay then. We'll need you for phase one when we can find Lincoln."

Caine nodded. "Not going anywhere."

With Caine on board, we stood a chance. If he siphoned the information we needed and then decided not to join the actual rescue attempt, we still had a leg-up.

Hope was a dangerous drug I could carry around in my jock all day.

I headed for the office where I left Kim and Hall, seeing the back of Hall's blond head and Kim's red mane bobbing in the crowd walking away from me.

"Hold up, bitch!" I sent into Kim's far too accessible mind.

Kim spun in search for me, Sophie's cousins Kevin and Shannon nearly barrelling into her and Hall, the big guy snapping up a muscular arm saving them all from collision.

Always on high alert.

Lifting a few fingers and motioning them to follow me, we re-entered the office.

"Bitch? Really?"

"I haven't seen Denise much. Needed to hit quota."

"Does this playful attitude mean Caine's in?" Hall read me well.

"He said, 'Sure'."

Kim crossed her arms. "And you actually told him everything and didn't trick him?"

"No tricks. All areas covered, all negative consequences explored. He still said, 'Sure'."

Hall leaned down close to Kim's ear in a mock whisper. "Guess you owe me one-hundred bones, kitten."

Kim huffed and popped up her shoulder to knock him in the chin.

Hall gave a deep-chested laugh and pushed his hands into his pockets. "Caine knows what it's like to be left behind. No way he bows out of this."

"Whatever," Kim mumbled. "Fine. I'll find Sophie and let her know it's in the works. You guys round up Lincoln."

"One more thing." Hall stopped her motivated steps with a

gentle hand on her waist, contact she didn't balk at. "Going in for Vincent may also mean leaving a blood trail. Not everyone in-house is Tainted or deserves to be cannon fodder. Be them lowly pencil pushers or Alasdair himself, if anyone dies, we better be sure we get Lewy back. If not, they'll move Vincent, tighten protocols, and it'll be another six decades until we find his location and then longer to dig him out of whatever lowly cell they stashed him in. Plus, we kill Alasdair or Chase during entry or exit and still don't free Lewy, no cave or hovel in the world will be sufficient enough to hide in."

"I get it." And I did. If we messed this up, we were all fucked.

"I hope you do, because you won't be invited into my burrow." Hall winked at Kim. "Don't worry. It'll be big enough for two."

She raised an eyebrow. "Perfect. You can steal a dog and save on flea shampoo."

"I envisioned more purring and less belly rubs, kitten."

Kim rolled her eyes and left to find Sophie. Hall chuckled in a way that said he didn't believe she was as put off as she wanted him to think she was.

We left in search of Caine in the cafeteria, hoping Lincoln was somewhere easily accessible.

"You gonna keep pressing until she gives in?" I asked the big guy. "People call that coercion nowadays."

"You assume she hasn't given in already."

I side-eyed Hall.

"Not in that way, you fiend. Not like I would gossip about it."

"As if everyone couldn't tell if you did. You'd probably beat your chest to a Viking chant while the sheets were still wet."

Hall chucked. "Try and stop me. Nah, nothing of the sort. Not yet. But in other ways that prove far more intimate than something as pedestrian as sex."

"Right. Well, people have noticed you're always together, sneaking off, or doing that intense stare thing you did before giving in to my plan. You don't care what people think, but she does. Something's changed."

Hall sanded his palms together. "Small place. Privacy equipped with locking mechanisms are in short supply."

I whistled and waved at Caine from the cafeteria entrance.

He lifted a finger for us to wait a second and then returned to the card game.

I hoped to see Lincoln in the mix of Magics milling about. "Frog's still an obstacle, last I heard."

"Not the man himself, only the prospect of a questionable future she once held hope for and doesn't see so clearly anymore. Even with awareness of her power, he knows nothing of her worth."

"And she's not convinced you do?"

"Oh, she knows. Complications arise when considering a future involving someone who has spent the majority of their immortal years in my line of employment."

"Right. Recondite Magics aren't exactly known for honesty. Plus, immortality means she doesn't want to be another toy you break and relocate. Frog's a safer choice."

Hall chuckled. "Like Caine was a safer choice for Sophie?"

If the Soul Magic wasn't a factor, he was probably right. Though, the fact Caine could use his persuasion to control her wasn't a positive relationship trait.

"I'm not a man who wastes his time with shallow conquests. Too old for the drama. Played it in spades and now I invest energy where I see a high percentage of success. Not cocky, I see it as it is. Though, I could ask my contact about any beach bunnies Frog's been spending time with on that Caribbean resort he ended up at if she requires the proof. I guarantee a few are tending to his bruised ego."

Caine started our way.

"You hired a tail for your future girl's current boytoy?"

Hall shrugged. "Had to confirm he followed through with Caine's instructions. For all we knew, the persuasion may have dropped with the significant distance he travelled. He could've also bailed or told his buddies all about what happened with Loring."

Caine approached us. "What's up?"

I turned to him. "Frog made it to the beach and your persuasion's held up."

Caine narrowed his grey eyes. "Didn't know it was in question."

I turned to Hall. "Neither did I. Did Ranlyn ask you to check in on Caine's froggy buddy or were you bored?"

"Plenty entertained, just thorough."

I looked back at Caine who was clearly confused. "Lets find Lincoln and fuck with his head."

2

PINKY TOES

Sophie

Why I thought I could be a psychologist of any sort was a sad TV sitcom cancelled mid-first season. Like my degree, which has been relegated to "waste of time and money" status for too long. Half of the time I was a headcase, struggling for cultivated coping mechanisms learned from what felt like a literal lifetime ago. Deep breathing exercises fell flat against the grief of family murdered by Tainted evil who were actively hunting me. Plus, the Ballard Estate was a heap of twisted metal, crumbled stone, and family history.

Nothing I said or did could console Olive or anyone else, except finding the aunts and delivering them their prized pet for Olive since it was the only thing she asked of me.

I held up the semi-translucent, dark red, container housing Ferdinand the Pompeii Worm by its braided rope handles into the Prison Creation's lobby lights, watching it squirm and thinking about how it spent time in Donovan's brain to connect him to Caine in Diluculo. Poor thing.

"Hey, you!" Kim and her bright, sunny attitude came towards me through the crowd.

"Gotta deal with this." I headed off in the opposite direction in search of my aunts. Did Olive tell me where they were? Shit. I can't bother her again while she was a bag of tears and exhaustion.

"We've got a V-man plan."

I stopped and whirled on Kim. Ferdinand's container clanged off of the ground, my arms having dropped in shock of what Kim said, hoping 'V-man' meant Vincent and not some weird porn name. I lifted Ferdinand up. He wasn't leaking, but if he had ears beneath his fuzzy, white, body they were ringing.

"What are you talking about?"

Kim slid a suspicious glare around us.

"Think about whatever you can't say." If I could read her mind, she wouldn't have to speak aloud. Others could still listen in, but it was less chancy.

Kim worked through the plan.

"Did Donovan manipulate Caine? Caine doesn't need the hassle after—"

"Whoa, whoa. Be real, Donovan can't manipulate Caine. But we need more information—"

"Okay. Fine." I left to head somewhere, then remembered I didn't know where. "I need to find my aunts."

"On it."

Kim took a second and then pointed towards the cafeteria, her guiding light leading us right to them. I handed off Ferdinand without a word to my hat-wearing, scowling twin aunts playing some kind of card game with my Aunt Priscilla and Tapi and then joined Kim in her search for Caveman. Since it was Donovan's plan, you'd think she'd be looking for him, but her thoughts were on Caveman more and more these days.

Maybe Donovan wouldn't be with him. For some reason, I wasn't looking forward to seeing the guy. Certainly not as excited as Kim was to see Caveman.

The Soul Magic was fixed enough for us to feel each other's emotions again and I felt completely different now than when we talked in the lobby, but something changed. Again. Not fully, yet enough to second-guess his motives for every single thing he did. Including saving Vincent. Why was he gung-ho to go after him and without the help of the Tactical Team or the Elders? Suspicion was thick and murky across the connection. All mine? What was he up to?

Kim led me to one of the smaller offices and knocked. Hall answered, confident about letting the knocker in as if he knew who it was. Was he dialled into Kim's mind twenty-four-seven? Or did she reach his somehow?

We hustled into the room. Hall closed the door behind us and murmured a lock spell. Caine's casual voice pulled my attention to him sitting in a chair facing us, but his grey eyes were focused on Lincoln, the Tactical Team Leader seated in a chair across from him.

Donovan's attention flitted to me as I entered, his emotions flickering with expectation and disappointment.

I found a spot to stand, one away from him. Kim joined Caveman who explained something to her in a hushed voice too low to overhear. His icy stare settled on her with an intensity I envied as I actively tried to ignore Donovan's pining by concentrating on the men in the chairs.

The racing thrill of awakened energy hung in the room, nudging mine to join in the fun. It took me a beat to tamp my power down so it wouldn't switch into party mode without my say-so.

How long ago was it since Caine discovered his gift? Less than a year? It seemed like yesterday as well as a decade ago. Too much had gone down. Now look at him. Cool as a cucumber with no visible conflict for removing Lincoln's free will. And Kim possessed her own magic and was sidled up to a literal immortal Viking as they looked over at their comrades like this interrogation was an everyday garbage run.

How did we get here?

"What Sovereignty department does John Weaver work in and what does he do?" Caine asked Lincoln, arms folded across his broad chest as he awaited an answer.

"Account Services, payroll, bookkeeping, both sets on and off the ledgers," Lincoln responded in a robotic-detached tone indicating Caine's full control.

Caine turned to Caveman in silent question for confirmation. He nodded and returned to whispering to Kim.

He continued. "What do you know of the Magic guarding the Sovereignty cells?"

"Jim. Alias. Birth name unknown. Worked in the department for two years. No Tainted affiliations. Teenage son with an ex-common-law partner living in Toronto."

"How can we reach Jim?"

"Through an off-grid burner phone."

"Do you have the number in your cell phone?"

"Yes."

"Unlock your phone and give it to me."

Passing it over without hesitation, Caine took the unlocked phone from Lincoln and tossed it to Donovan who caught it with little effort and began searching its contents.

"Are there other numbers on your phone of Sovereignty insider contacts?" Caine asked Lincoln.

"Yes."

"Who?"

"Chase Llewellyn, Patricia Sparks, Jeremia—"

"Stop," Caine said suddenly as he and the rest of us did our best to keep our chins off our shoes when Lincoln mentioned Vincent's brother. "Why is Chase Llewellyn considered an insider contact?"

"Chase is who I speak with when providing information regarding the Mother Coven."

The hammer dropped so loudly we all spun to each other in awe. Caveman swore in a foreign language and Caine raised a hand to settle the small crowd and sat forward, elbows to knees, in his chair.

"How long have you been providing the Sovereignty with information regarding the Mother Coven?"

The air in the room thickened with the tingle of power each of us was dying to use on the guy we thought was acting in our best interests, and we held our breaths as we waited to hear how long Lincoln had been betraying everyone.

"Since the Diluculo Creation was sealed."

A chorus of "What the fuck!" filled the room as the timeline of Lincoln's deceit set in. It had been many months since Caine jumped back into the Diluculo Creation seconds before we locked him and others, including Evaristus and Loring, inside. Months of Lincoln siphoning intel to Chase.

What could Chase have known? What injuries and deaths was Lincoln responsible for? The list could be extensive.

Caine raised a hand again to stop anyone asking their own questions and messing with his process.

"Why'd you start secretly communicating with Chase when the Creation was sealed?"

"Anne-Claire was killed during that battle. She was my everything. I went to Chase Lewellyn for justice. He promised me it would come. When there was talk of immediately re-opening the Creation, I went to Chase again, asking about the lack of progress. He offered more promises and in payment insisted he know everything about the Mother Coven so when Loring and Evaristus were released, he could bring them in in a way that would circumvent any interference from Vincent."

Of all the excuses for such treason, Anne-Claire being killed made the most sense. Everyone loved her and she loved many of them in return. Or at least a part of her did according to Donovan who claimed to have "loved" Anne-Claire at least once.

Working with Vincent for however long Lincoln was on the Tactical Team should have been enough for him to know Chase's promises held less value than penny candy. Was he truly so desperate? Why not exact his own justice? Or go to Vincent?

Caine scratched at his five o'clock shadow and took a second in thought. "Did you believe the Sovereignty would try Loring and Evaristus in court for their crimes?"

"Yes."

"Do you believe that now?"

"No."

"Why not?"

"The Sovereignty will ensure Loring dies."

"Then why do you continue to funnel information to Chase?"

"The Sovereignty does justice how it should be done. Murderers of innocents should die. Others deserve worse and end up in the cells where they are punished until they wish for death."

Umm, wow. How did Vincent miss this?

"Do any of the Elders know you speak to Chase?" Caine asked once Caveman prompted him.

"No. They are contributors to the problem."

Okay. So, one of Vincent's biggest weapons against the enemy didn't even trust the Elders he protected.

"Does Vincent know you speak to Chase?" Caine continued.

"No. Vincent is the worst of them all. His rebellion is tentative. His faith in his people is presumptuous and ill-directed. He only cares about Cora-Lynn's soul and his Charges' life and death cycles."

Lincoln has known Vincent in this lifetime longer than I have, but I knew he was wrong. Vincent cared about a lot of things and saying otherwise sounded like a bunch of whining.

"Go find Ranlyn and Veata," Caine said to Caveman and then refocused on Lincoln as Caveman and Kim left. She presumably used her guiding light to find them. "Do you know where Cora-Lynn's soul is?"

"In her body."

"Whoa, whoa, whoa." This answer confused everyone and stopped Caveman in his tracks. He did a double-take, standing close to Lincoln. "Pause the interrogation." Caveman then picked up the office phone, spoke to the front desk guard and gave instructions to find the Elders immediately and meet us in the office as we were interrogating a newly discovered mole.

That should get Ranlyn and Veata moving.

When Caveman's call ended, Caine asked Lincoln what he meant by Cora-Lynn's soul being in her body.

"Cora-Lynn's soul is in her body," Lincoln reiterated without further enlightenment.

I gasped. Everyone's attention shifted to me. "Holy shit. Cora-Lynn's alive."

My surprise echoed through the connection within Donovan and tennis-matched back at me, stuttering my control.

"Ask the piece of shit if Cora-Lynn is alive." Caveman was a wall of clenched muscles and a menacing stare trained on Lincoln.

Caine asked Caveman's question.

"Yes," Lincoln answered.

I wanted to strangle the fucker. Not just Lincoln for being a deceitful little mealworm, but Chase. Chances were Lincoln only knew about Cora-Lynn because Chase bragged about the end-all leverage they held over Vincent, it being some kind of proof or carrot to keep Lincoln on the hook and willing to provide information when Chase came calling. As long as the jackhole thought he had one-up on Vincent, Lincoln would continue to lead the Tactical Team and feed any and all information Chase's way.

So much for loyalty.

"Is Cora-Lynn in the Sovereignty cells?" I heard Caine ask through the onslaught of anger railing through me.

"Yes."

"Is Vincent and Cora-Lynn together?"

"Yes."

Ohmygod!

Caveman shook his head. "Why give Vincent what he's wanted all this time? Makes no sense."

Caine asked Lincoln if he knew why Vincent and Cora-Lynn were imprisoned together.

"They've been grooming Cora-Lynn to kill Vincent for centuries."

Grooming her? Holy shit.

Caveman paced, anger sloughing off of him in waves of repressed power. How long was Cora-Lynn imprisoned? Vincent said she died a long time ago, but how long? Decades? Centuries? Caveman probably knew.

The Elders entered the room, the confusion plain on Ranlyn's expression as he stood next to me and saw Caine and Lincoln. After seeing the blank look on Lincoln's face, he gestured to Lincoln as if to ask what was going on.

"It's bad, Jeeves," I said to Ranlyn. "Real fucking bad."

"Of course it is," Ranlyn mumbled. "Catch us up."

Caine refocused on Lincoln. "How long have you been providing Mother Coven insider information to Chase Llewellyn?"

I saw Ranlyn's shoulders drop in my peripherals under the weight of another crisis.

"Since the Diluculo Creation was sealed," Lincoln answered again.

Ranlyn exhaled, closed his eyes, and rubbed his fingers into his forehead to ease his building exhaustion.

"Who is in the Sovereignty cell with Vincent?" Caine asked.

"Cora-Lynn Llewellyn."

Ranlyn's attention sharpened.

I managed to pull my glare away from Lincoln to face Ranlyn. "She's alive. And they were put together hoping Cora-Lynn would kill him."

Ranlyn fought to swallow his shock as Veata asked, "Why keep her alive at all?"

I leaned to the side to see Veata around Ranlyn. "'Cuz they're sick fucks who enjoy a good laugh."

Ranlyn crossed his arms, his dirty-blond brows scrunched in thought of the game-changing information.

Caine went quiet, holding Lincoln's will, awaiting a directive from the Elders.

Donovan came up next to me, focused on Ranlyn and Veata. "We need to go in now."

I stopped myself from cringing away from his close proximity, reminding myself hours ago—at most a day—I hugged him and didn't keel over. Though, the sensation of disgust slowly seeped in and I couldn't shake it.

"Do the Llewellyns' know where this Creation is?" Ranlyn prompted Caine, who then posed the question to our newest enemy.

"No," Lincoln answered.

Okay. One good thing to come out of the asshole's lips.

"Why didn't you tell Chase where the Prison Creation is?" Caine asked Lincoln.

"I didn't trust Chase to follow through on his promises if I provided the entirety of my information. I was waiting until the Sovereignty killed or imprisoned Loring. And since I'm currently hiding inside of the Prison Creation, it didn't make strategic sense to put my own life in danger."

Selfish bastard.

Ranlyn nodded with relief and rubbed a finger over his bottom lip in thought. "Are any of the other Tactical Team members in on this with him or aware of his connections to the Sovereignty?"

Caine rephrased on Ranlyn's behalf.

"No," Lincoln answered.

This too came as a relief to Ranlyn, and I wondered if it wasn't his way of confirming the other bodies in the room weren't traitors as well.

"Jeeves..." I waited until Ranlyn focused on me. "The longer we wait, the greater chance we have of losing Vincent. We don't even need to worry about a side-mission to find Cora-Lynn's soul since they're together. And while we planned on doing this without you so you didn't have to decide where you stood as an Elder, a Mother Coven member, or Vincent's friend, clearly things are complicated. We came to you and Veata. Should we regret that?"

His stare was hard. I couldn't read his mind, but he was likely unhappy it was another mission we were cutting him from, even if for good reason.

"Here's Lincoln's phone." Donovan passed it over. "He said there're other Sovereignty contacts in there and was listing them when we lost it over Chase being named. I'd bet my pinky toes if you let Caine at him for a while longer we'd discover more in an hour than in the last three months."

The pinky toes comment flashed an image of Donovan shirtless and barefoot in low-hanging lounge pants to my mind. I flushed with unwanted heat which switched to discomfort of a different kind when I realized Donovan felt as I did. Like I needed him getting all hot and bothered right now.

Ranlyn briefly glanced at Veata behind him. "I'm not arguing the urgency here—"

"But you *are* arguing when it should be a cut and dried move." If he was seeking an ally with Veata, she wasn't sticking up for him as I continued to pressure Ranlyn for action. "For all we know, Lincoln has a system with Chase. Some scheduled time or date and he'll stand Chase up while we're busy interrogating him."

"Lewy wouldn't leave any of us in there." Caveman's voice was lined with a growl. He had remained quiet since the truth of Cora-Lynn's condition dropped, yet every part of him appeared to fight a constant motion, full of wrath and at risk of exploding. Kim side-eyeing him as if she expected him to blow up any second was slightly off-putting, though Caveman detonating may help convince Ranlyn to move his ass.

"No, he wouldn't," Donovan agreed, surprising more than me. "We need the rest of the Team on board, find out who's on the night shift at the Sovereignty, and slip in while the head dick is snuggled in his Blind-skinned duvet cover."

"Learn some tact, boy." Veata shook her head and *tsked* him.

"Born in it, but not of it. Even Loring displays better political prowess with his enemies than you of your own kind."

Donovan craned his head around Ranlyn to glare at his biggest critic. "My own kind is my enemy. You want politics, fetch the only other Elder this Coven has so you can work on your voter base."

Veata braced her weight on her cane. "I know your tongue seeks action, but I assure you it is nothing to be proud of and amounts to rallying a frog to leap in front of the wheels of your car." She *tsked* him again. "Ineffective."

The woman wasn't finished with Donovan. "If you worked as well with your words as you do with your hips maybe your soulmate wouldn't detest the very memory of your half-naked form, right down to those pinky toes you mentioned, and you would have earned your Elder's ear."

Great. Outing me to prove your point. Thanks, girl.

She raised a brow at me, maybe overhearing my thoughts and dismissed their importance.

Donovan scoffed. "I don't want your ears. I want you to pop your head outta your ass—"

"Okay, okay," Kim interjected and glared at Caveman still pacing behind her as if he was going to start throwing office décor if they didn't quit arguing in circles. "Fine. If you don't want to do it this second because of whatever reason, what are your timelines when considering the priority of Vincent's life?"

"See?" Veata smiled, showing her yellowing teeth. "The Kitchen Witch is a fit politician."

I knew Kim well enough to see the pride in her carefully collected expression.

"Our timeline *was* more along the line of weeks," Ranlyn said this with a hint of agitation for the banter.

"Weeks?" Caveman roared, his voice echoing off of the walls with a ripple of power he was failing to contain and had most of us flinching.

Kim turned to Caveman, trying to calm him. He fumed, red-faced, hands fisted, as he continued to pace like a caged tiger.

I leaned into Ranlyn's view. "Vincent doesn't have weeks and you know it. Lincoln didn't even tell us about Vincent being in the cells for a couple of days. If Cora-Lynn was really being conditioned to kill him, he could already—"

Ranlyn raised his hand to cut me off. "With this new information, as I was trying to say before half-naked pinky toes and power dumps, was we will hit the Sovereignty in search of Vincent immediately, but not at night. While I don't like putting the Blind in danger, unless we have knowledge of an ulterior entrance into the Sovereignty, we'll have to enter through the Blind's courthouse. That's not something we can do at night without facing greater issues concerning security. A daytime approach with a bit of ingenuity may work better and result in less casualties on our end. Sometimes chaos is your friend."

"I can see if Lincoln knows anything about another entrance." Caine was still in front of Lincoln who hadn't moved an inch while Caine's persuasion was still active.

"We can ask, but his verification may not be needed." Ranlyn reached into his pocket and removed a keyring holding a few keys and a small cylindrical container reminding me of something to discreetly store a bump of cocaine. Though, maybe it was having seen them regularly at the bar.

Since this wasn't a party, I waited in anticipation with everyone else but Veata, who appeared unsurprised. Ranlyn twisted off the lid of the small container and fished out a tiny scroll no more than an inch and a half long. Placing it in his palm, Ranlyn uttered a few words in what I assumed was Latin, but could have been anything. Without a shimmer or shake the scroll grew to two feet long. He sat at the office desk and unrolled the now four-foot wide scroll full of nonsensical lines.

We gathered around Ranlyn. Caine gave the directive for Lincoln to "Stay and don't listen to what anyone is saying until I tell you otherwise" like he was ordering around an obedient dog. Caine was fully confident in his command as he put some distance between them and joined the rest of us.

After a few more words from Ranlyn, the lines on the paper shifted around to reveal a blueprint. The magic words let us see what was on the paper, but I was still clueless to what I was looking at.

"This is the Sovereignty Creation connected to the Blind's courthouse." He planted his finger near the bottom where the Blind's region started. Details were slim since it wasn't the focus of the map. "Vincent hadn't been through every section of the Sovereignty Creation when he last updated this, so it's incomplete. It's likely much greater and doesn't outline the specifics of the Sovereignty cells since his father didn't trust him."

"Vincent gave you this?" I asked because it seemed odd for someone so secretive as Vincent.

"Gave is a stretch." Ranlyn straightened. "When word of his incarceration hit, certain protocols were enacted, including the handover of this blueprint. The man has more contingency plans than any conspiracy theorist I've ever met. The fact he was thrown into the cells shocked the hell out of us. Giving over the Sovereignty blueprints and his Prison Creation plans was a required failsafe for those left behind to operate the Prison Creation and to organize a rescue from his father's cells. Something he clearly saw as probable at some time or another."

Ranlyn looked to me at his left shoulder. "Leaving Vincent to be treated like a goldfish in his father's shark pond was never anyone's intention. Going in at all is a long shot but otherwise necessary because Vincent is a Mother Coven Elder. The fact he's also the Sovereignty Leader's legacy is unfortunate and means no attempt at brokering a deal is worth a second thought. Alasdair would never give Vincent up and we have nothing to bargain with, the location of this Prison Creation included."

I wasn't sure why he pointed this statement at me, but he made sense. Alasdair had what he wanted...Vincent. And if Vincent's father somehow didn't know about Vincent's capture, Chase would keep it a secret long enough for Cora-Lynn to do what she was conditioned to do and hope Daddy forgave him for it when it was all over.

Envy bloomed, tickling down my spine. Donovan didn't appreciate the explanation directed at me, either because of Ranlyn's attention or because he thought Vincent would want me to know. Whatever plucked his jealousy, it passed when I gave him an internal shove at his audacity.

As Ranlyn explained his plan, I was wholly impressed. Reckless and flashy came to mind, especially for the Blind. Ranlyn was a military-esque man until he became an Elder. A mystery of a person, but great at his job, even when I made it difficult for him. I still knew nothing of the child's bedroom Donovan and I stayed in at Ranlyn's Slovenian home, though his slowed age and no mention of a wife or partner meant he might have outlived them. No chance in hell I was asking. I figure the loss, or losses, granted him laser focus on the job. And this plan of his painted a picture of the Elder he became and was a whole other side of the man I liked a shit-tonne more.

A plan didn't mean we were strapping up and hitting the road, it meant waiting until 1:30pm the next afternoon when our scene would be set. Which meant Vincent was spending another night in his father's cells while we were still resting up from the battle with Loring at the Falls mere hours ago. Or was it a day? My grasp on time was slippery. We weren't planning for more death. However, everyone involved knew our path wasn't paved with cotton candy, but saturated in the hubris and gore of all those who fought the Sovereignty and failed.

Unfortunately for Caine, rest was far from on the menu as he and the Elders hammered Lincoln with questions involving more than his hand-holding with Chase and the Sovereignty. If we were to amp up our chances of winning, every pinprick of data collected could add to our arsenal. And when they were done with him, Lincoln would become the first official prisoner of Vincent's new jail system as soon as Vincent was free and put someone on the bench to prosecute him.

Exposing Lincoln's treason to the rest of the Tactical Team was not without disbelief. Once they stopped arguing and were given a demonstration of repeated questions straight from Lincoln still sitting in the office under Caine's control, they had no other excuses to defend their leader. Gregor, Ismail, Arden, and Bronya lost two from the Team. The whiplash was too much for them to see the truth right away. Jessabelle was dead at Loring's deadly attack and Lincoln let driving grief dictate his allegiances.

The Team was pissed.

"How could he hide this?" Gregor said aloud to no one in particular.

Ranlyn replied anyway. "No reason to question him. He said none of you knew anything about his communications with Chase. I understand Lincoln's justification, the death of someone you love can result in actions you may not normally take, but he will be tried for his crimes. We didn't know how far-reaching the damage from his actions had spread. And time spent in a cell won't be anything like how the Sovereignty does it, no matter how much you feel he deserves it."

Judging by the locked-down expressions on each of the faces of the Team members, an execution was too light a sentence.

"The container..." Ismail's gaze was unfocused.

"What container?" Ranlyn asked.

"In the lower decks of The Chiff, Lincoln had me swim to a particular floor and cubicle in search of a container."

"The drink canister thing?" Gregor remembered.

Ismail nodded.

"What was in it?" Ranlyn asked.

"I never asked or opened it. Lincoln said it held something important for the Mother Coven. Or, maybe I assumed he meant it was of great significance for the Mother Coven." Ismail swiped his hand over his hair in frustration. "The water was not of my liking considering the dead, but I thought—"

"Lincoln lied to many," Veata stepped in to stop Ismail blaming himself too harshly for whatever was in the canister. "The question is, what could the container have held since it was not on request of the Elders?"

Ismail ground his teeth together, shifting his weight from foot to foot as if he was ready to go after Lincoln himself for putting him in the position of potentially helping the enemy, even if unknowingly.

I thought it was weird at the time, but no one had treated me as an equal. They all thought I was being dramatic for insisting on answers. Guess they wish they had a few more now, didn't they?

"We'll question Lincoln more on this," Ranlyn said. "Now, this Team is not mine and I intend on handing you off to your maker so he can redistribute duties. Can I trust you to govern yourselves without Vincent or Lincoln's leadership? I'm happy to provide oversight where needed, as I have since Vincent was forced to leave you to me. Because I'm not always alongside you in the field, and no one needs ego fighting for a promotion while face-to-face with our enemies, speak up. With any luck, Vincent will be back at the helm in twenty-four hours."

The Team all looked at each other, considering his words. Donovan, Caveman, and I were all new, so if anyone was lobbying for a new title, it was none of us. Caveman wasn't engaging in conversation. More like intently observing, keenly listening, and silently judging. Kim was the only one he complained to. As a Recondite Magic, he was probably used to swift action designed and implemented in the height of need.

Ismail ended up answering Ranlyn. "We will remain a functional team and will defer to you if management is required to bridge operational gaps."

This satisfied Ranlyn as no one argued or appeared to be seething at Ismail's response. I didn't get a vote, but following Ismail was preferable to Bronya ordering me around. Though, letting Caveman head the Team would have been less restrictive.

Ranlyn went on with a mix of logistics, motivation, and cold reality. Each person in the room was on board judging by the nods and clarifying questions. Enlisting the entire Mother Coven to retrieve

Vincent was overkill, but key players would be included. Caine would work on Ness, but he seemed rather confident, or at least hopeful, of her involvement.

After Ranlyn's audacious plan was set and the Elders and Caine were left to squeeze Lincoln's memory like a rotten lemon, I stood in the lobby amongst passing Magics...with nowhere to go. Many hours were left until we were setting off for Vincent. I saw enough of the inside of offices and boardrooms while in the questioning and planning stages, and I wasn't hungry or tired even though I should be starved for both.

Oh, fuck me.

Before I could decide on how to waste time, Adam and Serena headed my way. I should have ducked into a cell, but the set of confrontation in my brother's shoulders rooted me to my spot, igniting an antagonistic part of me happy to bite back at whatever they seemed so determined to say.

Adam stopped in front of me, dark glasses in place to protect his sensitive Soul Seer eyes, hands in his pockets, overreaching to appear casual when we both knew he was pissed. "Hey, sis. Nice to see you alive."

"*Pfft*. There's always tomorrow."

"What's happening tomorrow?" Serena's anger slipped and she failed to fight the curiosity in her tone.

I shrugged. "Another day."

She rolled her eyes and set a smile saying, "Yeah, I thought so." She knew I wasn't going to share unless I needed to, and right now I didn't need to. Serena and Adam wouldn't be infiltrating the Sovereignty, so I wasn't going to waste the energy explaining.

A part of me knew I should care more, say something to right things, tell them what was really up, and trust them to stay quiet. I couldn't and didn't want to. As soon as I opened my mouth, Adam would tell Denise who would pirouette like a ballerina so fast to tell the entire Sect, and Serena would tell Jared who would tell Blake who would tell the rest.

Lincoln was one mole. The possibility of more was as high as my irritation from and for different factions.

And while I did feel more myself after Donovan forced his mediocre healing on me, the creeping of annoyance was steady and worsening.

"Why'd you dose my drink?" Serena was an award-winning actress when she wanted to be, handing me a drink spiked with memories of how others perceived my and Donovan's relationship. All outside POVs quick to jump on his harebrained manipulation scheme.

Serena levelled a blue-eyed stare at my bluntness. "With your soul all tore up—"

"Not my soul. Just the Soul Magic."

"Call it what you want. Point is, if the drink killed you, it would've been an improvement."

Wow. I guess I asked for the truth.

"I don't want you dead," Serena amended. "Donovan had a good idea, and you were too messed up to see how bad things were."

"You made it worse."

She raised a blonde eyebrow. "Sure seem better to me."

"I'm not."

"Yeah, you are," Adam cut in. "Your soul glow isn't as dull as it was before the memory bomb. A little worse now than right after it happened, but better than it was. And you're actually talking to us instead of sitting in your cell like an emo kid. Write any good poems in there?"

"Yup. Call me So-So Poe."

"See." Adam smiled. "And telling lame jokes. Practically normal."

"Have you been calling Mom?" I abruptly shifted topics.

Adam huffed. "Yes. I'm still her favorite, by the way."

"She still at Elizabeth's?"

"Grandma Lizzie's? Obs. Where else would she be?"

A wave of heat and something else flushed through me, clearly a Donovan thing, whatever it was. "Where's Dad and Ben?"

"In between hotels and Uncle Joe's, waiting for the insurance money to rebuild since Loring torched his house. Arson equals an investigation even though the Magic at the fire department knows what went down. Plus, if you're actually interested in how they're all doing, pick up the damn phone. If you can shoot a gun, you can dial a number."

"Right. If you can be a dick, you can go fuck yourself." Right or not, my patience for my brother was down to mere droplets as another flush of heat washed over me and settled within my gut.

Oh, I get it. Donovan was drinking.

"What's the matter with you now? Your cheeks are red." I couldn't concentrate on who said it, but mentioning it had my blood punching my temples.

Warmth beneath my fingertips when I pressed them against my face confirmed what I felt through the rest of me. "Donovan found a bottle. Besides the spiked drink you fed me, my alcohol consumption has been lacking. Guess I forgot the sensation."

"Still not sorry I did it."

Serena's comment sparked another round of anger. No one knew how to get under your skin more than family.

"And I wasn't sorry I broke your hand. You're lucky I didn't rip your whole fucking arm off. Pull that shit again and I'll do worse."

Serena shrugged, not put off by the threat. "At least it's honest for a change."

"I wasn't lying then either. I just wasn't talking to you. Bigger things to worry about."

"And now?" Adam asked.

I scanned the lobby, letting go of a heavy breath to off-set Donovan's intoxication, the circulating air doing nothing helpful. "I gotta go."

"Nah." Adam stepped in my way. "You were saying?"

I ground my teeth together. "I was saying, although you both deserve to be hated for the rest of your existence for colluding with Donovan, a twinge of guilt sprouted, and I thought I should apologise. Moment gone. Now, move."

Adam pursed his lips and stepped aside. I couldn't tell if it was the alcohol scrambling my emotions or the fact I might have actually felt bad for all the shit the guy has gone through lately. Regardless of the reason, instead of taking off, I reached up to hug him, ignoring his flinch that told me he thought I was going to attack him.

We may have been ten months apart and were mistaken for twins as toddlers, but hugs were few and far between.

Before he settled into the embrace, I was already backing off. A hug didn't change the fact I was a bitch or that he and Serena conspired with many others to dose my drink. In fact, it didn't solve anything. I should've kept walking.

"It was *my* hand you broke!" Serena called after me when I escaped.

I walked backwards to blow her a kiss and flip her the middle finger, then I raced off for the cell console without waiting for Serena's response.

Fucking Donovan. My head was alternating emotions like an Olympic gymnast, and he was at the peak of those to blame. Not the top flag-bearer but pretty damn close. With the torn connection mended with the equivalent of a racecar Band-Aid, he knew damn well I would feel everything he did. We've played this game.

Punching his name into the cell console, a flush of a different kind stopped me. A hoof of pleasure to the pelvis tingled down my thighs to my knees with a recognizable floating sensation. As my fingers hovered over the console's touchscreen, the sensation grew to include hands on me that didn't belong to a visible body.

Was Donovan having sex with someone?

A nightmare flashback flared, dropping me into the Sorrel cells. Invisible hands were all over me, someone I couldn't see or touch riding my body as I had no hope of shoving them away.

I opened my eyes unaware I closed them. Seeing the Prison

Creation around me snapped me from the Sorrel cells memory. I wasn't imprisoned in a cell with no door and guarded by Magics in the midst of an evil flock. I was free and able to stop this like I couldn't then. If Donovan was in the beginning stages of getting laid, I sure as hell was going to be a contributor of his blue balls.

I fought to focus beyond the alcohol-induced lust loosening my shoulders to finish entering his name. I walked into the cell, ready to take on him and whatever stupid vagina he sweet-talked.

The bed was empty, white sheets crumpled.

Running water droned on above the blood pumping in my ears. Steam rose from behind the cinderblock dividing wall to the shower area.

A bottle of whiskey stood on the ground outside of the shower as if on guard, water dripping down the glass neck and saturating the label.

Apparently, this was an aquatic session.

Sprinting the few steps to the shower, I found Donovan.

The only person entertaining him was himself.

His hand braced his weight against the wall, his bicep hiding his bowed expression. He leaned into the hot spray hitting him in the chest and rolling over his tattooed shoulder and down his back, chest, abs, and hips. His flexed thigh slightly in front of the other concealed the hand stroking himself, causing the slow sensation of sex I couldn't escape.

Donovan lifted his head a few inches, his dark eyes cutting to me through his wet lashes. Water from his hair ran over his cheekbones, hard jaw, and dripped off of his parted lips. Noticing he wasn't alone, he didn't stop the motions slowly weakening my knees.

"You know..." With intentions on berating him lost in my throat, I tried and failed not to stare at the water sliding down his hard body and landing on his handy work. The bold and encapsulating scent of his soap in the shower steam overwhelmed me, further obscuring my drive to punish him for—

I flinched when wetness hit my hand. The cast off of water from his body dappled my skin and I realized I was closer to him.

He now faced me, stance planted, still under the hot water, keeping up a languid rhythm.

I wanted to shrink away and race my heartbeat out of the cell, but I couldn't force myself to do more than face the cell wall behind me in hopes of breaking away from his enticing invitation.

The loss of visual temptation did nothing to cut the cravings to stay and accept his offer.

His hard body was now at my back, impossibly close, somehow managing to remain hands off yet feel like he was touching every inch of my skin.

Pressure within me let off. He dialled down his lust a notch as if realizing his was crowding mine, his distance allowing me to sense his purposeful retreat and decide to close or widen the contentious gap between us. I still couldn't think rationally enough to do anything. Or reach beyond the conflict in my brain trying to work out who I was when it came to this man and who he was to me and versions of me in the past.

Soft lips pressed onto the side of my neck, the shock of contact snapping the tense muscles in my shoulders. My head fell those crucial inches against his chest. He gripped my arms, firm and steadying. Water from his damp skin seeped through my shirt sleeves and back, his heated fingers trailing from my arms, down my ribs, and to my hips as his tongue grazed my throat and jawline.

His hand snaked down my side, across my stomach, up between my breasts, and gripped my throat with enough pressure to retain my stuttered breath yet lock me against him and his erection at my lower back.

"No visions in here. Just us."

Right. The cell's power-dampening meant Donovan couldn't view past versions of me. No peek into rosier times when I didn't war with hating or loving him. He couldn't read my mind or the conflict swimming within it. The ritual stone magic was packed away and our telepathy was mute inside these walls. The single extra sensory ability left was the live wire of the Soul Magic connection flowing sensations between us.

He kept his hand on my throat, caressing the length of it with his thumb as his other fingers slid under my shirt hem, grazing tender skin. I involuntarily reached for his hand, not to still it, but to add pressure, and drink in the small amount of contact.

"It's just us," Donovan said again, his voice low next to my ear, his hand wandering further over the skin of my belly, fingertips playing with my waistband. "Be it right now or forever, it's just us."

Right now or forever. I didn't know which I was hoping for. Or maybe I was praying for someone to interrupt us or for him to say something stupid and make the choice for me.

I let rational thought drown beneath the weight of Donovan's inebriation, my desire to endure something more than anger or nothingness, and closed my eyes to revel in his leashed yearning. Giving in to our combined compulsions, I focused on the wet and naked body against me and guided his hand with mine beneath the fabric where his fingers teased.

Pressure on my throat tightened as he slid his fingers under the waistband of my tactical pants and underwear. His hiss brushed my ear when he found wetness beneath his shower-slick fingers.

My knees loosened at his touch, his chest bracing my weight as he delved in and out of me.

A spark of something slammed into me. Not power. Panic? It bunched in my gut and shoulders.

I spun from Donovan's hold. Not to leave, no part of me wanted to escape him. I wanted...I needed...a shift. To stop him from guiding this interaction.

He raised his hands. "Whoa, I—"

I didn't let him finish. I grabbed hold of his wrists, forcing him backwards through the hot shower spray, and shoved him into the shower wall. The jarring impact of his skull barely registered in my own, same with his shoulder blades digging into the cement block. The unmoving surface was an alcohol-softened buffer to our surroundings, forgotten with a bruising kiss.

Donovan tugged at my pants, the material sticking at my hips and giving a little easier when he dragged them over my thighs. He bent to remove my boots as I tried to rip my shirt over my head. The wet fabric stuck and popped a couple of stitches before I was free and dropped it to the shower floor. He was quicker with my laces and soon the shower steam coated my newly exposed skin.

I stopped him from standing by draping a leg over his shoulder. His enthusiastic revelation of what I craved drowned his initial confusion. Not a question or an offer, but an expectation. If he wanted this to continue, he was going to spend time on his knees.

Donovan's mouth was on me, licking and sucking his way into me. His fingers joined the effort to work me over the edge. Nothing within the connection told me he wanted to be anywhere else. And I tried to ignore the intrusive thoughts telling me his commitment to the task was for some other shady agenda. If I let them win, I'd think my way out of the building orgasm I needed more than wanted.

I let my head fall back into the spray, the water running down my body. His fingers still inside of me matched the unrelenting rhythm of his tongue outside of me. If I was waterboarding Donovan, he didn't complain. Talking would mean removing his mouth from me and he was too busy for something as mundane as breathing.

A pulse of pleasure brought on by his dual stimulation raced through me. Falling over the ledge felt too far away, like I was chasing it instead of being taken by it. I gripped his head and found room for added pressure by squeezing the leg over his shoulder to keep him in place. I planted a hand on the wall to retain balance as frustration started to cloud my mind.

As if he read my growing restlessness, Donovan grabbed my elevated thigh and cradled me to swiftly lift me off of my feet and place me onto my back on the shower floor. With no door or lip into the open shower, room wasn't an issue for him to splay me out or gain leverage for what he thought I needed while pinning my lower body to the tiles.

No.

I don't know if I said it aloud or if Donovan felt the tug on the thread between us, but he popped his head up from between my legs, mouth open in concern, brows cinched, water falling down his face from his hair.

I swept my body to the side, bringing him with me, and spun him onto his back, ending up with his face still between my thighs, but with me on top instead of trapped beneath him.

Surprised at the shift in position, Donovan hesitated until I lowered and repositioned myself to where I wanted him, ignoring the rasp of floor tiles against my knees.

His desire roared forward, and he grabbed hold of my ass and resumed with passion to finish the job as I rode what I was aching for.

I expected him to fight me for the upper hand. He didn't. He was seemingly content for me to grind the back of his skull into the floor as long as his tongue was buried and busy.

An orgasm hit me.

Rearing up, I braced my hands on the porcelain sink at the end of the shower-bathroom combo area. A strong grip under and around my thighs was Donovan trying to hold me in place to draw out every pulse of pleasure from me. I could have squashed his brain between my thighs, but I shoved the visual aside to focus on my pleasure and not his pain, illusion or other.

Landing on my back when I couldn't hold myself up anymore, I expected the few breaths of thick steam to usher in a shift in duties to Donovan's needs, even though he would have felt everything I did through our bond. Donovan's hand on my belly slid down over my hip, between my thighs, and slipped his fingers inside with a careful drawing in and out as his teeth and tongue found my nipple.

I moaned with inescapable pleasure as his renewed attention was meant to build on what he already created instead of used as a transition in a "his turn" ploy.

No, he wasn't done with me, because I still wanted more, and he knew it.

3

DOOR STOPPER

Donovan

Oddly enough, I had no intention of leading things here. Drinking myself unconscious was a routine plan before Sophie popped into my life. In a shower I took to loosen muscle tension, it dawned on me that the agitation I was feeling wasn't mine, it was Sophie's, spurred on by the whisky-burn simmering in my gut. Since the connection was re-established, I hadn't drunk much alcohol, but infiltrating the Sovereignty was a big fucking deal and very little sleep came to me lately, especially after narrowly losing Fox to his power drain.

The flush of my pickled veins clearly irritated Sophie. This brought on thoughts of what else she could feel. With the curious thought weakly formed, I was hard, and my body wash was suddenly my best friend.

When she appeared next to me in the cell bathroom, I expected a hailstorm of insults and threats or a butt-naked ass kicking in front of an audience...again.

By some flick of luck, the dreamy hunger in her eyes mirrored mine. I sensed her conflict when she turned her back on me. She enjoyed what she saw and what she felt, however, she fought the impulse to lose herself with me. Or at least she wished she didn't want me as clearly as she did.

Was I a bastard for exploiting the small window of doubt?

Abso-*fucking*-lutely.

Did this realization stop me from leaving the warm water and kissing the pale skin of her slender neck?

It probably should have. It didn't.

Masturbation was a hollow act I hoped would spark a reminder somewhere in Sophie that, at one time, she wanted me as much as I wanted her. Maybe this would melt some lingering ice between us, make her dig deeper into what we were to each other.

She used to trust I would protect her, would love her for lifetimes, would do anything to give her everything she desired, and strive to create her happiness. We lost that. Sex wasn't the end-all answer, but it could jumpstart a patch over the denial she held onto since the hate my father planted.

Grazing my teeth along her neck added to her building hunger, a need I fed with bites of desire until it met my own. I pressed myself into her back as a clear indicator of where I stood and an invitation for her to accept or reject. I may be basting her brain with the idea of sex, but she could leave as quickly as she appeared.

A snap of sexual tension landed me on my knees. Her insistence on this power dynamic revved me up and I happily ignored the stabbing floor tiles into my kneecaps, even when they cut through the skin and a hiss from her lips could have been a mirror of pain or pleasure.

Whatever she wanted, she could have.

She wasn't fully in this with me. She never met my eyes, hers closed, riding emotions and sensations from one second to the next. Her desire and conflict were as intoxicating as they were confusing, and I worked to dance around them when they took a nosedive into muddy waters. Whatever she was thinking about, she stuck around and didn't flinch in concern when she ground my gourd into the floor while she rode my face and nearly popped my head like a grape when an explosive orgasm rocked us.

She was greedy. Not to be worshipped or for more than what I could give, but greedy to feel everything and nothing and was satisfied with my involvement if I could provide the escape she was desperate for.

A moan fell from her lips when I slipped my fingers back inside her and took her nipple between my teeth, her pleasure rolling through me, gripping and quivering around my fingers.

She wasn't done.

Her nipple was pulled from my lips with a smacking sound, a sudden roar of need flooding from her as she pushed me away to then straddle me, driving herself onto me, enveloping me within her. Our dual moans echoed in the small cell over the shower still running off to our side and dappling our skin.

For whatever reason, she craved control, and I craved her.

A few strokes of her on top of me and something chilled through the connection, her thoughts imposing on the present enough for her to open her eyes and survey her surroundings as if needing reassurance of where she was.

I reached between her thighs. She dragged in a ragged breath, closed her eyes, and dropped her head back. I fought to remain active as she let go. She resumed riding me as I churned tight circles with my thumb, maintaining pressure while we moved together.

At this pace, I could have been any dick and heartbeat, which defeated the purpose of being with her, so I kept this up, feathering the gas pedal to keep her in comfort while pushing her boundaries. Not in hopes of her loving me again, but to show her I loved her regardless of how she felt about me. She needed this but didn't go to anyone else for it. That meant something.

When her moans became a frustrated whimper, I quickened my pace as she hurried hers, and I knew the game was done.

Another orgasm shot through us. Every muscle burned and

twitched, our cries in pleasure bouncing off the walls of the small cell. I milked the orgasm to its last few strokes. She gripped my thighs behind her to keep her balance. The blissful feeling drained from my body, toes tingling something fierce right up the back of my calves until it hit my ass cheeks, which were probably chewed up as badly as her bleeding knees from the cell floor.

Braced forward onto her hands now on either side of me, Sophie's head remained bowed. Punching exhales dropped from both of us as our surroundings came back into reality, though I would have locked us in the euphoric bubble if I could. If I let it, this would be the moment where she allowed the damaged voice inside of her to creep up and put miles of space between us.

So, I didn't move or say anything.

Sophie hopped off me without a warning and then sort of slunk to the outer wall across from the shower still raining water onto the floor. She pulled up her scraped knees to rest her arms on them, face still mostly covered, eyes closed.

I measured her emotions through mine and attempted not to scare her off, but sat up to mirror her own movements. Turning off the water would drop the cell into a silence neither of us could stand. Being the first to say anything may be as equally detrimental.

Shit. She wasn't going to move, and panic was starting to slink in. Mine? Hers? Probably both.

Too antsy to remain in that realm, I moved a couple of feet to grab each of us a towel. I wrapped my lower body in one and sat down where I was to hand her another. Water seeped through to my ass, but at least I was covered in case my nakedness suddenly bothered her.

Since her eyes were closed, she didn't see me holding the towel.

Fuck, this was brutal.

"I'm not kicking you out," I heard myself say in a low, strained voice, as I tried not to be too loud or jarring. "Far from it, actually, but I understand if you feel the need to leave."

She opened her eyes without raising them to meet mine.

Water dripped from her hair down her face and shoulders, the droplets ignored while palpable conflict flooded her. It felt as if I strained hard enough I could see the split in her desire. One path was to continue on in this life next to me and the other was the downslope to turning back into the furious woman I forced to heal. The fact the broken Soul Magic impacted her personality so greatly yet did nothing to me, was torture to watch her struggle. Her pain was still my pain.

She wasn't about to let me use the ritual stone magic to heal her more, not so soon, and I wasn't about to overstep my luck after she was so vulnerable with me after so long. I was a step in the door now. I needed to a add a door stopper until I found a cure.

Could regular healing sessions with the ritual stone magic be the answer? Maybe. But not right now.

"It doesn't match," she said without looking at me, her voice thin and disconnected, on the verge of cracking.

She grabbed the towel and stood up in one swoop, wrapping the fabric around her body, then started picking up her drenched clothing.

I stood and watched her, wanting to shake her and make her talk to me. Instead, I was stuck in place, trying to jigsaw puzzle the emotions across the connection and what she could have meant. "What doesn't match?"

She found her second boot outside of the shower area and hugged it to her body with the rest of her dripping wet clothing. "You. You don't match."

Me? I don't match what? "I—I don't understand."

"Neither do I."

I tried to close the distance, but couldn't as she walked straight through the wall to exit the cell leaving nothing but her wet footprints behind.

4

DIFFERENT PROPOSITIONS

Kim

Hall suggested a little timeout in Italy, insisting since sleeping so soon after the attack from Loring was impossible. I fought with the desire for safe freedom outside of the Prison Creation walls and what it meant to him for me to delve into his private world inside his memories all for a distraction. More than an illusion spell, more than a weekend with some stuffy posers in re-enactment garb, these trips into Hall's head were as real as it got without experiencing the place firsthand.

Amazing gift.

Anyone not on the Tactical Team spent the majority of life these days either in their cell or in little pockets of groups wherever they fit within the Prison Creation. Some focused on learning or perfecting spells, exercising their abilities so they didn't get rusty. Some kept up daily and routine rituals we would perform on the outside. And many were grieving for the dead from the hit on Niagara Falls or those from The Chiff attack or the safe house raids. When it came to the dearly departed, the abundance of ritual and witness to their life and their passing was endless.

Not a bad thing, but I have cried enough. I needed a break.

I needed space from the sadness, but in this place where more and more Magics required a safe place to hide out, it equalled less elbow room unless you wanted to sit in a small cell and stare at the walls.

No thank you.

I wanted a break from this place, even if through a mental vacation while sitting on a Prison Creation bench in a corner of the lobby.

Still, this escape came with strings, evident in the weight of Hall's stare as we casually strolled down a crowded Italian sidewalk circa 1901. Not like I could help looking at him with that ridiculous mustache.

His chuckle was a low grumble in his chest. He swiped his fingers down his once-upon-a-time facial hair. "Look around, kitten. I'm in style."

He was right. Almost every man we passed sported some sort of mustache configuration. Thankfully, Hall's wasn't super long and swirly like some blowing in the light breeze.

Yikes.

"How're you finding your fashion experience?"

We stopped outside of a *Dentista*—no translation required to guess what the business was—to check ourselves in full length in the front window's reflection. The champagne-coloured silk day dress was fancy by anyone's standards. The boned corset cinched my waist and pushed my ass back to create the highly unrealistic body shape of the century and was far more uncomfortable than any historical romance movie described. Yet, there was no denying the absolute perfection it created for the lines of my body underneath all this heavy fabric. The hat I could do without, same with the Gibson Girl hairstyle underneath, though like Hall's mustache, the female pedestrians all pinned up their hair under some hatted situation. Hall claimed the hatpin was useful as a weapon. Since pockets were scarcer than in the real world, a sharp metal rod to the eye or the side of the neck would work in a pinch.

Sophie's aunts would be in heaven.

"The high collar's restrictive and my ribs are aching. These shoes take the cake for being equal parts beautiful and torturous. Worth it for the sake of this escape, but it would be enough for me to strive to be a kept lady so I didn't have to walk anywhere." I pulled up the heavy hem and pointed a matching silk heel with delicate, embroidered flowers, twisting it to show off the design and to ogle them again.

Hall slid his hands into the pockets of his dapper dark-grey suit and gave me an up-and-down once over, his brow popping up with obvious interest. "Hike your dress up any higher and people will think you're for sale."

I rolled my eyes in jest and dropped my skirt. If this was the first time I visited his mind worlds, I would've freaked a bit, but I knew any reaction from those around us would only impact our direct interactions so much. No one here could kill us or do any true harm because it's not what occurred when Hall was here in real time. He didn't comment on instances where his interactions with others in this reality included violence and chose these little interludes with care to ensure a pleasant experience without the danger.

Hall laughed again, straightened, and extended his arm for me to hold. I did, fulfilling the role this particular landscape entailed.

The sound of horse-drawn carriages was noisy on the cobblestone roads. Lovely ambiance. The smell was something else and a detail of his worlds I could do without. A mixture of horse shit and human shit and whatever else was lingering in the air was extraordinary, in its own way. Hall didn't seem to mind.

"Smells like nostalgia to me," he said, answering my unmentioned comment, hearing it right from my thoughts. "When Giolitti needed someone to lead a crew, I was brought in to work at his side and behind the scenes when necessary to ensure his re-election."

"The name drop would mean even more if I knew who Giolitti was. Not that I ever pictured you in politics."

He chuckled. "Giovani Giolitti was the prime minister of Italy 1903 to 1914 primarily due to my efforts in the year or so leading up to the election. The man was considered Liberal and built a reputation amongst the Blind, but an even greater one with Magics of the political and not-so-political variety. Our brand of difficulty spilled over to the Blind resulting in striking workers and riots. Some we could use to our advantage, others proved more problematic. I could have shown you Palazzo Chigi, the official residence of the prime minister, but something told me you'd appreciate a walk amongst the people in relative fresh air than being stuck in more marble-covered pretention."

"You nailed that one." He really did. The breeze on my cheeks was fake, but my mind didn't know the difference. "You score extra points for the fashion choices, and I won't even ask how you could possibly know what it feels like to wear a corset so well you could replicate the feeling for me in this place." I still didn't understand the intricacies of how his power worked.

"You don't need to ask, but if you did, I would have no problem explaining to stop your delicious brain from filling in the blanks. If my life had started soon before meeting you, then I wouldn't have such experiences to draw from and impress you with."

"Mhmm."

The double-edged sword was a difficult one, and I reminded myself it didn't matter either way. This wasn't a date. We weren't dating. I was in his mind, and he had full access to mine because I was in here with him. Easy to recreate my desires when you could access the cheat sheet.

"Speaking of your delicious brain, did you give any thought to what I said?"

What he said? Oh, right. Not what he said right now, but what he said that made this timeout into his brain a tad more awkward. "You've been rooting around in there, why don't you tell me?"

During the fight in Niagara Falls with Loring, Hall couldn't get a hold of me while he was with Donovan and Fox to ensure I was still alive or to know what was happening. I wasn't in the position to answer my cell as I was trying to ensure the safety of every other Magic and civilian in the way of Loring's dramatic plans.

Having a frenzied Viking squeeze me until my insides creaked in full view of the Sect, and then declare he would henceforth be my devoted protector until his last breath was...confusing. And while his feelings for me and my preoccupation with my "Blind companion" had until that point landed Hall on the sidelines, he could no longer allow his love for me to go unknown, ignored, or hidden beneath niceties and deflected humour. He added that his service was not dependent on a love match, that he would protect me regardless of our relationship status, and his love would endure and outlast all others.

Talk about the shock of all shocks, even after the bloody carnage of the fight.

I didn't answer him at the time. I couldn't. He spilled his offer at my feet and left without giving me the chance to respond even if I had had the words, which I definitely hadn't. I didn't even have the words now.

"You *can* tell me to leave you alone," he said as we continued our slow stroll.

"After all that, you'd be satisfied with walking away and letting me live on as if we never met, even while in the Prison Creation together?"

He stepped in front of me and faced me, the pedestrians of the busy Italian street bypassing us without notice. "If I truly believed being far away from you in every aspect was what you desired, yes, I would." He reached up to run his fingers along a strand of hair in the front of my ear left to curl and twist in the wind. "You waffle in indecision yet never seeing me again is not within your thoughts."

"If you're so intuned with my brain, why bother asking what I want?"

"Because the acceptance of a declaration of protection is a spoken bond between individuals, be it two people or twenty. A promise, a commitment, an understanding of duty, of responsibility, and of expectations. It cannot exist without mutual testimony."

Wow. Sounded like a marriage.

"It is, of sorts," he said, answering my thoughts. "Though, could also be a marriage of a more traditional definition as well."

I tried and failed not to roll my eyes. "You said they were two different propositions."

"They are."

"Doesn't sound like it."

"They are." The second time he said this his voice was harsher, but his eyes were sadder, like he wished I wasn't separating the roles.

If Hall wasn't on mission, he was my shadow. His offer did state "until I ordered otherwise".

"And if I decide to accept it and then change my mind at some point down the line?"

He inhaled, swallowed, then ran his fingers over his mustache again. "Then a divorce of sorts would follow. Be it from my duty to you or our love...or both."

Well, damn. It would never work.

"How so?"

My head tilt was an unmentioned *"Duh"*.

"Making my feelings for you plain was supposed to answer your questions, not create excuses."

"I didn't ask any questions."

He tilted his head as I had. "The Blind man is a waste of your time and since I do have the ability to hear the thoughts you hide, I know your interest in me goes beyond visual accoutrements."

"Are you talking about your muscles again?"

"Kimberly..." This was said with a seriousness that tripped me up. I was pretty sure he never spoke my full first name from those lips before. Half the time he called me kitten. "To say this stand of yours is beyond my patience would defeat the reasons I love you, for your defiance is a part of the drive confirming my emotions are not wasted. Understand, I will not stop because you've erected a wall of false justification for turning me down. I also see that while events are currently in chaos and you can't find it in you to break things off with Frog, you also know you feeling the way you do about me, admittedly or not, means your Frog is already a moot point."

"You can't throw 'love' around and automatically assume the one you say it to is going to swoon and kneel in gratitude."

"You don't have to kneel, however, the position can be favourable. And I will kneel if we seal my declaration of protection."

Now it really sounded like a marriage. Or least an engagement. Probably something he's done quite a few times.

"Officially? One time in formal marriage and none bound by a promise of protection to this degree."

Hall looked around in a bit of discomfort and needing to focus elsewhere as some kind of emotion bubbled up. I minutely felt...bad. Sorry was not on the menu since it didn't fit, but I had no context for whatever story was behind his expression.

"My expression..." he spoke slowly, again reading my mind, "is because I know too well what it's like to live beyond those I love and to wish I possessed the forethought to include a declaration of protection."

Someone died. Either by violence or by death in old age. "Your wife?"

"Yes."

Huh. And only once, he said. I figured the lone-wolf Viking either never took on a bride or swooped them up by the dozen.

Vincent did warn me against getting close to Hall and how others ended up hurt via proximity. He never detailed his old friend's history, and I didn't care enough at the time to insist. I probably should have. Or at least told Vincent to mind his own business. He must have seen something happening that I hadn't since I never anticipated this situationship with a Viking at any time in my life.

The scene around us dimmed and swayed. Was Hall losing the

handle on his power? He closed his eyes and twisted his neck to the side in a short struggle before everything around us ran clear.

"Hall, I have no clue what it feels like to be married or to lose a partner in any form other than a crappy breakup, but you and I have known each other for how long? Weeks? Not enough for you to hitch yourself to my potentially short future." I continued so he couldn't speak over me. "The protection aspect of things, I get...maybe. I could use you, even if I don't understand why you can't be the barnacle you've been since we met without the extra title. The ritual and promise you described sounds, I don't know, hardcore and more permanent than you're letting on. It's something you can't simply walk away from, right?"

He didn't answer, his ice blue eyes communicating a quiet pride because I was on the right track.

I exhaled in a huff. "Without all the details, how can I decide this for the both of us? I need to know more, but I will tentatively agree to—"

He grabbed the sides of my head and pulled me into a crushing kiss. The intensity of the emotion he put into it washed over me until I blinked back into reality.

I shoved my hands into his hard pecs and pushed him away from me.

The scene around us dropped to reveal the Prison Creation. Hall went flying off of the bench where we sat and slid along the floor. Guards rushed towards us as power railed through me, and Hall righted himself.

One guard stepped in front of him in way of shielding him from me, throwing his arms in front of Hall and sending a blast of energy at me.

Some kind of noise squeaked out of me the second I realized I was in big trouble.

Energy hit me, encapsulating me like a latex suit. Zaps of power filtered pain through my entire body, striking every nerve. I felt everything.

Moaning filled my ears as yelling surrounded me. Deep punches of agony throbbed from head to toe and back again, my limbs moving on their own in response to the pain.

Movement and more yelling.

Murmurs I couldn't understand were at my ear, then more pain. My scream filled my eardrums and then relief took charge.

When I opened my heavy lids, Hall's beefy arms cradled me, but Ranlyn's hand was on my arm. Did he heal me? The ache slowly retreated.

Far too slowly.

"Thank you." Did my lips actually move?

Ranlyn gave my arm a light squeeze as if he heard either way.

Hall picked me up and carried me to a closer bench.

"I will not stand for your delinquent members attacking my people!" Edson's voice rang across the lobby.

Ranlyn was now defending me, his and Edson's raised voices bouncing off the walls and ringing in my brain.

No wait, Edson was talking about Hall. Hall attacked the guards?

Uniformed Prison Creation security members helped a few of their men to their feet, grumbling and sending daggered stares our way.

"They will consider the consequences before attacking you again." The depth of Hall's growled words was a guarantee, though they were protecting another Magic from harm and didn't realize Hall was in no danger from me.

I lifted my hands to his justifications. "If they hesitate to ask questions, they could be killed or held by other consequences for not acting quicker." I rolled my neck and shoulders, still stiffened by the attack.

Others questioned if I was okay. I waved them off and smiled until they went about their business, Ranlyn and Edson having left the lobby to discuss the incident privately.

"Nice energy dump, by the way," Hall projected into my brain. *"I more than deserved it."*

"More than, you ass. Though, that's not an actual apology. Why do guys think lips and dicks are the answer to everything?"

He smiled in a guarded way and reached for my hands. I didn't flinch or move away as they completely enveloped mine, though I braced for whatever came next. *"Please know I mean everything I say. Even in times I jest, I understand where your reservations lie and merely need you to comprehend my intentions."*

"Being?"

"Being that I have the mind and heart of a warrior and do not accept defeat, even if it chucks me across the floor. Romantic idealism is also not within my roster of weaponry. Loving you is easy, and I'll creatively enjoy convincing you I mean it. I'm a cut-the-shit kind of Magic in every respect and refuse to overanalyze this. Knowing personal tidbits of someone's life is not how I measure love. I'm sure Frog didn't know everything about you before you started dating."

"No, but he's also not using the word 'love'."

His blond brows tightened at the comment I immediately regretted making. *"He either loves you and is too proud to make it known or he's the stupidest man on earth."*

Hall was from a different time, literally, so I understood what he was trying to get at, but people don't declare love so easily these days, or at least they don't in my experience without being love-bombing, manipulative assholes. I could go for skipping the dramas of dating, but Frog and I were already in the midst of it. And who knew what he thought of me now. Maybe nothing at all since jetting to his island paradise. My imagination was full of ways he must be spending his imposed vacation.

Hall inhaled audibly through his nostrils, refraining from commenting on anything he heard in my thoughts. He sat forward and sanded his hands together, making me wish I could hear his mind as easily as he heard mine. I'd feel a hell of a lot better about his intentions if I could. Sophie and Donovan had no clue how lucky they were to be able to feel exactly what the other one did and detect any shadiness or lies.

"If you want to prove you're dedicated to my protection, I need to learn to cover my thoughts. Whether it's a spell or an unconscious act like so many other Magics do."

"Hmm. Leaves me at a disadvantage. I can teach so much else."

"Yeah, I'm sure you can, but this is what I'm asking for. It's not just to keep you from using my thoughts against me or for your own gains, but to protect myself from our enemies. There're not enough herbs to go around here after dispersing it to so many others. I need something more than my Kitchen Witch knowledge."

He narrowed his eyes. "You are much more than a Kitchen Witch."

"It wasn't a self-loathing dig, simply reality. Being a Kitchen Witch isn't a derogatory title unless used like one. I need to develop beyond my current skills, and I haven't been doing that while focusing on everyone else's needs. You happen to know more, or at least say you do. So, if you can put aside the goal of getting in my pants and focus on the protection side of things, then I may take you seriously and make it official."

"I know you were in too bad of a way to see what happened, but you only have to ask the guards to know whether or not I am serious about your protection. Or think back on countless other acts of service since we met."

I tilted my head, silently calling him on his stall tactics. If he wanted the job he was lobbying for, this was his chance.

I stood, strapping on a judgey face. He stretched to standing height, maintaining eye contact, and then stared down at me.

He cleared his throat. "Fine. But it goes both ways."

"What does?"

"I will fulfill my promised and professional role on a probationary basis as long as you fulfill yours as my protected. Under my watch means wherever you go, I go. You don't fight me."

I crossed my arms. "Is this some pervy tactic to watch me pee?"

He shook his head and fought a grin. "I will loosen my detail here in the Prison Creation since there are obvious protections in place.

Other locations will be appraised on a case-by-case basis. Otherwise, expect me around even if you don't see me."

"Hmm. Sounds a little stalkerish."

He shot me a crooked smile.

"What about the Tactical Team?"

"What about them?"

"What happens when you go on mission? I'm not going with you. And I do have a Sect to run."

"I have no problem quitting the Team if your role as a Sect Leader requires it. Until the day my position on the Team poses a threat to my duties to you or if your role in the Mother Coven advances and requires an elevated level of defence, I will, again, require your cooperation with our current occupations. If I'm on mission, I need to trust you won't put yourself in danger. I leave. You stay. Simple. Outside these walls, again, case-by-case basis and something we decide together unless you're unreasonable and fight me on it."

"And if I'm unreasonable, then what? You lock me down? Bind me?"

"If needed."

What? Shit.

"You're a smart and level-headed woman. I have great faith we can work out something mutually beneficial."

"Mhmm. Guess we'll see."

"Yes. We will."

Ranlyn exited the office where he and Edson met, his quick steps bringing him towards us en route to keep going. I mouthed a "Sorry" his way. He returned a tight and stressed smile and slid it towards Hall with an extra dose of tension without missing a step as he continued on somewhere else.

A loud laugh and murmured talking sounded from people in the lobby. Sophie appeared, exiting from a cell, sloppily dressed in a towel. Her soaking wet hair clung to her shoulders, so did the clothing in her arms, the water dripping off of them as she stormed off to the cell console and disappeared into a cell. Why would she leave her cell and then go right back into it? Did she forget something besides how a towel works?

Someone called for a mop from one of the guards, but another Magic used a pulse of energy and dried it up in a snap.

Donovan appeared from a cell, he surveyed the lobby quickly and he headed towards the cafeteria, looking angry and blank-faced. Whatever was happening, his hair was slightly drier than Sophie's. Oooh! Did they shower together? If they did, it meant sex, unless they happened to shower in their own cells at the same time. If so, why would Sophie leave a cell and then re-enter another cell?

No, they had to have been together.

"I wouldn't expect any true relationship happiness until their Soul Magic is fully healed."

"How do you know it's not?"

Hall's expression pinched. "Do they look like the happy couple they once were before the Sorrel cells?"

"You didn't meet them until they were in there."

"I've heard more than I've ever needed to know about those two from Lewy and seen them in your thoughts as well as in the memories from the failed memory bomb of Donovan's. Not to mention the endless perceived betrayal in Sophie during their time in the Sorrel cells. Their Soul Magic is still fractured and it's leaking onto everyone around them." He leaned forward to block my view to where Donovan and Sophie disappeared. "To be clear, if need be, I will protect you from them as well, so I hope you're taking this probationary period seriously. When I proclaim protection, I mean in its totality be it of your person or your emotional wellbeing whether you like it or not."

Right. I may completely regret this arrangement. I didn't need protection over my emotions. I'm stronger than he realized if he thought differently. Physically, a towering six-foot-seven beast of a Magic shield or going in alone or with lesser experienced fighters to battle was a no-brainer. A Viking who has fought and survived countless wars is offering to keep me alive and I'm going to sweat the relationship complications? I'm not a moron. Though, I did still need to be schooled in covering my thoughts in some way.

He narrowed his eyes, not liking whatever he was reading from my mind again.

"Come, kitten." Hall grabbed my hand and pulled me through the crowded lobby.

"Hey! Where're we going?"

When he reached an office door, I dug my heels in. With how we just fought and him dragging me from the scene, shutting ourselves up in an office is going to look like we're shacking up.

Hall chuckled. "They already think we're sleeping together. Besides, they can interrupt if they wish and will find two Magics practicing to shield the mind or at least a spell for it. Scandalous."

"What?" I wrenched from his hand and crossed my arms.

He kept a hand on the knob, door partially opened. "Is it really so bad if people think we're romantically involved?"

I scoffed. "It is if they know I'm still with Frog."

"Believe me, kitten. No one's thinking about Frog."

Ugh. That was a horrible truth. I didn't want to forget about Frog even if he possibly prayed he never met me. The opinions of others shouldn't matter when I knew the truth, but they did. I was supposed to lead some of them. I wasn't their mother or here to shake a finger at them, but still.

Following the bouncing ball of my thoughts, reading my disappointment in myself, Hall held the door fully open. He waited until I stepped through it, and then closed the door behind us.

5

WINDOW OF SUCCESS

Caine

Hours of interrogation had me cross-eyed. Throbbing above my brows lessened when I pressed my fingers against them, enough to clear my blurry left eye. Since Gareth's hitchhiking soul was ripped from me and destroyed, using my power felt experimental. When Donovan asked me to trick Lincoln into telling us contact information to access the Sovereignty, I never expected the guy was a traitor. By the looks of everyone else who met the man, neither did they.

Lincoln was so fucked.

He was going from a position of trusted advisor to the Sovereignty heir and Tactical Team Leader for the Mother Coven to a traitor and prisoner in the span of hours. Vincent wouldn't be happy. Heartbroken over Anne-Claire's death, sure. But she was a warrior. Potential death came with the package. Betraying your coven and providing sensitive information to the enemy, compromising the lives of countless, was inexcusable. Or at least, he should have covered his ass better and found a way to block my persuasion. He must have known we would learn the truth eventually.

"Am I done here?" I really needed to pee.

Ranlyn glanced over from where he and Veata stood in close conversation with the Tactical Team members, trying to think of more questions they might need Lincoln to answer. Or that they needed me to make Lincoln answer. He definitely would never have volunteered any of what he said. He was stupid for trusting Chase and anyone else in the Sovereignty, but not that stupid.

Ranlyn took a few steps towards me and glimpsed at where I left Lincoln, his will still in my hold. Not my hand, though it may as well have been. I felt it in my brain, not my palms, but it was there, an unseen fog I vacuum-sealed around the guy and could do whatever I wanted until I pulled the fog away.

"We're done with interrogation for now, yes. If you could get him into a cell before you let him free so we can avoid an escape attempt, it would be appreciated."

I smiled. "I don't need to be there for that. I'll give him his instructions, and he'll follow them until he's completed his task."

Ranlyn's brows raised a bit as he nodded. "He'll remain guarded…just in case."

I chuckled. "Whatever works."

Ranlyn extended his hand to shake. I returned it, trying not to think about the lemonade a guard brought me during the interrogation sloshing around in my bladder.

I stood to Lincoln's side. "Stand."

Lincoln obeyed.

I met our docile captive straight in his clear and non-confrontational eyes knowing he would be anything but at ease if I wasn't holding his will. "Lincoln, you are now in the custody of the Mother Coven and the governing body of this Prison Creation. You will follow Ranlyn to the cell console. You will not deviate from the path Ranlyn takes you. You will not speak or try to fight or leave the Prison

Creation. You will enter the cell assigned to you, again, without a fight or a spoken word, and you will remain in custody until otherwise instructed. Once you have entered the cell, my persuasion will leave you, and you will retain all memory of our conversation including your admission of guilt. At some point, you will be provided with legal representation. Your charges will be known to the Magic public, and you will be stripped of your Mother Coven and Tactical Leader positions, permissions, and titles."

I looked at Ranlyn to confirm if all I said was appropriate and to give him a chance to add anything else. He didn't. I instructed Lincoln to follow Ranlyn from the room and to abide all of the instructions as I described them.

Maybe I should have been surprised at how submissive Lincoln was, but I wasn't. The Berisford way included far more influence and degradation while taking over another's will. I knew I could make Lincoln do absolutely anything I wanted. Anything. Chances were I could implant responses to my questions if I wanted. No one could prove I did, except maybe Sophie. They should be lucky I'm nothing like Daniel.

I pushed aside the image of my father's face as I stabbed him in the heart. Was he relieved? If he was, I didn't understand why.

Ugh. Fuck him and the rest of the Berisfords like him.

It reminded me to check up on Jet and Andy again. She pretended she had it all together, but she was hanging on by her fingernails and probably needed a break. She didn't say it, but she still hadn't checked on her parent's home, her home, even though her parents were now dead. Maybe I could convince someone to let me take Andy outside for a bit. I tried to ignore the little voice in my head reminding me my persuasion was always an option no one here could ignore. I didn't want to end up caught and questioned. Others with persuasion powers existed, in the Berisford family and maybe some they didn't know about, and Ranlyn could probably find them to interrogate me.

Lincoln disappeared through the cell console, oblivious to the countless stares from confused onlookers as he was escorted like a prisoner. If people didn't know what was happening, they sure did now.

Damn. I still needed to pee.

I raced for the bathroom and did what my bladder was screaming for me to do in the first stall since the urinals were at the other end of the room.

Again, as with every time I used indoor plumbing, I thought of the countless times I pissed or shit in the forest in Diluculo while I was trapped in there. Evaristus wasn't above having the greenery come attack your balls, and even if the plants weren't alive, you kept your attention trained on the trees in case someone was alive and looking to off you mid-stream.

"Caine!"

Whatthefuck?

Felix's voice bounced off of the public bathroom's walls. The kid was freaked about something.

"Caine, I know you're in here."

"Yeah. Hold up." I shook and flushed.

When I left the stall, Felix and Derek were waiting for me, Derek's expression a stern look of warning Felix ignored.

"What's going on?" I pressed the soap dispenser and rubbed my hands together.

"She's leaving. She's making me go, too. I don't want to go. I want to stay here and fight."

I rinsed my hands under some water. "Whoa, whoa. What are you talking about?"

Derek reached for Felix's arm as if he was going to try and drag him away. "Come on, man. This isn't what—"

"I don't care what she wants. I'm not going!"

"Stop!"

They both dropped their stare down quickly.

Shit. Did my raised voice contain persuasion influence? It had been switched on for a long time, maybe it was still wading beneath the surface.

I grabbed some paper towels to dry my hands. “You’re talking about Ness?”

Felix scoffed. “Obviously. Who else would you care about taking off?”

“Okay. But what do you mean she’s leaving? Leaving to go where?”

“It doesn’t matter. I’m not going. I don’t care what she says.”

Derek piped up again and he and Felix argued over each other.

Fuck it. I’ll ask her myself.

There were two places I might find her: a cell or the cafeteria.

Derek stepped in front of me, blocking my way. He lifted his hands. “Hold up a second. You should know...I plan on going with them.”

“I’m not going anywhere,” Felix huffed in defiance when he caught up.

I focused on Derek. “Going where?”

“I don’t know the exact address. Somewhere in Chile.”

“Chile?” I turned to Felix. “What’s in Chile?”

“Nothing.”

Derek looked down at Felix. “It’s got safety.”

Felix rolled his eyes.

“Safety?”

“Yes, safety. Something we haven’t had since getting trapped in Diluculo with Evaristus and his rotting playthings. Something safer than in another Creation where Elders are kidnapped and their members are traitors and no matter what battle you fight, there’s another one right after it. We didn’t survive Diluculo only to die in this shady-ass town because your ex has a death wish and—”

“This is about Sophie?”

“Yes!” Felix was quick to answer. “It’s always about her.”

"No," Derek argued, "it's not about her. Though, it's a bonus for everyone to be as far from the chick as possible since she attracts bad luck like flies to a corpse, which is what we'll end up as the longer we stick around. Since you're going to barge in on Ness and try and convince her to stay and fight at your side no matter what I say, think about what her life is worth to you, and Felix's life, and mine. We can't save the whole damn Creation and fight a war against the Tainted or even the Sovereignty, but we can save ourselves and we can do it even easier with you next to us."

Next to them? They want me to leave with them? "She..." I didn't understand. She wanted to leave? "I need to talk to her."

I took off again to the sound of Felix and Derek's continued arguing, my thoughts racing as I pushed through the crowd to the cell console and punched in the information to pull up Ness's cell. When I entered, Ness was folding something, her bag open on the bed and everything she owned spread across the surface.

"You're leaving?"

She spun at the sound of my voice, shock on her face at my intrusion. She rolled her shoulder and started folding a shirt she snatched from the bed. "Felix is such a little rat."

I didn't know what to do or say as she put the folded shirt in the bag and picked up another. "You're leaving," I said again, this time in realization of her determination. Whatever was between us wouldn't be enough to convince her to stay. With no bargaining chip in my pocket, I stood in silence, my thoughts flicking up and discarding pathetic things to say to her before potentially never seeing her again.

"You could come with us."

I looked up at her in surprise. Her attention was on folding the pants in front of her. Did I imagine her saying that?

She shook out the next item in her hand and glanced at me. "It's what you want me to say, even though we both know you would never leave. Do I want you to come with us? Yes, I do." She tossed the pants into her bag and faced me, crossing her arms. "It would be better if you came too, but you won't. You'll stay here and be at the

Mother Coven's beck and call every time they need a human lie detector. And, yes, for Sophie whenever she needs you because she always needs something."

She took a step towards me, arms still crossed. "You'll continue to be sucked into their agenda until it becomes your agenda, as it pretty well already has, and you will die fighting their fight. Be it in actuality or in spirit or whatever you wanna call it. Who you are will die and you'll be an extension of the Mother Coven's arm of justice. If you want to be that person, then me leaving won't change anything."

"Of cour—"

"Felix and I shouldn't have been outside Diluculo, fighting immortals and saving everyone else so they can die bloody on a different calendar date. That's not what I wanted, not for me and definitely not for Felix." She returned to the bed and grabbed something else I couldn't focus on, looked down at it and packed it with her other stuff. "You want to stay? That's fine. Actually fine. But I'm not sticking around to watch us be taken down too because our specialties stick a target on our foreheads or for the Mother Coven to turn us into Tactical Team members they send on missions with low survival rates."

I cleared my throat, struggling to call her out on anything she said while knowing so much was true. "Where... Chile's where you're going?"

She unzipped a small front pocket of her bag and grabbed something inside. "Yes. I can't tell you where unless you come with us." A second passed and then she held up a slim piece of paper.

I took it, her hand steady with decision, and went back to packing. On the folded piece of white paper ripped from a book was a number written in blue pen.

"It's a contact where you can reach us. I know the number here." She zipped up her and Felix's bag. No other items remained on the bed.

She was ready.

I gripped the paper in my fist. "This is...this is happening too fast."

"We shouldn't have come here at all. We should've left for Chile the second we were rescued from the Creation."

"But you didn't. You came here for a reason."

"Do you want me to say that reason was you?"

"No, I—"

"A part of it probably was, but I also needed a breather. To stop moving for longer than a few hours where I could think and plan. I can't stick around and do this with you. Not when you're determined to be at the center of more fighting."

"I didn't choose this. I—"

"I know you didn't. But you also haven't chosen against it and wouldn't have given it a second thought without me leaving. They're hitting the Sovereignty next, and I can't risk Vincent's sick family getting their hands on Felix or me. They won't kill us. They'll force someone like you to do whatever they want, or they'll use us against each other. I can't give them the chance."

"You can't—"

"Caine, this is—"

"Stop interrupting me. Please. I know you're leaving and nothing I say will change that. I'm not the priority here. And I'm not even trying to convince you that I should be. I'm just trying to wrap my head around you not being here. You've been a part of this and a part of me for a long time, and I meant it every time I said I wanted to be with you. You leaving won't change how I feel. But now?" I fought not to glare at her bag as if it was a thief stealing her away from me. "You're leaving right now? Right this second?"

"A family friend arranged transportation without our names ending up on any manifests where Loring could have his minions follow. It took some time but there's a window of success. We may not be Loring's main targets, but we hit him with a few hurts inside the Creation in the months we were trapped there and we helped kill his Master plus some devotees. We're loose ends. And loose ends don't remain loose for long. They'd use us up like they tried to do to Jet. An opportunity exists now. We need to take it."

"Sure, sure." I understood, but the rejected tone in my voice said differently, and I couldn't hide it.

She propped her bag up against the wall. There was nothing left to do.

"That's it, then?" I took a step towards her, touching her arm and feeling her rigidity soften. "I don't want you to leave and never see you again." I lightly gripped both of her arms, holding her in however she allowed for potentially the last time. "You're right, I can't leave with you right now and I *will* regret the decision. The Mother Coven may expect too much from me. Or the next battle could be my last. In the hands of Loring or the Sovereignty is not where I want to be." I tried not thinking of my father again and how he ended up like so many others in my bloodline. "But I also can't up and leave Jet and Andy."

"I know, which is why I didn't ask you to. This life sucks, but it's what's in front of us and I can't follow you into a crash and burn situation. I put my power in when I thought it could make the most difference and when Felix wouldn't let me run from it. This will end badly if we don't leave now."

I nodded and leaned down to hug her tightly. She reciprocated without her usual pause. "And what if I manage to live through this? Can I come find you?" I pulled away to see the answer in her eyes, still holding her close.

"I'm not running from you, Caine. I'm just running." She pushed up onto her tippy-toes to press her lips to mine.

I met her halfway, gripping her to me, memorizing her soft lips like they might be the last time I felt or tasted them. She didn't fear me and that made a difference, but she would be a world away, and not seeing her every day would be a loss. Ness was all about actions above words and she stuck to her plans. Following through with this one had already been in the bag long before Felix told me.

She wrapped her arms around my neck and deepened the kiss,

stroking my tongue with hers, drawing me in with her hands in the back of my head.

I held her tighter. I didn't want to let her go. Once I did, she was in the wind. A number to reach her and the name of a place I may never see was nothing to having her within arm's reach. She was including me by giving me the information, but there was no end date for this war. If I had to wait to see her again until it was over, I may never see her again.

Ness broke our kiss and grabbed for the hem of my shirt.

"Really?"

She paused. "Are you saying you don't—"

"No, no." I whipped my shirt over my head and kissed her again. "Just surprised."

Ness pulled off her own shirt, tossed it to the ground, and then worked on my jeans button and zipper. A fever in her movements meant this was happening now or never and I was on board once I shoved away the thought of it being the last time.

Ness yanked my jeans down over my sudden hardness and sat on the side of the bed as she did. I leaned down, my lips to hers again as I kicked my jeans all of the way off and worked on hers.

Everything happened so fast. I heard about her taking off literal minutes ago and now she was... Oh, damn.

Ness was naked from the waist down and was taking off her bra. The deep red and lacey fabric was now on the floor in a pile with the rest of our clothing. She moved to the head of the cell's crappy bed with the thin pillow and laid down in a clear invitation.

No matter how long she was gone for, I could never forget her like this.

I leaned over her to feel her full lips again and found a position that didn't equal squishing her or falling off of the far too small bed.

She reached down between us and grabbed a hold of me, stroking me like she was afraid I might be too grief-stricken by her leaving to get it up.

No problem found.

My dick couldn't convince her to stay, couldn't even guarantee Felix or Derek didn't interrupt this spur-of-the-moment goodbye, but it found no issue ensuring she also remembered our last time together.

She guided me into her, wet and ready, and wrapped her legs around my waist to keep me close as a collective moan filled the space.

Fuck. I wanted to be angry at her as I matched her pace. I wanted to beg and plead for her not to leave me. With her smell in my nose and her breath on my neck, I couldn't do either and she would think less of me if I did.

Ness moaned again and pulled my attention from the negative shit in my head still circling with the whiplash of a situation. She held me by the shoulders, her nails digging into my skin, and lifted her hips to meet mine over and over again with an urgency different than the last times we were together. The cinderblock wall next to us and the hospital-grade sheets beneath reminded me there was no magic in this room. None of her illusions or my persuasion.

No hiding.

Ness's breath quickened. Her hold on me tightened into a grapple. She cried out, spurring on a rush of pleasure in me at the sound.

Driving into her to drain the orgasm from her sent me over the edge. I would have loved to last a night and a day, but control went out the window when she lost it herself.

In a huff of breathless exertion, I fought to keep myself from crushing her while my limbs turned to Jello.

I shifted to the side when I was soft enough to manage the maneuver and rested next to her.

Physical satisfaction filled every part of me. The tense silence afterwards left me hollow.

A blur flashed over me. I blinked as Ness got up from the bed. She wasn't running, though in my orgasm-inebriated state, she may as well have been. Instead, she quickly used the washroom behind the small cinderblock wall. When she returned, I spun around to sit up as she picked through the pile of our clothing in search of her own. She wasn't rushing, but everything still felt too fast.

"You're sure about this." I cleared my throat. "Not a question...a statement. Your mind is set, and I can't change it."

Was I saying this to hear my own helplessness or force her to feel some guilt? If she felt any, she wouldn't have said so and my helplessness wasn't her fault.

This fucking sucked.

Ness pulled her shirt over her head and righted the fabric. I pictured her pulling the same deep red bra strap down her shoulder and then flashed back to her getting dressed.

She sat on the edge of the bed to slide her underwear and pants up her smooth legs, stood to tug them into place, and then sat again to pull her socks on. In more silence, she untied her shoes and then tied them properly. Most times she would slip them on, bending the heels down instead of tying them. Not only was she tying them, but it also meant she was leaving now and needed to wear them properly in case she had to travel a significant distance or run for safety.

I hated the thought of her in trouble without me there to help her.

Fighting the scenarios in my head of her in danger, I reached for my clothing and dressed in a fog as my mind raced over picturing the aftermath of her leaving. Derek was going with them, which was comforting since I knew he was capable in a fight, but it wasn't the same.

She was ready first, arranging her bag and Felix's by the exit wall of the cell.

Once I was finished, there was nothing left to do.

I stepped in close to her and risked her rejecting a kiss. She reciprocated in a way she never did, leaning into it.

She settled back on her heels, hands resting on my arms. "Again, Caine. I'm not running away from you."

"I know, but the result is the same. You won't be here for what comes next, and I won't be there to help you with whatever dangers you face while outside of this place. I know my opinion means nothing, but it's how it is."

"Yes, it is." Everything in her dark eyes spoke of her wanting me to make this easier. To accept this for what it was. "I have to go."

I nodded and exhaled with defeat, picking up her and Felix's bags and leaving the cell.

At least she let me help her.

No one paid us any attention in the lobby. I may have been carrying Ness's and Felix's worldly possessions, but it wasn't uncommon to see someone walking around with their stuff. Not everyone trusted leaving what little they owned in a cell since they were unlocked and accessible to anyone.

Felix's shoulders slumped when he saw us. Ness took the bags from me and held up her brother's for him. He refused to take it for a few seconds until he huffed and snatched it from her hand. When Ness didn't want to be pushed, she couldn't be.

Felix knew he lost this one.

Derek held out his hand for me to shake. I took it and we pulled each other into a half-hug and clapped each other on the back. "Don't worry, if she won't, I'll call when I can."

"Thanks, man."

Derek let me go, shook my hand one last time, and stepped back, pulling his backpack onto his back. He had less than Ness, and I hoped he took some supplies while he could.

Felix dropped his bag and hugged me tight without any regard for if anyone was watching. He didn't have anything to say. We both knew we weren't on board with this plan and wished each other well, knowing we were headed into different brands of danger.

When he pulled away, I leaned onto the guard's desk, and Liam looked up at me, his jaw set as if preparing to tell me to go fuck myself.

"Do I need to persuade you to activate the elevator? I'll take the heat from Ranlyn and Edson. Either way, these three are leaving."

Liam did a show by thinking about it for a few seconds and then rounded the counter, saying what he had to to turn his hand into the proper key shape and revealing the lock to manipulate the elevator.

Ness, Felix, and Derek stepped into the elevator when it opened. Felix gave a sad wave, Derek pursed his lips and nodded, and Ness just looked at me until I was staring at the doors instead of her deep eyes.

They were gone.

6

NOTHING TO IMPART

Vincent

Blood spurted onto my shirt, covering me from chest to thighs and pooling beneath Cora-Lynn's jagged stump of an arm onto the dirt-encrusted floor. Her cheeks were flushed and blood-spattered, and her blonde hair was streaked with grotesque strawberry highlights. Cora-Lynn's screams echoed off the factory walls, and people all around us scrambled, shouted for help, or retched in disgust. Most fled the floor and were content to observe from a distance.

I ripped off my shirt and fashioned a tourniquet around Cora-Lynn's arm. The intense pressure caused her to gasp without sound.

She kicked her feet in involuntary agony. "Vincent, please..." she begged, though I did all I could.

The blood slowed, nevertheless, a constant fount of impending death I possessed no hope of delaying continued, just as it had when my father drowned us over and over again. Nothing I could do would best my father's efforts to torture me with this new brand of misery.

Blinding pain was prescribed for Cora-Lynn and the sickening loop of witnessing my greatest love die was on tap for me.

The perfect mix to guarantee our suffering.

Our new tortures consisted of nothing more than replays of how Sophie and Donovan died in their previous lives including some I never experienced firsthand, like this current death in this factory.

Somehow, the mutant or maybe my father, gathered knowledge of the ways in which Sophie and Donovan died in the years I did not encounter them or in ones I chose not to connect in fear of losing them again. To think, I assumed I kept them safe when I restrained myself from entering their lives and, all of those times, my father knew of their existence anyway.

The chances of my father taking Cora-Lynn's arm permanently was small yet not implausible or beyond his doing. A lump of flesh to remind her she was lesser of a human being to him. Her arm was likely still attached, and an illusion caused me to see it as severed.

I see through the narrow window my father and the mutant Sovereignty cell warden allow and nothing more.

Amputation via industrial equipment resulting in death by blood loss was common in this timeframe, though I could not recall this end for Sophie. Maybe this was how Donovan died, and the machinery took Sophie's life along with his. They must not have discovered healing prowess in this life. Enough time passed for them to heal if they possessed the ability. Maybe my lack of presence in this particular life cycle is the reason why or maybe their powers were different in general. Unless I left this place and peered into Sophie's soul along with her as she read her past lives, I would never know.

If Fate allowed, I did wish to find Sophie again. With Cora-Lynn is where I needed to be right now. I refused to live outside of this cell while she remained.

"Please..." Cora-Lynn grabbed my arm with waning strength in her remaining limb. "I need you to tell her... I need her to send for—"

"Not a worry. Quiet now," I said to bring an ounce of comfort to the woman I loved who, in these scenarios, thought they were real, and she and I were still lovers, dying from some horrible ailment or accident. Cora-Lynn didn't remember the years she spent in my father's cells while in these replays of horror. She lived the life Sophie and Donovan did, thinking those memories belonged to her and me.

Until…

Cora-Lynn blinked, rapidly taking in her surroundings. She saw her mangled arm and then looked up at me knelt at her side.

She was herself again. Not the husk of a memory my father's cells replayed, but Cora-Lynn herself was alive in those eyes.

"Yes, we are still in the cells," I told her. "I am truly sorry."

Cora-Lynn dropped her head back onto the floor, her chest heaving as her heart worked to fight mortality with no hope of succeeding. A sheen of sweat covered her, the bleeding stump now a trickle as she closed her eyes and paid no attention to the frightened murmurs from fabricated onlookers.

No parting words crossed her lips. The moment she was granted comprehension as part of her torture, she knew she was close to death.

This reliving of Sophie's and Donovan's death occurred well over forty times in forty-plus different ways. In each instance, I could not refrain from coming to Cora-Lynn in her last moments of rapt understanding and then passing in confusion. If I could separate myself from the dramatic ending, especially of those I never experienced in person, maybe the mutant behind the button would choose a different line of torture. Sophie and Donovan existed long before our meeting, living and dying with their Soul Magic intact. No matter the effectiveness of such a punishment, the material the tortures consisted of was not infinite.

"Not infinite, no."

I sprang to my feet and spun to the voice returning my inner thoughts. My father and brother stood on the dirty factory floor, my father the one who spoke as Chase found himself unable to refrain from peering around our staged surroundings as if the realism impressed him.

The scene around us paused. The pool of blood under Cora-Lynn no longer spread, the voices of horrified onlookers switched off, and none ran to free themselves of the gore or seek help. I glanced at Cora-Lynn and saw her relaxed in a way I hadn't observed in many years. They created the illusion of hair in this scenario, and she appeared more like my Cora-Lynn than ever.

"Why recreate their deaths? They continue to live regardless of any intervention of my own. Is your mutant's imagination faltering?"

Alasdair flashed a small smile. "Sometimes simplicity proves most effective."

"I'll never understand why you bother with those two generation after generation." Chase's glower rolled over Cora-Lynn. "Their goldfish existence must be infuriating."

I prayed Chase was never gifted the task of Overseer. Present involvement in Sophie and Donovan's life may not have always been my top priority, falling to the wayside when my heart was too battered to fulfill the post again.

"Overseer..." Alasdair put his hands in his pants pockets. "A position without compensation. I will never understand it."

Chance scowled. "Overseer? Mismanagement at its highest."

I glared at my brother, yet spoke to my father. "This is what is left of your legacy. One rebellious son imprisoned by your hand and the other so irresponsible and untrustworthy you would rather continue your position centuries beyond duty than risk the world existing under his reign. You must be swimming with pride."

Chase moved towards me. He was stopped after a step by my father or the mutant, I was uncertain, but he ceased his path and stood silent and fuming.

My father bypassed my brother without addressing him to stand and peer down at Cora-Lynn. While I knew anything he might do to her was nothing compared to the centuries of abuse he passively approved, I still tensed to strike him down if he dared touch her now.

"She appears deceased, yet is merely deactivated. You know this and still allow unsubstantiated fear and grief to convince you it may be her true end. Maybe such empathy is what makes an Overseer of Fate's design, one who refuses to let hope die. In some lives you certainly disengaged your hope in favour of self-preservation, ignoring the needs of your Charges, as with this life." His motioned around us, confirming my memory was not lacking and I was not present for this death of Sophie and Donovan's. Since the roles were mine and Cora-Lynn's, I could not know if Sophie and Donovan were together or experienced this dual loss separately.

My father repositioned himself to peer down at Cora-Lynn to better see her face. "Until you found this one, your Charges were the singular beings keeping your hold on immortality." He met my eyes with true question in his own. "Why not end yourself? We immortals are not impervious to death, as you well know." He looked down at Cora-Lynn again. "I could have the Warden force you to relive finding your mother's remains, but it's a waste of time and wouldn't fill an hour let alone a day. And this one has not attempted to end her own life since her fifty-second year."

Chase shifted his stance in what seemed like annoyance and frustration. He was always quick to anger when mention of our mother entered the conversation. In the midst of an argument, he once said she betrayed him in her death by choosing to orchestrate my finding her instead of him. Imagine, someone so concerned with themself that they could be jealous of such a thing.

My father's cold features remained stoic at the mention of her death, the memory of her bolstering my resolve instead of the opposite of what my father hoped. She hated who he became and knew about his dark plans too late to stop them. I always wondered if she truly died by her own hand or if my father had played a role in her death beyond conditioning her with a sense she could never find freedom outside of his influence.

"She knew she did not possess the ability to end your supremacy, and she found an avenue of freedom you could not prevent. Death is always on the table when other viable options cease to exist. I promised her the day prior to her finding her freedom that I would live long enough to see your empire lay waste at your feet. That whatever nefarious plans you devised would collapse and drag you under with them. Even in here, my fight has not been lost. Thank you for the reminder."

He clenched his jaw and pinched his brow. "You have failed for countless years."

"Years, yes. Each contained their own brand of success. A war which will continue to be waged in my absence." Alasdair let this be said without comment. "You have surrounded yourself with others who also enjoy the vengeance you dole out against perceived weaker Magics because you could not punish my mother in the way you deemed she deserved. In planning her own death, she found an escape far from your reach, so now you refuse to allow those you punish to perish. Your prisoners are nothing but a representation of retribution which has not given you the satisfaction you have sought all these years because they will never be her."

"That's quite an assumption."

I shook my head. "If you had found solace in your approach to civilised order, you would have handed off the company years ago. If not to Chase than to another. You remained and grew colder. You created in Chase a thirst for punishment. Now you live knowing you have lost control of him and cannot reverse the perversions he has developed instead. Kill us for good if you desire. I will never take up position where you have always envisioned me, and you will still be left with Chase as your legacy as he will see it burned to the ground if you do not gift it to him. That is if you do not orchestrate his death or imprisonment as well. Though, I assume he implemented a myriad of failsafes to prevent such maneuvers or you would have already." Neither my father nor brother commented on the potential of such a possibility, however, I knew them both well enough to believe in a high likelihood of such behind-the-scenes safeguarding. "I have witnessed their deaths in a plethora of tragic ways. You being here and designing Cora-Lynn's continued deaths proves you have never changed and are still everything my mother could not bear to live with another second."

The tragedy of the truth was that no matter how much I railed against injustice, it changed little. Alasdair revealed nothing and remained resolute in his frigid response, choosing to stare at me from across my wife's deactivated form.

"What brings you here now?" I asked. "Did you have a break between meetings and decide to check in on your handiwork? One can assume you have more pressing concerns on your agenda. You can collect any of my Sovereignty contacts from reading my mind, so they are already dead or you find them useful or unthreatening and have left them alone until they prove otherwise. What could you possibly want from me?"

Alasdair retained his heavy glare as he rounded Cora-Lynn's body to stand in front of me. "Your experiment, as it were, to replace the Sovereignty's rule has failed."

"Failed, as in fallen?" I glanced at Chase whose expression always betrayed our father's intentions. If the Prison Creation truly fell, Chase would be gloating, and he was still fuming from father restraining him.

My father was bluffing.

"Without your presence, it will."

I smiled. The Prison Creation still stood, and he was desperate to find it. "Contingencies were created for this exact instance. You think me ignorant to believe I would not end up right where I am? True, I never anticipated Cora-Lynn's involvement, she was a genuine surprise, though not an all together negative addition." I leaned forward and closed the distance a bit. "Thank you, for giving me the gift of seeing her again." I straightened. "Those whom I have worked within your organization and outside of it, know I am here. And whether I have been here for days or years, they will continue their search. Until I am fit to retake my position or if you prove to them my true death, they will enact certain protocols to ensure our systems continue.

"Now, I have yet to see the inside of a courtroom, so you have no plans of following through with judicial process. Return to your desks knowing I am right where you left me. But know I will be retrieved at some point. Your methods of punishment against your prisoners are ineffectual, as are your techniques in convincing me to be anything akin to you. All your teachings have done is ensure I am strong enough to endure whatever you throw at me. If you were in my position, would you reveal the information you have come for?"

No. Alasdair would never give up the type of intel he expects me to divulge. Those I love were already targets of his attentions, so they are in no greater danger for me refusing to reveal the processes which may lead him to the information he sought. He shoved me into a cell because I attacked him. He could have done so decades ago. Now that I am here, he is conflicted on ending me and has no way to retrieve the data he needs otherwise, and he knew it.

Brisk air invaded my lungs, riding the stale scent of car exhaust and the heaviness of saturated filth. A fog rose in front of my face, startling me until comprehending it was my breath. A dank alley boxed me in on both sides, it too narrow to accommodate a vehicle. Garbage bins and various forms of refuse lined the alleyway, seemingly a rear exit for businesses and pedestrians.

Honking blared from one end of the alley, as did the voices of passersby. A tug on my arm snapped my attention to the forefront, the action done by a woman wearing a felt cloche. Droplets of rain and intricate beading from her dress caught the harsh glare of an exterior light.

"Come on." She tugged my arm and wrapped a gloved hand around my elbow to propel me forward. "You know the code. Lets put this in the rearview so I can return to Jesse and the others."

Confusion set its heels in as I fought to remember this. Realization of the memory came when I saw the woman as Cora-Lynn yet knew this was Sophie, or Virginia as Sophie was known then and affectionately as Virgie. I barely recognized Cora-Lynn with a face full of makeup, elegantly dressed, and in heels. 1926, southern California, prohibition era. Magics never went without alcohol. The substance ban halted the import business in a multitude of ways, trickling down to Magics requiring places akin to the Blind's speakeasys seeking required elements of spell work. In this time, we needed feathers from a Black and Chestnut Eagle, unavailable to many and possessed by a paranoid Necromancer. Which meant... Oh, no...

I did know the password and once I recited the code the man on the inside of the steel door ahead of us required, we would enter. Only I would exit. Not through this door, but by a secret tunnel for this decade's bootleggers, popping up in a public restroom a block over.

In this life, I forfeit the ability to bury Sophie and Donovan as I had in the past, choosing to save myself as they had already been cut down too far away from each other to cling to one another's company. Some knew nothing of their eventual re-entry into existence. Those with the knowledge would care for Donovan's body, I was certain. What became of Sophie's or Virgie's, I never knew. I left for Europe as soon as I could arrange transportation.

"Vincent..." Cora-Lynn in Sophie's clothing urged me again to step to the door and recite the required code. She could not know what was about to happen, my father choosing another way for Cora-Lynn to die in front of me and to come into reality moments before death. In this case, death came via a spell-choked bomb laced with household nuts and bolts, glass, and various scrap metal. Shrapnel put me down for weeks once I escaped and it was removed, the remnants of a lingering substance I never identified poisoning me until I met Moira, an Alchemist in search of refuge for herself and her family and who eventually became a trusted friend.

Moira. I wondered where she was, shifted my worry aside, and then refocused on the green peeling paint of the steel door in front of me.

I grabbed the doorknob. A zing of sensation rolled through me as it read me as a Magic and took stock of my power as confirmation I was not some Blind stumbling upon the location.

The door ran translucent, enough for me to gaze upon the mug of the Magic who eventually gets twitchy and sets off the bomb which ends my short-lived happiness in this life with Sophie and Donovan as Virgie and Jesse. I set my jaw and braced for the scene to conclude as I knew it would.

7

SUCH FEARFUL MEN

Kim

"Come on, come on." It took me an hour to convince myself to call Frog and now no one was picking up.

I hung up the office phone, ignoring Hall's pacing shadow at the bottom of the closed door while he insisted on staying "on duty", and dialled Frog's cell again.

The line clicked. "Hello?"

"Hey, Reed, it's Kim. Sounds like you gargled rock salt." His voice was so groggy I almost didn't recognize him.

He groaned. "Remind me to ditch tequila shots whenever we pop our heads up outta these groundhog days of fun and sun. Hold on a sec. I'll see if Frog is vertical."

I had to chuckle. "Thanks."

As Reed navigated through the hotel suite, voices grumbled in the background. Dom's low complaints were recognizable, the higher-pitched voices of company were not. Were they there for Frog? Some of the other guys were single, so they wouldn't hesitate to bring women back to their rooms.

A scuffle of the receiver, Reed calling Frog's name a couple of times, more complaints. Like the rest of them, Frog was still sleeping.

"Hello?"

"Sounds like you spent as much time with tequila shots as Reed did. Fun night?"

Pause. More scuffling of the receiver.

"Frog?"

Another second passed and he cleared his throat. "Wha—? What's going on?"

"Ah, I just thought I'd call. I ha—"

"Haven't called me since I got the beating of my life and was forced to go on a vacation and ignore every instinct I have to do the very opposite?"

Okay. He was still pissed. Guess Caine's persuasion was still working or Frog would have left by now. "Yeah, since then."

"Mhmm."

"I'm sorry. I didn't have anything new to tell you and was trying to give you space. You wouldn't've been interested in any updates, anyway. I've barely been outside." He could be angry all he wanted, but I wasn't having the time of my life.

"The thing in Niagara Falls...were you there? Was that a Magic thing?"

I exhaled, feeling trapped into an answer that would only vindicate whatever negative argument he had in mind. "Yes, I was. And, yes, it was."

"Of course it was. I may be on vacation, but I call home and it was all my mom could talk about. Jessica and Travis were there."

His niece and nephew. "Crap. Are they okay?"

"Yeah. They hid in the wax museum until the worst of it was over. A tad traumatized, but uninjured."

"Good." Ugh, this was bad. "Frog, we're doing the absolute best we can. That was a really, really hard day for a lot of us and the last day for far too many. We didn't create the situation. We were trying to stop it. This'll continue whether or not I have anything to do with it. I can't just walk away."

Scuffling on the other end was maybe Frog getting up from a bed. The dull metal on metal noise and then a light wind blowing against the receiver told me he was now outside. "Meet me here."

"What?"

"This place is perfect. Beautiful. Has everything you could want. Much safer than where you are. If you really want to survive whatever's happening there, meet me here."

I pressed my fingertips into my temple and glanced at Hall's stilled shadow beneath the office door, knowing he could hear everything. "Leaving isn't the answer. If it was, I'd have jumped on the plane with you. But that's why I called you. One of our own was captured—"

"Not *our* own."

Silence was heavy for a beat, the creeping anger in his tone piggybacking his rejected offer. "Fine. One of *my* own, Caine's own. One of our leaders, was captured. We're getting him back. I just wanted to talk with you beforehand."

"Why? It's not for my permission. If it was, my answer's no. You've done enough. Hop on a plane and we can discuss it face to face. But you're not going to, are you, Kim? You won't because I'm not a priority. Sure, I'm on the list, but not ahead of your coven. Not even ahead of Sophie, who, by the way, put Caine ahead of everything, including herself, to be with him. More than once, to hear him tell it."

"And since they're not a couple, they're not exactly the blueprint for happiness, are they?"

"Maybe not, but he mattered to her even when she was with that other dickbag. She sacrificed herself to save Caine. You said so yourself, she was willing to do absolutely everything to see him safe whether it messed with her relationship or not. Whatever you want to call that kind of crazy, at least it was some brand of devotion."

"Devotion?"

"Yeah, devotion. I never expected you to be a doting wife. I thought I'd be killing myself to keep your fashion obsessions flush, not be magically banished and kept away from scary things. If I wanted to pick a fight across the world, I'd join the army. I want to live a life, not spend every waking moment defending it. Can't you see how destructive this kind of thrill-seeking is?"

"Thrill-seeking? You think I'm getting off on watching people I care about die?"

"What I know is that I'm never, ever, going to join your coven or be a part of those people. I can't. Maybe Sophie was so quick to save Caine because they're both Magic people. Maybe that's the trick. Finding someone who's also fine with waging war every day. What's real clear to me now is you're never going to leave those people."

I clenched my teeth at 'those people'. "You're absolutely right. I won't."

"Exactly. So, how do we bypass this?"

I didn't even know what to say. Him bringing up me being with my own kind was what everyone warned me about. If he wanted to work on it, he would. Others have found a way to balance this life and one in the regular world with the person they loved. I thought him at least knowing about it would remove the paranoia of what I do and where I go, especially when it sometimes included being with Caine.

His ego was too bruised and he couldn't handle it. Quitting was easier for him. Easier than fighting for me or fighting for a solution so we could be together.

I wiped away wetness on my cheek with anger it existed. I didn't want to shed angry tears or let him hear me upset. He would think I was heartbroken, and I wasn't. I was pissed.

He continued when I was too busy trying not to scream through the phone. "If you have any ideas of how to make us work, I'm game to listen, but the way things have been isn't working for me. And even after this emergency or hiding period is over, you'll still be a coven leader and a—"

"A Magic? Yes, yes, I will be." I found my voice. "And you're right, I don't plan on being anything different than myself. Someone who truly wanted to support me and who cared about me wouldn't expect anything different. I shouldn't have to explain to you that I'm not going to abandon people in danger to stick a bandage on your ego. But if this life isn't what you want, I'm not wracking my brain to come up with ways to make you comfortable enough to love me."

A few moments of silence hung across the line. Maybe it was the L-word as neither of us used it with each other.

I didn't expect this call would end with us being over. I just wanted to hear his voice and gain a little bit of strength from knowing there was something on the other end of this waiting for me. He was one person I knew was safe from Loring and all the Tainted circling us. Guess Frog wasn't the waiting type. Damn Donovan for being right. I shouldn't have told Frog anything at all. Maybe I shouldn't have bothered getting serious with him in the first place.

I sniffed. "Okay, well, regardless of me being in your life or not, you may still be in danger. Loring and his chums don't exactly get updates on my relationship status and could still be after you if they think it'll give them any type of information or leverage. I doubt they would bother, but you never know. If you think anything is off, contact Caine. Yes, he's a Magic as well, but he's powerful and will always be your friend whether you've accepted him for who he is or not. Plus, you still can't tell the guys about Caine or about the existence of Magics. And as you know, it's better they know nothing about a world they can't do anything about, especially when they have no interest in joining it."

"Please. As if I would do that."

"You almost already did. Regardless of us being a thing, I don't want you or any of them in danger. I could erect a warding system for your place—"

"No, thanks. Besides, I could have Caine do that kind of stuff, right?"

"Right. He's a champ at that kind of…stuff."

I tried to think of anything of mine I may need at his place or vice versa, but we didn't do that kind of thing. I carried my Vintage Check, briar brown, Burberry overnight bag from his place and he shouldered a Nike backpack when he stayed over at mine. We never once cleared a drawer or left behind a toothbrush. I never even considered giving him one or saw him struggle through an awkward invitation to offer me space. Once this conversation was over, nothing was left for us.

Maybe I was more prepared for this than I thought.

"Okay, I'm going to let you go, so I can, y'know, get back to my people. Enjoy the rest of your vacation." I hung up without giving him a chance to say anything else that might have me on a plane with my feet in the sand on route to ramming the phone through his perfect teeth. I wasn't an easy girlfriend, and I know our relationship began with me hiding who I truly was, but I wasn't a Sect Leader or in the midst of a war back then. Life was simpler when he and I met. I was really into him.

Damn it. I stood and clenched my fists as tightly as I could, standing in place with my eyes closed until power bunched up in my muscles. Actual power. If Frog could stop and feel how delicious this could be and how much good it could do if it was wildly known, he wouldn't be such a freakin' idiot.

Tears hit my cheeks. Goddammit! Anger pulsed through me.

I've craved true access to tangible abilities for as long as I knew Magics existed. Now it draped itself over me like I flipped on a hoodie, cascading over my skin. My hands remained in fists as I tried to swallow my anger.

Why couldn't Frog just fight harder? Why couldn't he use his beautiful skull to understand something, anything bigger than his stupid truck tires or his stupid ego? He could have had so much more, but he's scared. Too scared to try. Too scared of me.

Why? Why can't he see? Why can't he see me and see how I—

Gentle pressure gripped my arms. I gasped, the hoodie of energy snapping off, sliding down my back, and dissipating in a pool at my heels. Anger dissolved into more tears on my cheeks and cramps in my ribs. I fought for an even breath as I realized the steady hands around my arms were Hall's. Did he drain my power? Or did I lose it?

I didn't hear him enter the room and I didn't want him to see me fall apart over a man he already deemed below himself and other Magics.

"Pathways to happiness are obscured in darkness for scared men, Blind or Magic, lost in their desperate need to fight or run until their landscape fills with familiarity." His already deep voice found room to fall lower, bringing with it the remainder of my power and seeping through holes in my ragged disappointment in myself for seeing a different outcome for Frog and me.

I grabbed the back of the chair in front of me to keep myself upright on weak knees, my fingers digging into the fabric. Hall let go of me as I did, without moving away from me. I wasn't pulling away from him. I needed room to breathe. Room to think.

"You will heal from this." Hall's tone found a softness. I couldn't say anything or turn around to face him. "Not because you didn't care for him, but because you have healed from greater losses. Those who have not suffered as you have suffered cannot see how helpless one can feel in the throes of such loss and how they would do everything within their limited strength and resources to gain such power. Frog cannot see reason behind your fight because he cannot see the grief you carry and cannot hear the internal war you wage for the unfairness in life's timing that you should know such power too late to use it for those who truly deserved your love."

Images of my mother and Aunt Lacey popped into my mind. Both died while I was too weak to save them. If Aunt Lacey had found me sooner, she could have saved my mother, or I would have had greater ability by the time Loring moved against Aunt Lacey. The fact Hall made this connection told me he knew a little thing about powerlessness. Looking at the man and experiencing a taste of the power he could wield, it was near comical to think of him as anything close to weak.

I straightened and swiped wetness off of my cheeks with shaking hands, knowing I couldn't catch it all before turning to him.

His ice-blue stare connected with mine. "I cannot read your mind with the spell protecting your thoughts successfully activated, but I know and have known such fearful men as Frog and I know the helplessness that brought you to this grief all too well."

He did know.

Nothing in his demeanour or stare told me he was lying. He was a con for hire, but I didn't think this was another job to him. Not an angle to play or a ploy to gain my favour. His usual flirtation or joking was stripped away. Even anger for whatever he might be referring to from his past was absent. His concern was calming me down and preventing my power from overtaking me. A perfect opportunity for him to swoop in and insult Frog, but he didn't. Instead, Hall gave me understanding for Frog's reaction, something that could have me trying to get back together with him.

Nothing Frog said created any peace between us, but I can understand why he felt the way he did even if I completely disagreed with him. Frog wasn't able to see himself in this life because he didn't fit here. Or he was scared he wouldn't fit here. Scared I wouldn't see him as someone who would fit here. And so he pushed me away. I'm not going to try and pull him back. I still think he's where he should be, but the immediate anger I felt towards him was extinguished.

It's a sad and shitty situation because break-ups suck.

Hall knew all this, and he put my welfare first, risking the chance I may jump a flight and talk Frog into giving us another chance. If Hall was fishing to give me a reason to agree to his protection gig, he sure found it, but by the look on his face, he wasn't happy to have discovered it. He didn't want me hurt and he was doing his best to let me feel my feels while lessening the unnecessary wounds I could've caused myself if my thoughts remained where they were.

"I'll do the ritual."

His light brows pulled together as he studied my face.

"Not until after Vincent's back. I'm assuming it's an involved situation to go through the process and, honestly, I don't have it in me right now. Regardless of Frog, I'm a bit stressed. I know I said I'd consider it after a trial period, but I don't need more time. I know all I need to know. I'm in."

Tension hung. Did I misread him? Maybe he wasn't serious about—

Hall lunged to kneel at my feet so fast I yipped and jolted back a step into the office chair.

"Kimberly Wheeler, co-Sect Leader of the Niagara division of the eternal Mother Coven, will henceforth be under the protection of Halsten Amund Holgata until my dying breath and beyond if the Gods would allow it. Be it from those who seek vengeance, negative favour, or wayward torment, I will abolish all who threatens, all who schemes, and all who dares to act against you even if it requires me to sacrifice my life."

I didn't want to think he would ever die because of me, but I wasn't exactly the strongest Magic in the Prison Creation. Requiring his protection meant being responsible for his life as well as my own. I wouldn't put him in danger without good reason. Plus, he seemed capable of handling most anything thrown at him. He helped rip up Evaristus and has infiltrated many Tainted factions. I wasn't worried. Not really. Though, thinking of him dead because of me caused a bit of internal panic.

I shoved the thought aside and placed my hand on Hall's shoulder. He grabbed my hand and pressed it against his scratchy, short-bearded cheek, seemingly drinking in the contact or something, though he didn't say. I didn't know what else to do. His declaration seemed complete and silence was stretching.

He hadn't looked up at me since he knelt on the office floor. I couldn't help but run the fingers of my other hand over his pulled-back hair. His head hung at the contact. Wherever his thoughts were, judging by the passing heartbeats as he stayed on his knee, they were someplace dark.

He rose to his feet and wrapped his arms around me, squeezing me to his hard body until I couldn't breathe. "You cannot comprehend the trust you have handed me." He stood back, his arms on my shoulders. "No matter if my dear friend falls in the attempt to free him from his family's cells, you will survive. I promise you that."

"Hall—"

"He has lived many lives and wouldn't fault me for making such a choice if it came down to it. The Coven would suffer, as would Sophie and Donovan, so it is not my desired result, however, it is imperative you survive."

Of all of the things he could promise, protecting me if it meant Vincent dying was a huge deal. Not only because Vincent was a Mother Coven Elder and important to so many, but the reality was he and Hall were life-long friends. Or friends over many lifetimes. I still didn't understand why he thought I deserved his focused attention, and his claim to put me first in all situations was about to be tested.

8

FOR THE NEXT ROUND

Sophie

The group recruited to retrieve Vincent met in the lobby an hour prior to go-time, talking gear and strategy to ensure all involved knew their part. Running on little to no sleep since the Niagara Falls attack, everyone wore a cast of depressed determination. Though I probably needed it after the incident with Donovan, I couldn't risk sleeping and having them leave without me.

As soon as I left Donovan's cell, the connection was a fluctuating torrent of feelings. All of them uncomfortable and confusing, be it his or mine.

I wanted to feel the dull bliss of nothingness, but he was a live wire, too amped with hyperawareness for me to switch off.

Busting Vincent out was the perfect distraction for the both of us. Or so I hoped as I ignored his side-eyed attentions as we prepped for the infiltration.

Since we were hitting the place in the middle of the afternoon, we couldn't waltz in with our faces displayed for witnesses to recite to a sketch artist or for the copious numbers of cell phone cameras to splash on the nightly news or social media sites. Even though we planned to block any phone capabilities and general security cameras, witnesses would keep the tips rolling in and the risk of failing to cover this detail could cost us in unforeseen ways down the line.

Ranlyn's solution? Glamour spells set to alter facial features every thirty seconds. This wouldn't change anything else about clothing, body shape, hair—even our voices would remain—but it would be enough of a change to result in conflicting reports.

Thinking Kim's red hair was a dead giveaway, I suggested she use her hair colour changing spell to further disguise herself.

"Like you can talk," Kim returned. "If Chase or Alasdair sees the group, they won't have to guess which one you are."

Of the women who were going, I was the only one with long dark hair. I never cut it after doing the spell with Kim back in Diluculo. Girl-time in the cabin bathroom felt like an eternity ago and since then my hair grew faster than normal. Sticking it in a bun wouldn't trick anyone.

Watching Bronya flip her head over, collect her blonde tresses, and flip back to create a sleek ponytail, gave me an idea.

I nudged Kim's arm. "How'd you feel about being a blonde?"

Kim's gaze shifted to Bronya and then back to me.

She laughed. "Let's go."

I tried to flat-out ignore memories of our first venture to Diluculo for a Lughnasadh celebration before I ruined everything with Caine, Loring slaughtered Aunt Lacey and the Elders, and Caine's father tried to kill him but ended up dead himself. The attempt against the Elders was successful, and splashes of visual gore, the scent of the barn, and the film of power-reducing concoction over Aunt Lacey's barbed-wire trapped body lingered as we crossed the lobby floor to the bathroom.

The last time we did this spell, it was a flippant experiment. A way to test my power and for Kim to teach me everyday magic. The spell was pragmatic, even if it doesn't end up making a damn bit of difference. Using it for a mission stained the original memory of something fun and playful. Now it was a mode of survival. Of trickery.

No candle in hand, Kim recited the spell so I could repeat it. Apparently, I couldn't read her mind anymore even if I wanted to pilfer the spell myself.

Leaving my eyes open to watch the result in the long bathroom mirror, I directed my power to my head and thought of the colour I wanted, ensuring to match my eyebrows, my near-black colouring lightening until it matched Bronya's.

Kim tilted her head as she scanned me in the reflection. "Huh, I'm actually surprised you can pull off blonde."

I shrugged. I was blonde many years ago, but didn't care to delve into that time of my life. It was also fucked up in an entirely different way.

I fussed with the strap of my tactical vest. "You're up."

"Umm, you might be all-natural and greatness, but I can't pull it off with the power of my mind, Obi-Wan. I'm gonna need supplies and—"

"Nope. Now." I gripped Kim's shoulder. She flinched, not in pain, but contemplating pulling away. "You have power, but I'll cover the energy bump. Recite the incantation."

"What? That's not—"

"Recite it." I repositioned her so she could see herself in the mirror.

She huffed and rolled her eyes, but stood, now looking at me in our reflection.

I filtered some energy through Kim, noticing how it awakened her own now meeting me beneath my palm. The flavour of her power was familiar even if Kim's was newly awakened. Something within her remembered me. And even though she was nervous, her power nuzzled closer like a friendly cat.

"Remind me to hug you when you're more huggable," Kim muttered and set her shoulders to dive into the spell.

With a press of our collaborative magic and Kim speaking the words, her thick red hair lightened to the exact shade as mine and Bronya's.

"See. Blonde isn't better, but it is when it means pretending to be a someone you'd rather see in crosshairs than yourself."

Kim was still looking herself over as I went to leave the bathroom.

Caveman stood outside of the door.

I stopped in front of him, having nowhere else to go. "Stalker much?"

He glanced at my head in slight confusion. "Yes, actually. What are you—?"

Kim came up behind me.

Caveman's jaw dropped. "Whoa! I hope that's temporary."

"Or what?" Kim pushed passed me and Caveman.

He followed close behind her.

Why would he give a shit about her hair colour? Maybe they *were* fucking. Even then, Caveman knew he couldn't tell Kim what to do. Literal caveman or not, she wouldn't allow that kind of backwards opinion to tailor her actions. She'd probably shave her head rather than let someone dictate what she could do with her body, even if the dictator was a Viking warrior god.

Heading back to the lobby, I pulled my hair high into a ponytail like Kim. We both braided it to mimic Bronya's addition. As everyone else was getting ready, a low whistle from a normally quiet Arden caught my attention. "Guess change isn't always bad."

Bronya found a smug smile and crossed her arms over her tactical vest. "Imitation is the highest form of flattery."

I glared at her. "We were hoping you'd be taken out first."

"Us?"

I chinned in Kim's direction who was standing off to the side talking with an intense-looking Caveman. What was up with those two?

Arden laughed.

Cue the evil eye from Bronya.

She was too easy.

Camouflage aside, we were about to attempt something unprecedented in the hopes Vincent wasn't already dead or killed for our efforts. I had to believe this fight was worth the risk. If there was another way to guarantee success, I would take it. No one had come up with better, so this was it.

I checked and double-checked my gear, nervous and working myself up, repositioning my weapon holsters and placements of my knives. They wouldn't be my first choice, but given that everyone would be bringing their perspective powers to the table, they didn't always expect a crude weapon of choice. Since this whole well of enemies opened up and pissed in my cornflakes, I learned the winners were prepared for anything and that a blade could kill as easily as a spell.

Plus, there will be the Blind to contend with.

"Listen up!" Ranlyn's voice echoed off the marble and everyone quieted whether they were joining us or not. "The plan is still on as discussed, with one change. The Illusionists have left."

Ranlyn paused long enough to allow people their shock. Murmuring amongst people heightened as I scanned the crowd for Caine. He was a head above most and not easily missed. Others did the same. He knew it, too, and was looking at his feet, arms crossed, jaw clenched. Ranlyn said they "left". Not that they decided not to be a part of the mission, but left as in gone. Why would Ness leave? I didn't see the other one who was in Diluculo with them either. Did he also leave? How could they do that to Caine?

"Caine?" Ranlyn called for him.

Caine's brows pitched into points as he faced his Elder, a shape I recognized when he's pissed off and holding it together.

"Without their illusion distractions, it may mean requiring your ability more. Does that work for you?"

Caine's smile cracked at one side with something other than humour. "As expected."

Ranlyn clamped down his reaction, but I knew the man enough

to know he wasn't satisfied with the response even if he was confident Caine would follow through with what was asked of him.

Caine's gaze fell back to the floor as Ranlyn went on, a small shake to his head as he inhaled and exhaled with purposeful control. Something big happened and Caine was barely holding it in.

While my heart hurt for the guy, I couldn't help pre-emptively cursing him if he let whatever it was mess up Vincent's rescue. We all carried around a sack full of trauma and angst over something. The Mother Coven needed Vincent back at the helm. I needed him now.

Whatever Ranlyn continued on saying didn't register, but I doubted it was anything more than an ice cream scoop of terrified encouragement and cheerleading with ammo clips for pom-poms. I knew the plan. With or without Ness, Felix, and Derek's special skills—whatever Derek's special skills were—the goal was getting Vincent clear of his psychotic family. Anything else was a fail. My survival wasn't necessary, though I would prefer to see him one last time if that was the case.

Liam the elevator guard did his job, and we crossed the veil into the parking garage. We climbed into vehicles to meet at the exit, leaving as a group to meet up with Miklos.

He and his crew were tasked to put his money where his mouth was and would meet us closer to the Sovereignty, as were other devoted Mother Coven contacts staying somewhere outside of the Prison Creation. All-in-all, Vincent's rescue group consisted of a relatively small cluster of individuals against the biggest corporation of Magics they knew, all to retrieve one man. The political splash it created was some other's true goal, but I didn't give a fuck about that playground.

This was it.

All my begging for Ranlyn to prove he possessed the bravery to face this threat finally amounted to something. This was happening. It could kill us all, but it was happening. At least if I died, this wouldn't be the end. I would probably see Vincent again when I recycled into another hell. After all the shit this life shovelled at my feet, dying wasn't the worst possible thing.

"I'm right with you." Donovan's voice sounded in my grey matter. He sat in the row of seats in front of me in the van.

Fucking flabby powers.

Not thinking of his comment as being an intrusion in my mind, Donovan kept talking. *"When we escaped my father's cells and I saw how you looked at me with such disgust, I contemplated ending it for us so we could start again."*

"Sounds like something you'd do," I thought, without the ability to filter.

"Know why I didn't?"

"Let's not pretend you won't tell me anyway."

"Vincent."

A pause piqued my interest. *"What about him?"*

"When my father came after us during our escape and we were separated in the tunnel, I was thinking in a real bad way, with mental barriers as pathetic as yours. Vincent heard the snowballing ideas in my head and ended up convincing me you deserved this life in full."

"Vincent's been proven wrong on many occasions."

"Nah. Self-serving, but usually accurate. And he was. Your family doesn't deserve to lose you so young. Plus, according to Vincent, this is the most we've ever had our eyes open to the truth. The most we've participated in our own destiny since we created our Soul Magic."

"I don't believe in destiny. Only people like Nya and Gareth trying to control life and death. Just like we did when we started all of this."

"Well, if we die with our Soul Magic still damaged, there's no telling how we may end up next time. I won't risk us. We may be fucked up in this timeline, but I'll do everything I can to fix it for the next round. I managed to slap a bandage on the issue, but something's still not right and it's getting worse. So, don't think dying in there will help anyone including you."

"My objective focus is Vincent. If I die freeing him, then so be it, but I'm not planning a Romeo-and-Juliet-style ending here."

"Good. They were morons."

Considering they were two teenagers who couldn't organize a plan to save their lives, I had to agree with him.

Donovan slipped out of my head as seamlessly as he barged in. And since we were only driving to Montebello Park to meet up with the others joining us, the ride was over in a matter of minutes.

Miklos parked in the roadside lot next to the large park, waiting to stick his nose up Ranlyn's ass and pray for chili day if he thought it might get him what he wanted. A tall, bearded man pacing in all-black tactical gear wasn't the stealthiest way of passing time. Looking like you're about to wage war on the fringes of a popular downtown park where cops frequented was plain stupidity. The man was a constant heat score. We should have kept driving.

Caveman pulled up behind the car with the Elders and a few others inside. Miklos approached the passenger side door. They exchanged few words and then we all left as a convoy up Church Street. After obeying traffic lights and passing the sign for the Robert S. K. Welch Courthouse of St. Catharines and unlisted gateway to the Sovereignty Creation, we parked on the street for an easy escape.

The spaces were empty. A clear sign someone orchestrated our arrival since street parking was impossible this time of the day. Exterior surveillance was also noted, and we fell under some kind of invisibility cloak as we drifted into the open spaces.

There it was. Such an innocuous building for people who don't mix it up with the criminal element of life. I didn't have the floorplans etched into my mind, but I have been inside over the years for 'Take Your Kid to Work Day' and to meet my mom on her lunch breaks and knew the general makeup of the Blind side of the property.

Where it crossed over the veil to the Sovereignty was a complete mystery to me.

First things first was slipping by the Blind civilians going about their everyday, plus the Sovereignty guards posing as the Blind to prevent such attacks from annoying their boss and crossing into the Creation and posing a threat.

My heart pounded so hard my vision spotted. I squeezed my eyes shut, pausing for a last-second weapons check to gain control, and picturing Vincent needing me to get my shit together like he's managed for me too many times. If they signalled to move right now, I would've raced on, but I might have stumbled a step, and I didn't need to fuck things up by staggering inside of the building like a drunk.

As per the plan, Ranlyn and Veata moved first.

This was happening.

The Elders led the mission at the forefront. Veata leaned more heavily into her cane than necessary, playing up the helpless old lady act as Ranlyn held her arm and guided her as a perfect gentleman towards the doors. The half light-coloured flat stone and half artistic glasswork windows appeared artsy in a way no true criminal would admire if they were marched through the doors. Can't have civilians complaining about an institutional aesthetic, something Alasdair paid an ass-load for someone else to deal with, no doubt.

Ranlyn paused under the stone overhang held up by thick stone columns meant to keep people from the rain who had lawyers and officials in mind. He reached into his jacket pocket for something, and then guided an annoyed and over-acting Veata to one of the metal benches, pretending to have forgotten whatever he'd been searching for in the car. Since the spell Veata needed to perform took a minute or two, Ranlyn's ruse was to position Veata so she could accomplish this. Once completed, she would let the others know when it was time to move.

They were both already spelled with the face-altering cloaking and, since Veata was some random old lady now alone on the bench, security wouldn't pay enough attention to note her facial features.

Ranlyn returned to his vehicle. It wasn't under a cover spell like the others. We enacted the spell to trigger our disguises and spilled from our vehicles. Ranlyn then climbed inside of his car, but disappeared to the Blind going about their busy day to join the rest of us undercover.

We wound around Blind pedestrians while invisible to the public and remained impeccably silent in the hub of afternoon downtown activity.

When Veata's magically fuller lips ceased to move, the immortal braced her weight on her cane to stand. The subtle action cued us to her successful warding against the Blind from coming near the property and deterring Tainted Magics from entering at all. If either were already in the building, oh well, we could deal. If they called for re-enforcements, however, they were sunk. No cop or Tainted bodyguard was rushing inside to save the day.

It was go-time.

When the automatic doors opened, we slipped in behind a short-haired lady in a Nike windbreaker with matching white sneakers on her way out. The doors closed on their own, slowly, and then re-opened again to accommodate more foot traffic. The walking brand name billboard had no idea how lucky she was to skip an extra trauma for lunch by heading outside.

Our cover spells also skipped the metal detectors, allowing us to hop protocol since all the heat we were packing would set the alarms to scream mode.

Inside the courthouse and amongst the Blind milling about in a spectrum of cheap suits and worried faces to five-hundred-dollar heels and confident shoulders, I knew not to ignore any as a potential threat. Alasdair's protocols to douse his employees' soul glows was still in effect. The uniformed guards were typical working-class civilians, but would be an easy plant as would any number of people walking around.

I squeezed my sweaty grip around the handle of my gun, not fully remembering having pulled it from its holster. No matter what happened, I wasn't leaving without Vincent. In hand or dragging behind me, Vincent wouldn't spend another night in his father's torture chamber. No Magic could force me to let him rot here, not even Alasdair Llewellyn himself.

Adrenaline and nervousness were a blended smoothie through the Soul Magic connection. Donovan was not a fan of what he was sensing from me.

Waiting for everyone to file into position was the hardest part.

Risking telepathic communication was too dangerous given the mission's importance, forcing all spell-covered Magics to cool their heels and dampen their powers begging to be utilized. Lust for battle would inadvertently break our cover spells if given into.

Telltale signs of the Sovereignty's soul glows may have been missing while I hid behind a potted plant taller than me, until a couple of men in suits wearing superiority like a headdress exited an elevator and split up. One stood in line at a coffee shop and the other took up space by a pillar and took out his phone. Both appeared to focus on their mundane tasks while they discreetly surveyed the lobby. I saw them as exactly what Alasdair trained them to be. Useful protection, yet visually unimportant to those on the daily grind or preoccupied with whatever court case brought them to the building. Others on the rescue team must have spotted them. Were they obvious on purpose? Pulling our attentions to their threat or a passive warning from Alasdair to tell us he saw through our tactics, and we should back down now or he would send in the big guns?

Could they be immortals? Nah. Alasdair wouldn't potentially waste the lives of such important Magics, so these were exactly what he wanted them to be...effective, disposable, guard dogs. We would encounter the true threats once we crossed over the veil into the Sovereignty itself.

I kept my eyes on these men, trying not to hyper-fixate in case others were creeping up on me from somewhere else. The goateed guy in a suit closest to me peered down his nose at his phone, feigning interest while still surveying the room.

Finally. Veata's familiar form came through the doors. Her face was altered from the original disguise while outside, though her clothing remained the same and her immortal soul glowed as bright as a search light.

The crafty Elder breezed through Blind security protocols, the officer barely pausing to check her over. Nothing in her hands but her cane meant nothing to search and she was directed around the metal detector which would have beeped when she went through it if she hadn't already disabled it. She was betting on the guard's impatience with her deteriorated state and was not disappointed. If he was a Magic, he had zero intuition or resented his boring job so much he was checked out.

Veata retained her slow pace to sell the ruse and re-enabled the detector as not to draw too much attention or so she said in the planning stages as she did nothing overt to showcase the use of such a spell. Maybe a twitch of her cheek, but nothing any bystander would catch.

Her bypassing the security station and slowly ascending into our enemy's domain was the flick of the first domino I was itching for. Tense, I readjusted my grip on my gun to a surge of anticipation from Donovan as he, too, readied for the next stage of the plan.

Fire exploded at the front doors sending the Blind into a chorus of frenzied screams. If they ran for other emergency exits, they would find the same fire blockade. Miklos spell-locked the doors from his hidden location and another on his team was responsible for the flames. Not as effective as Ness or Felix's illusions, but the spell was so real it threw off heat felt from across the room.

To the outside world, if someone managed to bypass the spell Veata erected, the entrance would appear closed due to some type of undisclosed emergency construction. A sign on the door listed an apology from Niagara Region officials and a contact number, one people would have to leave the property to connect to since all cell phone activity was a bust.

No need for magic when a cell signal blocker would do.

Cries for fire extinguishers and call outs to the fire department went half-addressed. The extinguishers did nothing to beat the phantom blaze, and the landlines were as mysteriously unavailable as cell signals—Miklos's team also responsible for setting this up.

To ensure the chaos caused the greatest distraction and difficulty for any Sovereignty guards to operate around, Miklos's team dropped their cover spells, the first to do so, coupling the action of their sudden appearance in tactical gear with crackling shots of magic into the air, replicating the sound of true gun shots. Since guns weren't an everyday accessory around our pocket of Canada, more screams and chaos kept people on the edge as they fought for higher ground up some stairs or racing into offices. The fact they were all equipped with tranquilizer weapons went unnoticed by the Blind.

Caine popped into view off to my left. I recognized him by his tactical gear and his height since the spell to disguise his facial features darkened his grey eyes, smoothed the edges of his jawline, and added a trimmed moustache. He leaned towards a woman in a green blouse and yelled into her ear above the panic. Her eyes widened, reacting to whatever Caine said and then she ran off shrieking at the top of her lungs through the main area. He then moved onto another person and another and so on, sending them all into elevated panic to retain the chaos in the room and ensure security—Blind or Sovereignty—were busy fighting through the madness.

He may not have enjoyed his power when he first developed it, but damn, he was good.

Ranlyn dropped his cover spell and the rest of us followed.

A gun shot went off, a real one, the blast adding to the overwhelming commotion. Caveman jumped on the security guard who tried to shoot out a door he thought was on fire. Quickly stripping him of his weapon and shooting him with a tranquilizer was the easiest solution before the rent-a-cop tried to play hero or actually killed some unsuspecting bystander. The Blind were meant to be our smoke screen, not our sacrificial lambs. Not even Vincent would approve of innocent deaths to spare his own.

With the Blind already amped, the guard's shot revved up the mayhem meter to shit-your-pants terror.

A few from Miklos's crew stood vigilant at the exits, playing up their true-blue burglar roles about to shoot everyone who tried to leave. Most on this level who weren't running in circles frantically seeking help were cowering in corners and blubbering or praying.

Veata sat to the side on a thick windowsill, watchful over the panic-filled lobby, ready to intervene against any outside threat if one popped up as well as escape and retreat back to the Prison Creation if we all failed. We were already down an Elder. Losing all of them again, so soon after the Mother Coven did the last Elders, would be crippling in a way the Mother Coven may never survive.

As soon as shit hit the fan, my muscled and suited target disappeared in the fray. Time to move forward. Passing a few doors on our left at a quick jog, Ranlyn led the group with Tactical Team members close on his tail. Donovan stuck close to me, his face not his own.

As long as he didn't get in my way, he could ride my ass all he wanted.

Anticipating the enemy lurking around every corner, I was twitchy and ready to pull the trigger. Power simmered along my skin, as primed as my trigger finger, itching to punish anyone stupid enough to try and stop me from retrieving Vincent.

A few others broke off and performed lock spells on all necessary doors to different court rooms and smaller mediation rooms, even to offices. The Blind were tossed inside if they were anywhere near the doors. Some may have been Magics, though I couldn't tell unless they used their power.

A man with a loosened tie, dishevelled dark hair greying at the temples, and a cropped beard stepped in front of the group with his hands up.

Ranlyn lifted his hand, ready to counterattack.

"Picnic basket!" the man yelled and braced himself.

A code word?

Ranlyn paused. "Name?"

"John Weaver. We gotta go, now."

We followed behind an agile John who led us through a hallway full of still-frantic people in our way pushing by or screeching when they saw us. More offices dotted this hallway with a door at the end I could see around the shoulders of those in front of me. If those offices were full of awaiting Sovereignty goons and the door at the end was locked, we would be trapped in what was essentially a seven-foot-wide tunnel. We would be royally fucked and nowhere near Vincent.

The man in front used a series of codes and a pulse of magic to open the door.

Okay, not trapping us. Though, we would never have breached the door without him.

Through the door was another hallway like the one we came from, again, pinning us down within a small space if this John Weaver guy was a Sovereignty plant pretending to be amongst those in Vincent's rebellion.

Instead of going through the door at the end of this hallway, we were led to the left through a different door, one leading to a stairwell we raced up. Our boots echoed so loudly that if someone else entered the stairwell from above, there was no way we could hide the group.

I wanted this over with. Not to retreat, but to hurry the hell up, grab Vincent, and get the hell out of this place. Cora-Lynn was important too, but he was my main concern. Every second we wasted between infiltration and escape was a second closer to potential capture.

Let's do this already.

My chest burned with adrenaline and punching breaths, Donovan and I sharing in the discomfort as we pushed up the stairs.

After a handful of floors later, it hit me that we must have passed over the veil. The courthouse was three floors, maybe another for storage plus a basement. The Sovereignty was old, ancient even, so they must have updated their veil entry process over the years so it was painless, unlike the excruciating entry into Diluculo. I didn't see security cameras in the corners as we kept climbing floors the Blind outside couldn't see, though maybe Alasdair implemented an upgrade for that as well.

Panting left a tingle of magic in my lungs as my power amped up my stamina and eased the pressure in my ankles after so many steps. I wasn't the only one gulping for air, Kim needing periodic healing energy Caveman was eager to provide. He fussed over her in a way she appeared grateful for receiving yet annoyed for needing.

Everyone remained focused as our guide finally stopped on an unidentified floor and waited for the group to join him on the landing.

John peered through a small window in the door. "I've taken care of what I can."

"Meaning?" Distrust coloured Caveman's tone. The guy must not be Caveman's contact if he questioned him.

"Meaning the bullpens are loaded with entry-level Magics who could still dismantle the operation. The route around them is guarded. Right now, one of those guards is currently in the can puking his guts up and the other two are on Vincent's payroll. All other guards on this level are taken care of."

"What were they guarding?" Donovan asked.

"The same as those downstairs. Courtrooms, offices, boardrooms, mediation rooms, staff from potentially disgruntled clientele... anything and everything."

"And they're taken care of how?" Ranlyn asked.

John's expression crimped. "We're wasting time. It's taken care of. Word of what's happening with the Blind will spread quickly. We need to go."

He motioned for everyone to stay low, swinging the door open once we all mirrored his postured ducking. The half-wall we walked into was topped with glass, giving a view into the "bullpen". Even without seeing the Magics directly, we still heard the spillage of their conversations. Judging by voices alone, there were dozens of Magics. John was absolutely right in saying we had no chance of taking on the whole lot.

In a back-cramping crouch, John led us to a hallway where we could finally stand up. He spoke with two of the guards he said were on Vincent's payroll, and waved us through without a word.

The enormity of the Creation was surprising. It wasn't a huge visually-open playground like Diluculo and Pario, but this sandbox was saddled in the midst of downtown without notice from the Blind. Genuis. Somehow the Prison Creation in a high-rise parking garage seemed more probable.

"Hide your thoughts better." Donovan's mental lashing came without him slowing.

I huffed at the intrusion. A part of me wanted to tell him to shut the fuck up, but he was right. I tried to clamp down and spare some of my frenetic energy for my thoughts, refusing to be the reason Vincent's baby—the Prison Creation—was infiltrated.

Another door required an additional set of access circus tricks and another pulse of energy, a different kind than the last. Those from the Team in front of me crouched. The sudden movement had me wildly doing the same, thinking an attack was hurled our way. Instead, we bypassed beneath another half-wall and another bullpen filled with more Magics.

Why the fuck did the Sovereignty need so many Magics? Beings with immeasurable skills in cubicles doing what? Data entry? Cold calls? I've worked a call center job. Sure, it paid well, but the verbal abuse and tight oversight wasn't worth a cent of it. If they were anything like the Blind, most of these button pushers probably wouldn't engage if we popped up and did an interpretive dance since it would add some spice to their mundane shift.

At the end of this pool of cubed sadness was a door, but a different kind of door without the special codes. Inside was a cement-walled room full of light shining over a grassy patch lined with flowers. Small tables and comfortable-looking chairs dotted the lawn as birds chirped, though I couldn't see any actual birds.

This atrium would be great for a lunch break, though it was nothing more than simulated yard time for the overworked. The weather outside of the building was not nearly as perky.

Another door? How many freakin' doors—?

"Patience, babe. This place is a maze and every door could be a portal to somewhere else."

Ugh. If Donovan was answering my thoughts again, it meant I was too unfocused to cover up my complaining. When Ranlyn briefed us on the mission, we got as far as the lobby in way of details. Nothing about the cells and definitely no mention of bullpen paper pushers. How deep could we go and still find our way out?

When we approached yet another door, I ground my teeth in anticipation of our guide's song and dance with the keys and codes, but this time he knocked. Not like he was a delivery man, but it did have a particular sequence.

The steel swung open and a tall, dark-skinned Magic stood in standard security gear.

The man nodded at John and then his eyes widened when he noticed our group, a shrewd smile stretching in Caveman's direction. "I should've known you'd be a part of this," the man said in a heavy French accent.

Caveman pushed to the front of the group and the men clasped their non-weaponized hands. "Can't leave my man inside, now, can I? Didn't realize you were the coward too afraid to lose his job."

Wait… How did the guard recognize Caveman at all? The facial glamour must have busted somewhere along our trek here.

The man gave a hard grin and tilted his head. "Kid to feed, my man. Becca might always think I'm a mangy bastard, but holding down a job means I can be a dad. Those weekends go smoother if I'm breathing, yeah?"

"Yeah, yeah," Caveman answered with a light-hearted lilt to his voice. "What we facing inside?" He motioned behind the man, the space too small for me to see into.

"No clue, other than this door leading to another," the man answered. "I stand in this tiny ass room, no windows, all day, with no clue what's after this cement box. All I know is it's a protected sally port where they usher in prisoners. I don't got an interior layout for you."

"Come on, Brad," Caveman hedged.

Brad shook his head. "No joke, Bash. This place is a Rubix Cube of fun. The boss decides who goes in and who don't come out. When he exited with one less rebellious son, I knew the Team would come for him. Didn't know you were signed up with Vincent's tactical outfit."

"Every man needs a job," Caveman said and paused, no one taking the opportunity to call him out on the name Brad used. Made me wonder if Hall was his real name or if it was just another of his undercover monikers. "How do you want to stay clean of this mess and keep your weekend dad schedule? Your choice."

Brad motioned towards Caveman's tranquilizer gun. "How many hours will that thing put me down for?"

"Does it matter?"

"Shhhhiiit," he mumbled and wiped his hand over the stiff bristle on his face. "You fucking owe me."

With a devilish smile, Caveman nodded and raised his weapon.

"Hold on!" John rushed forward between the men. "We need your access first."

Brad scoffed. "You can replicate an Extractor's power?"

"Enough to bypass the system."

Brad raised a brow as if skeptical and the two ran through some kind of authentication to access the inner door. Brad lent his codes and then John spouted off a spell and used a dark red liquid on an electronic pad of some sort with a pulse of energy.

Caveman's buddy leaned away from the access panel as if waiting for the thing to explode.

It didn't.

Instead, it chirped, and the door cracked open.

John stepped away, satisfied.

A whoosh, a thud, and Brad flinched hard, swore, and lifted his arm to see the tranquilizer dart in his shoulder. A gruff grunt escaped the man as he glared at "Bash" for shooting him, even if he knew it was coming.

Brad swayed a step. Some jumped to help him to the ground when Caveman stopped them.

"He can handle a bump on the head. More authentic."

"Ostie..." Brad slurred in French. His eyelids sagged as he slumped into a heap on the floor.

Caveman grabbed his buddy's arm and dragged the guy from the path of the door with a little extra care than he would a stranger, but only marginally, again, he wanted to ensure it appeared as natural as possible to keep his friend's cover.

"Wish I knew it was Brad." Caveman nudged the guy's leg out of the way with his boot. "I could've skipped a few steps in the contact pool."

Kim looked down at the man now snoozing. "Maybe you shouldn't know so many shady people."

"Shady people are my people, kitten," Caveman returned with a wink.

I scoffed. "While you two work on foreplay, Vincent's being tortured. Can we move the fuck on?"

In case his persuasion was needed, Caine led the way into the tiny space Brad called his office. Ranlyn was behind him, Caveman with Kim on his tail, and then Donovan and I followed. The others remained outside to cover our backs until we knew what was on the other side of the door.

I was ready to shove my way in front when Caine whipped open the door, then I remembered Donovan's nagging voice saying every doorway could be a portal. I wanted to find Vincent as quickly as possible, but that needed to include getting him out.

9

SHED NO TEARS

Sophie

Every tranquilizer gun was raised in anticipation when Caine opened the door.

"Stop!" Caine yelled and then more calmly said, "Move against the wall."

When I finally shoved my way in, I had a hard time fitting, the small room another cement box about ten-feet by ten-feet at most, forcing everyone else to remain exposed in the hallway. No furniture, only one tall black-clad body standing and cowering against the wall where Caine ordered them.

Except...holy shit. That wasn't a person. It was a living wax mannequin. Shiny skin on what was its face featured no eyes. Where they were meant to be were two slightly sunken divots in the skin, and yet, the Magic seemed to be looking at us. Tiny nostrils broke up the face, though they were almost gill shaped they were so slight, same with the lips.

I didn't understand what this alien-like entity was, but it was as tall as Caveman and clearly in this small room for a reason.

Why was Brad guarding them?

"What is your job here?" Caine asked the creature wearing dark robes after Ranlyn prompted the question.

With a mouth that split open as if with disuse, a resonant voice answered, "Sovereignty Warden."

"Okay." Caine gathered himself and said, "Release Vincent Llewellyn and his wife Cora-Lynn."

Without hesitation, the warden raised what was a hand without separated fingers, light escaping from the appendage. Light enveloped the cement walls and filled the cement space with two extra bodies. Caine ordered the warden to do something that made the Magic cower against the wall, but my attention was on the extra people who dropped into the room.

Kim surged forward to the person in front of her and I followed in a rush of emotion as Vincent laid on his back, coughing, dust flying and settling around him.

We have him. Oh my god, we have him!

Vincent partially sat up after I pulled back from the embrace I assaulted him with, and he raised his hand to keep everyone at a distance. "Are you real?"

He scanned my face, his warm, dust-covered fingers running over my cheek. Why was he so dirty?

My vision wavered with tears as I nodded. "We've got you."

His shoulders slumped, trusting what he saw enough to wrap his arms around me and squeeze.

A flush of jealousy splashed across the connection. I ignored Donovan as Vincent's stare panned around the room, grateful recognition in his thoughts as he tried to tell himself this was real, that he was saved. I've only heard his thoughts a few times, maybe twice when he didn't allow it. His vulnerability made me uneasy. He always seemed so in control.

A low growl and then a grunt and scuffle sounded behind me.

"No! Don't hurt her!" Vincent was up on his feet and trying to push Ismail aside.

He turned to a dirty, bald, and raging woman. Her bright, toxic-looking soul glow was confusing. Not Tainted. Something was wrong with her. It didn't help that she plastered herself into a corner and crouched as if she was half a second from turning into a pouncing mountain lion.

"Cora-Lynn..." Vincent spoke with a softened tone and waited until her wild eyes found his. "They are friends."

Cora-Lynn? His wife? How was this feral woman his wife?

"You?" Cora-Lynn said, and those calculating eyes locked on me and narrowed. "Your face?"

Moira, Vincent's Alchemist friend from The Chiff, told me the story about Cora-Lynn's death, or what Vincent thought was her death, and mentioned how I apparently met Cora-Lynn in a previous life.

"We met many years ago in a different lifetime for me. I don't remember."

Cora-Lynn's brow pinched further, her muscles tensed.

Whatever I said made things worse.

I touched Vincent's arm to gain his attention. Cora-Lynn tracked my hand. She didn't like that either. "You okay enough to walk out of here?"

Vincent ran a hand through his hair, dust falling into his face. He swiped fingers across his eyes and repeatedly blinked, looking more worn than I have ever seen him.

"We need to move," John called from outside of the room.

As everyone started to file out, Caine took over with the warden, telling them to sleep until someone found them. The long limbs of the Magic went limp beneath the black cloak as they slid to the floor.

I looked between Vincent and Cora-Lynn, and then focused on her. "We're getting you both somewhere safe, but you gotta stay close to Vincent and the rest of the group."

She didn't nod or utter a word for or against the plan, and I didn't have time to convince her I wasn't a threat.

Vincent waved Cora-Lynn on in front of him to follow others

through the door, Donovan and me being the last to leave the small warden's hole of an office. I uttered a lock spell to keep the warden in his pen as long as possible, and we hit the hallway knowing our job was only half done.

"Have you encountered my father or brother?" Vincent asked in a low voice.

"Nope," Arden answered.

Whatever Vincent was thinking, he kept it to himself. Alasdair would have already been notified of the commotion down in the Blind's sector of the building. He may have thought it wasn't his problem or he might see through it as a smoke screen for something much more.

We had to move fast.

When we reached the cubicles and everyone crouched, Cora-Lynn dropped back. Vincent didn't realize she wasn't following him. I tried to usher her forward and told her to crouch, but she refused and started making a weird, panicky noise.

"It's okay, it's okay." I dropped my voice. "We're getting outta here."

Nope. Cora-Lynn wasn't having it. She started walking backwards towards where we came from.

Whatever I said, it did nothing to reassure her.

Deciding she was taking things into her own hands, Cora-Lynn bolted down a different hallway, definitely somewhere we weren't supposed to go or John would have taken us that way.

I called her name, trying to keep my voice down. Since I failed miserably, I ran after her.

The sound of Donovan's boots slammed the marble floors behind me.

Before Cora-Lynn got everyone thrown into cells, I pulled the trigger of my gun. The tranquilizer dart stuck into her lower back and sent her to the ground in a screech of mostly dirty and naked limbs versus marble flooring.

Vincent yelled Cora-Lynn's name, pushed past me, and dropped to the floor next to his wife who was slowly succumbing to the drug when he flipped her over like a breakfast pancake. She fought him, shoving at his shoulders with failing strength until her arms fell to her sides and all of those tensed muscles relaxed.

"It's only a tranquillizer." Donovan came to my defense, checking around us at what attention we may be attracting as Vincent yanked the dart out of Cora-Lynn's skin.

Voices from an adjoining hall came closer. If they turned right at the intersection of hallways', they would get an eye-full of two unauthorized Magics and another two who wore the sheen of escaped prisoners in their head-to-toe dirt-bath. Plus, chances were they would recognize Vincent and have heard the rumours of his imprisonment.

People came around the corner too quickly to pull off a cover spell or utter a healthy "*Ohfuckingshit.*"

An older man's eyes were on a dossier in his hands while he talked to an annoyed-looking Chase.

Chase grabbed the man's arm and halted their progress with a sharp, "Father."

The man's attention cut from his paperwork to our half-tactically geared and half-dishevelled and unconscious group.

Just fucking wonderful. We were eyeballing the two people we wanted to avoid most.

Maybe Brad missed a check-in, or Alasdair inspected his cells when chaos hit the fan in the Blind side of the property.

To give the chaotic shitshow of a situation an extra dose of fun, a set of armed guards on their heels snapped into their roles, surging forward.

Alasdair raised a hand to stop their action.

"Son?" Alasdair's face was lined in concern I couldn't read as genuine or not. Chase stood in complete shock, his expression a mix of disbelief and anticipatory satisfaction. "I see your Charges have arranged for your release."

Alasdair clasped his hands casually in front of him, the dossier still in his mitts. His gaze fell on me and Donovan with an uncomfortably familiar ease considering we had little acquaintance.

I hesitantly chanced a glance at Vincent. Donovan stepped closer to me, as his fear and drive to escape ran through us. A darkness clouded Vincent's gaze, his mind still easily accessible. He thought of himself and Cora-Lynn in a barrage of different scenes moving too quickly for me to see in full or understand what they meant beyond danger fueling a current of vengeance, most involving screaming and blood.

What was clear was that Vincent refused to lose Cora-Lynn again.

Vincent bared his teeth, raised a hand towards his father, and snapped his power up and into the surrounding area so quickly my diaphragm cramped. I pitched forward and grabbed at my gut, but Alasdair gasped the loudest and dropped his papers, peppering the floor like snowflakes.

Vincent clenched a raised fist and pulled it towards him. A ghostly light encased Alasdair and then shot away from his body as Vincent partially extracted his father's soul. Alasdair's mouth hung open, his eyes wide in shocking pain on both his physical body and his separated soul.

Chase roared in anger and rushed towards Vincent.

Surprise hit me too late as Chase bypassed his brother and came for me, hands raised, filling me with agony.

Donovan's shouting and my gargled groans echoed in my ears. The walls around me faded and sharpened in pulses of agony as waves of pain and then disconnect rolled through me.

What was happening? I tried to move my limbs. Am I moving? Oh fuck! Stop! Stop this!

I fought to see around me. The overwhelming static of Chase's attack caused me to lose time to spasms of pain. The Sovereignty guards were fighting...someone. I couldn't see. No, Vincent. They attacked Vincent. He was on the ground, sprawled next to Cora-Lynn's still unconscious body.

Chase. His fist was in the air like Vincent's had been.

I'm so fucked.

Chase was keeping my partially extracted soul in his grasp. He berated the guards in a stream of threats. Over what, I couldn't concentrate enough to hear.

I strained to see and understand what happened, bringing on more and more confusion.

Donovan? He was on the floor in the fetal position. If he was somewhere in our connection, I didn't know for sure. Everything was pain and more pain. Mine? His? Didn't matter. I wanted it to stop.

"It is done, Chase. His reign is over." Vincent was speaking, his voice warbled in my ears.

"Shut up, Vincent! You had no right." Less clashes of fighting sounded as Chase continued to yell at the guards.

Had no right to what?

I couldn't... What was...?

I missed time again as a spike of pain took over.

"Your own people caused this." Vincent was talking again. "I shed no tears over father no longer being one with his vessel. The blame falls on those he pays for their service, not me."

Ohmygod. Alasdair was dead.

Vincent was partially extracting his father's soul when the guards attacked him. When he did the same to Donovan's sister-slash-promised wife, Joelly, he explained that if he didn't put the soul back properly, it was torn from the body and could never be stuffed back in again.

Alasdair, the King of the Sovereignty, was a wayward soul without a body.

Wait, no. Alasdair was staring down at his body. He had to know what happened to him and what it meant.

Would he go on to some kind of afterlife? Would he haunt the hallways of the empire he built for an eternity?

Alasdair's hard stare swung my way. In his ghostly form, he could see my soul was also partially extracted by Chase. He hesitated a moment and then walked straight through his son, who felt and saw nothing.

Pain rolled through me. When a beat of it subsided enough to concentrate, I could see Alasdair standing inches from me.

As a living, breathing, Extractor, Alasdair couldn't see my soul outside of my body even if he was the one extracting me, but in his newly ripped-free status, he saw me as a floating soul, and something in his gaze sent me into greater panic.

He reached forward and stepped through my soul to my body.

"No..." I tried, but I couldn't force the words through so much distorted pain. I flailed, still stuck in Chase's grip, remembering the horror of being trapped in my body as the ancient Nya took over whenever she wanted and left me to abject loneliness. Alasdair wanted to control my body since his was toast, and if he did it, he would never allow me an ounce of control ever again. And I couldn't warn Vincent about what Alasdair was trying to do.

A bright flash lit up the hallway and a *whoosh* of pressure and relief filled my entire body.

I sat up mid-scream. Holy shit, my soul was back in my body.

Vincent exchanged a few blasts of energy with the guards. Chase was kneeling over his father's body, checking his pulse, swearing when he didn't find what he was looking for.

I scrambled to my feet with the ghost of pain straining my muscles, tripping before I could make it vertical. Tingles of awareness struck my semi-useless limbs when I flexed my fingers and toes, neither waking up the urgency.

Donovan recovered faster than me. He tossed a hit of energy across the way at one of the guards and threw up a shield in front of me while keeping up defensive hits alongside Vincent until I could get my shit together.

Mid-extraction or not, my soul-seeing ability let me see Alasdair's soul outside of his body. My power was spilling from me, not impacting the room in a blast, but as it did when I was in the Ballard Family Estate's attic and I could see all of the soul glows around me even through walls. Reading all of the Magics in the hallways and beyond was blinding.

Even if many were Tainted, they still emitted light, and it was overwhelming.

In soul form, Alasdair was easier to focus on. He came after me with confidence he could bypass Donovan's shield, and he did, forcing himself into my space.

Pressure on my chest cramped my ribs as he tried to push his way into me. I tried to scramble away. He followed, the strain persisting when I tried to back off, his attempted invasion crippling me further.

Did Nya leave a window cracked when she was evicted? I was born a vessel. Did it matter who was trying to slip into me? Could any phantom do it?

I saw myself in Alasdair's mind, saw his intentions, saw his desperation to recapture the control his bodiless state would leave him without.

Energy tingled along my skin, a defensive response rising. As soon as I registered what I felt, I dug for more and spread it all over me like lotion without moving a muscle. The pressure of Alasdair's effort didn't lessen or increase. The second skin kept him from getting what he wanted, however, I wasn't spinning winning moves either.

Donovan had no idea what was happening to me, unless he was reading my thoughts while busy facing off with more and more guards at Vincent's side.

"Stop all fighting! No moving!" Caine's booming voice crashed over the hits of power and the weight on my chest vanished in a snap.

Shit. Caine's persuasion worked on spirits?

More surprising was how everyone listened. Not a few, not for passing seconds, but his voice had a firm hold over every single Magic within earshot.

"Sophie, Donovan, and Vincent, you're free to follow me. Chase, come with us without fighting or talking unless otherwise instructed."

The hold on my will eased and I felt Donovan's relief as it did.

"All Sovereignty personnel, leave. You never saw us." Caine

continued. "Tell all others there is no cause for alarm and return to your posts."

As he willed it, the Magics still alive and guarding their employers turned and left them completely alone including Alasdair's dead body still on the floor as his ghostly form stood staring at us. He didn't leave, maybe because he didn't have a post to guard, but he didn't move against me either.

Vincent picked up Cora-Lynn. Her limbs were limp and draped over his arms. We headed towards the hallway we were originally supposed to take. Caine waited until the others followed through with his command and Chase came to stand beside him, obeying calmly without resistance.

As we continued down the hall the relief in my chest radiated to my extremities and I realized it was Donovan. He remained close, his lungs heaving with exertion of the fight and lingering anxiety of us getting caught, plus that heavy relief.

"I thought I lost you," I heard in my mind.

I realized his relief wasn't for Caine saving our asses, but was directly related to my welfare. Tears gathered in my eyes and I looked at him again, but he kept his attention forwards and trained on the corners, his weapon raised in case we were stopped.

When we finally reached the others, they were surprised Chase was with us. Caveman stepped in front of Kim to protect her and then realized what was happening. "Can you keep him in that girdle until we get back to the Prison Creation?"

Caine gave a crooked smile. "I'm confident I can." And he was. There was neither cockiness nor hesitance in his tone, a simple statement of fact.

Instead of running out as we did on the way in, we waltzed through the hallways and passed the bullpens. When we were about to be stopped, Caine commanded Chase to tell every person we passed to "get back to work" and kept walking.

No one would dare question Chase. He may be a psychopath in a suit, but enough staff were smart enough to fear him.

Caine's power was incredible.

When we reached the lobby, the walls and corners were full of people cowering with tear-streaked faces. Veata sat in her spectator seat off to the side and rose without a hint of alarm as we walked with Chase among our group.

"That leash good and tight, Berisford?" Veata asked Caine.

"Yes, ma'am. Would you like a pirouette demonstration?"

Veata's smile grew.

"We need to go," Ranlyn interjected, and her smile dropped.

"Such a wet blanket, Ranlyn." She tsked and took a minute to undo the spell she erected when we first came in the door.

As soon as she concluded, we were outside in the cold afternoon, the whole mission taking less than thirty minutes.

Miklos argued with Ranlyn, his thick accent rose in the street about fairness and urgency of need. Whatever Ranlyn told him had him shaking his head. And then Miklos called for his people to follow him, and they climbed in their SUV and took off in a rush of squealing tires.

I guess Ranlyn still didn't trust him.

John was allowed to come with us. He was in too deep for the breakout not to be traced back to him. Same with the two guards on Vincent's payroll, whatever their names were.

As we piled into the vehicles a figure stepped clear of another parked car. Everyone dropped into fighting stances, guns drawn, and power at the ready.

Rosemary stepped into full view, all long, sleek hair and casual threat, her eyes on Chase as Caine told him to sit in the vehicle. "Guess I'm too late for the good stuff."

"Alasdair's dead," Donovan informed her.

"And his lackey child is a prisoner. Good to know." Her dimpled smile was small and vaguely sinister.

"You coming with us?" Donovan asked, his guarded hope stirring.

"I suppose," Rosemary said to his relief and stepped up to Ranlyn. "Do what you need to."

So, no Miklos and his cronies, but Rosemary who was literally Tainted was okay?

Maybe because Vincent was busy fussing with Cora-Lynn, staring at her like he couldn't believe what he was seeing.

Rosemary wasn't stupid. Just because no one contested her joining us at the Prison Creation, that didn't mean she could access its location or be given the allowances of trust from anyone other than Donovan.

Vincent settled with an unconscious Cora-Lynn on his lap in the trunk of the SUV, looking utterly exhausted and still dirty, or dusty, maybe with a thick sand. The background song of the courthouse's alarms blared, and the Blind fled from the building since the fake fire was removed from the exits.

Rosemary was equipped with a backwards balaclava for a hood and strapped into her seat between me and Donovan. The effects of a confusion spell had her head swimming and shaking as her brain tried to right what was wrong, where she was, and who was taking her there.

The short trip to the Prison Creation was longer than necessary as Vincent didn't want Rosemary or Chase memorizing where we were going in case they were strong enough to withstand the confusion spell and Caine's persuasion.

I couldn't stop peeking at Vincent and Cora-Lynn. She was nothing like I expected—hard-bodied, bald, and so dirty. Alasdair imprisoned her for a very long time. Whatever I saw in her didn't matter, as by the way Vincent was cradling her in his lap she was nothing but his wife, though his expression wasn't one of satisfaction for getting her back. His thoughts were covered better now and I couldn't see what caused his drawn expression. Maybe because his father was dead or a ghost or whatever Alasdair was now. He dethroned the man after all this time and had Cora-Lynn back in the real world.

Everything he fought for was his. Why wasn't he over the moon with unhinged excitement?

Donovan stared out the window, his trance pulling at my focus as his teeth bit into my thumb, his anxiousness beyond hiding. Ebbs of emotion flowed through me. He would gain control only to be nailed by them again.

Apparently, I was responsible. I could tell this without reading him, though I didn't know exactly why. Whatever. If it was because Chase almost went all Pez despenser on my soul, there's nothing I could've done about it. I didn't invite him to separate me from my vessel. Though, I wondered what it would've done to Donovan if Alasdair had managed it. Would he be a ghost, too? Both of us wayward souls stuck wandering the Sovereignty halls with Alasdair?

Movement ahead of me caught my eye. Caveman reached over from the driver's seat while we sat at a red light and held Kim's hand. An even bigger surprise was that Kim didn't pull away. She didn't glance over at him either, but still her fingers squeezed his, trying to convey something through touch. They lingered until the traffic light changed a few seconds later and his hand returned to the wheel.

What was going on with those two?

Imagine being able to explore a relationship that way? Kim and Frog may flourish into happily-ever-after, they may not, but I envied her choice. I wasn't going to hit up a club and hook up with the first smile attached to a cute guy, but if I felt like whoring it up for a night, I should be able to do what I wanted. Plus, Caine moved on from me, even if Ness left, so he wasn't an option and anyone else in the coven wouldn't keep their mouth shut.

Before Donovan and Caine, I was happily single for a couple of years. Or at least semi-happy. I could do it again. It wasn't like a guy at my side was my sole version of happiness. I had more self-respect than that. At least now I did. And sleeping with Donovan again didn't necessarily stick me right back into the fire of our connection.

A clenching in my chest and a pressure behind my eyes warbled my sight, confusing me since I didn't feel weepy. Wait… Why was Donovan crying?

"Because I can hear everything you're thinking."

Ugh. Of course he could.

He leaned forward around his mother still writhing in a confusion spell, the dark pools of his eyes glassy tar pits. I always anticipated his default anger. He didn't get the response from me he hoped for. I felt nothing but annoyed. Instead, he felt something I couldn't quite place.

"It's called helplessness. No matter what I do, I can't make you see me differently. All I want is to have you understand me like you did before my father's cells, but you won't even try, so I'm SOL because, same as you, I'd rather be alone then resort to whoring it up around town."

I reinforced my neglected mental barriers and focused out my window. He was all talk. The tears were a shock, especially since now a few actually fell and the tightening in my chest worsened. So, maybe he was genuinely upset. It's not my fault I can't have a random thought without him dissecting it. As if he hadn't fantasized about shoving me into oncoming traffic a time or two lately.

After a few minutes of Donovan struggling to collect himself, I decided the show of waterworks didn't change anything. He was right. Things weren't the way they used to be. I can't change how I feel because he wants me to. I'll forever be tied to him which isn't true freedom no matter how much our past selves thought we were destined for each other.

When we finally gave up the ruse and returned to the Prison Creation, I went to remove my gear, but Vincent asked me to follow him as he still cradled Cora-Lynn's limp body.

People roaming the lobby gasped and applauded when seeing Vincent had returned. Then again with renewed vigor when Caine brought Chase to Edson to register him as the Prison Creation's second official prisoner.

Vincent butted in front of the console line, chose a cell, and asked me to follow him in. Whatever he wanted to tell me, I was eager for a moment with him, so I followed.

Inside a cell like all of the others, Vincent laid Cora-Lynn down on the small bed.

He then stood and braced his hands on his hips, his head bowed, eyes closed. "When the sedative wears off, all those people are going to terrify her." He pinched the bridge of his nose and smoothed back his hair still covered in dust. "At least this is a cell she can free herself of when she wants."

I didn't say anything. I knew I should, but nothing came to mind.

He turned and pulled me into a tight embrace. "I am eternally grateful for your persistence."

I squeezed him back, thankful to be able to. "It was mostly Caine."

"His skillset was indispensable. Though, I would wager you insisted on making the attempt in the first place."

I had wanted to go in immediately and was blocked. Donovan technically organized this push of a mission, but it didn't matter when Vincent was finally in front of me.

I squeezed him tighter instead of explaining the finer details of who did what.

When we pulled apart, I did feel the compulsion to fill him in on a few other things. "While Chase had me partially extracted, I saw what happened to your father."

"His detached soul?"

I nodded. "He couldn't get back in his body, so he tried hijacking mine. If Caine hadn't showed up, he may be walking around in a less fancy suit than he was used to, though he might have enjoyed the boobs."

Vincent's head hung. He shook it and hugged me again. I drank in his contact, updating the feel of his comfort in my memory.

"There's probably a spell to lock souls from using me as a vessel. We might have to look into that." Caine too, I mentally added, since he was also a vessel.

He pulled away again. "Even if he is aware of his surroundings, my father cannot initiate change. The ultimate Hell for someone like him." His laugh was soft and hollow. "Far less deserved when considering the suffering he has inflicted on others."

Quiet dragged, Vincent staring at his wife.

"She is not the woman I married," he finally said. "My father has twisted her. I question if she can—"

"It'll work out." I wrapped an arm around his ribcage. He put his arm around my shoulders, the weight filling me with such relief. "Introduce her to the new world. You've done it for me countless times. Knowing the place where she was imprisoned has fallen should help."

"If only that were the case."

"What do you mean? Your dad's a ghost and Chase is probably busy counting his heartbeats."

"My father may be dead and Chase in my cells, but the Sovereignty will survive without them. Granted, we have crippled production, but the lines still move."

Great. "So, what now?"

"Well..." He exhaled heavily. "My hope was to transfer innocent inmates from their current cells to mine and assist with reintegration efforts as I will with Cora-Lynn. The rest will be ended humanely when we destroy the Creation. However, this will impact the Blind as it did today. My hope was for it to happen all at once. The board will appoint a new leader and seek reinforcements. More innocents will suffer."

"Hmmm. I don't know if I can survive another Creation blast."

"This would be more of a controlled detonation."

"Why doesn't Caine compel as much information from Chase as possible first? You could build a team to strongarm the board or sic Caine on them. Work on the transfers here at a reasonable pace and retry the others to be sure they're where they should be or if their term of punishment should have ended last century. The ones who deserve it could still have their sentences downgraded to a normal prison experience until you decide their fate."

Vincent laughed and planted a kiss on my crown causing a

prickle of giddiness to tickle my nose. "I suppose the Sovereignty Creation could remain until greater plans are constructed."

"Plus, by the looks of those bullpens, a lot of Magics work for the Sovereignty. Keep the administrative wheels turning and run it as you want. Or have someone you know who will do it right. With Caine on the Mother Coven's payroll, options are raining four-leaf clovers. You might wanna send him a fancy basket full of chocolate and sour candy. You wouldn't be breathing fresh air without him."

Vincent laughed again. "I will think of something."

"Will you try cases yourself?" I asked, not wanting to leave his side.

"I want to see how Cora-Lynn adjusts before I attempt to commit myself to any one role. We are not free of danger," he said with regret in his tone. "Sovereignty devotees will rebel against a new system. Assassination attempts will become common."

"Thankfully you built this Prison Creation to hole up in."

He smiled and rubbed my shoulder as quiet resumed.

While we waited for Cora-Lynn to come around—or Vincent waited for her and I still couldn't compel myself to leave—I updated him with what happened in his absence, including Lincoln's betrayal ending in incarceration and the partial reconnection of my and Donovan's Soul Magic which now seemed to have dwindled down to its not-so-healed state.

"I see happiness has not followed such a renewal. Re-establishing the connection could save you both. Why resist?"

"You learn that the leader of your precious Tactical Team fucked you over to your brother and you're more interested in my relationship drama?"

"People will always discover ways to satisfy their own ends while deceiving all others, including those I misplaced trust in. While Lincoln's treason is an unfortunate development, I am unsurprised. Actionable consequences have already been employed in my absence, so there is no place for my immediate concern. As for understanding your reasoning for denying an easy solution to the problem of your broken Soul Magic, my question remains. Why resist?"

I crossed my arms. "He forced the reconnection. It wasn't like I forgave him and it mended on its own. And now I can't differentiate... Well, anything about him before or after. None of it makes sense in my brain."

Thinking about it all caused a crawling heat up my neck.

"How exactly did he force you?"

I recounted the memory bomb drink and the knock-down, drag-out healing where Vincent's memories were not included. Maybe if they were it would've changed things, but I doubted it. It was still against my will.

"Donovan does not possess the power to pull off a healing within the cells."

"Apparently, the ritual stone from our original Soul Magic spell provided more than enough magic to make it happen." I punctuated this with an eyeroll.

Vincent was lost in thought and then he inhaled and placed his hands on my shoulders. "Allow Donovan to repeat the process."

"Wha—?" I knocked his hands off of my shoulders. "No."

His green eyes locked on mine. "I love you. As my oldest friend and one I have witnessed in pure bliss and tragic death in countless lifetimes, I beg of you, allow him to try."

How could he ask this of me?

"Do you see the difference in yourself? I have witnessed many sides of you, but this version marinated in anger and willful defiance is not the vision of you I hold close."

"You'd rather the meek, self-loathing Sophie instead? Easier to deal with, right?"

"Certainly easier to converse with."

I didn't respond.

He raked his fingers through his messy hair. "Do you remember your life before learning of our history together? Before you lost Aunt Lacey? Before the Sect and the knowledge of Magics?"

"Vincent—"

"Do you?"

"Don't try to guilt me about life events I couldn't control."

"You misconstrue my intent." Somehow, he increased his intense stare, hitting me harder in his dishevelled state. "You ensured your survival after another treated you as less than human. You nearly died to protect a neighbour from living with much the same disregard and abuse. You have learned from the scars of your journey and carry them into your future as trophies of your refusal to bow to defeat. Now you are letting this additional scar conquer you, and I sense you would be satisfied in walking away from Donovan and your promises to him without care."

"I didn't promise anything."

"Did you not? If you forgo ones forged in this lifetime, you cannot deny the promise the Soul Magic created. It is grander than any marriage could recreate."

"We zip-tied our souls together in a completely different life, different bodies. You can't expect me to feel the same now?"

"Prior to the Sorrel cells you did."

I squirmed and couldn't stop myself from the disgusted reaction.

"Your love for Donovan was—"

"Unhealthy."

"Uncorrupted." Vincent straightened. "I can see the Soul Magic is still too broken for you to fathom how damaged you are, but I am determined to see your soul remains true to the love you shared before Tobias twisted it. Like my father has done with Cora-Lynn, I have to believe the twisting can be repaired. You owe it to every life you have lived to try. Millicent would be disappointed. As would Elysande. And Anya. Galina. Virgie. And so many others."

I tried not to react to the names he spoke that I heard for the first time. "No, I don't. I'm not any of them."

"You are them, as well as all the others. You are as much a victim in this as Donovan so you will not appreciate my method of management, but as Overseer of your soul, I must act."

I waited for Vincent to drop the grenade he was holding, seeing it in his exhausted eyes.

"The Tactical Team was created to operate behind the scenes where not all Magics are permitted. I have granted you a position to channel the excesses of your anger as you worked through what was done to you. Now I see the role has reinforced your rage and provided the tools to arm yourself against further recovery."

"Don't." My voice was a soft, desperate plea.

"Effective immediately, I am suspending your employment with the Tactical Team."

I stepped forward with a raised finger in his face. "You said the position was mine as long as I wanted it."

"It still is."

"Based on if I snuggle up with Donovan? A little creepy, don't'cha think?"

"Call it what you will but your current behaviour is beneath you. You are headstrong and although your stubbornness is usually endearing, your pig-headedness when concerning yourself, and the harm it causes others, is not worth keeping my word."

"Of all people, I thought you were on my side."

"You did not ask me how to regain your position," Vincent said when I turned to leave the cell.

"I have to kiss and make up with Donovan. Kind of obvious. Which is bullshit and just another way to entrap me."

Vincent closed the gap between us. "No. You and Donovan will reconnect naturally once the treatments are successful."

"Treatments?"

"You stated Donovan used magic from the ritual stone to repair part of the connection. It stands to reason a greater range of restoration will occur if given the opportunity."

"Letting Donovan put his hands on me over and over is your solution?" Vincent didn't need to know about the fact Donovan and I slept together recently. It shouldn't have happened.

"Yes."

"Your father really fucked you up in there."

"Yes, he did!" Vincent's rage poured from his voice so loudly I'm surprised Cora-Lynn didn't wake up. "He used our history to enact the worst of tortures. And at no point did I think if I was lucky enough to escape that I would return to you still clinging to such foolish ideas of breaking the Soul Magic or allowing it to decay." His expression crimped as if he wished he could throttle me and hand in his Overseer ID card. "You have no idea the gift you have in the mere existence of a choice to fix what needs mending. You have no idea... no clue."

"Because you wish you could have it with Cora-Lynn? Should I have somehow saved her from your father back when I was whomever she thought I was? That's something I'm paying for now too?" He shook his head. "It doesn't matter what else is happening. I tried, and I almost felt normal, and now I don't. Enjoy your Tactical Team and your fucking fairytale reunion when she wakes up. Happy you're fucking home."

I stormed out of the cell, pushed aside whoever was standing at the cell console, punched in my own cell number, and disappeared into it while the person was still bitching behind me.

All I wanted was to see Vincent alive and outside of his father's cell. And now that he was, he was playing favorites with a guy who occasionally breaks his face.

What a load of shit.

10

NON-LETHAL MEASURES

Kim

"I could've done more." So much more. He practically parked his big body in front of me every chance he could. "Protection or not, I need to stretch my powers and defend myself in real-life situations or I'm never gonna gain—"

"Death?" Hall interrupted.

I stopped walking and pushed up the sleeves of my green, cable-knit sweater to my elbows, frustrated and heated, and glared up at him.

"You'd gain death." He went on, "Your heart stopping isn't a learning experience, it's the absence of life and the opposite of what I signed up for."

"You haven't signed anything official yet."

Hall leaned in closer, leering down at me with his big arms across his chest. "I made expectations clear."

"No, you didn't." I stormed off, winding around others towards the office for a Sect meeting, knowing Hall would follow. "And even if you did, what happened in the stairwell shouldn't have happened."

"The team was divided when Cora-Lynn took off. Whatever happened with them, they weren't the ones trapped in the stairwell with a bunch of Sovereignty guards up their asses and no Persuader to clear a path. Plus, you were blonde. I was mixing you up with Bronya and overcompensating."

"I'd be insulted by the comparison except that was the whole point of the colour change." I was happy to be back to my normal red.

"I wasn't about to let our first mission together be our last. The more field experience you gain, the less I'll need to step in, but don't expect me to play eyewitness to someone threatening your life without jumping in guns blazing. It will never happen. I said I would loosen my detail on a case-by-case basis. A historic Sovereignty infiltration was not one of them."

"Fine." I stopped outside of the office where the meeting was set. "Valid. But know that I wouldn't put you in more danger by sticking myself in harm's way for no reason. You have to trust I can handle myself."

"I appreciate you clarifying. And I will. When you can."

"Hall..."

"Don't be naïve, kitten." He raised his hands as I went to bite back. "You will be able to handle yourself. I'll see to it. Until then, how about you let me take point? Not because I'm a big strong man, but because I'm a very old man with far too much experience killing others. Okay?"

His argument drained the fight from me. Not his words, but the expression on his face when he said them. He didn't feel good about being an expert in spilling blood. If he wasn't, he wouldn't have lived as long as he had, but that wasn't a part of his thoughts right now. I let him take the win, knowing we would butt heads on this matter a million times over until we found our rhythm.

Time was a difficult thing to track with any amount of accuracy sometimes. Some crises cost us days, but others made a few hours crawl by as if they ate up a week. Because of this, the Sect meetings didn't occur as regularly as they should. After recent developments I wasn't answering the same question individually. A meeting did the job in one go.

Hall held the door open for me. "I'm attending the meeting."

"What?" I didn't go through the door, instead stood staring at Hall.

Hall let the door close, leaving the room full of Sect members mumbling in confusion. "I said I would back off in the Prison Creation. Give me a day or two and I will. Since the promise, we gained Rosemary, John Weaver, two extra Sov traders, and Cora-Lynn. Each of them has good reason for being here, but all of them are potential plants either for the Sovereignty or another Tainted faction."

"Sure, but the Sect—"

"Is angry and grieving their friends' deaths and not just from Loring's last attack. They could have established contacts with the enemy outright or sought justice themselves and landed in bed with the covers pulled over their heads like Lincoln. Unless Caine interrogates every person in the Prison Creation, anyone else could be a treasonous mole. For all we know, Cora-Lynn is a walking timebomb and doesn't even know it."

"Don't repeat that to Vincent."

"I wouldn't dare, but he's smart enough to have thought of it himself."

Everything was getting so messed up. The Prison Creation was supposed to be our safe haven and Hall was right, there's so many of us in here now keeping track was getting a little more difficult. Caine could persuade them all for answers, though Vincent might have a mutiny on his hands.

Hall extended his hand towards the door in silent question if I was going inside and taking him with me.

I huffed and pushed through the door with Hall probably close enough to get whipped by my hair.

He was winning too many fights.

Hall closed the door behind him and planted himself in front of it. If anyone tried barging in they would hit him in the ass first. And since I was standing closest to the door, he wasn't going anywhere.

"We good to go? We got a poker game and another dub to steal." Blake had his legs stretched out in front of him, using one of the few chairs in the room.

With so few Sect members left in the Prison Creation, we didn't really need the large boardroom. Depressing. Far too many of us were gone and quite a few were out in the world living on a prayer hoping Loring didn't track them down wherever they decided was safer than the Prison Creation.

"Nah. You're cooked," Deirdra said, igniting fire in her palm and letting it climb to her elbow.

"*Pfft*, please." Blake spun to eyeball her. "Brick was mind reading and counting cards. They're against the—"

"Shut up." Donovan had no patience for their banter.

My co-Sect Leader didn't try and run the meeting. His heart wasn't into it since Aunt Lacey died and gave him the title. He surprised me by showing up in the first place. Though, I saw that Sophie wasn't around. Usually, she attended in tense silence or mouthed off or something. But to not show up at all? Nothing was right nowadays.

Caine was even in attendance. His grey eyes were set, trance-like, either overtired or in his head about Ness. Something told me it was Ness-related.

"We have new additions to the Prison Creation that have cause to be here, as well as some more over-reaching news about Magics in general. I figured you've all heard the meat of it or at least the appetizer platter and deserved the whole story. Plus, if you had questions, I could answer them now. Let me get through it first."

After I outlined all of the details I knew of from Vincent's Sov escape, Hall and Caine filled in a few of the blanks, and even Donovan tossed out a couple when the Sect members kept asking the same questions Hall and I couldn't answer since we were stuck in the stairwell. He didn't respond with any gusto or even care if they were properly informed.

"We didn't even know the Sovereignty existed until recently. Now they've imploded and we're potentially greater targets because of it? How perfect is that?" Denise asked with a heavy amount of sarcasm.

"Not if Vincent takes over," Gwen added.

"Did you see that happening?" Jared was quick to ask.

Gwen straightened in her chair. "I didn't say that."

"You kinda did," Deirdra joined in.

Gwen rolled her eyes and shook her head. She was a Prophetess and things she saw have come true in the past. I couldn't blame the others for questioning everything she said, but Gwen looked like she wished she kept her trap shut. Though, I did wonder if maybe there was something more to what she said. Vincent running the Sovereignty had to be a win for the Mother Coven, no?

After quieting the group when conversation devolved into arguing about something none of us would have the answer to until Vincent informed us, it turned into more tense conversation about Loring, where he could be, and when he might slither from his hidey-hole to torture everyone again with the help of Sophie's ancestor, Issát.

"He can release and then alter souls whenever he wants. Can Sophie do that?" Denise's question was for Donovan.

He glared at her and refrained from answering. She acted like he was rude for ignoring her, but even I knew that if Sophie was capable of releasing and altering souls, her brother would know, so in essence Denise would already know. If doing so was among Sophie's weapons belt, she wasn't strong enough or maybe not old enough. Issát was ancient. You learned a lot of tricks by his age.

"He'll probably be given the key for here. Everyone else is allowed in," Blake complained. "Why are you in this meeting?" He motioned to Hall. "Does shacking up with the Sect Leader gain you exclusive access?"

"Not shacking up." I needed the rumour to end here. "Hall has agreed to expand his normal duties on the Tactical Team to include an extra protection detail. That's it."

Gwen narrowed her eyes at me.

"Are the rest of the Tactical Team members taking on other key members or Sects?" Deirdra asked.

Shit. Everyone's eyes were on me. I flailed for a believable answer. "They certainly can if they want to."

Good enough. And not a lie.

I continued on to encourage them to hold certain rituals and rites with regular frequency to create a sense of routine and normalcy.

Jared interrupted to ask about Rosemary. Donovan shot him down and sparked an argument I then had to deescalate.

I swear. That guy does nothing but make my job harder when it's supposed to be his job as well.

The Sect members weren't stupid and felt insulted when kept in the dark and treated like Seedlings. In some cases, they were, but then so was I. Pointing this out seemed to calm them a bit. Complaints about the lack of social media and familial contact was expected. I just let them vent. They had a right to be upset about it, but they were lucky to have access to streaming services and games even if the cooperative modes and any kind of communication options were disabled. Still, their options were better than others who were stuck outside of the Prison Creation. And Caine knew what it was like to pass your days running for your lives. The Prison Creation was cushy by comparison.

"Use this time as the best vacation you never asked for. Do whatever you want, whatever you can, and keep your drama at a minimum."

Jared hit Blake's arm as if to blame him for whatever drama they found themselves in.

"That includes getting laid," I added. "STI's are one thing. Babies are another. And there's already too many people in here missing parts of their kids' lives."

None of them looked happy to add parenting to their resumes, so at least it was one thing they agreed on.

"Plus, we may also need any of you for your ability at any time, so keep your skills primed. You can practice all you want if you don't hurt others, even if in small increments. No tornados or burned-the-roof-down fires, but there're options. Be creative." No one needed Jared and Blake sweeping the lobby with tornados or Deirdra scorching the place.

"What about physical combat skills? Or weapons training?" Denise surprised me by asking. "Can't the Tactical Team run classes or something?"

Blake raised his hand. "Second that."

Jared nodded, the idea intriguing him as well. Same with a few others.

"That's actually a good question." I looked to Hall. He lifted a shoulder slightly. "I'll try to set something up. I need more chances to hone those skills, too."

Hall's slight head tilt said he understood my implication since we argued about it before the meeting.

The meeting ended because I had nothing else to say and the complaints could send us in circles for days.

Donovan left without a word as we dispersed. Maybe he was off to find Sophie. Or maybe his mother. Wherever he was headed, he was unconcerned with how the meeting went. He better cover my ass one day if my life becomes a trainwreck and I can't perform my co-Sect Leader duties.

"What now?" Hall asked. "A trip to Rome 46 BC? Interesting times."

"No trips. What about the training thing? I want to figure out a way for people to solidify their basic skills, if needed, and develop greater ones outside of their everyday skillset. We don't know if Loring will find a way to disable—"

"We can't use guns indoors."

"Not ones with real bullets. What about riot bullet type things? Those exist, don't they?"

"Non-lethal measures do exist, yes. Space for a shooting range does not."

I looked down the corridor to the lobby and then the other way towards the cafeteria. "Sure it does. I just need Vincent."

The moment I thought about him, my guiding light snaked its way towards the lobby and my feet took off in that direction.

Hall followed closely, throwing out advice to leave Vincent alone.

Yes, Vincent had been through a lot lately, and once my plan was implemented, his flock would run themselves instead of cramping up his to-do list with inane issues born out of boredom.

When we reached a tired-looking Vincent and I shared my plan, he couldn't or didn't have the energy to argue the need. He couldn't even deny the availability of members who could teach. I would be present, so Hall would be available, and if he didn't want to play teacher, at least people would have the ability to pull a trigger at a target and do something active, even if it meant learning they wanted nothing to do with guns.

With a few contingencies and safety protocols, Vincent approved stating he would deal with Edson, and if the need grew he would expand the Prison Creation to include space for larger group physical skills development.

Perfect!

Energized by having something to do could enrich Magics inside and outside of the Prison Creation. The drive in my motivated steps was unstoppable as Hall was forced to follow me to the cafeteria where I announced my plan and set in motion the people needed to spell the room as well as gather the equipment needed to pull it off.

An hour later, the cafeteria was split in half. With plenty of room for people to eat and relax, the shield splitting the room was clear for true transparency of our actions inside, as well as soundproofed. Guns were spelled with fake magic bullets which operated the same as real ones and shot down range to awaiting targets in the shape of Loring instead of the standard target.

Magics were equipped with ear protection if they wanted it, Hall was available for weapons information and tweaking people's form, and even Ismail and Bronya joined the classes. Without Donovan to distract her, Bronya had some skills she was happy to show off.

At the far end was a second smaller section, equally soundproofed, and equipped with other targets for hand-to-hand combat. Something Gregor enjoyed teaching. When he wasn't available, Edson's people took over while on their breaks, and the space was always stocked with the standard weapons a Tactical Team member would use, so someone could familiarise themselves them.

Denise left the gun range area through its transparent walls and came in behind me in the food line where I was getting the trainers some drinks.

"You're welcome," she said with a heavy dollop of smugness.

The weapons training was her idea and a good one. She may have had nothing to do with its execution, but still. If there was any proof that sometimes a meeting was a good use of time, this was sure it.

Anyone who didn't want to participate didn't have to hear it and could sit with their backs to it. Others could watch and see other's skills, plus it was something to blow off steam for those without intentions to fight a true enemy. Plus, *plus*, it was safe. People couldn't shoot each other with the fake magical bullets, and if someone pulled a knife on someone or attempted true harm against others within the combat room, they were hit by incapacitating pain. Same with trying to remove a weapon from the room. Since we were inside of the Prison Creation, it came equipped with greater safety features than if we were on the outside.

Failsafes were in place and a sense of rejuvenation in the Prison Creation lifted the tension enough to inject a few smiles including Hall's. He was wholly in his element teaching others how to inflict the most damage with minimal effort and leverage their unique qualities.

I found myself watching the way he handled each Magic and the questions they asked. If his motives were performative for my sake, I couldn't tell. No, he was enjoying himself and routinely checked to ensure I was near and safe and happy with how he was training the others.

So far, Hall was everything he promised he would be.

11

THE ENTITY YOU SEE

Vincent

The choking scent of dust and dirt lingered in my sinuses. The remnants of my father's tortures were equipped with staying power. What existed within the cells should not live outside of them, and somehow it survived in the literal fabric of reality. Maybe due to the swiftness of our extraction?

I decided to wash away the heavy reminder of the desert and dust storm which snuffed out Sophie and Donovan in another life while Cora-Lynn remained tranquilized. Leaving it on me felt like carrying my father into this place of safety and I wanted him off of me.

The yank and broken tether of my father's soul lived in the muscle memory of my hand. The sensation of his removal from this world replayed in my mind over and over again.

Chase's hasty attack was the true culprit. However, a full soul extraction could not have occurred had I not first gripped my father's soul.

Whatever awaited our presence after this life, my father was now experiencing it firsthand. Did a Hell of sorts await him? Did greedy demons rub their hands together and salivate to torture him the way he tortured others?

The Sovereignty Creation still hosted his wayward soul, unless those demons broke through the fabric of the veil and dragged him into their ring of karmic payback. As far as us Soul Extractors are told, my father's soul would not pass through to his natural afterlife. He is doomed to oversee the passing days without the ability to impact change. Maybe the most fitting Hell for Alasdair.

Would a crossing spell force him through the veil to his next phase of death? I may have to seek an opinion of ridding the world of him.

"Not as much of an issue as pining down Loring, but he's still popping up in random locations and freaking out the Blind. Some Magics also made an ID. They didn't act fast enough for photographic proof."

"Sorry… Photographic proof of…?"

Arden's expression remained passive, concern floating within it. "Gualichu. The demon-possessed Architect is easy to spot. His activities sound more observational than active. Sightings, no chaos. And no sign of Loring in the region, however, we are tapping into Recondite Magics to assess local factions. Communications are slow."

"Okay. Keep me informed of any changes."

Arden nodded, clapped me on the shoulder. "Of course."

Kim ran up to me when Arden left, Hall close behind her. She summarized a plan to train or entertain others in basics survival tactics. Edson would be cantankerous with the addition, yet I bet the guards would appreciate the diversion. Boredom was rampant for those not enmeshed in activities outside of the Prison Creation.

No argument came to mind to counter her proposal, and I approved it without true emotion.

Hall appeared surprised, saying nothing. He wanted Kim to have all she desired. Where this emanated, I had no mind to ask my old friend about it now. A later conversation would occur once the capacity to juggle another matter returned to me.

Maybe those two could create something together despite their vast differences. I was no matchmaker.

As quickly as she arrived, Kim was gone to implement her vision and Hall followed.

Acceptable clothing choices for Cora-Lynn were slim. Now free of my father's cells, would she prefer a dress, a familiar choice of her original time, or something she felt safety and empowerment wearing? A basic tactical outfit and boots were the extent of the available options. The durable fabric would cover her body, and was a better option than nothing at all.

An echoing growl filled the lobby.

The familiar sound gripped my insides. I dropped the clothing on the lobby desk and ran in a stunned panic. Cries followed by more growling filled the space.

I arrived to find Cora-Lynn in a bracing stance. Her posture had reverted to the form whence we first met in the Sovereignty cell forest. Animalistic fear and a drive for survival was alive in her eyes and in the snarl of her teeth. She was covered in the dirt I already freed myself of, her clothing torn and hanging off of her thin, muscular frame.

"Cora-Lynn!" I yelled over the fray of terrified Magics, stepped between Cora-Lynn and the Creation guards, and sliced my hand towards the ground. The marble flooring broke with a crash and lifted into a jagged rampart at the guard's feet.

The ten or so guards stood with their power at the ready, looked to each other, and then to Edson also behind the chin-high destroyed flooring.

"What happened here?" Edson asked. "Allow my guards to assess—"

"Do not force me to remind you who forged this Creation," I said to my carefully appointed Creation Warden. I needed to reestablish my position of boss. This hedging for alternative leadership was unacceptable. "Use lethal force against her now, or at any time, and you will meet a swift end."

With all of the abilities at their disposal, their emanating power was panicked retribution and not an appropriate level of intervention. Especially since Cora-Lynn had not displayed any power.

Shock overtook the guard's complaints. Edson ground his teeth for having been put in his place.

Ranlyn split the crowd with a tranquilizer gun in hand.

At least he had the presence of mind to arrive useful and not intent on spilling blood.

Cora-Lynn sprinted in the opposite direction. Those in her path scurried aside as she pushed through a door she must have mistook for an exit.

A few Magics ran out of the bathroom, fleeing Cora-Lynn.

I telekinetically stole the tranquilizer gun from Ranlyn and tucked it into the back of my waistband, ran towards the bathrooms, composed myself for a second, and pushed the door open an inch. "Cora-Lynn, it is Vincent. You are no longer in my father's cells. You are safe here."

The banging sound of the metal stall doors punched the space. She must be seeking another exit.

"We have been rescued by trusted allies. My father is dead and my brother imprisoned. We are safe."

The rush of an automatic toilet flush preceded another crash of a metal door.

I risked entering the bathroom, my hands up and empty.

Cora-Lynn stood in the middle of the floor. She flinched and growled at the sight of me.

I pointed at the bathroom stall. "Not a means of harm. Modern convenience and nothing more."

She made another feral sound in the back of her throat and then jumped onto the bathroom counter, balked at her reflection, slipped on the slick surface, and fell off.

I surged towards her and then stopped myself. "A mirror. The entity you see is your reflection."

Cora-Lynn was in a squat like a skittish feline, her movements rigid and calculated as she stared at herself in the streak-free surface. She took a step closer and then another a second later. Tension hung. I waited for the next explosive reaction. Instead, she touched her cheek, then turned over her hands, rubbing them together as if she felt the grit of the sand on her skin from our torture.

She assessed her reflection again. Silence remained and I watched every tiny movement while she acquainted herself with how others saw her now.

Her expression changed, tears fell. She swiped at them with angry impatience, becoming increasingly upset at the tears and the brown smudges they created across her cheeks as she attempted to erase them.

Cora-Lynn screamed with a heartbreaking fury that shattered against my bones. No terror, no true sadness…fury. So much was stolen from her: people, time, innocence, peace, her visage included. The mirror did not reflect the woman I fell in love with, and it did not display the lovely person living in the small town where I found her. Magic had warped her, not unlike the Sovereignty's Warden's twisted body. She did not appear anything close to the woman I used to know and she was now grieving this with a wild anger she could not direct at the person truly at fault.

Tears sprung to my eyes for my role in bringing her to my father's attention by existing by her side. While I ended the life of the person who ruined her, she would never garner the chance to face the one responsible. She was not even afforded witnessing my father's end and I knew the telepathic process of showing her how it occurred would terrify her.

She wilted and sat on the marble floor, emotion spilling from her. Instinct screamed for me to hold her while reason reminded me this was not about me, not about us, and she needed space to fall apart now while she was safe to do so.

This realization did not yield any amount of ease to stand idly by.

A minute or two fell away as she emptied some of the poison that infiltrated her heart. Her breaths came in heaves and she let her head fall back to draw in oxygen in stuttered pulls. Exhaustion clung to her dirt-streaked cheeks and eventually lessened. Not to a smile, but to a present state of awareness. She was not in my father's cell anymore. She may not understand her precise location or time, nevertheless, she knew she was free and that freedom from his chains was something she never envisioned.

Her thoughts swirled with visions of her tortures and the associated emotions she now experienced rather than words. They flowed in splashes of sensations. She inhaled deeper, her shoulders slumping, her planted hands on the floor keeping her upright.

"It is gone," she said in a meek, exhausted voice with her head bowed. "It is all gone."

I gently cleared my throat of the emotion which choked me. "What you knew is gone. Not everything, but most, yes."

"My parents?"

"A long time ago. They were not practicing Magics, so they could not extend their lives." Lying to her would be unhelpful and after all of the deception she experienced, I refused to add another.

A few moments passed. "Morgan and Henry? They lived many lives?"

"Yes, and we experienced their many deaths. They are here now," I was quick to add, then minutely regretted it. "They have also endured much in this lifetime and are known by different names."

"They trusted you and died anyway."

"Fate's design does not allow me to save them, only to experience their lives alongside them for a time."

She grew quiet again, collecting her thoughts. "When we lived and died as they did, I saw many things, understood many things. Tall homesteads, bright lights, fast...everything. Everything moved faster."

"You caught glimpses of the evolving world changing through the eyes of Sophie and Donovan in each life they lived and died. You will see those things and more, firsthand."

She knew more about those timelines than Sophie and Donovan did themselves.

"I—I know not how to live. How to endure." Her voice was still laden with anger and resentment.

"You will learn, and you will decide what living for yourself looks like."

Cora-Lynn gripped her head. I refrained from accessing her mind for glues. Her thoughts should be her own.

"The others I saw...out there...?"

Her question dissipated, yet I understood. "Some are employed to protect those who are here. They do not know you or what you are capable of, so they overreacted, but this place is mine."

Her head snapped up, her gaze a spotlight.

I spoke quickly. "It *is* a prison, of sorts. However, it does not operate as my father's and right now is not a prison at all. It is a refuge for people in hiding from those who wish them harm. As you experienced, you can leave the cell whenever you please and enter at your own will. They are a place to rest, not to contain."

She straightened, and I felt my opportunity to explain slipping away.

"Those you saw do possess abilities. They do not wish to use them for harm. It is a simple matter of how they were born. You may see inexplicable things. No one here intends to harm others with their abilities. They just want to live." I tried to explain that others who were true evil existed. The sheen of desperation to absorb all I claimed was awash over her eyes, overwhelmed. Again, I fought the urge to comfort her.

"Would you like to clean yourself of my father's cells? I found it affirming of the escape. I could help you return to your cell and explain the facilities, if you wanted. Afterwards, you can eat. No one here goes hungry, and options are endless."

Cora-Lynn examined her arms and body and then her reflection again.

Without answering, she started towards the exit, and an inner panic took up space in my chest for what may await us outside of this bathroom and how she may react to it.

Noise from the Magics rose in the lobby. The marble floor was smooth with no perceptible damage.

She peered way up to the ceiling and at the brick wall as people appeared seemingly from nothing when they exited the cells. "How do I know any of this is real?"

Not an easy answer. "You will experience more and more until it becomes normal. You will ask questions, I will answer them if able, and then you can construct your own conclusions. Your distrust is expected. Many thrust into this world tend to need time to come to terms with how Magics are normal people who can do abnormal things by comparison. We are no better or worse for having these abilities.

"You will also see that no matter how many nights you sleep, your surroundings will go unchanged. You will remain essentially the same, only now with the ability to impact your life."

Cora-Lynn walked instead of commenting. I pointed where we needed to access the cells. I did my best to exist as close as possible in case something spooked her.

While some were more subtle than others, far too many stared and others scurried away from a perceived potential follow-up attack.

Ranlyn started towards us. I discreetly waved him away. He complied. Whatever he needed could wait. And then I remembered I left the clothing I found for her at the lobby desk. I nudged Ranlyn's mental walls in a way Elders could to remain connected. He dropped his defences an acceptable degree and I requested he bring the clothing to us.

I explained this to Cora-Lynn and took the clothing from Ranlyn at a safe distance. The introduction to another Coven Elder was quick and probably meant very little. Ranlyn took no offence or used the introduction to segue into his brewing requests.

Explaining a digital touchscreen and cell entry process was beyond the understanding of anyone detached from modern technology. Cora-Lynn contained no real-world reference to use such a thing, so I kept my descriptions light and stuck to practical application, directing her to myself or the guards if she required assistance.

When we popped back into the cell, she was unafraid and reacted well-acquainted with the process, lest she display weakness. I stuck my hand through the wall to prove she could leave again and then explained the shower and toilet use. Toilet paper did not exist in her time, and she found the automatic flushing mechanism obnoxious, fighting the flinch at the brash sound.

I remained in the cell at her request. I was unsure if this was due to distrust of whether or not she could leave. Her invitation was surprising and made it harder to remind myself she was no longer my wife and had too much healing ahead to predict if she ever would be.

She dressed in privacy while my back was turned, and once done, I saw my clothing choices would suffice until she decided on a style of her own.

After some conversation on how her body's needs would have been in suspension while in my father's cells—I strayed from mention of her menstrual cycle since this was never something we would have discussed in the past—we headed for the cafeteria.

Seconds into our objective for food and I remembered Kim's request. I hastily explained the training center now included in the large space and found it divided into sections by glowing transparent walls. Crowds sat and stood outside of the walls to observe those inside shooting targets and practicing hand-to-hand combat.

Cora-Lynn seemed to absorb all of this while we waited in line. When our turn arrived, she requested foods she would have cooked in her time, foods she had not tasted in many years including beef pot roast with parsnips and potatoes, chicken and vegetable soup, and strawberry tartlets. I ordered a few modern staples in case she wanted to try them and assured her she was not expected to finish everything.

She found the process easy enough and remarked it preferrable to endless farming and preparation. I wholeheartedly agreed and remembered a time when if you did not seek the particulars of your meal, you went hungry.

We found a seat near the wall where she would not be surrounded by others, her attentions on the new training facilities. She was cautious with the food. It was not exactly as she remembered, however, served a pragmatic purpose. One day I hoped she would be at a point where she would desire something and find pleasure in acquiring it. Survival mode would no doubt persist for some time.

I chanced a peek into her mind while she observed the others training. She deserved her privacy and I found it impossible not to overhear her open thoughts.

The images in her mind centered on the day my father's goons came for her. She did not recognize Loring in the picture on the targets, but understood he was an enemy. She wished she possessed such weapons and knowledge to protect herself then. She counted many in the cafeteria and believed she could outwit and outmuscle them. While the cells were a Hell, they equipped her well for this stage of life where people possessed god or demonic powers and strife was at our door. And if the Devil had corrupted her, then the people accepting her among worse evils meant she was amid her peers.

I hated this perspective and the reason she now saw herself as corrupted.

12

FAIR TRADE

Sophie

I couldn't force myself to leave my cell. I sat or paced for hours and eventually passed out, probably Donovan's exhaustion forcing me under now that the connection was back online.

I tried avoiding sleep as often as possible or else splashes of Donovan's face plagued my dreams. Memories of us together, a sense of satisfied companionship, a peace in my heart I hadn't felt in a long time. It all sank into my languid limbs as Donovan held me tightly. Then he was ripped away and I was left sitting up in bed in an otherwise empty prison cell alone.

Why would I dream about someone I wanted nothing to do with? Too much talking about him with Vincent. Too much trying not to think about him at all.

The comfort from my unconscious state morphed into a seething resentment for the inability to escape him. The memory of his body on mine was so fresh I could feel my skin move beneath his embrace.

I needed him off of me.

After a shower that did nothing to permeate and clean him out of my mind, I left my cell when the walls felt like cling wrap. Everyone was eating. Or staring at an enormous translucent and glowing wall.

A new addition to the cafeteria?

The crowd was so thick at ground level I couldn't see what everyone was gawking at. Whatever was inside the big glowy box, they were hootin' and hollering about it like they were at the horse track and had good money riding on how much someone had drugged the horse. Or the jockey.

With all of the bloodshed, how long ago? A couple of days? You'd think they would be going through tissue boxes and running through every funeral ritual in their magical toolboxes. Maybe they had. No one bothered to tell me about it if they did.

Caine sat with Jet. Andy was perched on the side of the cafeteria table to see a head above the crowd. Caine wasn't anywhere near as happy as his nephew and neither was Jet, nevertheless, they painted on smiles for each other as they chatted.

Kim was next to one of the glowy walls. Caveman wasn't with her surprisingly. No wait. The top of his blond head was inside the glowy box. He may be a Viking, but he wasn't worth the upgrade if it meant she was cheerleading on the sidelines.

Even my brother hung out with some from my sect, and the rest of the Ballard Coven enjoyed some food as they checked out the others practicing. Watching the young ones blow off some steam was all the entertainment the old timers required.

Too many happy people.

Seeing all these cheerful smiles with the peaceful romance of my dream still alive in my nerves caused an achiness for something easier, lighter. Nothing specific, and not the literal events of my dream, but the sense of belonging that comes with being with the person you love or the people who give a damn about whether or not you're breathing. A contentment that couldn't be faked. I did have something close to it. Losing it was worse than never experiencing it at all and I couldn't recreate the joy. I wanted to, but it wasn't there.

Wow. Even Vincent and a conscious Cora-Lynn were together at the end of the cafeteria. The former Sovereignty inmate settled into a perfect position to watch everyone. She was dressed in tactical clothing and looking like she could take on three-quarters of the room before Vincent could use the tranquilizer gun tucked into his waistband.

Guess that was love.

"You okay?"

The shock of Donovan's voice sent a shudder screaming down my spine.

A gasp fell from his lips as it affected him.

I turned and saw something glittering in his eyes, something I was content to ignore.

Fuck food. I'd rather starve.

I took off where I didn't have to pretend everything was A-okay.

Inside of my cell, time crawled with nothing else to do but pace and stew about my conversation with Vincent and everything that led to it, plus him ousting me from the Tactical Team. My spinning thoughts riled up my anger more than I wanted them to, but I couldn't help but dwell on Vincent breaking his promise and taking Donovan's side.

Nothing about this was right.

And it sure as hell wasn't fair.

"You gonna keep the blonde?"

I spun, Kim yelping and raising her hands. "Geez, Soph. Check your freak. I'm not here to fight. You want any of that, line up at the range or for a round with Gregor."

I didn't consciously spring towards her into a fighting stance, but I guess it happens when someone walks into your space unannounced. The rest was gibberish.

"What do you want?"

Kim straightened and flicked her red-again hair over her shoulder. "To be yelled at for asking a simple question, apparently."

I hadn't cared enough about my hair to carve out the three seconds needed to change it. "It's just hair."

Kim scoffed. "Okay."

"Why are you here?" She had to have had a motive to leave Caveman's side since they were so attached these days. Unless the glowy box in the cafeteria was some kind of a cell he couldn't escape.

"The Team was sent on mission about an hour ago. Another safe house was hit by Loring or his devotees. Donovan tried to get you but Vincent told him you were off of the Team. What happened?"

"Ha. Yup. Vincent stripped me of my gun-pointing privileges until I learn to play nice doggy with Donovan."

"Hmm. You guys seemed a lot better."

I shrugged. "Didn't stick."

"Okay. Well, Donovan tried to boycott it. Insisting he wouldn't go on the mission without you."

"Let me guess, he got over it pretty quickly."

Kim lifted a brow. "Vincent took him aside. I don't know what he said but Donovan ended up joining them."

I nodded, having no idea what Kim thought I should do with this information. "What's up with you and Caveman?"

Kim raised both her brows now.

"Yes, I changed the topic. An indication I have no interest in continuing what we were talking about since there's nothing I can do about it. On the way back from saving Vincent, I saw Caveman hold your hand. You're always together. Something more than nothing?"

Kim's lips twisted. "Can't help but like the guy, I guess."

"He *is* sexy as hell."

She chuckled and sat on my bed as I remained standing. "He's more than his packaging though the packaging is deliciously pretty." She rolled her eyes. "We have an arrangement. One I may need you to solidify as a witness. I just hope he isn't screwing with me."

"Good luck with figuring it out. I can feel everything Donovan can, and I still can't tell what his intentions are. Wait, are you getting married? Frog might have some thoughts."

"God no. Though, Frog's opinions aren't my business. We broke up. He can't handle me being a Magic and doesn't think we should be together."

"He broke up with you?"

Kim pursed her lips and nodded.

"Asshat."

She laughed. "Yup."

"Well, Caveman seems genuine, in general, anytime I've dealt with him. Not much you can do but try."

"Yeah, we'll see. What about you and Donovan? You thinking of playing nice to get back to guns and body armour?"

I sank onto the end of the bed opposite Kim. "Not so simple. Vincent stipulated I participate in 'treatments' where Donovan hits me with the ritual stone magic. Not something I can fake. Not like I have the energy to pretend."

She turned her body to face me more. "You know, I hate that every time we talk these days I'm giving you the 'mom look' and ending the convo with a lecture. But I do have to point out that Olive lost the Ballard Estate, the Sect lost members as did the Mother Coven. A lot of people have died in the safe house raids and in The Chiff, and by the sounds of it more are goners right now since the Team was dispatched. Cora-Lynn lost countless years of her life. Your dad lost his house, your mom can't return to work—"

"Your point?"

Kim sighed. "Life is beyond shitty right now, but what's going on with you has to be pretty bad for Vincent to give you problems, cuz that man would move mountains for you. Literally. If he's worried, as a guy who's known a version of you for centuries, then yeah, I'm worried too. Which evokes my mom face." She pointed to her face to prove her point.

I didn't want to laugh, but a chuckle escaped. "Sorry. I can't help it."

"I know you can't, even if you don't seem to understand why. Plus, I really didn't like seeing you and Donovan beat the crap out of each other. And not for the obvious reasons considering how toxic it is. Donovan was always a drunk and angry guy. Now, he's sad and you're the one who's angry. And there's not enough alcohol to go around."

"I can't say I care about how Donovan feels in a way you would believe, Kim. He's responsible for his own emotions."

"Bullshit."

"You can leave at any time."

"Sophie," she said my name with great patience, "I'm calling you on your bullshit because I'm your best friend. I'd back you up on almost anything, I truly would, and have even when you didn't deserve it, but I wouldn't be your bestie if I let you lie to yourself. Not letting you pass with bullshit lines is what true friends do."

"Let me guess, you would do the treatments."

"Do you want to be on the Tactical Team?"

"Yes."

"Sounds like a fair trade."

"How could coercion into a relationship be considered a fair trade?"

"Are you in your right mind to decide? Maybe the people who know you best are better suited to see the things you won't let yourself see. Until the Soul Magic is fixed, I'm not so sure you could make the decision."

On my feet again, my blood was pumping double-time and I was trying my damndest not to lose my shit.

"I don't know if you recognized them, but I was a donor of some of those memories from the memory bomb spell Donovan stitched together. I've seen how intense the love between you two is, even before you were ready to admit it. It existed in everything you did. Completely unmistakable even to a stranger. I know you love him."

"Like you loved Frog?"

"No. I was never *in love* with Frog, and we weren't arguing about Frog and me."

"I'm not arguing at all. I'm telling you facts."

The sound of my stomach growling stole the momentum.

Kim's eyes widened and she failed not to smile. "You're starving yourself in here to avoid seeing Donovan and Vincent. Let's hit the caf. Donovan and the Team are gone. You can see the new training grounds, catch up with some family you've been ignoring, and fill your gut."

The family part wasn't a concern. It should have been, but it wasn't. Family equalled a barrage of questions I didn't feel up to answering. Keeping up my energy was more important when I was on the Team, though I could at least eat enough to stop my stomach from gnawing on itself.

I gave in and we exited the cell. Caveman's booming voice reached across the lobby.

Shit. The Team had already returned. So much for avoiding them.

A person wearing civilian clothing turned to speak with Vincent. The sight of the man stopped me cold in my tracks from heading to the cell console.

"I wonder who he is?" Kim asked.

"Mr. Smiley." I started forward, Kim keeping tight to me.

"And Mr. Smiley is...?"

Donovan's attention flipped to me from across the lobby. He remained stoic while his chest rolled with jealousy.

"A pleasant complication," I murmured and crossed the way to unapologetically interrupt Caveman and Mr. Smiley a.k.a. Jordan the extra cute hacker we met on mission recently. "Drink for the road? Or are you staying?"

"Hey!" Jordan responded with excitement. "Whoa. Look at you, blondie. I like it."

I was aware of the eyes of the group on me but focused on the stretching smile Jordan flashed as he lifted an arm over my head and leaned in for a natural hug I happily reciprocated.

"A temporary alteration." I waved it off when he let me go. "I was on my way to the cafeteria. Need some fuel?"

"I sure could." Jordan bent to pick up a heavy gym bag he slung over his shoulder. "You've got yourself a tagalong."

As we left the group, Donovan's anger beat in my chest and the burn was a ripe satisfaction I couldn't help but get a high from. He wanted me miserable unless I was with him. Well, he didn't get to decide when and who I would be happy with. Right now, at Jordan's side on our way to join the food line, was exactly where I wanted to be. And Donovan could sit his ass down in a cafeteria chair next to us and see firsthand how he wasn't the center of my universe anymore.

In fact, I welcomed the audience.

13

PATHETIC ADMISSION

Donovan

Watching Sophie walk away with Jordan boiled my insides. A heat in my chest and throat blazed. No way she missed the internal reaction. She couldn't.

Sophie and Jordan were shoulder-to-shoulder as they wove around the crowded lobby, too comfortable with casual hits of contact. She smiled so big my cheeks registered the muscle tension. The tech weenie was basically a stranger, and she was tripping over herself to treat him like a long-lost friend.

"Donovan." Vincent's voice yanked me away from imagining I could shoot lasers out of my eyes. Maybe with the ritual stone magic enacted. Instead, a belly full of flirtatious laughter made me want to disembowel myself jack-o-lantern style.

"We should've left him to burn with the others."

Hall laughed.

"You performed your duty," Vincent said. "Once Jordan is settled, we will extend inquiries into if he knows anything of import."

"Looks cozy enough." Hall earned a backhand in the arm from Kim.

I was all for violence and a light smack was not what I was itching for.

"Unhelpful," Vincent directed at his old friend. "Most lost their lives when the safe houses were targeted. Jordan may contain important information he is not aware of."

"How about questioning why he was there at all? I thought Mr. My Talents Aren't for the Frontline was skipping town."

Hall tucked his thumbs into the arm holes of his tactical vest. "He said he sought safety where he could finish a few things up. And he was sleeping when the fire started. No alarms, no warnings. Loring's people strike quickly."

"And no one else survived? A bit convenient, no? The burn he sustained was an easy heal." The house was full of Magics, and not one of them noticed the fire quickly enough to do something about it? Everyone else was found crispy in their beds. Loring could have used some kind of spell to incapacitate the Magics inside. If he did, why was Jordan left unaffected?

Something didn't feel right.

"He was lucky," Vincent concluded. "I am going to check in with Cora-Lynn." He stuck his finger in my direction. "Be cordial to our newest guest. If you are beyond capable of witnessing Sophie's interactions with the man, remove yourself from their vicinity before you...do something you would do. Understood?"

I stood soldier straight, receiving his order as the most important thing to happen to my day. "Affirmative, Master."

Vincent's expression wilted into exhaustion as he left for the cell console to see Cora-Lynn.

Cordial? I refused to make this easier on her.

"Hold up, cowboy." The drop of Hall's heavy hand on my shoulder did nothing to stutter my steps towards the cafeteria, but he followed anyway. "I'm all for setting Sophie straight, but Jordan's a pawn. All this guy knows is a good-looking chick is hitting on him. Anyone in his position would welcome it."

"Are you suggesting I set up their honeymoon suite?"

"I'm suggesting you let her have her fun."

This stopped me, tripping up Kim who was apparently tailing us.

I turned and eyeballed Hall for the audacity of his suggestion.

He raised his hands. "I meant the fun she's having screwing with you."

I started walking again.

"Once she sees it doesn't get her anywhere, she'll back down," He went on. "You rolling in there to mark your territory will have her pulling away more and drags Jordan into the middle. It happened at Jordan's apartment, and she pushed it to mess with you. Which I know, because I read her mind back then and warned her against these games. Nothing's changed. Whatever's happening with her, you're making it worse."

Hall's heavy hand gripped my shoulder and stopped me with a small injection of power. "Let's do our homework on this guy. Distract ourselves with anything that doesn't involve you stalking Sophie until she jams her tongue down the guy's throat to prove a point."

Everything in me wanted to boot-stomp the smile off of that keyboard-humper who never earned Sophie's happiness. The last time I experienced anything close to mild contentment from her, it lasted shorter than a sneeze.

A giddy thrill went through me, sparking a smile. Not my smile. Sophie's. I growled and felt her corresponding amusement with my reaction. Fine. She can have her fun. Something was still wrong with her and whatever it was, this was a part of it. At least no matter where I was, I'd know if things went further than vapid flirtation.

Fuck, I hated that guy.

We turned away from the cafeteria, and headed back to where we left Kim, waylaid by Gwen at some point. I focused on putting one foot in front of the other to stop myself from breaking Jordan into Humpty Dumpty pieces and watching the blood of his yoke run—

"Whoa," Hall interrupted my fantasizing, "seriously, man? Your imagination would disturb my ancestors. The visuals..."

Kim chuckled, having overheard Hall. "I'm pretty sure they bathed in the blood of virgins, so that says a lot."

"We'd never waste virgins in such a callous manner, kitten."

She rolled her eyes and flashed a flirty and dismissive smile.

Gwen smirked at the exchange.

Ugh, those two. How were they not fucking yet? Whatever it was, I didn't have the brain cells to spare if my mental barriers were already slipping so much that Hall heard me in the first place.

I channelled some passive energy to re-enforce my thoughts. No one needed to know how desperate I was to get Sophie back to the woman I loved. The fact everyone knew as much as they did was a pathetic admission I was willing to bypass because I couldn't hide it anymore and only cared so much about what anyone thought.

Fine. Research it was. Something about Jordan didn't sit right, and it wasn't the fact Sophie was weaponizing him against me.

Once Vincent returned from checking on Cora-Lynn, he found us with Arden looking into our new visitor. He was already attached to his computer while keeping an eye out for any word on Loring's antics or even Gualichu the demon so we could stifle any damage ahead of corrupting the Blind.

And since Vincent gave me the skimpiest reason for kicking Sophie off of the Tactical Team, I insisted on a full explanation.

When Vincent finished, it took me a moment to decide if I was pissed or impressed.

I wanted a drink. "Something really messed up must have happened to you inside of your father's cells for you to put your foot down with her. You're usually all about giving her everything she wants."

Vincent narrowed his stare, choosing his words. "Her happiness is important to me."

I glanced at Hall who smirked and shook his head at Vincent's gross understatement. And it was. Maybe Vincent didn't realize how wrapped he was.

"Do you really think more of the ritual stone magic will work?"

Vincent went to push his glasses up his nose and then stopped midway since he no longer wore any. "You tell me."

"*Pfft.* Maybe. While I was doing it the first time, intuition dictated I push through. Whatever it was inside of me understood the issue and was driven to fix her. I thought it..." My voice trailed off, dripping in disappointment.

"When I spoke with her at the meet with Miklos, she was... untethered, raw, reactive, hardened by her experience and what the broken Soul Magic inflicted on her. Now it seems she endures all she must and battles the rest with bared teeth and claws while trusting very little. And while it appears most dire, feeling nothing is worse than a show of active aggression."

"Is this what she thinks using the ritual stone magic is? Injecting her with fake sunshine like some kind of mind-control, Stepford Wife spell?"

Vincent gave a slight head tilt, assuming that was the case. "As I have stated, this is the first life in which I can say the Soul Magic has been tested to such degree. Marital separation is sometimes needed to remind both parties why they are together. Have faith the both of you will survive this."

"Marriage?" I sputtered at the term. Not that I wouldn't marry Sophie, but in this lifetime, we were far from making it official.

"She laughed too, but this is a marriage of souls not defined by unflattering bridesmaids' dresses and expensive rings."

Hall sucked his teeth. "Sophie and Caine wore rings and that didn't work so well."

I glared at the big guy, trying not to recall Sophie and Caine being a happy couple and vessels to Aunt Lacey's dead son and daughter-in-law. "Thanks for the reminder."

He shrugged.

"My hope was Sophie would come around on her own, however, it is possible the fracture will not allow her to. Intervention may be the sole course of action."

"And me forcing the ritual stone magic on her will put her back on the Team, but nothing less?"

"Nothing less than her returning to a person I recognize, capable of reasonable decisions based on more than paranoia and distrust."

The fact she would rather be benched then let me work a little magic and save her was another kick to the beanbags. She saw the good it did the first time. How could she think that was some kind of mind control or fake happiness?

What if forcing it the first time is why it didn't work? I'd top her up every day for our unnaturally long lives if it meant an ounce of happiness. I just wanted her to look at me like I wasn't the vilest thing she ever let herself care about.

14

BERATING THOUGHTS

Sophie

Turned out Jordan possessed uses beyond keeping me company and pissing off Donovan for doing so. Over the last couple of days, Jordan was a ripe source of information, a previously untapped reserve. Who knew freelance tech work for Magics was so lucrative in both money and contacts?

His specialities were Recondite Magics, those working behind enemy lines with freelance agents and handlers. His fingers were in everything.

The Team came into the boardroom where Jordan and I were working on a spell to speak with him to confirm a few things about the safe house they brought him from, and they got to talking about his history in a business some were all too familiar with.

"I've never heard of you." Caveman leaned against the board-room wall, his arms crossed. "My career as a Recondite Magic is extensive. I would've heard of you."

Jordan swivelled in his chair, a hint of a smile on his lips. "You know me by a different name."

"Being?" Vincent prompted.

"Neo?" Donovan's deadpan attempt at comedy gained him a "tsk tsk" from Veata.

I loved how easily Donovan was irritated with Jordan. The second Donovan saw my ass in the chair next to the guy, Donovan bristled and hadn't smoothed his hackles since.

So easy. So satisfying.

Jordan managed a small laugh at Donovan's quip, making me happier to see Jordan was as tickled to antagonize Donovan as I was.

"The rights were already sold on that one, champ." Jordan refocused on Caveman as Donovan's fury simmered along the connection. "We've even spoken. I've provided you intel on dozens of cases, a few in a tight pinch, and created the identity and background required for you to squeeze in with Tobias Sorrel."

Donovan's father's name alone made my insides cramp enough for Donovan to shift his stance.

Caveman's ice blue eyes narrowed. "Scourge?"

Jordan leaned back, swivelled his chair, and lifted his hands as if to say, "That would be me."

"Hmm." Caveman side-eyed Arden, the hacker of the Tactical Team, sharing a skeptical glance.

Jordan stopped swivelling. "What? Not impressive enough for you?"

"Plenty impressed. More surprised you're alive. I heard you flipped on a contact, and they removed you from the playing field...in pieces."

"Nah." Jordan sat forward. "A plausible cover for my disappearance. I knew all of this would come to a head when The Chiff was flooded and you all knocked on my door, so I crashed my handle to stay free of the bullshit. Can't exactly be strong-armed into joining one faction or another when they think the applicant is ritual ash."

"Again," Donovan interjected, "instead of stepping up, you hide. Bit of a character flaw for someone who claims to be doing such noble work, no?"

"Right. I forgot all about your perfection when training to lead your father's troops into a righteous incestual future." Jordan's tone was one of knowledge, not assumption, and Donovan glared at me with no trouble guessing where he learned it.

Okay, I talked about Donovan. So what? Not enough to be all pissy when Jordan likely heard the information through the grapevine. The last thing I wanted was to talk about the bastard, but when Donovan got into a scuffle while on a mission the day prior, Jordan saw my bloody knuckles spontaneously appear and I let go of a few details packaged into a profanity-laden rant. Nothing anyone else inside of the Prison Creation wouldn't learn eventually.

"We should be making rounds of the safe houses again," Ranlyn said, interrupting the stare down. "Those and local Magics' houses have been Loring's focus. Ignoring that could be our downfall in bolstering their view of the Mother Coven as a viable ally."

"Most are scuttling like cockroaches," Veata said. "Not many places left to check."

Vincent agreed. "Tonight at..." He checked his watch.

"No, no, no. Don't go during the night again," Kim chimed in. "Banging on doors to say '*we care*' won't be welcomed or appreciated if you wake them or their kids up."

Not a lie. Not that it mattered to me. I wouldn't be allowed to go and thought the mission was pointless. If people weren't on our side after all Loring has done, they were already playing for the other team and would use the visits to funnel more information to the enemy. We had enough intel issues.

"Early morning then," Vincent decided. "We will start with the southern city safe houses and work our way up."

With an agreed upon plan, the meeting soon broke off, Veata and Ranlyn leaving immediately though Vincent paused and stayed behind, focusing on Jordan.

"Since you have experience infiltrating Tobias's security measures, can you provide supplementary intelligence other than what Hall would have already supplied?"

Jordan shrugged. "Doubt it. With Hall under for years and Tobias's own son in your ranks, including Rosemary inserting herself into the mix, you couldn't have compiled a camp of Sorrel flock exes any better except if Donovan hadn't killed off his supposed-to-be bride and captured Brandon instead of you offing him. If any more Tainted souls walk in here, we might have to sojourn to Ranlyn's Slovenian hideaway."

Wait a second… The shock of how much Jordan knew sat cold in my chest. A whole lot of people side-eyed each other to assess who let the information slip and questioned how much of what he said was common knowledge. A discrete head shake let anyone who cared know it wasn't from me.

"With any luck, Loring will be stopped without the need arising, and life can normalize." Vincent continued smoothly, "At this point, you have maintained some contacts, correct?"

Jordan hesitated. "A few."

"You will let us know if they reach out?"

"Of course."

Vincent nodded, slid a guarded smile my way, and left the room with the others following.

"What now?" I asked, though I would rather have grilled him about the information regarding Joelly and Ranlyn's Slovenian home where the covens gathered to prepare to fight Evaristus the Puppeteer. There must be a logical reason why he knew that, right? He knows a lot of things, mostly second-hand from his digital excavations. Many people had been at the gathering. Someone must have talked about it. But how many had witnessed Donovan killing Joelly? Most were gone from the field outside of the Diluculo Creation by then, but Donovan did admit what happened to his brother Brandon when he snuck into Donovan's house. Would Jordan have had any contact with Brandon? Or Donovan and Brandon's father?

I didn't want to admit to the flapping red flags.

Jordan adopted a relaxed smile. "We can go over that spell again."

"Which one?" We covered quite a few clever spells over the past few days, his instruction almost as delicious as the bump to my spell repertoire.

"How about the sight booster one you haven't memorized?"

He took whatever my returned expression was as confirmation of a plan.

"Head to my room, err cell, whatever." He laughed. "Those chili and lime peanuts you like are in my laptop bag. I'm going to check in with my aunt and meet you there."

"Sure." I felt his stare on my ass until I shut the door behind me. He'd called family in the days he was here and, even if it wasn't really family, it wasn't my business who he spent time on the phone with. He was supposed to have been leaving town when the safe house was hit, and he said he feared one of Loring's people following him to their home.

A plausible and relatable story from many within the Prison Creation.

I meant to keep walking with intent to chomp on some spicy peanuts, telling myself to shove down the paranoid princess I felt bubbling up inside of me.

Something stopped me from moving towards the cell console. The gut feeling begged to be soothed and proved wrong. I feared the instinct was right and something was off.

I turned and stopped.

You're being paranoid, Sophie, I told myself. This is weak and unfair and borrowed emotion from Donovan who detests the guy for simply existing. There had to be a reason he knew about Joelly and Ranlyn's home. Maybe he'd been there among all of the people fighting. Though, he was a hacker, techy dude who stated he was unfit for field work.

The feeling didn't dissipate.

Ugh. Fuck.

I was already standing off to the side so he couldn't see me through the little window. Those meandering around the Prison

Creation were into their own conversations. So many others who were victims, seeking safety in a trusting environment. Buuuuuutt, the niggling sensation was a swinging red flag in my face and it didn't care about the berating thoughts I tried to beat it away with by telling myself I was a stupid little girl for seeing danger where there wasn't any.

Whatever. Call me the asshole. I needed to know for sure.

I sputtered off a spell Jordan taught me, one to heighten hearing as he was all about elevated natural senses. Voices assaulted my eardrums. I fine-tuned my range and directed it to the office Jordan was in.

Soft patters were likely Jordan pacing while ringing over the phone line droned through the receiver.

A click followed by a deep man's voice gave a curt "Yes?"

"Put him on," Jordan said with equal annoyance.

More pacing sounded as he waited for many moments longer than Jordan seemed to appreciate. His audible mumblings and quick snap were him breaking tension in his neck as dead air waited with him.

"Yes?" A voice said with as much enthusiasm as whomever initially answered the phone. It took only a single word to pinpoint the voice's owner.

I stood frozen outside of the office in furious disbelief. The mention of Vincent pulled me back to Jordan telling Loring about Vincent sending the Team on the safe house rounds in the morning.

"And you feel I should do what with this information?" Loring asked the charming traitor.

"Head them off at the pass, maybe? Cut them down while they're outside of this fortress? I don't think you realize the foothold this place has. Vincent's followed in his father's footsteps with this one. I have what I need to move forward with the plan but no time to enact it."

"Spending too much time with our Firefly?"

My insides cringed at the thought of belonging to Loring in any way and him using Olive's nickname for me.

"Don't you worry about who I'm spending time with. Focus on—" A static-like burst preceded a grunt from Jordan so strong it rang in my brain.

What the fuck was that? Was Loring somehow hurting him through the phone line? Was Loring capable of long-range torture let alone while Jordan was inside of the Prison Creation?

"You grew bored of hiding behind your gadgets and came to me to quell your disuse by injecting you onto the fields where you so readily sent others. You *will* learn to curb your impulse to dictate what I should and should not do. Heed the warning or you will not return to..."

I raced away from a Loring-sized death threat in search of Vincent. With any luck, Loring will be as long-winded over the phone as he was in person.

There! Vincent stood with others. I ran up on them, my breath coming too fast, mirrored by Donovan who suddenly scanned his surroundings searching for me.

"He's guilty. That motherfucker."

Vincent put a hand on my shoulder. "Who are you—?"

"Jordan. He's on the phone with Loring right now."

Vincent's eyes widened. He flagged Arden over as Caveman, Kim, Donovan, and Ranlyn asked for details.

"I think he's trying to sneak Loring inside the Prison Creation or he might do something to take it down from the inside."

"What's up, boss?" Arden asked, his tone ready for instruction.

"Run a trace of the outgoing number from the office closest to the cafeteria, yes?" Vincent confirmed with me the location.

"Yeah. Now. They could be done any second."

Arden ran off to do his thing.

"Is Jordan aware of your eavesdropping?" Vincent asked me.

I shook my head. "I used an auricular amplifying spell and listened through the door."

"When'd you learn that?" Of course the question was from Kim. I didn't have time for details, remembering too fondly having fun when Jordan was teaching me how to roll my tongue to pronounce the words correctly.

Why didn't I see it when I've dealt with pretty-faced assholes too many times before? I should have known he was a sheisty bugger.

An anxious thrum had me watching the office door, waiting. "He's meeting me in his cell for more spell practice. He's Velcroed to his laptop when it's not in his cell, but I guarantee there's a shitload of info we can use on that thing. Maybe the plans for whatever he's trying to do are on there. If he knows we're coming for it, it'll be toast. No way he hasn't booby-trapped it in some tech-weenie way."

"Can you snag it?" Caveman asked.

"How? I just said—"

"Can you distract him?" Based on his tone and tilt of his head, the implication became clear.

I crossed my arms. "Of course I can."

"Sophie—" Vincent began in protest.

Donovan stepped in front of me, panic and dejection flooding the connection. "You can't be serious?"

"What about using Caine?" Kim suggested.

"He's working with Ismail on Chase." Ranlyn's voice was low in contemplation mode.

Instead of wasting time we didn't have, I focused on Caveman. "Wait no more than ten minutes once we're both in a cell. I'll keep his eyes away from the entrance and his laptop bag." I pointed at him. "Make it worth it."

I spun from the group for the cell console.

Donovan followed. "You can't do this to me. I'll... I'll..."

"Now you'll know how it feels."

Donovan's shock hit me deep in my chest.

Guess it was his turn to take one for the team.

In...hold, out...hold. Getting my breathing to regulate with overused four-square breathing exercises from anxious days in my past was the hardest part. Inside of the cell, I found Jordan's laptop bag already at the side of the bed, found the spicy peanuts to follow-through on the ruse, and toed the bag a couple of feet towards the entrance wall so it would be easier for Caveman to snatch. One great thing about being in the cells was that it would cripple Jordan's magic, though mine would be useless as well.

If something went wrong, my fighting skills might be more practiced than his. I could probably put him down. Or I told myself I could. The boots would help.

Unfortunately for Donovan, the cells didn't douse the connection, but I was ready to do this regardless of what it did to him. Jordan deserved what was coming to him for using me as a pawn in his bid to prove to Loring he was fit for the field. Another traitor was in our midst. Not a name in our contact pool, but inside of the Prison Creation. One that wholly blindsided me. If he hadn't slipped up and spoke about information he must have learned from Loring himself, I never would have listened in on his call and wouldn't be waiting to play slutty victim for the good of the Mother Coven. Or for a little revenge, which would taste much sweeter.

What does falling for his flirtatious banter say about me? Probably the same as it did when considering the male at the end of the emotional tether screaming for me not to do this. I couldn't hear him, but Donovan was freaking out.

"You ready for practice?"

I chomped some spicy peanuts to cover the surprise of him popping into the cell. I expected him to show up, but it was like waiting for toast to pop and then shitting yourself when it did exactly what you were waiting for.

"Memorization is always the tricky bit. We can run the true spell outside of the cell once your memory's on board."

His captivating smile was pinned in place, ready to resume his treacherous task of charming me. Did Loring orchestrate that as well? Was the plan to fiddle with my emotions and continue to drive a wedge between Donovan and me to fuck with our Soul Magic? What would Loring gain besides a little distraction? Maybe he thought I would switch sides if another dick was available to hop to?

Fine. Whatever. Regardless of what Loring wanted, I would play my role as well as Jordan, if not better.

"Well..." I put the peanuts aside, cleared my throat, and made a show of feigned nervousness with a slight head bow and a couple of languid steps towards him. "I'm definitely out of practice with something other than spell memorization."

Looking up into Jordan's hazel eyes I saw the light go on as he grasped what I was clearly throwing at him.

Not to be knocked off center, he played it cool, giving me a magnetic smile and a minutely cocky chin. "And what's that?"

I stepped in closer, drawing out the seconds to build tension between us as well as fill the clock until Hall would pop in. Ten minutes was probably too long a timeline. Too late now.

"I wouldn't say it's magic-related, and it doesn't entail much talking let alone memorization, but it does require a certain expression of...energy."

Fighting to hide my gagging from the cringe-worthy play, I tilted my head back to gaze up at his unguarded smile. Before Hall came waltzing in and ruining his chance to snag Jordan's laptop to find proof of his treason, I placed my hands on his chest and pressed my lips to Jordan's. His mouth formed to mine without hesitation, his hands on my waist, pulling me against him, and then moved around me to deepen the kiss.

Donovan's presence in the background of the connection was a voyeuristic Peeping Tom able to share in every sensation. My bottom lip depressed as my entitled soulmate experienced the kiss through the connection, fighting against it with his teeth.

All this did was spur me on.

Jordan's pecs flexed beneath my fingers when I slid them up and over his lean muscles, wrapped my hands around his neck, and then melted into the kiss. He took the eager invitation by pulling me closer. Instead of thinking too hard about Jordan using me for his own political and vengeful ends, I enjoyed the opportunity of being with an intelligent and charming man I wasn't infinitely chained to.

Without giving Jordan a chance to think twice about why I was suddenly so eager to throw myself at him, I waltzed us a couple of steps backwards. He followed me in perfect sync towards the bed. When the backs of my legs hit the bed frame, I did the most natural thing and sat down, and then tugged on the shoulders of Jordan's shirt to bring him along with me as I laid down.

Needing no extra incentive, he retained our kiss and hovered above me, his weight dipping the thin mattress and me along with it when I pulled him down to bring our bodies back together.

The hard ridge behind his jean's zipper sent a thrill through me causing a moan I didn't expect, and his answering groan was a low vibration against my chest.

Reminding myself this was a diversionary tactic for a mission proved difficult when he kissed so damn well.

Dragging my nails along the hem of his shirt and up his lower back was a cue he read. He straightened to pull his shirt over his head.

For the second his face was covered, I caught a glimpse of where Jordan left his laptop bag, now noticing it was missing. I was amazed I didn't hear Caveman sneak in considering how big the guy was. What I needed to do now was keep Jordan busy so Arden could access the laptop and copy the hard drive. We needed everything we could. If Jordan was stupid enough to call Loring from inside the lion's den, then maybe he tripped up and left enough accessible intel for Arden to go through.

We may get lucky.

Thankfully, the cells prevented Jordan from reading my mind and he had no clue I was enjoying this for the sport of the diversion it created as well as the big middle finger it sent to his future self when he realized what happened and why.

I smiled, pretending to enjoy what I saw, pulled my shirt over my head, led him back down onto me, and reached in between our bodies.

I could play this game all day.

15

FOG OF LUST

Donovan

A mission was one thing, what stemmed from Sophie was another.

The weight of someone else on top of her was not unwelcomed. She was enjoying every second of it. True attraction spilled from her, and it had nothing to do with me.

The deep breath I took in was all Sophie's too, her amped blood pressure causing a slow heat to flush over my skin. I couldn't see what was happening, but I didn't need to to know the guy's hands were on her skin. Worse was the fact that my own arousal wanted to jump in and play. Since Sophie was so keyed up, the thread of connection automatically dragged me into it as a willing participant, my body aching to tag in as a third player and enjoy the experience.

This was no threesome and I sure as fuck wasn't willing.

"Can you hurry the fuck up?"

Arden was tired of my complaints, tapping away at Jordan's laptop while that fucker was all over Sophie.

"He is doing what he can, Donovan." Vincent peered over Arden's shoulder at the laptop.

"I could knee you in the nuts, but I doubt that would help Sophie's cover." Kim stood somewhere in the room, no doubt with Hall.

I couldn't concentrate enough to keep track of the others, but the Team and the Elders crowded the office, investigating Jordan's laptop and planning on how to handle the information leak.

"If a kick to the nuts would detach my unit until this was over with, I'd pose for it." A gasp stopped my train of thought as a groping sensation between my legs. I went rock hard against my will.

Jordan clearly passed the over-the-clothes part.

My sweaty palms cooled against the wall when I leaned into it, trapped in this limbo. A wave of something close to possession left me powerless.

"Fuck!"

"She's definitely keeping him distracted." Kim's voice was an extra stab of annoyance as blood pumped to the head of my dick.

"We need another room." Hall grabbed my shoulder and started pushing me towards the exit on shaky legs. "Stay here," he must have said to Kim. "We'll be next door."

Making quick with the exit and entrance to another room so the whole Coven didn't spot my tented jeans, Hall pushed me inside and closed the door behind us.

I squatted to the floor, facing away from Hall as my erection throbbed. "I can't believe she's doing this to me, man."

"Neither can I actually," he muttered in true surprise.

I appreciated the fact Hall skipped the details of what he saw when he snagged the backpack from the cell. Not that the touchy-feely wasn't in live mode anyway.

"Flirting is one thing. This is—" My breath hitched— "Much more."

"Are you going to need a new set of trousers anytime soon? I'd rather not be present for the money shot."

"Fuck you." If only I could really be angry with him. I wanted to rip someone's head clean off of their shoulders, but not Hall's.

"Don't worry. I was in the audience at the Sorrel Compound during the Conception Rituals and guarding Sophie's cell during the second round. Nothing new to see here."

"Happy to be a bore," I managed and groaned through gritted teeth.

Someone knocked on the door. I heard it open as I felt Jordan's mouth on my chest and then as his teeth bite my, Sophie's, nipple.

"You need to go away," Hall told whoever showed up uninvited.

"She's my sister. What happens to him happens to her. I know something's going on."

Damn it. Adam must have seen us switch rooms.

"Let us in, dickwad. We've dealt with worse."

Denise? Serena and Jared and maybe even Blake were probably out there too. The whole fucking Sect was fixing to glimpse me writhing like a horned-up cat.

As Hall went on talking to them, a spike of pleasure hit, pressure welling between my thighs, tightening in a way I recognized and was stunned to feel.

"Oh fuck!" I yelled and heard the door slam shut as I rolled over the edge into an orgasm that shot through my limbs and left me a panting heap on all fours.

I grabbed the leg of a nearby chair as I clenched my teeth, pressure between my thighs a stroking pleasure I couldn't escape.

The release was vocal, but I didn't have any control of my voice any more than my bucking body, cursing Sophie as bliss morphed into an impotent rage and settled into the downslide of our shared climax.

When I could feel my feet again, I shot up and chucked the chair across the room and into the wall, exposing drywall.

When the orgasm fully settled, I could think more clearly and realized it hadn't been sex at all, but manual manipulation. All it meant was Sophie and Jordan weren't done. Or she had her turn and

Jordan's was next. With the appetiser out of the way, they may also be gearing up for the entrée.

This meal could fucking rot.

After reconnecting with Sophie in my shower and then having her walk away afterwards with regret, my body was starving for more of her, my dick still hard. I ignored the wetness saturating my briefs and noticed I was alone in the room. Hall had left while I fell to pieces on the office floor.

Outside of the room, I found who I assumed I would. Hall, Adam, Denise, Serena, Jared, and Blake hit me with questions when I blew passed them, barged into the office where Arden was working, and grabbed Vincent by the shirt. "Stop her, now!"

"Hold..." Vincent said, stopping the Tactical Team members ready to punish me for touching their leader.

"They still at it?" I heard Veata ask and then chuckle.

I retained my grip on Vincent's shirt. "I can't endure another orgasm. Get her the fuck out of there or I will murder you and then him. I swear it, Vincent. I don't give a shit about the mission. Get her the fuck out of there!"

"Oh my god," I heard Kim's light horror.

What did everyone think was going to happen?

"Okay, okay." Vincent meant this as a soothing gesture that did nothing to help the situation.

"Not okay, Vincent. Really not okay."

No coping techniques were going to ease me through this without turning murderous. The groping started up again and I was afraid the pause in action meant repositioning for something more vomit-inducing.

Vincent aimed his attentions over my shoulder. "Have we acquired enough of what we need?"

I shook him harder. "Now, Vincent!"

"Yup. Jordan's definitely a Recondite Magic for the other side, but there's no telling exactly..." Arden's voice faded into the background when I hit the hallway.

I grabbed Hall by the arm and pulled him along to the cell console, Vincent and Kim following. "Get in there before me or it's not gonna be pretty," I ordered the big guy.

If people were smart, they would stop Sophie's brother and cousin from coming in, but I couldn't think about them right now. Everything within me wanted to paint the cell with Jordan's innards. Regardless of if this was Sophie's doing or the fact Jordan was a treasonous piece of shit, I wanted him dead and buried for having been anywhere near her.

Hall was first as we dropped into the cell. I was right behind him and caught an eyeful of Sophie's fully naked skin along her side. She was on her back, her lips attached to Jordan's. The only thing covering her and preventing Hall and me from seeing everything was Jordan's body being accommodated between her split thighs. No penetration, since I would know, but he was as naked as she was and clearly expecting to put his cock to good use.

People were talking, pulling Sophie and Jordan apart, or maybe Sophie pushed him off, but I was rushing forward.

I shoved Jordan across the small room. He hit the wall and crumbled onto his naked ass in a grunt. He may have been magically mute inside of these walls, but I wasn't. Ritual stone magic flowed from my body without hesitating for direction.

Jordan's hands went up in front of him and then to his chest, grasping at it. The pallor of his skin bled away to a deathly paleness, worsening by the second and crawling to his neck, shoulders, and down to his stomach.

The attack was not for touching Sophie, the drama was between her and me, though it was a good enough reason whether she consented or not. It was for Jordan's audacity in messing with us, for playing people against each other, and for flipping sides to stroke his ego. For all of these reasons, plus a few more, I was a boiling blood bag of wrath with a worthy target.

The room spun in the opposite direction, my body with it, leaving nothing but the cement floor instead of Jordan's pain-ridden grimace.

What the fuck?

"Let Jordan live," Caine said, his hand on my shoulder, the command filtering through my revenge-clouded ears and bloomed with certainty that I must listen to him, I must obey.

The ritual stone power slunk into hiding.

Caine let go of my shoulder and released my will.

My power was gone.

Caine's persuasion overrode the ritual stone magic.

I stood and saw the man standing next to me. I guess he was done with Chase. Caine nodded, yet he appeared ready to take over again if I stepped out of line. If not him, Hall was close and prepared to step in, as was Vincent. I had my chance. If I tried again, I'd have to land a kill-shot and be prepared to remain in one of these cells for a long time.

Vincent took a couple of steps in between Jordan and me, blocking my view of the asshole. He detailed Jordan's reasons for being imprisoned including operating as a Recondite Magic for Loring, profiting from stolen Mother Coven information, causing the indirect deaths of Magics who sought safety in the safe houses, even working with the Sovereignty with Lincoln, our former Tactical Team leader. Lincoln didn't reveal this during his interrogation, but maybe Jordan used a different name with him as he did others. Either way, Arden must have found evidence of it on Jordan's laptop.

Sophie and I stared at each other. She was now sloppily dressed and standing next to the bed, unable to remove the almost-got-laid look of her non-her blonde hair and heated cheeks, our chests raising and falling for different reasons. The anger coursing through me didn't scare her. I didn't want her to fear me, but it would have been nice to see a flash of regret in her cold eyes.

I saw none.

To stop myself from saying exactly what I wanted to, knowing the response would be hollow and superficial, I forced my attention on Jordan standing fully naked, flaccid, and straight-backed as Vincent explained his imposed charges through the new legal system, and letting him know he wouldn't be leaving his current cell.

Unable to focus on anything but the tether connecting Sophie and me, as her arousal dissipated across the connection, she was left like her eyes.

Cold. Empty.

Why would she do this? She's not the one-night-stand or revenge-fuck kind of girl. I felt sorry for the woman I loved trapped somewhere inside of this messed up version of Sophie. Whenever she did find herself, she would regret doing this. She didn't have to go so far. And going there, with Jordan, just to fuck with me? Waking up, no longer in the fog of lust or desperation, with the monster of clarity on your shoulders, wearing a backpack full of regret, was my expertise, not hers. No, this was bad.

Jordan claimed nothing in his defence as Vincent clarified next steps. Instead, he rubbed his bottom lip, the other arm across his middle, his eyes trained on Sophie without a care he was still buck naked.

I didn't have the energy to force the ritual stone magic to resurface to invade the guy's thoughts. I knew what he was thinking. At no point did Jordan question Sophie's intentions. He was fully convinced he was going to cross the finish line and that Sophie was passionately in it with him. He was right to think so.

"Do you request representation?" Vincent was asking.

Jordan didn't respond. Too busy with his attention glued to Sophie as her stare was equally glued to his.

"Since you refuse to engage, we are done here," Vincent concluded, and we started towards the exit wall.

"You sure you don't want to finish what we started?" Jordan's tone was low, the target of his invitation unmistakable.

I felt my stomach cramp. No, Sophie's stomach cramped. Not the ache I knew too well in days when she wanted nothing but to touch me, but something reacting to Jordan's offer.

"No, thanks. I got what I needed." Sophie used a detached tone that didn't outline what exactly she was referring to. Was it her need to fuck with me, to satisfy an itch for Jordan, or to complete the mission to prove Jordan's guilt? Maybe all of the above and more or something else all together.

Vincent urged Sophie to leave the cell with a soft gesture, placing a hand on the small of her back to press her forward. The graze was enough to evoke my raw envy. All these people touching her when she was disgusted by me was driving me crazy.

Pain snapped the middle of my spine and shoved me across the small cell. I flew through the cell exit wall and into the lobby, the marble floor a punch to the skull.

I skidded to a stop in a screech of sticking skin. The voices of freaked and confused people warbled in my ears. Dizziness curled my stomach and had everything swimming.

Someone stood over me, my blurred vision taking a few blinks to clear. Jordan! A wave of energy shot above me, the heat a blast against my skin. More screams.

Hall, Kim, Vincent, Sophie, and a handful of others were on the ground. Jordan hit them all?

Jordan reared back and booted me in the gut. Another blast of power sailed over me into the crowd.

Ritual stone magic jolted through my veins and cleared away the dregs of what was probably a concussion and traumatized innards.

I sprung to my feet, seeing dozens of Magics writhing on the floor and Jordan stalking towards Sophie who was as healed as I was and busy trying to help Vincent.

With a step I ghosted next to Jordan, disappearing and reappearing next to him before he could hurt Sophie or drag her off to the nearest bed.

Sophie yelped in surprise as we appeared in front of her, her hands coming up to defend herself.

Jordan spun and drilled me with a quick pulse of power.

Everything went black.

16

TRADITIONAL MEANS

Sophie

Nausea rolled through me. Blinding light blurred my surroundings and pounded in my skull. I squeezed my eyes shut, the minute pressure hurting. I tried to grip my head. A thick sweat slipped under my fingers along my hairline.

Shifting to pull myself into the fetal position worsened the nausea. I moaned and ground my teeth. A violent cough gripped my ribcage in spiking pain. Vomit shot out between my lips, arching my body and cranking my spine.

Hectic voices surrounded me.

Something touched my face. An image of Jordan attacking Donovan shot to mind. I grabbed for the wrist of the hand touching me and squeezed, weakness in every finger not amounting to much.

Olive's face came into view. She leaned in close, her expression crimped, the hand of the wrist I was gripping holding a washcloth. She grasped my fingers that were trying to manhandle her.

Vincent rushed in behind. She said something to him and he stopped.

Olive leaned closer to me. "It's okay, Firefly. I won't hurt you."

Kim stood close by. Caveman was to my right on the far side of a bed with a hand to the shoulder of a crouched body. He peered at me with an unreadable expression over Donovan who was laying down and struggling for a comfortable position.

Olive was now caressing my hand to try and soothe me. I didn't feel myself let her go, but it took too much energy to prop myself up and I collapsed back onto the bed when I tried.

"Heal us." Vomit clung to my lips. I tried to wipe it away.

Olive swiped my mouth with a warm cloth as if she heard my thoughts.

Why was I so freakin' hot?

Vincent knelt at the side of the bed next to Olive and held my hand, folding my fingers around his consoling grasp as I was too weak to flex the joints. "We tried, Sophie. Physical damage healed as expected. This sickness... Jordan attacked Donovan with some kind of pestilence magic we cannot cure. We are treating your symptomatic aliments by more traditional means."

What? No. Jordan's soul glow wasn't Tainted. And they could heal everything.

As my lungs seized, I struggled to remember that blanket healing wasn't always true. I saw it happen with other Magics. Sometimes magic can't touch damage caused by Magics.

"Jordan can heal it?"

"Possibly. However, after his attack, Jordan used a spell on Liam, forcibly recalling his elevator access ability, dropped the Prison Creation in a temporary darkness, and used the elevator to walk out the front door. Security protocols will be revised."

"Don't forget he pulled it off buck naked." The added detail was from my brother. A muttering followed, probably people telling him to shut up since I didn't have the energy to do so myself.

Great. Jordan was responsible for this, and his bare ass was in the wind. But, again, he wasn't Tainted. How could this happen?

Vincent called it a pestilence. "Contagious?"

He shifted, uncomfortable. "No diagnosis has been agreed upon. If the disease is communicable, we are already exposed." He squeezed my hand tighter. "Contagious or not, I am not going anywhere."

My brother's voice came from a different place in the room.

I tried to turn to see him, and the movement triggered another wave of nausea. I groaned, grabbed my head with my hands, and rocked along with the throbbing pain in my skull.

The pulses of sickness settled a bit. Where are we? We're not in a cell. An emptied office?

"It's my fault," I heard Donovan say, his voice hoarse. "I'm so sorry."

"Cool it, buddy." Caveman's deep voice floated below the muddled sounds in the room.

"Sophie?" Donovan called to me.

In response, someone said something, the voice flat. Rosemary? I couldn't hear what she said. How could I miss Donovan's black-haired beauty of a Tainted mother in the room? Maybe I could if I somehow missed Jordan's Tainted soul, and it had to be if he was canoodling with Loring.

Donovan called my name again.

I tried to shift to my back. The small movement was enough for the room to sway. I pinched my eyes shut, riding the disorientation.

Others talked at me, trying to tell me to relax. Others, like my brother, asked questions and got testy when no one provided answers.

When the room came back into focus, Donovan was lying fully towards me, his skin shiny with sweat matting his hair, his eyes rimmed with dark circles, skin blotchy.

He apologized, telling me he loved me between coughing fits. "We can't let this life end like this. We don't know what it'll do—" Another coughing fit cut him off, shutting him up as everyone else fussed over us, getting water, herbal mixtures on cold cloths, and office garbage bins as puke buckets.

He didn't have to finish for me to know what he meant. He was worried about future us. The people who would know nothing of this life or any of our past ones unless someone was still alive to tell them about it. He wanted the Soul Magic to carry us through more torturous years of loving each other and dying early. Well, I didn't give a fuck about what he wanted. How could he not see how fucked up all of this was? Why put himself through it again and again? So he can own me in another life where fate decided we should be happy, so it squashes our chances at loving anyone else and forces us to love each other without the truth about what it meant for our souls' existence?

I turned away from him towards a scraping sound. Evelyn was mixing something with a mortar and pestle on a desk pushed against a wall. Kim spoke to her, pointing at ingredients and asking questions. Nothing like a medical mystery to hone her skills.

"Are we in quarantine?" I asked Vincent, who was still next to my bed, preoccupied with talking to Caveman.

Caveman noticed my attempt to communicate and motioned to Vincent who spun back to me.

"Quarantine?" Short sentences worked better.

"Contact between you, Donovan, and the others has already occurred. We are monitoring if any others fall ill with symptoms. Thus far, no one else has been impacted so quarantining is pointless. Until we possess concrete information, we will keep the children and any others with suppressed immunity safeguarded from potential infection. If needed, we can isolate others in cells."

Children? It took me a few moments to remember Caine's nephew, Andy, then another to remember the baby, Pheonix. There were probably others I never met who came from the safe houses.

Whatever the cause, the stress of being solely responsible for everyone else in the Prison Creation was etched in the lines of Vincent's face. This place was meant to house and protect those in the inside from the Tainted in the outside world, not imprison and poison the innocents who happened to be stuck while hiding in fear.

This burden was easier to see around his eyes without his glasses. I might not ever get used to seeing him without them.

Vincent laid his hand on my forehead. His cool touch was a small blanket of relief that released a sigh I couldn't supress.

He asked Evelyn for something. Evelyn pulled a cloth from the herbal mixture in the bowl she and Kim were fixated with. She murmured a spell and then handed it to Vincent. He placed the cloth on my forehead.

The escaped moan was replicated in Donovan's voice in the other bed. The popsicle temperatures were divine. I wished the cold spell covered my entire body.

Dipping into the relief from the supernaturally cooled cloth, I zoned out the others in the room moving around the best I could. They all did things I couldn't fully see or hear, talking to each other about strategy and solutions. And then further updating Ranlyn and Caine or whomever else on our condition and on whatever was happening outside of this room.

With Donovan refusing to let us sleep, I was stuck in reality alongside him when all I wanted to do was check out. I even asked for them to knock me unconscious with medications or some kind of herb, but Evelyn argued it may interfere with whatever this is and slow our heart rates too much when they still didn't know what they were dealing with.

At least they found a way to dim the overhead lights.

"Sophie..." I heard Donovan call for me too many times.

He wanted to talk.

I wanted nothing to do with him.

He may have been cool with chatting about what happened with Jordan or repeating himself until his voice croaked about our Soul Magic and fixing us, but I just wanted him to shut the fuck up. Words wouldn't cure us. They didn't turn back time or rethink casting the Soul Magic in the first place. They exhausted us and nothing more.

Every time he adjusted himself, tried to sit up or roll over, he doubled our problems, and we would end up puking or leave me wishing I could so maybe the nausea would subside.

After hours of this, nothing was left in my stomach and my muscles were achy.

"Please, Sophie..." I heard Donovan say again and felt his fingers brush my sleeve.

"Stop. Just stop." I tried to press my hand into my forehead over the still-cold cloth, but I missed and dragged my hand down my nose, my arm falling back into place.

I felt the brush on my sleeve again, a quick, light graze and then he slid his hand down my arm and his fingers touched mine.

The shock of a vision hit Donovan. I went rigid. Panicked voices around us yelled instructions and argued, their voices clambering on top of each other. My hearing blinked in and out, and there was a confusing gurgle in my ears. Hands were on me. No matter what anyone said or did, I couldn't respond, and I couldn't see to comprehend what was happening.

"Separate them!" Vincent yelled, his voice above me and louder than the others.

People shoved and grabbed at our hands. Rosemary screamed at Caveman, who was making the visions worse by touching us, but they needed us a part to stop this.

A point of pain in my fingers was a piercing above the rest of the agony, the injury a throbbing onslaught.

Gasping came from a few, the crowd quieting and then roaring into more yelling, this time between fewer people.

"You will be okay, Sophie." Vincent's calming voice came into my mind. *"The contact triggered Donovan's vision which caused a seizure. It should end soon."*

Could he hear me like I could hear him? This is what happens when Donovan insisted on being so damn pushy. I hope whatever he saw in the vision sticks in his nightmares forever.

In a sudden break in tension, the seizing stopped.

Moaning hurt my jaw, shifting my legs a few inches hurt more, as did moving my arms, but I couldn't stay still. Donovan's movements added to my own discomfort. He was freaking out about hurting me and then asking someone to fix it. Fix what?

I could open my eyes enough to see Caveman wrapping his hands with a small blanket from Donovan's bed, Donovan holding up a trembling hand, his middle finger bent backwards and clearly broken or dislocated. Without looking, I attempted to flex my fingers on the same hand... Fuck! That hurt.

"Don't!" Rosemary grabbed Caveman by the shoulder and put the man on his knees with a jolt of energy that had him roaring, his neck veins bulging.

A flash of light filled the room, blinding me. When the spots cleared enough to see where everyone was, Kim was standing over Caveman and Rosemary was a struggling lump on the floor, the carpet now featuring some new artwork in the shape of a body.

"You okay?" Kim was looking at Rosemary, but she was talking to Caveman, braced, waiting for Rosemary to attack.

Caveman cracked his neck and slowly rose to his feet. "I'm supposed to protect you, kitten."

Kim patted his arm. "Next one."

Caveman growled as he straightened in full.

Damn. Kim put Rosemary down?

Rosemary pushed Evelyn away when she tried to help her. Donovan's mother was pissed, but otherwise okay and staring at Kim as if she was seconds from retaliation.

"Mom..." Donovan tried, exhausted from the seizure.

"Attack again and you can consider your presence overstayed," Ranlyn made clear, having entered the room with Caine behind him.

Caine looked over me, Donvan, and the rest of the room with his brows creased.

"Donovan's finger's broken," Rosemary justified.

"To split them up!" Caveman yelled.

"I'm sure Hall had no choice, unless he and Donovan have

become sudden enemies." Vincent eyed Caveman. "No?" He returned to Rosemary. "You may—"

"Fuck!" Donovan and I swore in unison as Evelyn straightened Donovan's finger and rubbed the knuckle with a hint of healing magic. "There we go. Simple dislocation."

Rosemary surged towards Evelyn.

From where he stood at my bedside, Vincent raised a hand and telekinetically stopped her from taking another step. "You may protect your son in battle. Here? He is among people *he* trusts. If you attack another member of this coven or any within this Creation, you will have more troubles than a place to hide. You will not yearn for shelter or safety. My cells will provide adequate provisions."

Rosemary chewed on that, glaring at Vincent.

"We clear?" Ranlyn asked, forcing Rosemary to answer.

The most the woman would give was a begrudging nod.

Donovan's relief flooded the connection. Things would get really dicey if Vincent imprisoned his mother.

Once everyone reclaimed a sense of peace while trying not to upset us or aggravate our pain, the room remained dimly lit as the others moved about.

This time, I won the fight for sleep or maybe Donovan gave out under the added exhaustion from the seizure, and unconsciousness dragged me down into restless fever dreams.

17

AN ACCELERATED DOSE

Vincent

Sophie and Donovan slept deeply. Their minds remained open, showcasing dual dreamscapes of chaos and fights for traction over each of their trials.

I could not help but think that if this was the way this life ended for them, it was in relative peace. Unconscious and drenched in a feverish sweat may not mirror the harmony of an aged existence, but it was a gift not regularly afforded in their many lives.

With their numerous deaths newly stained on my memory after my father's cell experience, I found myself hard-pressed not to compare this possible end to those. Countless traumatic deaths for each.

Last I saw Cora-Lynn, she was in a cell, choosing to remain when the anxiousness of freedom became too great. No others presented with the symptoms Sophie and Donovan were experiencing. The likelihood of contagion low, though I feared infecting Cora-Lynn since she had lived a sheltered existence for over four-hundred years, leaving her immune-system potentially compromised or non-existent. An illness from the Blind was no concern. However, a pestilence such as this may prove quite difficult.

I had to admit an assumption of such was baseless and my fear of losing Cora-Lynn, in any form, terrified me.

Since my return from my father's cells, I wanted to spend more time nurturing Sophie's heart to foster a way back to Donovan, but reintegrating Cora-Lynn was my priority, one cultivating guilt and unfair inner conflict. Even now, my thoughts slipped to Cora-Lynn and what we endured.

When Sophie awoke, I wanted to be present so she knew I cared, regardless of the decision to keep her from active duty on the Team. She turned to so few confidants these days, I refused to erase myself as another.

I flinched when Evelyn leaned into my line of sight. She spread a moss-green paste from a mortar and pestle across Sophie's slick forehead and then ignored Rosemary's scrutiny as she did the same for Donovan.

Evelyn looked back and forth from Donovan to Sophie, and then moved aside the neck of Sophie's shirt. She revealed a cluster of small, discoloured pustules, finding the same on Donovan's neck and chest.

"What is that?" Rosemary demanded with her arms crossed like she was keeping herself from wringing the answer out of Evelyn.

"I've seen this," Evelyn said in her heavy Irish accent while examining Sophie's pustules again. "I'm sure you've encountered this in your time, Elder Vincent. And you, Viking."

I examined clusters of small, round spots spread across Sophie's skin. "Smallpox?"

Evelyn nodded.

"Smallpox?" Kim stepped closer in curiosity. Hall grabbed her arm to prevent her from coming nearer. "Isn't smallpox not a thing anymore?"

"No naturally occurring cases have been recorded in this part of the world by the Blind since 1980. If this was one of those cases, the disease would be no match for any healer, including themselves. The vaccine would have been given as children, no doubt for at least Sophie since she was raised by the Blind. However, this case is far more advanced. Symptoms rarely show in fewer than eight days after exposure and are merely flu-like in affect. What we see here is an accelerated contamination via spell or possibly Jordan's own specialty magic."

"His hacker moniker makes more and more sense," Hall pointed out. "'Scourge'. Everyone assumed it was a tech reference about computer viruses or worms and such, when it was really a bald-faced bait about his abilities. Bastard was waving it in our faces."

Jordan's technological skillset was useful on many fronts. If historical deaths were researched with greater scrutiny perhaps other deaths could be connected to Jordan's methods of disposal.

"Do you know what the medicinal antidote is?" Ranlyn asked.

Evelyn shrugged, staring at Sophie with sympathy in her eyes. "I believe one was created in recent years. If we can procure it, sooner the better. Until then, we treat the symptoms and pray for minimal damage."

"Damage? What kind of damage?" Kim asked.

"These pustules will spread over the entire body, harden, and scab. Depending on if they reach the ocular cavity, they may cause blindness. In a best-case scenario they will experience pain, headaches, diarrhea, and fever as they fight the infection."

Kim inhaled as if bracing herself. "And worst-case?"

"Statistically, thirty percent perish. I shouldn't need to further outline how this is no normal product of infection. With this a targeted assault, and at this level of acceleration, I believe the infection is contained within Donovan."

I could not allow this to be their end.

"Inform Arden. He can infiltrate major health systems. The

Team will retrieve what they need by any means." I shot a non-verbal command to Hall who left the room without a spoken word, though he paused and exchanged a mute communication with Kim.

I held Sophie's hand for hours, sitting next to her shivering, unconscious body as the pustules spread to mar her beautiful skin. Inflamed hard lumps filled with opaque fluid. Clusters quickly spread as both Donovan and Sophie twitched, mewling in discomfort, and in persistent unconsciousness from the overload of Donovan's vision.

If I was ever truly her Overseer, I was now being tested. So many years I held onto my mission to retrieve my wife's soul, to destroy my father's empire, and to bring my vision for a new method of justice to all Magics. Now, my vision was virtually a hotel and housed my brother and a once-trusted colleague as the only prisoners. My father's soul was lost to the ether, Cora-Lynn was a traumatised survivor navigating a broken vessel I once cherished. On top of the rest of my failings, I watched my Charges writhe with a sickness I was unable to heal after I foolishly allowed Sophie to engage with Jordan.

All I could do about any of this was sit and wait for a smallpox antidote.

Ranlyn thrust a phone in front of my face. "I need you to publicly confirm the death of your father and imprisonment of your brother."

Seconds passed as I peered up at my co-Elder. The man's eyebrows rose to urge me on. "Why is confirmation required?"

Ranlyn glared at me and hit the phone's hold button. "The Mother Coven needs solace. Word has spread that Alasdair and Chase Llewellyn are gone. Rumours are dangerous. People need to know the truth about them and about Jordan. The contact list Arden compiled from Jordan's laptop keeps getting longer. He could run to any of them for sanctuary."

I put the phone to my ear. "You either know me by name or by voice to trust the veracity of what I say. My father, Alasdair

Llewellyn, is dead. My brother, originally Charles Llewellyn, known as Chase, is now a prisoner under the new law for crimes to be outlined at his trial. A Magic known as Jordan Chapman is a traitor to the Coven and is responsible for information leaks to the enemy, Loring, and his devotees. If you are a friend to the Mother Coven, you will heed this warning and relinquish any valuable information or you will become another enemy."

Without a word from the party, I held up the phone for Ranlyn. He accepted the dismissal, his murmured voice pacifying whomever found the death and imprisonment of my estranged family their right to be informed of.

Arden entered.

"Where are they?" I asked of the Team.

"Still accessing health system contacts, but they're on point," Arden tried to assure me. He closed the door behind him, shifting his weight. "I've done all I can with Jordan's rig. Guy's a code-whore. Thinks his business is Big Brother important, but he's lazy with his creativity. His ego—"

"On most occasions I enjoy your banter, Arden." I rubbed my eyes with a free hand refusing to let Sophie go. "Unfortunately, I do not possess the focus to endure at present."

Arden gave a low chuckle, unaffected. "Bottom line?"

"Please."

"Our conniving hacker was elbow-deep in everything, playing every side imaginable, and operating under different aliases aside from 'Scourge'. Mostly to make bank, which is sizeable. An information hoarder. He speaks in as much code as he writes, but he won't go to anyone on our side after this." He motioned to Sophie and Donovan. "Loring's the only player in this game who wouldn't care that Jordan's a manipulative shithead. Plus, his power is clearly useful."

I nodded. How did I allow this man inside my Creation? How did I allow him to escape?

"My point," Arden went on, "none of us saw this coming."

And that was it. Arden saw the guilt I was too exhausted to

disguise. If I had instructed the Team to bring Jordan to another safe house instead of directly to the Prison Creation, Sophie and Donovan would still be healthy and bickering rather than fighting for every steady breath. Her wheezing was not comforting, laboured breathing a further sign of their degenerative health as pneumonia weakened their lungs.

"Every decision is meant to benefit—"

"You don't have to justify your decisions to me, Vincent. I can't count the times we've only survived because of your quick thinking. Or the times we've made a difference behind the scenes in a way that would change the course of events so drastically I would never have guessed it was possible. Questioning you now would do me no good. You need anything, let me know."

Loyalty in a time when few could be trusted was invaluable. If I had sidelined any of the others to hack a laptop, I would have met resistance. Never did I encounter this with Arden. He trusted me to assign him the right job to maximize success. Instead, Arden sat with me. After some time, he brought me a tea I sipped as thanks for his kindness, though thirst was far from my mind in my anxious distraction.

I have fought and staved off death for centuries in a war for justice due to the meddling my father has woven within the fabric of Magic law. Even so, if it meant being branded a hypocrite, if Sophie and Donovan perished from this disease, Jordan will meet his own death by my hand. And I will harbour no guilt for doing so.

Ranlyn made consecutive calls to warn others about Jordan possibly seeking refuge, though Arden was probably correct in assuming the man went straight to Loring. More often than not, the people Ranlyn contacted claimed no knowledge of Jordan and were more interested in details of the fall of Alasdair Llewellyn and the future of the Sovereignty.

He deferred to me to verify the veracity of his claims. People were untrusting of the current Elder regime and craved a tale originating from the horse's mouth to somehow elevate their importance.

While I understood Ranlyn was doing as the Mother Coven needed, I wished he would leave me be. I had no energy to campaign for the faith of Magics. This was a part of what stopped me from taking up an Elder role decades ago.

Whether times were imminently gloomy, Veata stayed the course. She never wavered from her demeanor and either slept or laughed aside any attempt to remain serious. Now she appeared troubled. After the Sovereignty break-in she adopted a scowl showing little and saying much.

Veata was worried.

For some reason this knocked me off kilter a toe further.

"What do you see?" I asked the quiet Elder seated off to the side of the room.

Veata inhaled. Her clouded eyes stayed searching. "I see too much, yet oh so little."

"And from that you take...?"

"Take? I take nothing. I watch. I see. Nothing to take."

"Any specifics?" Ranlyn asked as he was flipping through a book for his next contact.

"Change. Change is soon."

"Positive? Negative?"

"Depends on your perspective," she responded to Ranlyn and then flicked her fingers in my direction. "You will assume your father's role."

"To rule the Sovereignty?" Ranlyn jumped in where I was too stunned to articulate. "That is what you're saying, yes?"

"You requested specifics, yes?" Veata's parroting of Ranlyn's tone and question was delivered with heavy sarcasm.

I knew better than to question what Veata saw. She would never share another vision with me if I dared to. But this? How could such a future prove accurate?

"Is that all?" I asked her.

Her sightless eyes panned my way. "Is it not enough?"

She was right. Hearing I would command the company I hated

was more than enough. This news came with no timeline and I was too afraid to ask. Knowing my father was already gone and Chase was no longer a viable replacement, this left the company in the hands of the Sovereignty board. A fact that did not leave me any less worried about the fate of all Magics.

18

ABANDONED

Caine

Andy pulled himself between the front seats. "Aren't we going inside?"

Sitting in the driveway of my deceased aunt and uncle's home was not on my to-do list for the day, but when Andy kept pestering Jet for some things from his room, his real room, Jet asked if it was a possibility to return to the house.

I palmed the keys from Vincent's SUV. He handed them over without invasive questions and only a plea to call if I needed backup.

"Mom?"

Jet's knee shook as she peered through the windshield at her family home.

I put the keys in the center cup holder. "I'm going to go in first—"

Jet unbuckled her seatbelt. "No, it's fine. We can go in."

"You sure?"

She said something like "yup" and swung open her door.

I raced to climb out, Andy doing the same.

Jet knelt down to inspect the pile of half-frozen, mostly soggy mail on the cement stoop, the mailbox itself stuffed full.

"So many bills..." Jet muttered, sifting through the junk for actual mail, the paper disintegrating and indistinguishable between electricity bills or a pizza coupons.

I knelt at her side. "We can make some calls for the most updated ones. Is there a hidden key or can we spell our way in?"

After a moment of helpless defeat, Jet dropped the ragged pieces of paper in a splat on the front step.

I stood as she did and smiled at Andy, his shoulders up to ears against a chilled wind across the flat, surrounding farmland and landing his little squint on his mother and me. Andy may be a kid, but he knew when things didn't feel right. His mother fussing over demolished mail was one of them.

Turned out the front door was unlocked.

I insisted on going in first in case we weren't the only ones checking on the place. Considering how rural the house was, random squatters were unlikely.

A hint of hope Aunt Bernadine was alive, that maybe the others were wrong, and she wasn't killed in the battle outside of Diluculo to kill Evaristus, sank in my gut when I realized that if she was here, she was still an enemy. She fought alongside the Sorrels to kill Magics who belong to the Mother Coven. And to hear Donovan tell it, she wasn't exactly helpful while his brother sliced my uncle's throat open.

Inside the house, the air was stagnant and stunk of rotting food. The fridge and cupboards were probably hiding some real goodies. Off to the right of the door was the living room. Dirt and disarray were on every surface. Pictures and coffee table knickknacks were shoved aside. The whole space was messy in a way I never saw it while Aunt Bernie and Uncle Eli were alive, but no one was on the comfy couches or Eli's lounger.

"If anyone can hear my voice, come out now!" I yelled into the house loud enough and with an effective amount of persuasion.

Silence called back.

"I don't think anyone's here," I told Jet.

She came in behind me, a small gasp leaving her lips as she saw the same mess I did. Whatever Aunt Bernie and Uncle Eli got up to when they desperately brought in Tainted contacts to find Jet, it meant their home was no longer a home.

Andy ran to the left down the hall towards the bedrooms.

"Hey!" Jet called after him. "Don't pack the whole room."

Jet flicked up the light switch on the wall and the living room lamp in the corner spotlit the layer of filth on the carpet.

"Electricity's a good sign. Probably why it isn't freezing in here."

Jet was still looking around at the mess. "Mom and Dad paid the important bills with automatic withdrawal. They never wanted to risk losing the property."

I didn't know what to say. Commenting on the irony of them losing everything including their lives was already a fact Jet was thinking about. Saying it didn't make it any less sad.

Her eyes glassed over, her inhale deepening. "I should pack some things of my own and help him or he'll stuff his entire toy chest into his backpack."

I smiled and nodded. I would have offered to help, but getting in the way wasn't helpful.

Memories of the first time I was ever here came to the forefront. Bernie, taking one look at me, eyes widened, and knowing who I was based on my close resemblance to my father, Daniel. Uncle Eli filling in the blanks of my family history and teaching me how to control my persuasion gift. Homecooked meals, working on the farm with Eli, training with Jet. Later, Sophie would come with me, and Andy would predict her death... Nothing was so casually cozy after that.

Wait. The kitchen tap was dripping. Not a lot but enough to prevent the pipes from freezing.

Boot prints in a thin layer of dirt were scraped from the metal feet of the chair. Someone with large feet had been sitting at the table.

The prints were dry, but they appeared on top of the grime, as if it happened recently. Shit. How recent?

A choked scream came from the hallway.

I took off towards the sound and found Jet in the hallway, back against the wall, hands to her face.

"Mom?"

I put my hand up in front of Andy who was now at his bedroom door to stop him.

"Jet?"

She pointed across the hall. "He's still... He's..."

I looked through the open door and saw... Oh my god. Eli.

His body was still here.

Eli was on his bedroom floor, the comforter from his bed twisted around his body, his throat sliced wide open. Dried blood stuck to the fabric and on the floor beside him, as the rest of him was discoloured and rotting. Bugs. There were bugs.

He was still here.

"Mom?"

Andy's voice snapped us from the trance of staring at Eli's dead and decaying body.

"It's fine, buddy." Jet hurried to her son and gently pushing him back into his room coupled with an offer to help him pack.

The stench hit me. It was what I smelled in the rest of the house, the bedroom door letting it loose once Jet broke the seal.

I raced to close Eli's bedroom door and open a window at the end of the hall. It took some muscle, but it opened. I breathed in the fresh, winter air, hoping it would chase away the stink of my uncle's rotting body. My lungs might forget, but I never would. I've seen many dead bodies while stuck in the Creation, Evaristus loved the kill and kept his dead lingering around in festering piles, but none of those faces were family.

I was told Bernie was left with my uncle's corpse after Donovan's brother and father made an example of Eli for being a rat and talking to the enemy...Sophie.

How could Bernie leave him? How could she have left her murdered husband on their bedroom floor to rot?

I let my head fall back and sucked in a few breaths doing everything not to focus on the smell.

Fuck...the smell. I couldn't let Andy breathe in the stink of his grandfather's corpse.

I rushed to the bathroom, found some room spray, and doused the hallway in "Citrus Paradise". I kept spraying until it went from rotten fruit to a lemonade bomb. It could be skunk ass and it would still be better than what was seeping out of that bedroom.

"Bernie, what the hell were you thinking?" I said quietly to myself.

She was dead as well, her body left stinking on the battlefield, but still, it didn't make this any easier to swallow. The good people I knew shouldn't have ended this way.

Standing in the living room without a hint of what to do, I dialled the number Ness gave me. It rang and rang as long as the last time, without a voicemail to pick up.

"*Hola*?" A raspy-voiced woman answered.

"Hi, hello." I wasn't expecting anyone to answer and now the person who did spoke Spanish. Which totally made sense since Ness said she was headed to Chile. I tried to remember my high school grade ten language elective and couldn't have pulled up simple profanity if it meant Ness would appear in front of me on the dirty floor. "Umm, is Ness there? Or Felix? Vanessa and Felix Pleitez?"

The woman asked questions back, but she spoke so fast, I wouldn't have been able to answer even if I understood the language.

"Sorry...um, English? Does anyone there speak English?"

"Ingles? No, no Ingles."

"Not you, I know, but anyone..." I exhaled in frustration. Not at the woman, at someone finally answering and somehow it still getting me nowhere. If the woman spoke English, I may have been able to persuade some answers from her, but then I'd be stealing something from a total stranger who had nothing to do with anything.

"Thanks, anyways," I said in defeat. "Have a good day. Bye."

I ended the call, saving both myself and the woman any further aggravation.

Was Ness not there? Did she not arrive, or did she give me a fake number? She claimed she wasn't running from me, but maybe she thought this was easier or safer, to head to an off-the-grid location where she and Felix, and I guess Derek, would be free of the overbearing threat of being anywhere near me.

A scuffle was Jet opening and then closing Andy's door behind her. Her expression scrunched as she met me in the living room.

"Sorry, I tried—"

"It's fine. A wall of janitor's closet is better than..." She stopped, but I understood.

"Yeah. Exactly."

Jet's arms were crossed so tightly I braced for her to spontaneously vomit.

I felt pressure to say something helpful. "We don't know what happened, but we know what we're left with. What do you want to do with him? I can bury him out back in the field. Frozen or not I can move some ground. Or we can burn the whole place down. Truly, whatever you want."

She lowered her voice. "What if I sell the house? Do I then have to dig him up and bury him someplace else? I can't leave him here for the next owners to accidently unearth when they're tilling to plant fucking corn or some shit. And I don't want to watch it burn."

I didn't know how to answer her. And I didn't have property to start my own family plot. Though, maybe I could add Eli to Cole's gravesite. They never met as adults, but they were family.

"We can't leave him on the floor," she continued in a flurry. "My mom abandoned him. I can't leave him again. I can't leave him here, in that room, in this disgusting house. I just can't."

"I know, I know." I wrapped my arms around her. "We're not going to leave him. We'll figure something out."

She wiped her eyes when she pulled away, trying to keep it together.

"I can talk to Vincent about the legal stuff and selling the property if you go that way. You don't have to decide right now."

Other than Vincent, I had no other contacts to ask.

Jet sniffed and swiped at a fallen tear. "After Rob, they didn't talk about death or dying to me much. Not in terms of anything legal or their wishes for when it happened." I took a lagging second to remember Rob was Jet's deceased husband. "Andy seeing the death spots on unsuspecting people at the grocery store or the park was enough on all of us. I think my mom kept paperwork in their bedroom, but I'm not going in there."

Far too much death for one little family unit. And I forgot about how much of it occurred before I even knew they were my family.

We came up with a plan to wrap Eli in a sheet or two, including temporarily covering the spot on the bedroom carpet, and put him in the barn. Without him in the house, Jet felt more comfortable searching her parents' things for some type of paperwork. We had the time, and Andy would love spending it in his bedroom with all of his familiar things for a change.

I couldn't let Jet help me with her dad. Wrapping him up left me raw and empty. With some telekinetic influence, I managed to peel his stuck body from the floor, then I carried him through the house, and out the backdoor into the barn without Andy or the not-so-near neighbours seeing anything. And while I didn't want to leave Eli on the barn's cold cement floor, it would preserve his body better than the carpet inside of the house. Maybe a spell could help slow the process, but I couldn't think of one right now.

Wet boot prints on the barn floor caught my eye. Large, like the one in the kitchen.

I laid Eli all of the way down, retaining my power. When I released my uncle and ensured he was covered, I switched from telekinesis to persuasion.

"If anyone can hear my voice, show yourself."

A man appeared about fifteen feet away, built in the shoulders, wide grey eyes, short-cropped hair.

Shit.

"Stop!" The man said with his hand towards me. "Drop your power and listen."

My persuasion released like I let go of a heavy sack of potatoes, my attention all his.

He took a few steps closer to me. "I'm not here to kill you or anyone else."

Whoever this was trained his eyeline on Eli while I hung in anticipation of hearing whatever he said next. Instead of addressing me, the man said something in a different language. I heard something else, but I was waiting for the man to speak to me.

His grey eyes returned to mine. "You can't cart a body around or leave him for the rats in here. Find an urn or a Ziplock and tell Jet to take him along."

The man then gave me a visual once over while I waited to hear more.

"We are certainly related. Nice to meet you, cuz."

I blinked into attention, my will released.

The man was gone.

What the fuck? I didn't remember him leaving. What else did he say?

Eli.

At my feet were still the sheets I used to wrap my uncle's body, but they were nearly flattened.

I knelt and grabbed the fabric. A small plume of dust came from one of the edges. I dropped the sheet and reared back, realizing the dust was Eli.

The man cremated Eli?

Not a random man, my cousin, another Berisford. A strong one with the same persuader grey eyes as my father and me.

I tried to flip through the interaction with him, but it was one-sided. His power overrode mine. He disintegrated Eli's body, and then he left.

Why was he here? How did he know Eli was dead? Was he here because Eli was dead? If he was my cousin, who were his parents?

Shit. Now I needed something to put Eli into. And a face mask to do it. And to tell Jet about our visiting family member with Berisford abilities to watch out for. Claiming he didn't want to hurt anyone didn't mean anything when it came from the mouth of someone sharing our blood.

Fucking Berisfords.

19

MASTER OF ALL

Vincent

The door burst open. The Team filtered in with their hands full.

"Did you acquire—?" I stood, their presence stealing me from thoughts of my future.

"We got it," Hall interrupted, carrying over-flowing duffel bags.

I could not wager a guess at how most items would be used, but the stands Gregor walked in with were definitely to hang bags of intravenous medications.

Evelyn ordered the Team to move things around or set things up to best treat them. I assisted where I could, reminded of my mother healing the Blind when I was a child the first time I met Sophie. It was the same shift from wait-and-see to dropped into crisis and action.

Whatever was in the clear bags Rosemary and Bronya were hanging from the steel poles needed to work. Setting one up for Sophie was nothing more than discomfort in her half-conscious state. Doing so with regards to Donovan and his psychometry took Evelyn a few tries to access to a vein. Hall and Gregor held him still enough to avoid undue injury, even while unconscious.

Movement in my periphery was someone standing in the doorway.

"Cora-Lynn..." I rushed to her watching the goings on in the room.

She straightened and stepped back on her heel.

I apologised for advancing on her with too much urgency. "You are welcome to observe. I was merely surprised to see you."

Venturing from her cell alone to eat was not quite among her reintegration skills. Or so I thought. Inside of the Sovereignty cells, starvation—real or fabricated—was a near daily symptom of her incarceration rather than motivation.

She clutched a copy of Dante's *The Divine Comedy*. Maybe not my first choice after what she endured. Somehow it comforted her, and I was too happy she was engaged in something to ruin her solace by dissecting it.

"Have you eaten?" I asked when her attention lingered on the activity in the room. "Would you like me to escort you to the cafeteria?"

"No," she answered in a tone I was clueless to interpret. "What is happening to them?"

Her response took me aback. She wanted to learn about Sophie and Donovan from my perspective. She may hold misgivings about my answers, however, her tentative faith filled me with great relief.

"They are quite ill and their condition has since worsened. Newly-acquired equipment and medicines were gathered in hopes of healing them." Saying so was for me as well.

Evelyn added more of her slime mixture to their foreheads to aid with the fever. Cora-Lynn withheld any questions about the substance, the crease between her eyes asking for her, so I explained.

"Elder Vincent..." Evelyn approached. "I will continue monitoring and administering medications. If they are meant to remain in this lifetime, we will discover soon enough."

I nodded. "Thank you, Evelyn. Your efforts have greatly improved their odds. If you need anything, please do not hesitate to ask or ensure someone does so in your stead."

Evelyn smiled, patted my arm, and returned to a table at the side of the room where she continued to add and blend ingredients. Kim helped, distracting herself with learning of the herbal properties. With so many healers within this place, Evelyn was elite. If she could not turn the tide of Sophie and Donovan's illness now that modern medicine had joined the fight, recovery was hopeless.

A quick glance passed from Cora-Lynn to me. Having her hear me called "Elder" or be addressed with any amount of station evoked some unease. She knew the real me or as authentic as I could be without revealing my true nature while her husband. And that person was no one of great importance. A man with a certain amount of wealth or subdued influence, to be certain, but nothing akin to the individual I was to the flock inside of the Prison Creation.

"Tell me about them," Cora-Lynn said and stepped into the room.

I followed when she stood between their beds to stare down at them. Rosemary glared. I returned her warning as assurance I could handle Cora-Lynn if something happened and that any intervention on Rosemary's part would be met with swift correction.

Leaving Cora-Lynn between Sophie and Donovan, I rounded Sophie's bed and sat where I had for hours, holding her pox-ridden hand.

"They have smallpox," I informed Cora-Lynn and went on to describe the disease.

"No," Cora-Lynn interrupted. "Tell me of them as people in your past."

Shocked as I was that Cora-Lynn genuinely wanted to learn about my Charges, this to me was a sign of progress.

"They are great lovers," I began. "At some point they were strangers and they built a solid foundation of love. They harnessed that love to create their Soul Magic. And I somehow became their Overseer, destined to meet each incarnation of them."

She appraised one and then the other. "They are not the same people I met?"

"Not in blood and body, no. However, they are the very same souls you knew. They are created each time appearing much the same, besides a few genetic variations." Except Cora-Lynn would have no concept of genetics. Another mental note to remind myself of the information she went without that could assist her in acclimating to this time.

Cora-Lynn's brow creased. "I am not fond of Morgan's light hair."

"Morgan?" Kim asked.

"One of Sophie's previous names," I answered. "Thankfully, the colour is temporary as I am not too fond of it myself."

Something in Cora-Lynn's expression changed. "She and Henry… They experienced all we did in—"

"Yes. Yes, they did." I, however, did not want each of their deaths repeated in front of the others. I could not state why if someone asked, but I did not.

Cora-Lynn slightly nodded, gleaning my caution.

"Show me outside," Cora-Lynn demanded, her tone soft in a dissociation of sorts.

Although she was still looking at Sophie and Donovan, I knew she meant this demand for me and found I lacked reason to deny her. All of her time spent in the real world was unconscious or inside of the Prison Creation walls. Fresh air would connect her to this time.

Willing to satisfy near all of her desires to find peace in this new timeline, I laid Sophie's hand down and we left.

I stopped Cora-Lynn in front of the elevator and offered an explanation, warning her of what we may experience in the elevator and see upon exiting.

Cora-Lynn offered no nod in understanding nor did she express her own worries, instead she stared at me with those beautifully cold eyes.

I nodded to Liam, who accessed the elevator for us.

Steady on the way down, when the doors opened to the cold parking garage, I led the way. I scanned the cement ground and walls and the deep shadows hoping not to find an awaiting enemy. Although, none should be able to glimpse any Magics in the parking garage because of the perimeter spells.

Cora-Lynn surprised me by falling in step into the chilled space.

The elevator door slid shut.

"When you want to return, you can reopen the door."

She refrained from saying anything, standing straighter to display a lack of fear. Her discomfort was in her thoughts and the deep inhale of the cold air around us. Forgetting outdoor gear was an oversight I would not forget again. A spell to warm her would likely scare her. She held the tension of a stretched piano wire as it was.

"These are some of the vehicles of today," I explained to keep her engaged. "The way we travel around the city."

"No horses?"

"Not typically for methods of transportation, though they still live on various farms and are used for modes of competition or as pets. These modern vehicles are all metal and plastic."

"They are quite ugly."

I gave a small chuckle. "This one is, yes," I said, looking to the pickup truck closest to the elevator rusted through its wheel wells. "Their condition and performance depend on how much money you have or are willing to spend, which tends to determine how beautiful or efficient the machine is. A status symbol easily viewed by others or a simple vehicle to travel from one place to another."

"Do you own one?"

"A few, yes. A couple in this lot, though others sit at homes I own in different parts of this country and in others."

She took a few more careful steps towards other vehicles, bringing her closer to the mouth of the parking garage.

I followed close behind.

A loud hiss of air brakes and a high-pitched squeal preceded a bus whipping around the corner. Across the street, it stopped with a screech in one of the bays of the city bus terminal.

Cora-Lynn sprinted in the opposite direction.

"No! Cora—!" I took after Cora-Lynn, screaming her name.

Her tactical-booted feet and panic to flee the perceived threat gave her a considerable lead and blocked my desperate call.

She rushed through the large parking garage opening without hesitation and veered left.

I screamed her name again and chased after her in my unseasonal loafers, still too far away to interfere. Calling her name did not impact her speed, neither did invading her headspace and pleading for her to stop. Her fear relaxed enough to understand what I asked of her. She knew she was clear of the original threat. The knowledge of a forthcoming explanation of what she saw did nothing to stop her.

Cora-Lynn did not trust me. This was what kept her running.

She thought she may be better off on her own.

Everything she experienced so far was within my father's sandbox. She knew nothing of the real world.

We passed another open parking lot that serviced employees of the companies they backed onto. Cora-Lynn ran towards a major downtown road when a silver sedan headed for us. She pivoted and found an alleyway between two buildings.

I called her name again.

She stopped.

Finally.

Wait. No.

I dug in to rush to her when two Magics blocked her path through the alleyway.

"This way!" My voice broke with the warning.

She spun to flee the men and slipped. She could not see their soul glows to know them Magics, neither could I, yet they wore the drawn expression of clear danger.

I whipped up power and tossed it in the direction of the men, shooting for the walls of the narrow alleyway. A spiked energy form bounced off of the brick and into the men, dividing into multiple more spiked energy forms, and assaulted the men while they were trapped in the small space.

Cora-Lynn tried to dodge me again.

Now close enough, I telekinetically snatched her arm to pull her in the direction of safety. "You are unprotected this fa—"

Three more Magics came from the direction of road where the silver sedan entered, the driver now gone.

"Run!" I pushed Cora-Lynn towards the parking garage, though we still had road to travel until we reached safety.

Without another option, she took off where I needed her to go.

A force of energy missed its target and fizzled out on the road in front of us.

The deep yellow light and then flash of power scared Cora-Lynn. She slowed in a skid, slipped, and landed on the slushy dirt road.

I threw up a shield behind us and grabbed her by her underarms to muscle her to her feet.

Another hit of energy slammed against the shield and left the odour of singed rubber in the air.

My push and demand for Cora-Lynn to keep running was more brash than intended. I needed her to listen. Five Magics against two was not a successful ratio.

Dammit.

Another Magic revealed themself beneath a cover spell, standing down the road in front of us. She was poised to attack the moment we saw the flash of her wicked grin.

"Down!" I shoved Cora-Lynn to the ground and trapped her underneath of a tortoiseshell-shaped shield magically fusing it to the asphalt with her inside.

Now, I could focus on a target and not protection.

Six against one was not great odds, but these devotees walked with overconfident steps and quickened action with assumption of an easy target.

I rose power I inherited from others far more formidable than those now racing towards me and waited until they reached an advantageous distance.

A step close enough and I snapped up Extractor power and captured the six Magics barrelling towards me. The devotees' bodies slumped to the ground where their momentum dropped them in splashes of winter slush. Checking to see what damage I may have caused showed one partially-extracted soul in my right hand and five others in my left. If a few or all of their souls had become fully extracted in their attempt to kidnap me or use Cora-Lynn as leverage to corral us wherever Loring planned, I would feel zero guilt.

I surveyed the area in case others attacked while their comrades were busy in agonizing pain in their dissociated state. With no other enemies, I concentrated on holding the souls of my enemies. Unlike with Sophie and other Soul Seers, the devotees' souls were not visible to me in this state. I could hear their pleas, their confusion, their bodies relenting under the unyielding force in desperate hope I would release them.

I could also hear their prevailing thoughts surrounding wishing they never took the job to capture anyone who left the Prison Creation. They did not care about enslaving the Blind or Loring becoming the 'Master of All'. Not now.

As much as I would have liked to punish them with the full extent of my power, the strain of holding six souls aloft in partial removal was too great to hold for long. Safety for myself and Cora-Lynn was not far off, the entrance to the parking garage visible from our position.

Anyone could stumble upon us. This impasse could not continue.

I stepped on Cora-Lynn's tortoiseshell shield and dissolved it with a hint of power.

Cora-Lynn scrambled to the side in a heave of breath.

"Run to the elevator, now!"

She peered up at me and then saw those who attacked her on the ground, her eyes wide and wild.

"Now!" I screamed again to get her moving.

Cora-Lynn raced to her feet and ran towards the parking garage entrance.

"Hey!" More devotees arrived to check on their comrades' failure to report in.

Of course.

Cora-Lynn made it through the entrance. Elation flooded me to see she did not continue on where this road met another main street and potentially other devotees awaiting to ambush more Prison Creation survivors.

While Cora-Lynn would still take a moment to find the elevator, my time in this street had run its course with every pounding footstep of the encroaching devotees.

I dropped the six partially-extracted souls I held and sprinted off on the same path as Cora-Lynn, murmuring a stronghold spell. When close enough to use it, I slapped my hand on the entrance of the parking garage and watched my words enact a shield across the expanse of the entrance.

Devotees were on my tail and ran into a transparent wall where the stronghold spell would hold them back for a limited amount of time. A meat-fisted Tainted Magic pounded on the invisible barrier, his failure alive in his furrowed brow.

Where was Cora-Lynn? Already inside?

No. She knelt behind the bumper of a large SUV, peering over its edge.

"If you want to die, leaving the Prison Creation without a guide or resources is a surefire way to ensure that happens." Anger choked me. The thought of her alone in the world where my enemies could find her was terrifying.

Cora-Lynn stood, chin levelled, fists clenched at her side. "*If a fight is what he desires, he shall have one.*"

I pointed to my head. "I can hear you! I do not wish to fight, to punish, or to mourn you so soon after discovering the years of grief I endured was wasted."

She stood, unchanged.

"Do you wish to die?" I stepped closer to her aware of her fists tightening. "After all you experienced, I could understand desiring an end."

Cora-Lynn's shoulder rose ever so slightly, an anticipated move.

I caught her arm in a telekinetic hold before she could punch me in the face, and then caught the other, holding both in an unmovable grasp.

"Please!" I yelled above the screaming in her mind.

She stopped, panting through her clenched teeth and trying to pull away without hope of moving an inch unless I allowed it.

I held her close, ready in case she tried to thrash again. "Continue to fight, to escape, to place yourself in peril, and you will not be permitted access to anywhere except your cell. As much as you would hate me for removing your freedom, you would still live. And I would not worry my enemies were slicing you into pieces in order to extort precious intelligence from you. Information that would result in the killing of thousands within the Prison Creation by the very evil who ruined you."

Her muscles relaxed a bit in surprise when she surveyed my expression for an indication of a lie.

"I have not earned your trust. My failing to do so will weigh on me until the day that changes. Until then, the world you knew is gone and the one which has replaced it holds dangers you cannot foresee. A war circles around our people and the Blind. I hold the power of their futures and one...one...misstep causes irreversible disaster. The Cora-Lynn I knew could not live with the knowledge that her actions caused such tragedy. And while you are not the same, I refuse to believe the person I love has fallen so far that she would condemn innocents."

Cora-Lynn's lips were still pursed in defiance when I released my telekinetic hold. We stared at each other. She mentally attempted to connect with who she used to be and became stuck on my mentioning love for her. She did not want death for herself or for others due to her negligence. She wanted to live without fear, in a time she recognised, with the people she knew and loved.

In place of disappointing her with the inability to provide any of that, I lifted a hand towards the elevator, inviting her to return inside.

She hesitated and then relented. She did not feel safe within the Prison Creation after seeing so many use power she could not understand. Though, she felt safer inside than she did outside where people used those powers against her.

Without any of her thoughts spoken aloud throughout the entirety of the exchange, I settled on accepting her silence as surrender when she started towards the elevator. A speck of relief relaxed that choking feeling in my throat. This escape attempt may not be her last. She may not trust me, but I hope she would trust that I would follow through on my threat to incarcerate her against her will if she tried to leave.

Could I do it? Not without losing another piece of my heart I was not willing to relinquish easily.

The elevator doors opened to the Prison Creation lobby.

A brash exhale left Cora-Lynn. She looked upon some Magics using their powers in controlled bursts for fun or for menial tasks the Blind would not think twice about.

No matter where she sought safety, every place was another that was not her true home.

"I can help you through this," I told her. "Love for me is not required to be eased into this world. As the single living person from your old life, I have a rare perspective on what was, what is no longer, and what is now. If you can trust I have your best interests at heart, I promise to provide you any truth you seek regardless of how that truth may paint myself or those I care for.

"You survived my father's cells. You can survive this. Live the life you want, with whomever you want." The thought of her with anyone else set off a tightness in my chest. The unfairness of such reaction was not lost on me.

"You are free to roam. I need to check on Sophie and Donovan."

"I would prefer to see Morgan again."

"Of course."

When we entered the temporary hospital suite dirty and tired, we found Sophie and Donovan now surrounded by a few more family members. Both were still unconscious.

Cora-Lynn stood against the wall, arms crossed, settled somewhere between Sophie and Donovan's beds.

I motioned for Ranlyn to join me. When he did, I explained what occurred with Cora-Lynn and of the awaiting devotees who Loring had instructed to kidnap anyone who left the Prison Creation.

"We should move people," Ranlyn said and shook his head.

"You have to see the idiocy of such action?"

Ranlyn's nostrils flared. "During my calls were many questions about an expediated trial for Chase and Lincoln."

"Do you remember who asked you this? Chances are they are turncoats themselves."

"They weren't looking for them to be released, they were seeking to test how effective your new system is. We still need to bring in lawyers, a judge..."

"Officials are in wait of instruction for when they can safely represent the accused. The dangers surrounding this Creation were inevitable."

"Then why go through the trouble of hiding its location?"

"Because it had not yet been filled with personnel who could secure and react in the case of potential infiltration. No Magics under the protection of the Prison Creation can be seen exiting the parking structure. A circle of wards will not allow a Tainted soul access to the parking garage and is set around the block in its entirety. Cora-Lynn, unfortunately, ran outside of this barrier, inadvertently revealing herself. The Sovereignty has existed for countless years with Magics full knowledge of its location and still has few infiltrations on its record, one of which caused the true death of its countless evil practices. We will not fall so easily either.

"In time, others will fear this place as they do the Sovereignty.

For now, if they somehow surpass the wards to access the elevators, they will find themselves exiting without gaining access to their desired floor let alone the Creation. The process requires an array of spells and portals. You either trust the failsafes or you do not."

"Trust?" Ranlyn yelled, gaining attention of the whole room. "I trust knowledge and you have not previously shared anything regarding failsafes."

I peered down at Ranlyn. "Conduct yourself like the Elder you are and find blame in yourself for not inquiring of such basic information. Focus on the crisis management of our flock. With my father dead and Loring comfortable attacking, kidnapping, and killing the Blind in the open, we will have more enemies now than ever. Once we showcase our intentions with current prisoners, word of our process will spread. You may not enjoy your lacking knowledge of my plans, but know they exist to ensure the undeniable safety of this location and those within it."

Ranlyn crossed his arms. "This doesn't sit well with me."

"No? Then use your brain and cook up something more akin to your palate."

Ranlyn had no appreciation for the condescension. I was beyond coddling the man. He was an Elder. In the next few days, we would cross many paths and select the best for the flock or we would miss our chance and fail, causing them all to scatter.

Looking to Sophie and Donovan, I was reminded that not all of them could run, and I was desperate for the time for them and those traumatised, like Cora-Lynn, to heal.

20

A LITTLE LOYALTY

Sophie

An itch throbbed all over, one which ran deep and scurried under my skin with zapping strikes of pain.

I opened my eyes to check out what the itch was and saw a bald head too close to me through blurred vision.

Shit! Olson found me.

I scrambled to get away from the Apporter. Blood rushed to my head. Dizziness cranked the room to the side and almost pitched me off of the small bed.

How'd he find me? Was Loring here?

Wait...not Olson? Too short when they stood and stepped away. The eyes weren't right.

Vomit rushed up my throat. Something shiny and silver was shoved in front of my face a split-second ahead of my gut seizing and forcing frothy, yellow bile between my lips. The sound of Donovan doing the same came from somewhere in the room, if not a tad more dramatic, though I couldn't see who played catcher.

When the yakking settled, I curled into the fetal position onto an already sweat-soaked pillow. A stabbing jolt shot through my arm. An IV? Whatever bruising it might leave was nothing compared to all of the painful itchy spots covering the skin around it.

Evelyn put another cold cloth on my head, the chill driving into my brain in a most delicious way. I moaned and let my arm fall the few inches I managed to raise it.

Murmuring came from Vincent with Cora-Lynn backed into a corner. It was her bald head too close to me when I woke up.

"Sorry." The croak of an apology set off a coughing fit.

When it quit, Vincent held my hand and said something soothing I couldn't hear while my ribcage throbbed at the constant pressure. All I saw was the hand he was holding covered in nasty-looking bumps.

"What is this?"

"Treatable. Miserable, but treatable by means much slower than hoped. Expect to feel rather unpleasant for some time."

"Smallpox," a hardened voice filled in the blanks from the other side of the room. Rosemary.

Donovan's back was to me, yet he reacted to the news with as much internal surprise as I did.

I searched Vincent's tired green eyes. "You're sure?" I learned about smallpox from medical dramas and middle-of-the-night infomercials seeking donations for victims in third-world countries. Not here.

How could Jordan pull it off?

It was probably also too much to hope that Jordan was infected as well. If it was a vial from the grip of a terrorist, then maybe he would be exposed. In this case, the virus came from inside the man or from a spell as toxic as he was. Where was he now?

"Jordan's unfortunate escape is a future problem to be dealt with when necessary. We assume he will pop up whenever Loring resurfaces. Not for you to worry about." Vincent offered a smile instead of further bullshit he knew I would see through. Lucky for him, I didn't have the energy to argue about the importance of taking Loring off of the board.

"He wasn't Tainted."

The corner of Vincent's lips twitched. "He could have hid it."

"Usually the whole soul glow is gone, not visible but Taint-free. If Magics can completely alter their soul glows, my power is useless."

Vincent's slow nod told me he got what I meant, but it wasn't an answer to the problem. I didn't like the feeling of my failsafe being removed from me. Had I known Jordan was Tainted from the beginning... Which was another good question. How did Jordan know to cover his soul glow before I met him at his place with the Team? He was already in with Loring by then, had to be. Loring told him about me and my family power.

Did Issát warn them of this? Did he know a spell to hide the Taint of a soul glow? And, if so, why let them in on it when it would mess with his own ability to tell Magics apart?

Jordan was the last person I wanted to think about, the way he made me feel falling further from that. Donovan was a few feet away but I didn't want to see him either. I didn't need the judgement right now or his apologies because he was too scared to die with me still pissed at him in case it meant we flew solo in our next lives. That's not love. That's fear and desperation.

"Desperation to understand what's so wrong with you you'd hurt me like you did." Donovan's voice was another of his many invasions.

I couldn't even block my thoughts when I could focus on trying to.

"Can you not access your power at all?" Vincent asked.

When Donovan answered, "No," I realized Vincent wasn't talking to me.

"What about the—?"

"No," I interrupted him. "I don't need to read your thoughts to know how your mind works."

He squeezed my hand a little tighter. "The ritual stone magic can override my cell bindings. In this case, maybe it can override the smallpox or more. With treatment administered, you remain stable if not a hair improved. There could be a window of opportunity."

Probably for the sole fact that I didn't want to, Donovan flexed his inner strength to access the ritual stone magic. The vibration caused him physical distress and had us both vomiting again. Dry heaves ripped at my stomach muscles since nothing was left.

"I felt that," I heard Cora-Lynn speak in a small voice.

Vincent brushed my hair out of my face and Evelyn handed him a cloth to wipe my mouth.

I caught another glimpse of the pustules on my hands and arms. Nasty. Whatever punishment Donovan thought up for getting back at me for taking it as far as I did with Jordan, he likely didn't think of smallpox. Unless he thought he would enjoy going through it himself.

Vincent left my side to speak with Cora-Lynn. I couldn't hear what he was saying, but her eyes hesitantly left me when he called her name to gain her attention. She'd kept her arms folded since after I freaked out thinking she was Olson, but kept her stare locked on me.

Did she still not believe in magic or know what the feeling of magic was? With so many Magics around, it couldn't be the first time she felt it. Why bother convincing her of anything if she was too delusional to accept what was right in front of her?

"My wife cannot hear you, but I certainly can. Imagine living for hundreds of years somewhere where everything you experienced was most certainly an illusion. You may call everything else you see into question, would you not?" Vincent's restrained tone in my brain came while he simultaneously explained the basics to Cora-Lynn while maintaining eye contact with her. He obviously still saw her in the role no matter how long it had been.

"Nice trick." I was too exhausted to argue with him. His DIY project was not mine and I didn't have the mental bandwidth to hold up the flashlight to help.

When Vincent was done giving Cora-Lynn Magic Basics 101, he

took a few steps to the foot of my bed to talk to Donovan. "What about Fox?"

"No." A thread of insult yanked the connection.

"Donovan..."

Donovan rolled onto his back to face Vincent, the sensations this movement caused was uncomfortable. "I'm not doing this. He saved me, I saved him. He's barely recovered. Leave him out of it."

"I could talk to him," Rosemary said. "I've already called him. He knows what's happening and would do—"

"No!" Donovan snapped at his mother.

Vincent was now crossing his arms, mirroring Cora-Lynn. "Fine, but as soon as you can manage accessing the ritual stone magic without adverse effects, you will heal the both of you."

That was the end of that. If the ritual stone magic could bypass Jordan's power, then we would heal quicker. The question was, after what happened, why would Donovan want to heal me at all?

"Because I'm a masochist and still love you," he spoke in dark ripples across my grey matter.

Great. Like I needed his commentary every time I had a wayward thought.

"You can move to a different room."

"If I could move."

"Exactly."

Picking up the telepathic conversation, Vincent asked Cora-Lynn if she wanted to go to the cafeteria to give us time to rest, looking to the others with the same question. When Evelyn and Rosemary stated they were fine, Vincent shot them a stare hard enough to change their minds. Rosemary took an extra second and then gave in. Why he thought Donovan and I needed the privacy was presumptuous and annoying. Neither of us could handle the conversation right now and didn't need him meddling.

Alone and with the office door shut to block the sounds of passing Magics, the quiet was as itchy as the pustules.

Clearly, Donovan wasn't sleeping since I wasn't, but I could picture him on his back with his arm slung over his face as I felt the weight on my forehead. And, of course, he heard that too because he shifted the limp limb to his side instead and the pressure released. Though, my head pounded more without the weight.

"Why can't I hear your every thought?" I put out into the ether, not expecting him to pick it up since I wasn't projecting it at him.

"Because I'm awesome."

"Cocky asshole." Guess he could hear that too.

Silence.

"Why'd you do it?" he asked after another few silent minutes. *"You knew I'd feel everything."*

"Sucks, huh."

"You broke our Soul Magic over thinking I enjoyed being raped. I know for a fact you enjoyed that fuckers—" His thoughts were cut off as we both coughed. The strain too much.

After the fit subsided, he resumed. *"You wanted his hands on you."*

"Wanted more."

"Clearly."

"Did you see him? He wasn't ugly." May as well lay it all on the table since that's what Donovan was thinking anyway.

"Not the point."

"You think I couldn't possibly want anyone else?"

"Hoping you wouldn't, yeah. Banking on a little loyalty."

Loyalty? From him? Loyalty was a birdcage he held the key to and then perched himself next to me inside so we could enjoy the bars of imprisonment together. *"I'm done with this conversation."*

"Just know that when you realize what you did, what could have happened if I hadn't stopped you, I'll still love you when you feel like a dirty whore."

"Hey!" I was on my elbows facing him now.

He did the same as dizziness and nausea rolled through us. "Once you're *you* again and think back on it, you'll feel filthy, and I'll still love you."

He let that simmer, turning on his side away from me, no longer engaging though he could probably still hear everything I was thinking.

When Evelyn returned and asked if we wanted a sedative to sleep through the worst of it, we both responded with a resounding "Yes".

21

SPHERE OF PROTECTION

Kim

"Let's do it." I stopped mid-stride in the lobby on track to go anywhere not filled with smallpox and tension between... well, everyone.

Hall's boot squeaked as he pivoted after my quick stop. The pause and then pop of his eyebrow told me his thoughts turned immediately dirty.

"Not that, perv. The Verja Blota." I was pretty sure my pronunciation of the ceremony name was off.

Hall didn't notice the passing crowd as he closed the two steps between us and peered down at me. If he was any taller, my neck would be screaming. As it was, everything else in me was shrieking for him to do what I wanted and solidify him as my Verndari.

"The break-up with Frog—"

"Meant nothing a second ago when you thought I was demanding to ride your dick."

A small break in his lips was a tiny smile that glinted in his eyes as he ran his fingers down a strand of my hair. "If I thought you were serious, it would have meant everything."

The bass of his voice tingled in my eardrums, down my throat, and all the way down to my ass cheeks.

"Are you saying no?" I managed after a reorienting swallow and a straightening of my shoulders.

He dipped his head. "If at all possible, I would never deny another request formed by those lips. The Verndari agreement is not something to be entered on a whim when your heart is raw and the potent strain of ill friends and the grating responsibility of a grieving Sect occupies your mind."

"Exactly. All of it is shifting and tenuous. I need something, I don't know...solid. Something I can put my faith in as I move forward with all of this." I motioned to the Prison Creation around me, but I think he knew I meant life in general. "I don't need you to run the Sect for me or to help me navigate how to be an effective leader. I'm capable of those things on my own."

"Yes, you are." Nothing in his tone said he was mocking me, and this fortified me to continue.

"Like I said, I don't need you to survive, but I may need you to thrive in the roles I've fought for and with some greater roles I hope to eventually gain. I wasn't born to power, and compared to many Magics here, I'm a Seedling. You've been at this a long time. You have skills and knowledge and brute passion, plus a streak of conman intelligence that works to my advantage if I'm not on the receiving end."

His gaze fell to the ground. I didn't mean to shame him, but it was true. He made a living deceiving others. He could be conning me now, but I trusted that those around us, including the Elders, wouldn't let it happen.

I leaned in to regain his eyeline. "This was your idea. Waiting won't change anything. The amount of safety I may need now and in different roles, and being anywhere close to Sophie and Donovan, is automatically a test of luck." He shot me a hint of a smile again. "And I wish they could be there, or at least for Sophie to be, but she's not herself right now. And if this illness ends them this time around, we could be waiting forever for them to resurface, if they ever do again.

"And I know this arrangement doesn't end when this war ends, and it means having you follow me through life. Totally fine. For you, it might be incredibly boring. Though, I do need some more details, so I know the boundaries of your Verndari role. I'm in this, and I want to do it now."

His ice-blue stare captured mine and refused to move. "I didn't know you crafted such grand plans already, but I knew a woman such as you was destined to do important things. I would be honoured to live and die as your Verndari."

"Well, loose plans. But I can see my ass warming an Elder chair one day if I live long enough to earn it."

He chuckled at this. "I can see it, too, and will do all I can to assist your path to the throne. Though, speaking to as many Elders as I have over the years, the seat is not a comfortable one."

An image of Aunt Lacey and of her fellow Elders rotting in Loring's disposal pile came to mind. "I know."

He nodded, knowing what I was thinking.

Before my thoughts went too dark, he touched my arm and signalled for us to sit on a bench lining the lobby where we've sat together plenty of times. We did and I settled in, sensing the weight of whatever he was about to say that would toss the dice of our relationship be it business or awkwardness.

"There's no out for me," he started. "Entering a Verndari pact is a contract signed with life. Literally and figuratively. It ends when my life does and no sooner. Be it in battle at your side or by your hand if you end my service."

"Wha—? I'm not murdering you."

"I activated an extended life many years ago. If you do as well, there's no telling how long we may walk this earth together. And one day, releasing me from my service may become a waking desire. The future is a mystery, though I'm sure some around here could read into the coming years and tell us the flavour of our connection."

"Okay, so you do this, and you're stuck with me. But not in a relationship, if we don't want it to be."

"Yes. A Verndari pact could be between a king and his soldiers. It's not indicative of a romantic nature, but of course it can be."

"Right. I know where you land on the romance angle."

The sly smile he sent me reinforced his intensions.

"But what if we couple up and it doesn't work? Can I be with someone else? Can you?"

"Yes. We can be with others. In my case, you would still be my number one priority. Again, like a soldier promised to their queen."

"Okay. So, other than seeing your face every day for forever, what's the true downside for me? This isn't a Soul Magic thing."

"No. It doesn't follow us unto another life."

"Okay. Unless you have a history of brutalizing women and children and puppies in your past, there's something you're not saying. Drop the shoe, already."

He leaned forward, elbows to knees, and rubbed his massive palms together. "A Verndari connection can sour. I've seen it happen. Say you reject me. Not for former egregious acts against puppies and other vulnerable creatures, which I have not, but you decide you no longer require or desire a Verndari. You will remain as yourself. I, however, will feel the rejection in my bones," he said this with his fingers bared in a claw and jabbing into his chest. "My mind will become consumed with the original mission of protecting you. I will obsess with this rejection and failure and may act to forcibly steer the Verndari pact back on track."

"The fact you said all that with such, I don't know, careful emphasis is a tad concerning. Lay it out. What does cancelling the Verndari pact look like?"

"Generally, since I can't foresee what I may do in such a situation, cancelling the arrangement may mean me taking obsessive protection measures which may include things like..." He paused. "Kidnapping, forcible confinement, or spelled solutions leaving you alive, yet incapacitated, as I would justify it was the only way to save you."

"You'd be trying to protect me from myself, in a freaky, stalker, kind of way. So, you would become the threat I needed protection from?"

He nodded without looking at me as if he didn't want to envision what lengths he would go to protect me.

"I'm okay with that."

His brows crimped down into a straight line. "If you're not going to take this seriously—"

"I am. Relax. In the scenario you painted, while, yeah, it doesn't exactly sound awesome, it means you would become my enemy. It doesn't mean me or someone else couldn't kill you. It would mean planning or recruiting someone else to protect me from you if I didn't have the power to do it myself. And in killing you, I wouldn't die or have any consequences besides losing you and whatever you meant to me at the time. Which by that point, your death would be a positive thing because we would've fallen out and you'd be dangerous. Am I right?"

"Yes. Though, I've been alive a long time. If I was easy to kill, I would have been buried many years ago."

"Super fair. Your amazing skills have kept you breathing, which is why you're more useful to me alive and at my side. And speaks more to the question of why you would want to do this when you have far more to lose?"

He sat back against the bench and laid an arm on top of it behind me. "I've lived many lives over and again. Taken on many roles and sought information and favour for countless people in power. If I meet my end protecting you, it'll be a more worthwhile cause than many I have chased in the past. I'll follow my intuition on this one. You're important and worth the sacrifice. At least in a Verndari role, I'll know where to find you."

"Literally?"

"Yes. One feature of a Verndari's role is a keen knowledge of your whereabouts. No connection to your feelings or other such Soul Magic type nonsense, but a magical locator so I can best protect my asset."

"I suppose that's fair since with my power, I can locate you as well."

He smiled and nodded. "As fair as it gets."

"Okay. It's settled. How long do you need to gather stuff for the ceremony?"

"Don't you worry." He stood from the bench, and I did the same. "Take an hour to ready yourself and I'll handle the rest of it including the witnesses. We can do the Verja Blota ceremony as we are, but I have a feeling you'll want to get fancy and include others if only for proof we went through with it."

He was right on both counts. You can't enter such a life-changing deal in knock-off Gucci jeans and a Roots pullover. And I wanted people like Vincent to attend. If this was something he wholly objected to, there would be a good reason. Besides, people were going to find out about Hall's Verndari role anyway. May as well let them see how it started and give everyone something to do.

Hall strode away with purposeful steps to somewhere. I could still back out, and the thought of him one day coming after me if I tried to end his service was a scary one, but I've faced scarier already. This was going to happen. And whatever the ceremony entailed, it was going to end with me gaining an ally in life against whoever may try and hurt me and my coven next. Others had their priorities. Sophie and Donovan had one another, but I would be Hall's, and if a centuries-old Viking couldn't protect me, nobody could.

Forty-five minutes later, I was finishing up the last braid in an awkward behind-my-head maneuver as Gwen tied the straps of her green velvet wraparound dress, around my waist.

I added a piece of string at the end of the braid since we didn't have many hair elastics floating around. The bit of fabric would hold for as long as...well, I didn't know how long the ceremony would be, but it couldn't be too long, right? Hall does his pledge, I accept him into my service, and we probably drink ale or take a shot of something. Or we would if this was in the real world.

Damn. I probably should have insisted on specifics.

The door to the shared bathroom opened and Serena entered. She stopped and gave me a once-over. "Holy hell, girl. I thought this wasn't a wedding."

"It's not." I checked myself out again in the wide bathroom mirror that ran across the full length of the wall.

I saw Gwen and Serena exchange a glance.

"Shut up. It's not. I just want to look the part. It's an important ceremony—"

"Where a drop-dead gorgeous rock wall of a man vows his life to you. Sure sounds like a wedding. Or at least a rom-com."

Gwen laughed. "That's what I said."

I rolled my eyes as I had when she said it herself. "He can still marry someone else if he wants to. As could I. Hallmark wouldn't pick that up."

Serena dropped a pair of cream-coloured flats in front of me. They landed with a slap on the marble floor and rested cock-eyed. "Sooo, you're not gonna get freaky with him?"

I fixed the flats with my toes and slipped them on as I shoved aside the question of who Serena pilfered them from. They were a tad big, but would do. "It's unrelated. Being together in a relationship has nothing to do with him being in my service."

"It can happen. There're no rules against being together," Gwen said, leaning against the bathroom counter. She and Serena stared at my reflection, trying to get me to admit the ceremony was a preamble to something more.

"Stop it. Both of you." I shoved my hair over my shoulders and tried not to let them see the tendrils at the nape of my neck sticking with sweat to my skin. "This arrangement is just an extra security measure. Which neither of you can argue won't be needed soon and often. He offered, and I can't very well become the most badass Magic around without moving a muscle of my own otherwise. I may be strong-willed, but he is a physical weapon way stronger than I could ever replicate with my bird bones."

Serena and Gwen exchanged that same glance again and then Serena lowered her voice. "I'm betting his weapon is rreeeaallll substantial."

Gwen burst into laughter, Serena following, their cackles echoing off of the bathroom walls as they left the room.

I ignored them and swept the last stray hair into place. Hopefully Hall didn't see the style as offensive or laughable since I was channelling a shield maiden style I pinched from a TV show, and he's seen them in real life in a time they were relevant and culturally meant so much more.

Too late to change things now. It would take twice as long to undo everything.

The door burst open, Serena and Gwen returning wide-eyed with tight smiles.

"What?"

Serena broke their excitement. "Umm, your little ceremony's attracted a big audience."

"Big-big," Gwen added. "Like, the lobby is standing room only big."

"What? It wasn't supposed to... Hall said—"

"It's fine, it's fine," Serena said, waving her hands. Would be nice if they could flutter away my anxiety. "We wanted to warn you before you tripped over the people trying to snag a front-row seat."

A flush of heat hit my chest at the thought.

"Don't worry," Gwen said and rubbed my shoulder. "You look amazing. I've got a good feeling about it."

Gwen didn't say if the feeling was a part of her prophetess powers, a gut instinct, or her trying to ensure I didn't faint and dirty up her dress.

They left again with a couple of words of encouragement I didn't really hear, and I tugged at the dress and fussed with my hair in the mirror once more. Whatever brought me to this life, I didn't hate it, but I never would have guessed. I took a deep breath, rolled my shoulders, and reminded myself I was once an inexperienced Kitchen Witch, and aside from worry regarding the danger and loss we've faced, that Kitchen Witch would be so proud of where I was now.

Before I bailed on the whole thing, I grabbed the bathroom door handle, opened it wide, and walked through to the sight of the white marble lobby obscured by hundreds of people who one by one noticed me and were now staring.

Gwen and Serena disappeared into the sea of bodies. Oh wait, there they were. As some of those bodies moved aside to let me through, I could see them standing with the others.

Oh, damn.

In front of me was a large circle of...wait, were those knives? They were. Big, small, plain, and curved knives of all sorts. And guns. And a tactical baton I remembered seeing Team members carry. Weapons of all kinds made up the circle people stood at least ten feet from. Thankfully, those inside of the Prison Creation were generally trustworthy, but we had been burned by people lately. Traitors could easily hide amongst the others.

Ahh, Tactical Team members were dispersed in equal distances in the first row of people to ensure no one went for a weapon on the floor. They were strapped with their own weapons when they usually logged them back in when inside the Prison Creation and not on mission.

The illusion of trust was safer. I glanced at each of them. They extended a discreet nod when I did.

I wished Sophie and Donovan were amongst the onlookers. They should be. They were present for everything so far, but I couldn't wait for them to heal or die and potentially not recycle. None of these people had to be here, though I guess not much else was going on for them in the day-to-day hamster wheel of hiding from the enemy.

"Kim Wheeler..."

Vincent's voice rose among the hushed murmurs in the crowded lobby, and I found the Mother Coven Elder standing on the far side of the circle. Hall was next to him, but he was on one knee, a bare, thick forearm braced on that knee, yet his other arm was straight, his hand in a fist pressed into the floor. His head was bowed so he couldn't see me. His hair was loose from its normal tied-back style, two front pieces twisted and tied or maybe braided in the back.

I wanted him to look up. Was he as nervous as I was? It was his idea, but he hadn't expected it so soon. Plus, he could have changed his mind. If he ran away from me in front of all of these people, I might implode.

Behind Hall sat Veata and Ranlyn in chairs far too average when compared to the Elder thrones Aunt Lacey and the previous Elders sat upon. Nothing about Vincent's face warned me to run. He wasn't smiling either, though. He wore a serious expression. One a ceremony like this called for. The other Elders wore the same unreadable expressions, nothing jumping out in warning.

"Please enter the circle," Vincent continued.

Tension hung in the room, crawling beneath my skin.

Ignore them. This wasn't about them.

I lifted my hem and stepped over a couple of scary-looking guns. Vincent wasn't specific, and the circle was large, so I settled to stand in the middle with my shoulders steady and my hands at my sides as I resisted the urge to clasp them in front of me or cross them under the weight of everyone's attention.

Vincent took a few steps away from Hall and sat with the other Elders, his attention slipping behind him to Cora-Lynn. She stood on the edge of the group, her assessing glare shifting from Vincent to me and Hall who was still kneeling with his head bowed.

I couldn't imagine what Cora-Lynn thought of all of this. Probably not too much different than the rest of the Magics in the place, all waiting for whatever came next.

Hall spoke, his grave voice deep and resonating in a language I didn't know until suddenly his words translated into heavily accented English in my mind. "I, Halsten Amund Holgata, pledge my present and future in its entirety, to the protection of the one, Kim Wheeler, without coercion and with unbridled pride and humble gratitude. I vow to elevate her life to the greatest of importance above all others including my own, any family who may remain, and of those of my coven."

Given the not-so-subtle reactions of the onlookers, everyone else could also hear Hall's telepathic translations and were caught off guard by the promises he was making.

Hall continued. "I enter into my role as a Verndari with full understanding and relinquishment of my life into another's hands. A position of trust that ensures I will be treated with equal respect, led thoughtfully and with caution onto battlefields against grand armies or into backroom discussions in search of purpose.

"This is my pledge, my life to submit, my courage to provide all that is needed, and my devotion to your safety of body and of mind. Do you accept what I have to offer?"

Silence hung as everyone waited for an answer, Hall remaining bowed.

"I accept," I said so he wouldn't interpret my nervousness as reluctance.

A slight tension released in Hall's shoulders. Did he think I would reject him? Could he be regretting my answer? No, he wanted this. Regardless, we were in this together now.

Hall unfolded from his stooped position, standing in full, and raising his eyes to mine. His lips gapped a little when he saw me standing in the circle. His shining blue eyes saw me for the first time looking as Viking-like as I could in my borrowed dress and flats. His assessment wasn't overt, nothing creepy, but it stuttered something in his brain he then fought to realign to the seriousness of the ceremony.

Hall approached the weapons circle, reached down and picked up a knife with a leather handle, and then he slipped it into some kind of leather holster. It hung horizontally from his belt by two leather straps, and the deep brown material was branded or embroidered with some kind of a symbol. I would think it was a snowflake, except it was more like a spoked wheel without the circle around it.

Once the knife was in place, Hall stood soldier straight. "May I enter and let my sacrifice complete the Verja Blota?"

This part he spoke in English, but his voice remained so deep it resonated in my bones.

"Enter." He never prepped me on what I was supposed to say. Everything out of his mouth dripped with a heavy understanding of what would happen during the ceremony and afterwards. I was a bumbling idiot by comparison.

Hall took a breath in. Not a huge one and nothing that spoke of regret, but he was braced for something.

He stepped into the circle through the space that was left from him removing the knife. The moment his second foot landed inside the circle, Hall grunted, arched his neck in some kind of pain, his hands in white-knuckled fists. He swayed a step, but caught himself and straightened.

"Oh shiiit..." It was Adam. He stood off to the side with others in the Ballard Sect and some of my own. His reaction, as well as Olive's which included a hand to her chest, was off-putting.

Why would they act like that?

No, why would Soul Seers act like that?

Wait. He didn't.

Hall was suddenly in front of me and I searched his ice-blue eyes. "Your immortality? You sacrificed your immortality?"

His breaths were a bit punchy from the transformation, but it was clear he had no intention on commenting on his soul's new status. Instead, he inhaled with control and said, "Kim Wheeler, from this moment forward, my life is your life," and then put a hand to his chest and dipped his head.

The crowd around us erupted in applause.

"Kiss!" Blake yelled.

Jared backhanded his buddy in the arm as Denise jumped to remind him it wasn't a wedding. He rolled his eyes and argued that it looked like one to him.

The others talked amongst themselves about the things they saw and what they thought, some pointing to the weapons as Ismail answered a question and kept an eye on them to ensure they didn't do more with their curiosity.

"Here." Hall reached into the pocket of a pair of brown linen pants I had never seen him wear. They were the same material as the natural-coloured tunic he wore and folded the sleeves to his elbows. He held out a length of braided leather. In the center was some kind of metal symbol, an arch, but the ends were curled and crossed at its ankles.

He took my hand in his and started tying the leather around my wrist. "On my scabbard is the Helm of Awe symbol. One which creates a sphere of protection. Though, in our case, I am the sphere of protection around you. This—" He flipped my hand around to showcase the metal symbol on my bracelet— "is a Troll Cross."

"Troll Cross?"

"Not because you are one. As I assure you, no one would gaze upon you and label you anything resembling a troll."

My cheeks heated as his eyes moved over me in way that somehow didn't feel invasive.

"A Troll Cross is protection of its own, from dark magic. I will always be seen with the symbol of my new station as your Verndari. And you can wear your Troll Cross however you please. 'Round your wrist, your neck, or in your...lovely hair."

I couldn't help but smile. Guess the updo didn't offend him.

Then I remembered. "You gave up your immortality. You failed to mention it was a part of the arrangement."

He let go of my hand and stuck his thumbs in his belt. "I didn't give anything up. It was payment for a worthwhile adventure."

Adventure? Great. I knew he was putting his life on the line for me, but now it wasn't his life, it was life beyond this life. He may have lived many lives of his own already, but now I was responsible for getting him through this one and into the next.

No pressure.

22

WINDFALL

Vincent

Evelyn assured me Sophie and Donovan were sedated and would sleep for hours. With Sophie's thoughts an angry stream in her ill-rankled brain, whatever the two spoke of was nothing more than insults and shifting blame.

The day was full of stimulus and questions, risking Cora-Lynn retreating into her cell without comprehension of what she experienced during Hall and Kim's Verja Blota. She surprised me by occupying a cafeteria table for longer than previous. We sat among others discussing the ceremony and current goings on, plus the training spaces were in constant use.

Cora-Lynn and Kim were deep in discussion regarding modern gender roles and how Kim and Hall's arrangement challenged these in some ways. And while Kim explained the ever-persistent gender wage gap and a continued baseline of vulnerability of the Blind, Cora-Lynn seemed genuinely interested when it came to further explanations of how Magics tend to challenge such stereotypes.

Whether it was an attempt to acclimate or to discover weaknesses in others, I could not guess, and assumed the pace with which she pushed herself would inevitably stall.

Until then, I savoured observing her. She nodded while Kim answered and Hall adding his own brand of opinions. She ate fries without ketchup because she questioned the improbable colour, and sipped tea with honey since it was familiar from her time. I enjoyed the fact that after four hundred years I was able to have such a cerebral conversation with the woman I thought dead.

Liam started towards me. Whatever he had to say, it was not good.

"What is it?" I asked as he approached.

"Sir, you have an important call at the security desk."

I turned to Cora-Lynn. "Would you prefer to remain, return to your room, or join me?"

Cora-Lynn glanced at Kim. "I will stay."

Kim smiled and I gave Hall a guarded stare to communicate he may need to step in if something happened, receiving a slight head dip in understanding.

"Who is it?" I asked Edson who stood behind the security desk.

"Issát." Further explanation was not forthcoming.

I picked up the phone. "How did you acquire this number?"

"I would like to meet," said Evaristus's son and Sophie's oldest living relative.

I was struck silent for longer than a fleeting pause. "With you and Loring?"

"Only myself."

Nothing in the background revealed his location. "For what purpose?"

"To construct a plan to defeat our enemies."

"I was not under the impression our enemies were one in the same."

"You wouldn't have had the opportunity to believe differently until now. However, I assure you my presence with Loring pertains to personal motives and not lifestyle. Choose a meeting place, bring all Magics you require. I will arrive alone. This is not an ambush and I more than expect you to hold no trust for my word."

"You are right to assume I do not trust you."

"That will change." Issát spoke confidently. "When you have confided in your Team, contact me with details."

It did me no good for Issát to believe I required the Team's direction. "Meet at Jimmy's Reel Breakfast ten-thirty tomorrow morning. Are you familiar?"

"I will acquaint myself." Issát ended the call.

I offered Edson half-hearted gratitude and peeked in on Sophie and Donovan. According to Evelyn, once the pustules scabbed, they drew closer to the end of the illness. The hope was for maintained health to avoid complications.

I returned to my seat next to Cora-Lynn in the cafeteria.

"Upsetting news?" she asked, my silence causing her discomfort.

Her interest in the goings on of my role and her accurate measurement of my emotional state was so surprising I hesitated to reply. The drop of her concentration onto her empty plate was my cue to answer or she would never ask me another question again.

"Not upsetting, in particular. More so...unexpected."

Cora-Lynn nodded, having reached the extent of her questions.

"You win the lottery?" Hall joked.

The Team sat at the table next to us. Did they choose these seats to watch over Cora-Lynn?

"No typical windfall. We are meeting Issát over breakfast tomorrow."

This quieted the tables.

Gregor pushed away his plate of waffles. "I'm assuming the word 'trap' has sprung to mind."

"It has."

"But you don't believe it is." Arden guessed correctly.

"Did he say what he wanted?" Kim asked.

I sipped my cold tea and refrained from using a heat spell as not to bother Cora-Lynn. "To construct a plan to defeat our mutual enemies. Namely Loring."

"Huh." Hall leaned back in his chair, arms crossed.

"Precisely." The whole thing bloomed concern, however, no one attempted to talk me out of going or refused to participate.

Once Cora-Lynn decided she had enough of socializing, I walked with her to the cell console.

"Your decisions could kill them," Cora-Lynn said.

It took a moment to realize she was referring to the Tactical Team and the meet with Issát. "Yes, it could. And has. We used to have more members."

"And their deaths are acceptable?"

"Absolutely not. Death of a Team member rests solely on me, and I am not left without the scars of the choices I should have made. Even with you." Cora-Lynn squirmed at this. "Your incarceration was my fault and I will live in shame every hour of my extended existence, but it will not return you to your old life."

"Nothing can do that."

"I know." I wished it were not the case for her sake.

Cora-Lynn approached the cell console and punched in the information. A touch slow yet independent. She disappeared into a cell without further comment.

Maybe one day we could speak with less formality or contempt.

"You need another man?" Caine approached. He must have been close by in the cafeteria and overheard the Team talking.

Since Jessabelle's death and Lincoln's incarceration, as well as Donovan's illness and Sophie's suspension, the Team was low on specialized reinforcements.

"Are you seeking a permanent position? If so, you are welcome to one." A Magic with his skills was always useful.

"For now, I'll lend a hand when you need one."

"Commitment issues?"

"Nah. Just not so certain I want a career of it."

Ness and her brother were gone. Maybe he would soon follow.

Or maybe he no longer felt the pull of Sophie's orbit. If he truly planned to leave, Sophie would have an opinion about it and would ensure Caine heard every word even if it meant tracking him down.

Caine held up the SUV keys. "Thanks."

"Did you accomplish all you sought to?"

"Guess so. Though, I do have legal questions for you. Not criminal."

"If I fall short of accurate information I will garner the proper resource."

Caine explained his cousin's situation. And while the particulars were straightforward, he seemed to be safeguarding something. Perhaps it pertained to Ness.

He thanked me for my legal expertise and left with a promise to meet in the morning. While having Caine on the Team would prove invaluable, having him become another disillusioned or heartsick member created a breeding ground for dissension and potential sedition. He was one Magic I did not relish removing from the playing field or have standing opposite me.

23

TRUTH AT A GUT LEVEL

Vincent

Gregor blended into traffic en route to the meeting with Issát. His patient travels allowed too many aspects of concern to spiral and fester in my mind.

The countless steps paced from cell wall to cell wall, checking on my pox-covered and sedated Charges, plus fielding incessant issues Edson found dire, brought no sense of ease.

Was this meeting another fumbled decision in a host of wayward choices? Could Veata's claim of my Sovereignty rule be true? And were connections with Magics such as Issát a precursor to the future she spoke of?

After a perimeter search and boundary spell, we entered Jimmy's Reel Breakfast, a local diner I frequented when I could escape for a meal. A server racing from table to table informed us of a ten-minute wait. This time lessened when Hall and Caine claimed to be a separate party and sat at opposite ends of the breakfast bar.

Bronya and Arden occupied a table for two on the opposite side of the diner to cover our flank with a view of an exterior access point.

This left the Elders to sit together at a middle window seat in wait of Issát's arrival. The building was equipped with large windows on three sides for optimal surveillance and gave Ismail and Gregor a view while they worked undercover in case Issát arrived with devotees in tow.

An oblivious blonde took our drink orders and distributed laminated menus I knew by heart. This particular waitress's mind was consumed with a recent vacation alongside extended family. She found it impossible not to miss white-sand beaches and worried about a potential fungus now chafing her right heel.

Clearly not a Tainted affiliate plant.

A television played the original *Rocky* movie. The viewing was not uncommon for the diner covered in entertainment paraphernalia from posters to a cardboard cutout of Chewie from Star Wars manning the corner behind Hall.

Inside the condiment holder were movie trivia cards and survival tips for feisty morning conversation. Ranlyn and Veata were not good trivia company. Nor was Cora-Lynn, though the pop culture references may be educational. Sophie, however, would prove worthy.

Without Sophie's presence, our best guess was the other patrons were Blind. Any other of the Soul Seers would have sufficed, yet I would have given almost anything to see Sophie ordering enough food for three while arguing with Donovan. To think of them in their current state was a distraction I cast aside for mission focus.

Ahead of leaving the Prison Creation, I provided the Team few instructions. Unless Issát forged a full-out attack or if this was indeed a trap, the Team was to observe and nothing more. Angering a Magic older than any others in this space, including Veata, was unwise.

My cell phone chimed and vibrated in my pocket. The number displayed 'Unknown'.

"I've just arrived," Issát announced when I answered. "I wanted to ensure you knew I didn't show up early to survey the location."

He could have easily come at any hour. I refrained from arguing this. "We are saving you a seat."

Issát ended the call when he stepped through the door and pocketed his phone. With his hands discreetly opened, the ancient approached and sat in the booth next to Veata, facing me. At no point did he scour the establishment for other Magics. I knew this would be no hindrance for Issát identifying customers with extra gifts since the Mother Coven does not practice soul glow concealing procedures.

Our waitress served us tea and coffees, her blonde ponytail reminding me of Cora-Lynn many years ago. The faded *Teenage Mutant Ninja Turtle Movie* t-shirt collapsed the illusion.

"Can I get you something to drink?" she asked Issát.

"Herbal tea."

"What kind would you like?" She listed options while Issát sat patiently, her eyes closed in thought as she dabbed her pen on her notepad, her words increasing in pace.

When she finished, a little breathless, he asked, "What would you recommend?"

A rosy blush sprung to the young woman's cheeks.

No need to read her mind to know her thoughts of the man in front of her.

"I'll bring you something," she decided. Her shaky disposition flustered her further when she went to leave and then remembered Issát was but one customer at the table.

"Is everyone else ready to order?" she asked then returned to Issát. "Do you need a sec to look over the menu?"

Veata wasn't about to wait. "I'll have Hans Solo's Bootstraps, over easy on the eggs, with a Princess Leia cinnamon bun."

All the menu items were equally quirky.

Ranlyn ordered the Free Willy flapjacks with a side of Braveheart bacon. I asked for my standard order, the Back to the Future omelette without peppers and a side of Footloose home fries. Without perusing the menu, Issát requested the same.

The *Rocky* credits bored the owner sitting at the breakfast bar and he switched the television to *Indiana Jones: Raiders of the Lost Ark*. A peripheral glance showed Hall watching the movie, crunching on rye toast, causally sweeping the room for security concerns. Presumably Caine was doing the same, however, to confirm this I would have to turn to check.

The blonde returned too quickly to her favorite customer with his herbal tea and then let the rest of us know our order would be ready soon.

Issát sipped from a *The X-Files* themed mug. "Apparently, I look like a cranberry-apple kind of man."

I failed to disguise my smile. Winter tended to involve a lot of stereotypical spiced drinks and foods cultivated over years of altered religious perceptions. If only she knew none of us were standard holiday celebrants.

"Do we guess why you've called this meeting or are you going to broach the subject?" Ranlyn said with intended brashness.

Sometimes his impulsiveness was something to wonder at. One would think hooking the son of Evaristus the Puppeteer into a battle of wits while pinned inside of a diner booth would be enough to exercise caution.

Instead of answering Ranlyn, Issát focused on me with a raised brow that took all of my willpower not to reciprocate. "Am I correct in assuming my kin is not present?"

Momentary confusion passed until I realized Issát spoke of Sophie. "Are you aware of her condition?"

"I am," Issát confirmed, meaning he had contact with Jordan after Jordan escaped the Prison Creation. "My assumption was the Mother Coven fostered skilled healers."

"We do," Ranlyn said with a defensive edge. "You're old enough to know not all Magic-born illnesses can be healed in the same manner."

Issát's attentions remained on me. "Is Sophie in danger of demise?"

His genuine concern surprised me.

"On the mend," I assured, praying to every deity I was correct.

Issát's shoulders visibly relaxed, further masking his relief by sipping his tea.

"What can we help you with?" I asked in earnest.

Veata giggled.

I ignored her.

"My hope was for our mutual benefit." Issát placed his cup down.

Our waitress arrived, served us the balanced plates on her forearms, and then raced back for a few smaller plates of toast.

I added hot sauce to my omelette. "Benefit to what cause?"

Issát shook hot sauce onto his own omelette and then did the same with a pepper shaker. "With my father dead I can roam freely, have influence in the world around me without hiding behind a shill in hopes to surpass my father's recognition." He popped a fork full of egg into his mouth, and then said, "One cannot travel without learning of the pinnacle influence of this particular region. Alasdair Llewellyn and his heirs, one son ready to head the company for the next millennium, the other risking everything to cripple the same company. You didn't seek change, smart enough to understand the futility when your father's rule was unshakable. You sought a team of Magics who would deal with problems on a case-by-case basis, cultivating contacts, seeking weaknesses, and waiting for opportune moments to gain footholds. Some enough to cause kinks in the Sovereignty process while saving some in desperate need."

I waited patiently, dipping the corner of my whole wheat toast into a splotch of ketchup that reminded me of Cora-Lynn's distaste for the condiment.

"Do you think the work you have put into this plan has paid off?"

The question stopped me short. I would have preferred to respond with a resounding "yes" but feared my expression would falter.

Issát went on without an answer. "From what information I have acquired, until most recently, I would have said your efforts brought failure and not much else." Veata giggled with her mouth full. "Like my own, your father is dead. How do you wish to proceed with the company you so dreaded and have now inherited?"

I swallowed and wiped my mouth with a napkin. "I assure you, the company is not mine by any legal sense."

"And if I were to argue?"

"Arguments cannot change the name on my father's will."

"There's no need for change. I assure you his instructions in death outlined all details surrounding his funeral arrangements, which will commence in the next week, the dispersal of funds to those who bear importance, and the handoff to his assigned designee. The name is your own."

Locking with the dark eyes of the stranger, I detected truth at a gut level. "You have come bearing proof."

Issát placed down his fork and reached into the breast pocket of his black wool coat, pulled out a thick envelope, and slid it across the table.

I removed the papers and skimmed its contents.

"How did you obtain a copy of my father's will?"

"You're working with the Sovereignty," Ranlyn accused.

Issát bit off a piece of bacon. "Not officially, however, I wish to."

"Change is coming," Veata said in a sing-song tone and cut her breakfast sausage.

I scanned the pages. I was unsurprised to see Chase's name as beneficiary. A list of our father's properties in Germany, South Africa, and the Poconos were earmarked for my brother. Plus a luxury yacht, an antique pool table, and one-hundred or so other magical possessions and properties collected over my father's lifetime including a sizeable trust.

When I saw my name claiming heir to the Sovereignty in its entirety my heart nearly stuttered. A singular item with endless implications. My father was vocal about wanting me to one day lead the company. I wholeheartedly assumed the tactic was another manipulative ploy.

"The company became yours the day you dispatched of your father." Issát broke through my bafflement.

"I do not want this." I stared at my name in one of the most impossible places.

"You don't want to be your father," Veata chimed in. "Not the same."

"You—"

"Understand you better than you think," she insisted. "I already informed you of impeding change. No..." she paused, "change is here."

"Heading a company with the type of practises—"

"Troops follow their leader's directives," Issát said. "The ones seated around this establishment do nothing without your command."

"And you assume if I accept the role, they will follow? Relinquish centuries of my father's rule and opt for a leader my father hunted?"

Issát nodded.

I almost laughed. "Unfeasible."

"Three-quarters of your father's employees are run-of-the-mill pencil pushers. Some may revolt, opening coveted positions to those who will follow without fear of a life sentence accompanying your orientation package. You forget you have established your name in the Magic community."

"And you, Issát, what are your expectations?"

He sipped his tea. "My vision is to better emulate other regions where Magics have a say in their law. A say in how they work and live and punish those who bring harm to Magics when considering the Blind alongside them. An idealistic view of democratic resolution at this stage not unreasonable given the archetypes you live by. However, it will require work to first dismantle your father's legacy."

"I doubt you know much of how I live my life."

"You would be wrong. Nonetheless, you have the namesake, the allies, a suitable moral compass, and the gumption. Your newest Prison Creation can still be utilized."

"What do you know of it?"

"Only what our mutual contacts have informed me of."

"Jordan?"

"No." Issát popped a home fry into his mouth. "Although, that man is a talker."

"One who bragged about killing those in the safe house, no doubt?" Ranlyn assumed.

Issát nodded. "Incapacitated them with a fast-acting spell so Loring could set them ablaze unchallenged. Then he avoided the Berisford inside your ranks, knowing he could never hide the truth."

"And this contact you mentioned?" I redirected.

Issát inhaled, considering. "John has great confidence in your ability to drastically alter all your father has drilled into the minds of his employees."

"John?"

"Yes. John Weaver. He, too, sees use for your Prison Creation. Safe house potential, overflow of current Sovereignty cells, long-term holding for truly heinous criminals, anything other than an excuse to refuse the mantel where you are so desperately needed."

Of all of my old friends in a continual capacity to funnel information from inside the Sovereignty, John knew of Issát? Did he know of Issát's relation to Sophie? Or to Evaristus?

"By your word, you called this meeting to recruit me into greater political standing. Having a leader of our law also a Mother Coven Elder is of great conflict, no?"

"Stop being so obtuse, Vincent." Veata's features scrunched with distaste. "The fact the leaders of a governing coven have no presence in their own courtrooms is ludicrous and you know it."

Thing was, I have made the same argument. Why was I fighting my own principles?

"You have chosen your side then?" I questioned Veata. She was still comfortable next to our questionable ally.

"Damn right I have, boy. Step up or step aside. You can't expect to fool our Coveners into believing you can do better than what the

Sovereignty already has. Besides their underhanded practices, your father kept this region in harmony for years. Leave the practices that turn your stomach, alter the ones riding too closely to criminal themselves, and implement innovative decisions where needed. The Tactical Team can lead itself. Hire someone to head the company's day-to-day operations if you can't stomach the title. Decide now before the Sovereignty board topples the whole matchstick house fighting over the golden gavel your father fumbled on the way out."

Veata held no reservations in front of Issát. Was she so confident in his intentions or simply uninterested in hiding her opinion? No, Veata was never a danger to the Mother Coven. Even after Evaristus turned her into a puppet, she faced her Elders, accepted their mode of challenging her faithfulness, and continued on.

"Think it over," Issát encouraged, breaking my thoughts as my would-be enemy bit into his jam-slathered toast.

"What role do you play? A meet of this nature is not instigated without motive."

"This is my role," he said, motioning with his fork to the table in front of him. "Lobbying for you to shoulder yours. I do hope to work with you for our people. With Loring pummelling your defences, scattering the flock, and targeting the Blind, I have no doubt he'll aim for the secular minds of contacts he's built under your father's thumb. He sees the law is without a leader. You think he won't move on the opportunity?"

"Are you saying that is his plan?"

"Part of." Issát wiped his mouth and took another sip of his tea.

"And the rest?"

"Will you consider this conversation with grave sincerity? I am sincere when I say the Sovereignty and all it serves needs you. Speak to John, to your other contacts, to your flock, to Sophie and her family. Ask what they want for the future of the Sovereignty. I guarantee they would see your hand at the helm a positive."

"Same," Veata added.

"And I," Ranlyn concurred.

Surprised, I turned to Ranlyn. "Truly?"

Ranlyn shrugged. "He makes a good argument. If those documents are real, then you've been given the key to the city. A working city that's better utilized than destroyed or in the hands of your father's cohorts and whomever he led on that board. Why build from scratch if you don't have to?"

I was flabbergasted. Not by Ranlyn harboring this opinion, but by him openly voicing such in front of Issát.

"What of Loring's other plans?" Ranlyn asked while I absorbed the magnitude of the absurdity of myself leading the Sovereignty.

"To further his agenda while erroneously thinking he directs mine. With a Soul Seer under his thumb, he is under the impression I capture more Blind every day and corrupt them by releasing their powers. I have given him no reason to question the victim count I report. In truth, those taken during the attack on Niagara Falls are the only individuals who had lost their ignorance of Magics.

"In the broader sense, Loring wishes to claim himself as Master over all of the Blind after I release and Taint their souls in a forced exodus or to rid the world of them. Plus, exact revenge on those who oppose him."

"Is that all?" Ranlyn asked.

Issát looked across the table at him. "Does it have to be more complicated? Loring is an ambitious man with simple desires. The need to be heard, feared, adored, accepted even by those he hates. Envisioning him more dimensional may give you layers of reason to hate him, but all he does boils down to his ego being damaged worse than his body. He wants those enemies who have made him appear feeble to pay with their lives."

"Like Sophie."

He nodded. "He uses the death of my father and his Master to pad his speech to those below him. His true motivations are simply ruling by revenge."

I had to admit it was inline with Loring's behaviour. Another child in a man's body.

Issát went on. "While I've been hiding from my father, a man that makes yours look infantile," he directed at me, "I have been around the world many times over and have seen more than my memory can retain. The heinousness of the Sovereignty has reached far corners I dwelled in to survive my father's mission to slaughter his entire bloodline. With him dead, I have very few blood kin left."

"Your true goal is establishing a relationship with Sophie and the Ballard Coven." Connecting the dots should have come sooner.

He nodded. "In a world where we more often than not watch our family and friends waste away in old age, my hope is to know Sophie and her Soul Seer family descended from my mother's own blood and earn a place within it."

In her current condition, in illness and a victim of her broken Soul Magic, I could not speak to if Sophie would invite this connection. The Sophie before the damage may have sought me for counsel and opinion. Now her actions were unpredictable.

"You want me to command the Sovereignty and meld you into the fold. You want to help us kill Loring and disperse his devotees. And you want to merge into Sophie and the Ballard Coven's lives. Does that cover the main particulars of your agenda?"

"Yes."

I leaned forward. "If you know anything about Sophie, then you know of my role when it comes to her and her lives."

"And Donovan's. Which includes the Sorrels," Issát added.

More leaked information from Jordan? Or maybe Lincoln? Or circulating rumors since I found her in this life unconscious on Ranlyn's living room floor.

"Then you know the last thing I would do is put her in danger, from family included."

"Your Overseer status is not common knowledge, but I thought it possible considering you find her through her Soul Magic in every life she lives. This is also why I approached you. Your connection to the Sovereignty notwithstanding, I always intended to gain your trust, knowing without it I would never yield hers."

"And you expect this result based on this meeting?"

Issát flashed a smile. "For now, I will do all I can to prove my sincere intentions are without a nefarious agenda. I'm sure you could have her ex-lover test me. If his persuasion matches others of his bloodline, and I hear it does, he is more than capable."

"In way of an olive branch of sincerity," Issát continued, "I offer the location of the Blind Loring insisted I Taint during the Niagara Falls attack."

I leaned back against the booth. "An interesting concept for someone hoping to keep the world unTainted."

"A calculated modification I knew I could reverse. As I said, Loring thinks I have Tainted more. I have not. The people's power will remain released. They can never return to the life of the blissfully Blind, however, many would argue becoming a Magic is preferable to the permanency of death."

Some would argue this if it meant losing all they held dear to them.

"I will bring you to the location," Issát informed us. "And I will release the prisoners into your protective custody. Without control over their powers they would cause further chaos no Magics would relish dealing with. If I procure enough of your trust, and theirs, I am more than willing to mentor them myself."

How nice of him to drop the responsibility on the Mother Coven to become their shepherds and warden.

Ranlyn chewed on a piece of bacon. "What's to say it's not a trap?"

"I never claimed it was unmanned. The place isn't guarded well enough against me, and certainly not you or your team. When your meal is done, we can head there."

"Now?" Ranlyn asked with as much disbelief as I felt.

Issát nodded. "Until three o'clock, Loring utilizes more yet lesser-skilled Magics to secure the location. We could wait until later when fewer guards are present, however, we will meet greater resistance."

"If you meant to overtake us, getting the Elders and their security team together in a singular location of your choosing would be a perfect strategy. Play into our impulses after giving us the news of my inheriting the Sovereignty and pad the deal with the presence of innocents while in the light of day and with limited resources among us."

Issát took a bite of a home fry. "Yes, a perfect plan had I intended to deceive you. I don't. The nine Magics here, plus myself are enough to complete the job."

"If you betray us I have enough cause to arrest you, especially without my father's interference, for the unprovoked treatment of each Blind you forced to see this world."

"I considered my potential arrest when I contacted you and still believed it worth the risk. Your intuition should be enough to believe or condemn me. I won't betray you and my intentions do not include odious means. Even if I were to lead you astray, you have enough Magics to escape alive."

Trusting my intuition has landed me in hot water in the past. Unless Veata is also a part of some seedy plan, her instincts are telling her to trust Issát. If she sensed Issát's lies, she would have nailed him to the table, and she was content to finish her meal in peace.

Issát leaned forward, reached for his pocket, and placed a cell phone on the table between us. "Bind me until I have to clean those souls, use confusion spells...whatever you see fit to ease your suspicion. My single request is you bring me to Sophie."

Ranlyn made a throaty noise. "We still don't know why you went to Loring in the first place. You could've killed Loring yourself by now."

"Once I resurfaced after my father's death, Sophie, her family, and the connection to myself came to light, however, not until after I infiltrated Loring's people. Once inside, I learned who was involved in his Diluculo Creation entrapment and of his demise. John knew Sophie was a newer addition to the Mother Coven, but not the genetic connection to me.

"The destruction of a Creation and the death of an ancient is unheard of and to learn my mother's lineage was, in part, responsible for it was...frankly heartwarming. Sophie and the Ballards were already in the womb of your Prison Creation, so I remained where I could orchestrate our paths to cross while gaining intelligence."

"At the shoulder of her enemy?" Ranlyn asked.

"Precisely so, yes. I could think of no greater position to ensure I encountered Sophie. Especially once Loring mentioned how his efforts to gain a Soul Seer within his ranks had previously failed. Soul Seers are uncommon. It took some time to connect the bloodline to my own and how it enmeshed itself in this region. No talk of Soul Seers has been mentioned in decades."

With Olive institutionalized for thirty years most would have assumed the bloodline had died off.

Again, nothing about Issát's answers rang disingenuous alarm bells. The plausibility of events unfolding as such was not impossible.

Issát placed his silverware down. "If Sophie was surrounded by Magics who did not truly care for her, I would worry. My sources assure me she is loved by those stationed in this restaurant and protected inside of the Prison Creation. I trust your overseership. Jordan claims to have hoped Donovan would be the only one infected." He shook his head. "True idiocy. Whatever occurred between himself and Sophie, it left its mark, and the man still envisions a future with Sophie at his side."

"His side? Truly?"

"Again...idiocy. Sophie has an uncanny history of dying young. I want to know her in case this Soul Magic of hers and Donovan's upholds their routine and they perish under Jordan's impetuous assault. I may still be alive when their souls return. To my understanding, she wouldn't be my family. Not quite. So, please, finish your meals in thought. You know perfectly well you can hide your Prison Creation access from me. I'm not interested in it. I'm interested in her and her family, and they all happen to be within."

Eating and thinking commenced for the remainder of the meeting.

By the time the cheque arrived, my mind was set. What the Team did was up to me. If Ranlyn and Veata wanted to tag along that was their prerogative. As with the Team, the Prison Creation was also mine. I did not possess the ability to detect deception by any quantifiable margin, but my intuition was telling me to trust Issát.

A smaller part of me screamed of how this one mission could unravel all I worked for.

Caine could verify Issát's claims, however, leaning on his ability was a crutch I could not afford. Having him on mission in case I changed my mind was a back-pocket card to play if something went sideways. One I would use if the moment called for a Berisford's touch.

What Veata said stayed with me. Change was here. If Issát was evidence of such change, did it mean this partnership was a positive development?

24

HEAVY LIFTING

Caine

Razor thin trust brought us to a motel in Chippawa. One off a service road set away from Niagara Falls tourist traps where Sophie's ancestor, Issát, claimed it was abandoned. Judging by the layers of colourful graffiti and general lack of upkeep, no one gave a shit about the place.

"Loring chose this location from a few I researched when he planned for me to Taint the Blind, with hopes for more individuals in the coming days. The guards know nothing of my lies to Loring about the numbers of Blind within this location. They are kept isolated from the rest of the flock including the next shift of greater-skilled security to reduce collusion, so I risked no chance of my overcalculation of newly Tainted being discovered." Issát also explained transporting frantic newly Tainted was a hassle Loring left to his underlings. No one appreciated the babysitting duties.

We parked down the street from the motel and sat in the spell-covered vehicle while The Elders and Issát hashed out details in a private little conversation bubble. The whole Tactical Team waited for orders. Shiny tools anticipating a command, a target, to chase and to retrieve whatever we're told to fetch without knowing its importance.

Ness was right. We're walking, talking, weapons to be used at the Mother Coven's disposal. Which now includes the Sovereignty.

Other Berisfords were wandering the world, doing what? Was my supposed cousin I ran into at Jet's house listening to orders? I sent an image of the man to Jet when I explained why we needed some Tupperware to house Eli's ashes. Jet never met the man either. Her father wanted nothing to do with the rest of the family.

He was powerful enough to overtake me. Was he his own master or was he another talented weapon sent on a mission?

Hall hit my leg with his own while we waited in the car. "Quit with the bouncing knees, bro. You're shaking my balls. You square?"

I stopped my legs from running the speedy sprint my brain was racing and forced myself to nod.

"Good. No need for nerves," Hall said. "It's a grocery run. We bag the essentials and head home. Simple."

Sure. Easy-peasy. He wasn't wrong. The mission was likely straight-forward. Vincent was adamant about going with Issát under a cover spell while the other two Elders waited in the vehicle. Vincent was taking a huge risk trusting Issát would be at his side if shit went sideways.

No one on the Team complained about the simplicity or stupidity of the plan. Not even when the Elders were out of earshot. If they did, it was telepathically and not to me, but something told me they trusted at least Vincent's decisions when it came to their personal safety. They were all pretty powerful, so maybe they banked on kicking ass regardless of the inane situation.

Hall was wrong about one thing: the Prison Creation wasn't home. I didn't know where home was anymore.

Ranlyn and Veata returned to the vehicle. Ranlyn sat in the driver's seat to take off quickly if needed, ensuring the survival of at least two Elders. I think Veata just didn't feel like going. If Vincent had it covered, they didn't need her to.

"I don't like this," Ranlyn said out loud.

Veata shifted in her seat. "You never do unless you're doing it yourself. Let the control go. Fulfill your role."

"I come with word from the Master!" Across the large parking lot, guards started popping into view when Issát called out to them.

They met Issát at the halfway point near the motel's office entrance. Some practically galloped to learn what Issát had to say while others dragged their feet. Regardless of how excited they were to see their Master's buddy, they listened like Issát was middle management with decision-making authority.

None of them detected Vincent under his cover spell.

"Cover up," Ismail said and spouted off a spell. The rest of the Team followed and we all disappeared.

"I'll add a blueprint spell," Gregor's voice informed us. He left the vehicle door wide open for a quick exit. The rest of us did the same.

A couple of steps towards the motel and the other team members popped into view. I couldn't see their whole bodies while undercover, but their forms and weapons were all outlined with energy so we could still work as a team. Like with a blueprint. They looked like heavily-armed ghosts surrounded by a haze when their power fluctuated.

Effective.

Gravel crunched under our boots on the frozen ground, so we treaded lightly, letting Issát's voice drown us out until we rounded the back of the motel.

A shitty metal fence enclosed the property. Hundreds of pounds of Magic clanging the bowed fencing under us would tip off any lingering guards we couldn't see. Not a problem for the long-time team members who side-stepped Bronya in a practiced move. She ran her gloved hand over and through the snow-covered grass to reveal the ground and then motioned Ismail towards the fence. He stepped onto the now-empty spot and was propelled up and over the fence, landing silently on the other side. Gregor followed quickly and then Arden, Hall, and then me. It felt like I jumped on a mini trampoline. Bronya was the last one over.

Again, effective.

We didn't linger. Ismail led the group to a rear wall, whipping up a discreet wind to erase our tracks in the snow behind us.

Since this was a motel and not a hotel, there were no interior hallways to neatly lead the new Seedlings down and out of the building. Instead, we reached a window big enough for someone to stare at the bare trees behind the motel. Two smaller lower windows probably opened for fresh air, but a sheet of wood was nailed over one of them where an a/c unit fit in nicer weather.

"Wait!" Ismail's ghostly form switched places with Hall when I escalated my power. "Tripwire. Always assume exits and entrances are warded."

Frustration simmered as I waited for Ismail to interrupt a spell by rerouting it around the wood covering by pasting its focus onto the glass. Once the wood was removed, the warding wouldn't be set off. Smart. And I didn't see it. I'm not a trained officer and apparently have a lot to learn.

Once Ismail was finished, I shifted to the front of the group, bypassing their ghostly outlines. I stood in front of dirty window glass. Inside was a woman pacing like a caged animal. Her hair was greasy, clothing dirty and torn, and she muttered something to herself that I couldn't hear.

"Get that plank of wood off," I said to anyone listening. I could do it myself, but I shouldn't have to do all of the heavy lifting.

Hall grabbed the edge of the wood nailed into the half-rotted sill and yanked it off without using any power beyond his biceps.

The woman screeched, grasped at her chest, and stumbled onto a dishevelled bed. She couldn't see me, but she didn't have to for me to get her to do whatever I wanted.

"You're not scared." I sent the words into her open mind. *"Stand. Come to the window."*

The woman complied. Her dead eyes focused on the emptiness she saw outside of the window, and she was close enough now that I could see her tear-streaked face. Whatever comprised of their days since they were captured and turned into Magics during Loring's attack on Niagara Falls, it wore this woman down. I didn't have to see the bags under her eyes this closely to know she hadn't been sleeping.

With her exit unobstructed, I ordered the woman to crawl out of the old a/c opening. When her feet touched the ground, I told her she wasn't afraid and that she was going to follow my directions without question. Which included not fighting when someone else pulled her along. Since she couldn't see us under these spells, another Tactical Team member would have to direct her every step until we got back to the van.

The woman did as told.

We didn't check the room for any belongings. Loring didn't let them pack a suitcase when they were kidnapped, so nothing was important enough to risk their lives.

I left the woman behind to check the next room. This was a double. Inside were two men. One sat at a table, elbows on his knees, talking to another man lying on one of the beds with his arm over his eyes trying to ignore whatever his roommate was saying. Something about a political conspiracy theory he thought they were caught up in.

Again, Ismail rerouted the warding to exclude the wooden piece of the window and Hall manhandled the a/c cover off to reveal a big hole.

Before the men could react, I telepathically trapped them like I did with the woman and gave them the same directions as I gave her.

"Hey!" The annoyed man's top-half was halfway to safety when a voice interrupted the process.

A man outfitted in winter tactical gear barrelled towards the

Seedling now standing in the snow. Another guard popped into view and jogged towards the conspiracy theorist following my directions and climbing clear of the empty space.

"I got it," I told the others.

Damn. Their thoughts were blocked. Fine. Telepathy wasn't required to persuade them.

"Run yourselves into the wall."

The men stopped their course en route to the newly escaped, faced the motel's exterior walls between the room's windows, and ran into the brick without hesitation. The dull *thwack* when their bodies hit the wall was nothing to the second try when the one guard's head hit first. He stumbled and caught himself on one knee, stood up, and did it again.

This time, he didn't stand up.

The other guard took one more headlong trip into the brick wall and ended up like his buddy, bloodied and unconscious in the snow.

I headed for the next window.

"Thought you didn't want to end up like your forebears?"

I spun on Hall.

He continued. "You could've made those men thumb wrestle until nightfall. Or climb into those rooms and wait on the toilet until someone found them. Any reason you chose violence today?"

"They—"

"They'll always do despicable shit. You wanna end up like them, keep at it the Berisford way and you'll get there in no time."

The rest of the Tactical Team was close enough to hear everything. None of them added anything or argued with Hall's take on my way of dealing with our enemy. Neither did the three survivors still trapped within my persuasion and following in silence.

"Lets keep moving," Gregor said as more than a suggestion.

I could've let them find a way to get the rest of the survivors free and to keep them quiet. Hell, I could've released the three already in my persuasion and watched the chaos unfold. Those kinds of moves were something I couldn't explain away, not without sounding petty, because it was.

Feeling sorry for the guards still melting snow under their bodies wasn't going to happen, but I could've probably handled it differently.

I stepped in front of Hall. We didn't need him ripping the a/c cover off of its nails and freaking out the woman inside. Screaming would interrupt Issát's little chat out front. A silent infiltration and retrieval allowed us to escape with the survivors long before they were missed.

Survivors free of their rooms headed in a line beneath a cover spell to the vehicles like ducklings. Fitting them all into the limited space was a game of *Tetris*. A few apologies were thrown around when we doubled some up in the same seats with smaller people in foot wells or sardined into the open-concept trunk. It was either that or we left them behind. I kept them under my persuasion to save everyone the discomfort I told them they didn't feel or risk setting off their Seedling powers.

Mission complete, Vincent and Issát returned to the vehicle. Vincent took an extra glance around the interior at our newly stuffed-in Magics and then they both had to squeeze themselves in as well.

Issát got into the driver's seat in case anyone saw him, which meant Ranlyn and Veata had to move into the center of the front seats.

"Everyone comfortable?" Vincent tossed out to the rest of us.

"As comfortable as it gets, Lewie. Lets move." A skinny man was on Hall's lap, the guy stooping over to accommodate the roof.

Issát didn't hesitate to take off.

"Seems almost too easy," I heard Vincent say.

"In essence, however, by tomorrow when the change in venue doesn't occur like I told them would happen, they will report to Loring. The only way I can return to Loring's side now is if I can convince him someone impersonated me. Not all together impossible."

"Going to miss your Master?"

Issát laughed at Ranlyn's comment. "Loring was never my Master. Breaking contact is easy since the justification for joining no longer exists. My hope is that I don't need him for something of greater purpose in the coming days or weeks for myself or the Mother Coven."

"They'll figure it out soon." Hall joined their conversation. "Once a couple of guards wake up, if they wake up, they'll let the others in on the escape. Loring's smart enough to connect your presence and the missing Seedlings."

Vincent turned in his seat and looked over Veata's shoulder. "Anything in particular to report?"

"Yeah, my ass is numb. Lets get these people to safety before I lose my toes."

Vincent didn't press and I didn't offer up the information. Maybe I would tell Vincent what happened with the guards. Maybe another Tactical Team member would. I wasn't ashamed. Vincent sent me to do a job and I did it. Though, I guess Hall made a good point and next time I'll be more creative.

"To be clear," Vincent said as Issát drove us through the city streets, "when we reverse your damage, another Soul Seer will verify their souls are clean."

"Not a problem. We will also need to stop somewhere to switch places and have me equipped with a confusion spell or the like. While I appreciate my permittance into your sanctum, knowledge of the location is unnecessary."

Wow. Issát was volunteering to be magically black bagged. If Vincent was suspicious, he didn't call Issát on it. Issát could've already known the location and was putting on an act to gain Vincent's trust.

If I thought of it, I wasn't the only one.

No matter how welcomed Issát was into Vincent's Creation or Sophie's family, for that matter, the lives these people knew were over, and nothing Issát did would return what he stole. They were

Loring's captives. Now they were captives of the Mother Coven. Sure, they were safer in the Prison Creation, but they were far from free.

25

SOMEHOW DIFFERENT

Kim

"Watch your balls, Blake. I'm not warning you again!" One of the Prison Creation's guards got an energy ball to the calf that singed his pants as the guys tossed some magic around in boredom. The guard kicked at the pain and ruffled his pant leg, the scorch mark, and probably the leg hair beneath, mended in an instant as he went on with his lobby rounds.

Blake made another energy ball. It sparked blue in his hands. "What? It's not my fault Jer's swiping at 'em like a bear."

Jared scoffed. "Try aiming. I'm standing right here."

"You both suck. And we're supposed to be figuring out what to do for Deidra's birthday," I reminded them. Cabin fever was getting to them.

"*Pfft*. You say that like a trip to Belize is in our back pocket." The flash of light from Denise's hand and arm glittered like she was wearing a diamond-encrusted glove. The light itself was useless for anything other than a distraction, as far as I knew.

"Not Belize," I said with a quiet thought of Hall's ability and how he could probably zip me to Belize if he's ever been there. "Think smaller, but fun."

"How about a spell exchange?" Gwen suggested.

"Like giving her spells?" Jared asked and missed another energy ball from Blake. Both guys raised their hands, exasperated with the other.

"Yeah, adding some spells into a basket, something she could learn. Or add them to a book."

"Ooh. Yes, we can do that."

"Us Magic folk tend to call that kind of book a grimoire," Denise said with heavy sarcasm as she stood, rolled her eyes, and headed off towards the lobby bathroom.

"Okay. Yes, I guess it would be a grimoire," Gwen added in a small voice.

"Still a good idea and something she could keep for a long time." And we could ask people outside of our Sect as well.

Wait, if we approached everyone in the Prison Creation, we could technically create a huge Prison Creation collective grimoire.

Yes!

"Whatever side quest your brain just spat up, do it," Gwen told me. "The Mother Coven will benefit more than you realize."

I wide-eyed her, knowing she couldn't read my mind. "You don't even know what I thought about."

"Details are unimportant. I'm right and so are you. Figure it out."

Damn. Okay. When a prophetess gets a good feeling, you go with it.

New goal activated.

"What about some kind of contest?" Jared remade a sparking red energy ball. "She's competitive."

"A shooting contest!" Blake added. "Or archery. Or something she can light on fire. She's always complaining she doesn't get to go nuclear enough."

Very true. Not everyone in here could exercise their basic powers as much as they needed. A fire box or something to give Deidra and others the opportunity to let loose might be the key.

"You just want to shoot more guns. And destroy shit." Jared tossed his red energy ball so high Blake jumped for it.

Blake caught it, nearly landing on his ass on the way down. "Whoa, bro. And hell yeah, I want to destroy—"

"Kim!" Denise yelled across the lobby.

Denise was calling for me? This can't be good.

I jogged over to the bathroom, Denise impatiently waving me over. "What's wrong?"

"Hell if I know." She pulled me inside of the bathroom.

Whoa. A wall of throbbing magic stopped us.

I swallowed against the pressurized energy flowing from the stalls.

"Seedling," Denise whispered from her stance at the door.

Definitely a baby-fresh Magic fighting the build up of uncontrolled power.

Clearing my throat helped with the discomfort a bit as I stepped towards the stalls. The unfiltered force centered on a single stall. Knocking would scare the person more, but I couldn't say nothing.

The stall door flew open. Someone rushed passed me and then was stopped quickly when they hit the sink counter across from the stalls.

Shit. "Cora-Lynn..."

Flushed and wild-eyed, Cora-Lynn clutched the marble top, panting like she was running a marathon. Untamed power continued to pulse from Cora-Lynn's body. Sweat marked the back of her shirt. She reached forward to start the water, jabbing her hand beneath the faucet too quickly for the sensor to register her presence.

"I can help..." I lunged forward to activate the water.

Cora-Lynn flinched and let out a curt yelp in surprise.

"It's—"

The shock of pain and weightlessness turned to an adrenalized panic when I hit the ground and slid along the floor.

"Kim?" Denise was over me, shifting from staring down at me to glancing elsewhere.

A momentary second of confusion at what Denise was staring at hit me until I remembered I was on the bathroom floor because Coar-Lynn had busted her top and sent my ass flying.

I searched for Cora-Lynn.

She was sitting by the wall, hugging her legs and rocking.

"You okay? Should I find someone else?" Denise was more helpful than she had been in the past, but it was still a surprise when she extended a genuine offer.

"No," I said, keeping my voice low. "More people means more pressure. She doesn't need an audience."

"'Kay, fine," she whispered, "but I can't heal you and you look like you broke your ass."

She wasn't wrong. Leaning to the side lessened the sharp zing of pain in the hip I landed on. Lots of others could heal me once I ensured Cora-Lynn wasn't going to explode again.

Feeling the pull in my hip, I strained to stand and took a couple of soft steps towards Cora-Lynn. If she wanted, she could turn on me with enough power to do some hefty damage, but she was new to their abilities, confused as hell, and terrified of what her body was capable of.

"I'm pretty new at this too," I said softly as not to scare her again. "I knew about power and Magics, but I didn't actually feel it inside of me for a long time."

A spike of pain hit me when I attempted to lean against the counter. I swallowed the gasp as not to freak Cora-Lynn out.

For a woman who appeared so strong and in control of herself right down to her sharp, observant glares, Cora-Lynn seemed fragile on the marble with her legs curled up.

"You were an innocent person living their life. I know you didn't want this—"

Her wild glare landed on me. "What was that?"

I steeled myself so I wouldn't fold under the weight of her questioning. I also realized if I said the wrong things here, I could spook her. "We call it a power burst. When Magics are new to all of this, Seedlings, especially when they didn't discover it as a child, it hits them too quickly, all at once. And since they're not skilled at how to handle it, the energy rushes out of them."

I shifted my weight to ease my painful hip.

"Don't!" Cora-Lynn went to scramble away but she was already against the wall.

"I won't come any closer. I swear. I'm staying right here."

"I could hurt you. I'm unstable."

She must not have seen me fly or spotted the landing. Pointing out the fact she already technically hurt me was not going to get me anywhere.

Cora-Lynn's stare slid to Denise who must have moved.

"Ah, I will—" Denise reached for something to do— "stand at the door, so no one else bothers you."

I nodded. "Thanks."

Now what? Shit. Okay, okay. "You will learn a lot of things here. How to stop a magic burst from happening is one of them. They used to happen to Sophie a lot." When she kept staring at me, I took it as curiosity. "She didn't know her power until...geez, a year ago? Maybe not even a year ago? In this life, anyway. Since she doesn't remember her past lives unless she reads back into her memories, she didn't know how to handle them. Donovan taught her how to control her magic this time around. They didn't always hate each other." The small laugh I added fell flat somewhere between us.

Damn, I was flopping.

Whatever I said had Cora-Lynn on her feet. I tried a small smile she didn't return as she peered down at her hands. The tickle of power crossed the room, the little hairs on my arms rising at the sensation.

"I did not ask for this."

"I—I know you didn't. No one does. It's the same as being born a blonde or a brunette. It's a part of your genetic makeup. Passed down from your parents or someone along your bloodline."

Energy continued to build, Cora-Lynn closing her eyes to it.

"I saw a man...he turned into a coyote."

Yeah, that would be terrifying. "Right. A Transmutator. Someone who can shift into different types of animals. It's a specialty. Not everyone can do that."

"Sorry for the interruption..." Olive walked into the bathroom and placed her hand on my arm.

Oh, thank the goddess someone else showed up, but if Cora-Lynn accidently hurt Olive, Sophie might not be so forgiving when she's well enough to kick some ass again.

"I couldn't help overhearing. An old woman's bladder waits for no one," she added with a genuine laugh. "I also didn't have the pleasure of knowing Sophie as a child when I could have helped her the most. Our family knew nothing of their magic while I was locked away for many years. But you knew Sophie as Morgan, is that right?"

Cora-Lynn's chest rose and fell too quickly, the power in the room still elevated.

"Did you grow up with her as girls?" Olive asked. "I assume I didn't have a role in her life in your time either, but I find myself helplessly intrigued about her days without me in them, in this time and of the past."

Cora-Lynn's eyes darted from side to side as if thinking.

"Her hair...darker. Her hair was darker." Cora-Lynn managed as her power still threatened to overwhelm her. "Eyes the same. Mouth...somehow different. Nose, too. A little. Enough to appear different, and still remain the same."

I peeked at Olive. The smile on her face was kind and intrigued and I truly believed she cared about every detail Cora-Lynn described, because she likely did. Maybe she could see her through Cora-Lynn's thoughts.

Cora-Lynn inhaled with a ragged pull.

"Was she young when you met?" Olive continued, her voice a little bit louder as if to speak above Cora-Lynn's intense thoughts.

"Girls." She paused. "Small-town families, farms, church. Many hungered for...everything. Morgan's family was no different and joined my own to work the lands when we were quiet young. We shared the same fires, the same roofs...the same hardships."

"Sounds more like family."

Cora-Lynn nodded. "In all ways but blood."

"To see her now, in this place, ill, and without memory of your time together, must be quite difficult." She paused. "No one can know what it's like to be you and to have endured all you have. Not one single person. Not Sophie, not even Vincent."

Cora-Lynn's jaw flexed at the mention of his name.

Olive went on. "Whatever time you need to acclimate to this world, to your place in it, take it. As long as you don't seek to harm others, don't apologize for whatever is needed to make sense of your new world. Learning about your power might give you a chance to decide how you feel about it. Maybe your time around good Magic folk will also do that. Let you see how good people are Magics."

"Bad people too. What if I'm one of them? What if—"

"Your soul glow tells me you're good person. Soul Seers like me and Sophie and those in our family can see the difference even if the person questions themselves. Plus, those with a hint of Taint to their souls can still be good people if they want to be. But you, your soul is good."

Quiet fell over the bathroom, lasting long enough for me to itch to fill it. I didn't, waiting for Olive to say something, but she was letting the silence remain silent and, in that stillness, Cora-Lynn's uncontrolled power lessened until it was a low-level hum at best.

"Can you show me?"

Olive said a simple "Of course" without a big show of accepting.

Knowing she needed to be eased into the process, Olive explained she didn't have to touch Cora-Lynn to show her her soul glow, and then included what Cora-Lynn would experience. She spelled it all out so Cora-Lynn was comfortable with the process, and once Olive was done explaining, it was clear it worked.

Cora-Lynn crossed her arms, bracing to be shown her soul glow.

A moment passed and then Cora-Lynn gasped, and her arms dropped to her sides.

"As you can see," Olive said, "there's nothing evil about you. And we can discuss what creator or evolutionary hiccup made such a thing as Magics possible, but the truth of goodness would still remain."

Tears welled and fell from Cora-Lynn's blue eyes, shining against her flushed cheeks. Another gasp broke free from her lips and then a sob.

"You can hate this part of yourself," Olive went on. "You can curse it, suffocate it, ignore it, but I can promise you, from dreadful personal experience, your soul deserves better than the torment you would put it through if you did. You didn't deserve the hell you went through at the hands of Tainted Magics, but their Taint did nothing to darken the deepest part of you. It changed you, yes, but your soul remains pure."

I couldn't stop the emotion flooding from me. I choked it back, but stopping the tears was impossible, especially when Cora-Lynn dropped to her knees and cried into her hands. Some part of her must have believed she was lesser because of what was done to her and learning about what she was.

Olive didn't rush to her, so neither did I, but I felt like I should have. Did Olive know Cora-Lynn wouldn't want us to? She showed Cora-Lynn her soul glow, but I didn't know how much rummaging around she would've done while she did it. Knowing Olive, she did nothing but exactly what she said she would.

Again, Olive waited, letting Cora-Lynn fill the silence with emotion and nothing more. And no one else came in, so Denise must have let Olive pass on purpose and then held the line.

I wiped my eyes and peeked at the long mirror above the sinks to check that my makeup wasn't running down my face. Another few minutes passed until Cora-Lynn stretched her neck to each side, and then looked up at the ceiling or maybe to whatever Heaven or God she must have believed in at one time.

"You cannot tell him of this." Cora-Lynn wiped her cheek with the back of her hand and stood.

"Vincent?" Olive guessed.

"I don't want him to know about this power burst."

"Of course not," I promised. He was at the meet with Issát, but he would probably return soon. "Though…"

"With the abilities of those here, including Vincent, they may learn about it by overhearing your thoughts."

"Or Denise at the door might've mentioned it to people already. The rumor mill is lightning quick." I shrugged. "People have nothing better to do."

Cora-Lynn planted her hands on her hips, her eyes unfocused, panicking into her own thoughts again.

"We could spell your thoughts. Cover them so no one can hear. Well, maybe Sophie and Donovan could, their magic is… Either way, it would stop the common Magic including Vincent."

"Do it." Cora-Lynn took a few fast steps towards us. Her tense body so close was pure intimidation. Or at least, I was intimidated.

"Not a problem," Olive told her. The woman's voice was so tender it reflected back to her in calming Cora-Lynn down.

Cora-Lynn was a survivor. Whatever she went through, she learned what she needed to keep going. Now this was another thing she could do to protect herself and she was all for it even if it meant having magic used on her.

"Afterwards, maybe we can spend some time in the shooting range. Hardware isn't exactly my thing, but it does come in handy to unlock some tension."

Cora-Lynn hesitated. "I used to shoot my father's rifles. Coyotes or foxes would get into the animal pens."

"Oh, then you probably have more trigger experience than I do."

Cora-Lynn didn't comment. Whatever thoughts she had about the memory she kept them to herself.

"Also, remind yourself the cells are free of magic," Olive told her. "If at any time you need some space or a break from the others. Or even if your magic seems to be taking over, you can retreat to the cells so you can gather your wits."

Cora-Lynn nodded this time as if grateful for the safety net.

Led by desperation to safeguard herself, we went through the same process as Hall did with me to cover my mind. Olive provided most of the power since I didn't have quite enough juice, but in the end Cora-Lynn was satisfied her secrets would be safe and trusted Olive's say-so as proof.

Vincent would notice it soon and mention it. Or maybe he wouldn't say anything, but he would know.

Olive also suggested Cora-Lynn find a way to fill her time. A hobby. Sure, she had a lot to learn about the years she missed and of Magics, but Olive thought she would benefit from something more tangible, simple. Apparently, Cora-Lynn used to sew. As far as mending went, we didn't need the service with so many who could heal or fix things, but she could still create herb sachets and anything she wanted, really. She wasn't opposed to the idea and Olive told her she would handle gathering the supplies.

For now, Cora-Lynn wasn't up for shooting and opted to spend some time alone in her cell. Not that I blamed her. A hoard of thoughts was probably spinning in her brain right now. And after that cry, I could use a nap myself.

When we finally exited the bathroom, Denise released a sigh and complaint, but there wasn't a line since all of the cells had bathrooms.

"You play a good bouncer," I told Denise.

"I've dated enough of them to know the tricks." She added finger quotes when she said 'dated'. "I'll add it to my resumé."

Getting into clubs without paying cover fees was a practical decision on Denise's part. Sophie's brother was no bouncer, but they both fit well into the stereotype of hitting the bars on the weekend enough to know their way around the system. All of this hiding must cramping their social calendar.

I tapped Olive for a dose of healing for my hip while Cora-Lynn disappeared in the lobby crowd. When she was done, I nearly sagged to the ground in relief.

She patted my arm. "You know, many here are lucky to have you, my dear."

My heart clenched. "Thanks, Olive. That's really sweet. Same for you. I never would've gotten through to her like you did."

Olive shrugged. "It was a team effort with a successful result. And the addition of a thought-covering spell many others would love to have."

She wasn't wrong and I thought to add it to the list of spells for whatever future Prison Creation grimoire I might one day put together.

Before Olive walked away, I asked her about a few spells for the grimoire project. She agreed to put something into the pot and to ask the aunts and other Ballards for anything to add.

When Gwen says to jump on something, you do it.

26

STATE OF SUSPICION

Vincent

On the edge of a big box store parking lot under the guise of a cover spell, Issát cleansed the Seedlings' souls. While he opened his mind for us to remotely view the process of the blackened state of the soul shifting into the light, another Soul Seer would verify the result.

All the Seedlings knew now was that we were transporting them to another location where they would be provided answers to their rush of questions.

Caine's presence was paramount when a few fought against the plan until it was explained they would be safe from Loring and any others attempting to hurt them or their families. A few dwelled on the memory of Caine ordering two guards to harm themselves and the result they witnessed in a dissociated state while persuaded. I still had to speak with him about it when time permitted, as the Seedlings were anxious Caine would do so to them.

Once the Tactical Team members searched for tracking devices and weapons, we added spelled bindings against accidental activation of the Seedlings' power. We also ran Issát through the same procedure, minus the power bind. He did not voice offence for the other precautions. And while the man exuded sincerity, he was still a formidable Magic who possessed the ability to cripple a lifetime of my work in a single Prison Creation visit if his intentions were anything but pure.

Inside the Creation, the Seedlings scanned the lobby, while those already in the Creation surveyed the new arrivals. Team members stood vigilant, same with the Prison Creation guards. After their experiences with violence at the hands of Loring's people and witnessing Caine's, these folks required a softer hand.

Ah, there she was.

Kim stood with Caine's cousin, Jet, and her son. I called her over. She acknowledged Hall with a small smile. He nodded in return with a gleam in his eye foreign on the face of my old cohort, one he let falter when she approached me. Only eyes for her. I knew something was between the two. A Verndari arrangement, however, never crossed my mind.

"Would you mind showing the group around the facility and explain the finer details of accessing their rooms?"

She side-eyed the people too busy staring around the lobby. "Who are they?"

I explained and watched her expression harden.

She crossed her arms. "And you're hoping the office with smallpox victims, the other office with the growing altar of our dearly departed, and their rooms—" she stated with air quotes— "won't spook them?"

I inhaled deeply. "I am confident in your ability to reduce the amount of excess stress we cause them."

Her brows creased with suspicion. "I don't buy it, but I'll catch the hot potato. Do they know they're in a Creation?"

I gave her a universal look of "What do you think?"

"Do they know what a Creation is?"

I provided the same expression.

Kim huffed. "Fine. I'll start with the 'you're extra-special' speech."

"Issát has already provided an explanation, though they may want answers from someone other than the individual who propelled them into this life."

"Issát? Sophie's Issát?"

The man himself stepped up next to us. Kim gasped. "Yes. Sophie's Issát."

"If you could..." I let my words fall and motioned to the survivors.

"Right. Sure. Your hands are full. With Issát. The Puppeteer's son."

"And Sophie's ancestor," Issát added.

"Sure. Of course. Sophie's ancestor. Umm, can I..." She pointed towards Hall.

"The whole Team is at your disposal. Their presence may not foster ease, but until the Seedlings are orientated to the facility it would be smart to station guards outside of the room where you convene."

"Perfect." She took a couple of steps away.

"I will be along once I am able."

"Sure thing, Lewy." Kim approached the survivors and adopted a tour guide voice, instructing them to follow her to a boardroom. I would have to later address Hall's "Lewy" nickname she so casually offered.

"It appears his loyalties are with the Kitchen Witch." Issát accurately read Hall and Kim's relationship.

"When not on mission, yes. Where would you like to start?" I asked to move the focus off of my Team.

"Where is Sophie?"

Without the luxury of warning her, and anticipating a losing battle if I kept him away, I led Issát to my Charges.

Adam, Serena, Olive, Lewis, and Rosemary all stood or sat around one or the other while Sophie and Donovan slept. Their bodies accepted the IV treatment without notable side effects, however, they appeared no different than when I left this morning.

Rosemary shot to her feet, shielding her son. “What is this?”

“May we have the room?” I asked out of courtesy.

None of them wanted to leave their unconscious family with whom they believed to be a Tainted Magic.

“What do you see of his soul?” I asked the Soul Seers in the room.

All of them confirmed Issát’s soul was clear. If he could fake it, I was unaware of how, yet I did not ignore the possibility. Rosemary’s soul would be the most darkened in the room by quite a yard.

“I would love to meet with you all,” Issát extended the invitation to the others. “You are a part of me as much as Sophie is.”

Olive nodded with hesitation and agreed to leave. None of them commented on connecting old familial bonds.

Rosemary held out the longest and eventually left with promises of availability outside of the room.

Alone, I observed Issát analyzing Sophie and Donovan at a distance. He then reached for and held Sophie’s hand without fear of the smallpox pustule clusters, having likely seen many others afflicted with the same in his long life.

“Why are they unconscious?” Issát asked.

“To provide comfort where possible.”

After a moment of persistent silence, Issát stood between the two beds, placed a hand on each of their shoulders, and bowed his head.

A flicker of energy sizzled in the air.

I cleared my throat. “You cannot heal them in that fashion.”

“I’m not trying to.”

Issát lifted his head a minute later and focused on Sophie and then Donovan. “Their Soul Magic is so broken.” The heartbreak in his voice surprised me. “I see the fissure. Feel the damage it’s caused to the both of them. If she will allow, he can heal their Soul Magic.”

“How?” I asked, my voice thick.

“Exactly how you proposed. Their original power siphoned from the ritual stone can heal their illness once they are well enough to endure the onslaught. She will resist the process, but it isn't her. The break in trust causing the fissure prevents her acceptance of help. It won't allow her to believe anyone truly wants to help her without backhanded manipulation. Something dark is spilling into her, escaping the fissure. Her family would know all of this if their talents were better fostered. Something I plan to fix. As for Sophie, you may need Caine to persuade her cooperation."

Something poisoning her against healing this fissure explained why Sophie seemed improved the first time Donovan healed them and then degraded to her state of suspicion and hatred again.

The wound reopened.

Sophie's face shining with fever was relaxed in a way it wasn't while conscious. "I have threatened the possibility, though I would rather not. I would hate to strip her of this choice when so much is beyond her control."

"If this were merely a case of obstinacy, I would agree. Knowing of your relationship with the both of them, I would say your decision to allow her condition to continue is the result of personal guilt. It has nothing to do with Sophie's autonomy or lack thereof."

The audacity. "Easily said by someone who does not know her in this life or any other."

"Yes, it is. Though I do expect, in her right mind, she would see why forcing her hand was necessary and would be grateful you saw what she needed. Plus, you are not only her Overseer. What you neglect to accept is that Donovan is suffering and you're justifying his misery due to your closer relationship to Sophie. Healing her means healing them both. As Overseer this is your duty and your burden."

The thought of siccing Caine on Sophie was appalling. When I told her my conditions to retaining a Team position, I assumed she would be angry and fight to right her station. Instead, she grew evermore stubborn and turned to Jordan. Recalling Donovan's desperation during the incident, I knew Issát was right. Donovan was suffering. He may think he deserved such treatment, nevertheless, does his lack of faith in himself also fall to me?

Sophie and my relationship was always...easier.

"Call a Sovereignty board meeting."

I blinked into my present. Issát now faced me in full. "A meeting?"

"Your father's board will respond to a show of the region's Mother Coven Elders. You need to know who you can trust. Force them to show their true souls to Sophie or her family. Caine can surpass their mental barriers, seek those who will embrace change, and see who has already turned their backs on their people. I know of one such board member and believe there are more."

"And you would prefer to attend this meeting?"

"Yes," Issát stated bluntly.

"And I suppose you want this to be done now?"

He rounded Sophie's bed and stood beside me. "We would be stronger with them. We need her to be better," he said, pointing down at Sophie, "and not for the reason you think."

"What is the reason?"

"You are distracted. The meeting is important and we need your mind there and not here with them."

I exhaled. Issát's demands were already wearing me thin. "I agree. I am unfocused. However, Sophie is not why. Even if we can convince her to agree to Donovan's healing, neither would be well enough to attend. They require healing from more than illness."

"The meeting should happen rather soon. As Veata stated, they are probably already lobbying for the captain's seat. With them believing you are comfortable abandoning the Sovereignty to implode, they would never guess you would do the opposite."

I frowned. "I still question if I can trust you and your information let alone myself to shoulder the company."

"Another positive of having Sophie healed is that she can read how trustworthy I am. Unless her family is capable in her stead, I have no other means to prove myself. Hence, why we call it trust."

Touché.

"Who is the turncoat Sovereignty board member?" I asked instead of commenting further.

Ranlyn entered the room with none other than John Weaver, both waiting for the same answer they overheard me ask. Ranlyn's expression was one with less tolerance than John's who appeared to stand rather rigid anticipating my reaction regarding his prior involvement with Issát.

"Roger Offerman," Issát answered without hesitation.

John nodded as if this was common knowledge.

This alone gave the man a few points in the innocent column I was hesitant to admit was growing. "There must be more."

"I assure you there are. Some are questionable and I'm just not privy to which."

I focused on John. "You seem to have an ear against all of the right walls. What do you know?"

John refrained to comment on my petty dig. "Offerman's an easy bet since he has spoken to Loring in Issát's presence. Plus his financial dealings, ones I am not supposed to have access to, paint a dark picture of payoffs and funding for numerous Tainted operations spanning years."

Numbers were John's forte. My father trusted him with a spreadsheet and the bank codes. He had a knack for appearing unimposing and agreeable, affording the man the ability to occupy rooms without people realizing he took up space. And even when they did, they counted on his discretion and worked under the belief they received it.

"Can you contact Offerman?" I asked John and Issát.

They glanced at each other. Issát answered. "I can."

So, maybe John could not.

I nodded. "Have him call the board to an emergency meeting tonight."

"Wouldn't that provoke suspicions?" John questioned.

Issát looked between us. "Not with good incentive to attend."

Ranlyn gave a small smile. "What reason are we giving him?"

"Tell Offerman you have caught wind of an immediate coup. Truth is sometimes the purest motivation."

"Offerman wouldn't show for that. He would let it happen since he knows the board would also have the Sovereignty guard present. The guard would act against you, keeping Offerman's hands clean, which would allow him to seize leadership."

This was true. "Tell him Loring will personally be in attendance to ensure he is crowned company president once the rest of the board is slain. The kill will be blamed on me and my rebellious flock, and this will give public sanction to consider the Mother Coven, and me, Sovereignty enemies. Loring's involvement would remain underground and Offerman would have what he wants and will be able to appoint his own board if he attends to be hoisted as a survivor in order to take over."

Issát grabbed for his cell phone and searched his contacts. "Playing on ego is always a winner when dealing with Offerman."

"Drop your walls," Ranlyn commanded.

Issát's attention snapped to the Elder. "I'm sorry?"

"I want to hear everything. Since putting Offerman on speaker is too obvious, I want to hear it through you."

"You don't trust me either," he said, his stare flipping to me.

"Not without question."

Issát dropped his mental walls, allowing us to peruse his mind. While Issát was distracted by explaining to Offerman what we discussed, I took the liberty of searching his underlying thoughts. They laid primarily on me and Ranlyn's distrust for him and how this may impact his and Sophie's potential relationship.

Issát ended the call and pocketed his phone. "Satisfied?"

I had been too busy in these thoughts to hear the outcome of the conversation.

"For now," Ranlyn said and then left.

"I need to make a few calls," John informed me, "to family since I find myself here. I know you can listen in or record calls, or you are welcome to be present if you're finding yourself low on trust. I get it, and to be clear, my loyalty to you hasn't changed."

After a moment, I nodded. John was amongst my rescue team and had many years full of examples to lend to bolstering my trust, his knowledge of Issát notwithstanding.

I stopped him from leaving. "I want you to attend the meeting."

His brows creased. "I'm just the numbers guy."

"And the numbers guy knows the company inside and out. I want you there."

John offered his hand to shake mine and I took it. "Count me in."

When he left, I knew it was a good decision to extend an invitation. If for some reason he was hiding something, his presence would provoke thoughts of the others in attendance and would reveal any deceptions. And if his allegiance was as strong as I presumed it was, then he would be an invaluable addition to the board.

Issát didn't comment on my decision to include John. "Are you certain you don't want to wait for Sophie's and Donovan's involvement?"

I waded through Issát's immediate thoughts for the true meaning behind his suggestion and found them circling around thoughts of family.

"I can keep my walls down," Issát said, "but I refuse while attending the Sovereignty board meeting. Letting any of those Magics inside of my head won't benefit anyone."

I should have expected Issát to know what I was doing, the man older than me and probably skilled enough to pick up the sensation of my search.

"Why don't you check in with your Cora-Lynn and then we can see how the new Seedlings are getting on? I imagine they have questions not even your Kitchen Witch can answer."

The fact Issát knew so much about me, the Sovereignty, Cora-Lynn, the Prison Creation and those within it was unsettling, especially since Issát himself was much a mystery. Thankfully, John was now in the Prison Creation and accessible for a long conversation once I found the time.

The growing list of things to tackle was daunting.

27

SPILLING EFFORT

Sophie

If Donovan was listening to Adam and Serena talking at me, he was sticking to himself. Lying on a sweat-soaked bed facing away from him was as much privacy as I was going to get. Not that I asked my brother and cousin to visit. They showed up with questions and comments I didn't care about.

I didn't have the energy to host people.

The IV pumping smallpox-fixing juice was still in my arm, so it was probably doing something. Whatever it did, it didn't tickle the deep ache in my skull or the rest of my bones. Did nothing for the itchy, nubby sores all over me either. Itching made them angry, so I tried to ignore my twitching skin.

"You are awake."

Vincent's voice was unmistakable. I had reason enough not to turn to him, but I would use whatever excuse I could not to roll over and burst the thin balloon of bile always threatening to shoot out of my nose.

"Do you mind giving us some time?" I heard Vincent ask Adam and Serena, because why would he ask me? I didn't get a say.

"You realize she's my family, right?" Adam asked sarcastically. "Every time we're in here you kick us out."

"You can all leave." I cleared my throat, the action enough to add an extra pulse or two of pounding in my brain. I cradled my face and pressed my fingers into my temples, a cluster of pox there screaming like a disturbed ants' nest.

"Guess I'll call Mom with an update." My brother didn't sound too happy about it. "She doesn't know you're sick, but she still worries about us and is babysitting your dog at Grandma Lizzie's."

"Mhmm," I groaned, refraining from saying goodbye to Adam and Serena, my brother taking his guilt trip with him.

The brush of loafers on the floor told me Vincent filled their empty spot. The creak of leather of a different sort said someone else was with him. I opened my eyes to see who.

What the fuck?

The bubble of bile exploded in my gut like Issát threw a dart straight through my belly button. Vomit shot up into my mouth, through my lips and nose in a waterfall to the floor. More guttural sounds came from behind me as Donovan did the same. A female voice comforted him—Rosemary. My mind filled with panicked images of things I saw Evaristus and his son do. The piles of dead bodies in Diluculo, the colluding with Loring, the splash of soul glows that darkened in a snap. None of their calculated acts included the notion of either of them racing to find something to clean up my puke.

Holy shit. Evar's son is inside the Prison Creation and he's cleaning up my vomit.

What the fuck is happening?

"I'm sorry. I didn't mean to startle you." And now he's apologising? "I forgot you were unconscious last I visited."

"Wha—?" I couldn't think. Sweat punched through my pores as I rasped my pox-covered hands against my face to stop the room from spinning.

"Sophie," Vincent's voice was soft at my side, "I promise he is not here to hurt you."

"He...he's—"

"Not in league with Loring. I'm here to help." Issát's voice was as gentle as Vincent's.

To help?

I used to trust Vincent with everything. Then he kicked me off of the Team, insisted I play nice-nice with Donovan, and now he trusts the son of my ancestor who enslaved, tortured, and murdered our people. A man who also is already nuzzled up to our biggest enemy and changed all of those people into Tainted Magics.

Something about Vincent was still off. The way he moved around Issát. Always keeping him in view.

Issát added the vomit-soaked towels to the bag Vincent held. "That's because your Overseer loves you and fears my intentions are not as I claim."

I took the cloth Vincent offered me to wipe my mouth. His green eyes were guarded enough to confirm what Issát said without repeating it.

"Sophie..." Vincent started.

"I'll find someone to handle these." Issát took the bag of vomit cloths, which probably also contained the ones to clean up after Donovan, and left the room.

Vincent pulled a chair close to the bed and stared at my hand like he wanted to hold it. Either I assumed wrong, or the pox were too much, but he refrained. "I do have reservations regarding Issát's intentions. Thus far he has given me no reason to treat him as my enemy."

"Besides all the people he—"

"Those people are all here now. Souls cleaned. Issát states he is prepared to on board them as his responsibility after Loring forced him to release their powers."

"Doesn't make sense."

"I know. There must be more. Though the reasons may be personal and not nefarious in nature." Vincent peered up at the bag of liquid draining into me, hanging from the metal post. "How do you feel?"

"Ready for an all-night raver."

His eyes crinkled and then glazed with worry.

"I'm not actually dying, am I?"

"No," he said quickly. "I did not mean to alarm you. I was merely in thought. Much is developing quickly and my mind..."

"Is a Rubik's Cube and someone fucked with its stickers?"

He laughed. "Quite accurate."

I rested my head on the too-thin pillow and closed my eyes, exhausted of feeling like my stickers were fucked with as well, half of them replaced with the festering pox I tried to ignore. Jordan fucked those stickers up even if Donovan messed with them long ago. I didn't think Jordan would see outside of the prison's cells again, and now I'm brimming with the equivalent of a magically induced STI because Donovan turned his back on a naked guy.

His cockiness, my consequences.

"I should never have allowed it." Vincent's tone surprised me enough for me to open my eyes to his heavy guilt evident in his slumped shoulders.

I huffed and closed my eyes again. "I'm a big girl."

"You are normally a compassionate young woman who routinely places other's needs ahead of your own. In this life and in others. I have missed that young woman for some time now."

"Dramatic, Vincent."

Quiet fell. I prayed he would give up and leave.

"Issát assessed your Soul Magic while you slept. He claims Donovan can heal you."

Of course he wouldn't stop. "The ritual stone magic. We've already been over this."

"Same with the Soul Magic itself. Both were mere speculation until he read you."

I shot up in the bed. My stomach lurched and it took great control to keep from puking again. "You let him touch me?"

"He saw the damage. Saw the ritual stone magic could fix you."

"Not that she cares." Rosemary's voice rose in the room.

Donovan telling his mom to stop was accepted with gritted teeth and a narrowed-eyed reaction to the pox-covered middle finger I shot at her.

"You have to try." The softness Vincent used with the intensity of his stare didn't fit. The statement of "Or else..." hung in the air.

"And if I don't?"

Vincent didn't answer.

"Get out."

"Sophie..."

"You can't make me do it."

He stood. "Caine can."

"Bastard."

"I love you enough to do it. And Caine cares enough to know this is what you need."

"Says a lot about the both of you."

"I need to go." He ignored my comment. "The board is meeting. The Sovereignty is mine to run. Hate-filled as you are, you still know what that means and you know I want nothing of it. I want to think that while I am doing something I have battled against for centuries, you are here spilling effort into something you do not particularly want to do either. You are not the only one with regrets, and I am not enabling you to ruin your life or Donovan's any longer. Forge ahead of your own volition by the time I return or actions will proceed without your collaboration."

Vincent walked away, shared a guarded exchange with Rosemary, and left the room.

Forge ahead? He's going to do it regardless of what I want?

Asshole!

Impotent rage boiled along my skin, the emotion devoid of magic, which may have been helpful to have before they strapped me down and sent Caine after me. Rosemary wouldn't let me risk her son's life. And no one would miss me limping through the lobby, sloughing off skin as I went if I tried to leave. Maybe they would be too scared to touch me.

Vincent never wanted anything to do with his family or their business and now he's going to climb up onto his father's throne and rule his sadistic kingdom? He made it sound like he didn't have a choice. Clearly, he did, and didn't need Caine to steal his free will to force it. You don't want to do something, then don't. What the hell was the issue?

Damn. Sitting up was a chore. As was getting to the makeshift bathroom area on the far side of the room. Evelyn promised she spelled it for sound and anything we did in there was somehow magically destroyed in the same process as in the cells. I didn't know what that was, but I wasn't in a position to argue. Better than a concert porta-potty. A bedpan would have been less difficult, but like hell I was squatting over one with Donovan a few feet away and with people walking in any time they wanted.

When I was done and back in bed, I struggled to pull the thin sheet over me. The effort caused my skin to itch worse as I sweat and strained. Maybe if I was covered in my own filth Caine would decide touching me wasn't such an awesome plan.

"Not that he needs to." Rosemary's tone was flat and judgemental as she plucked my thoughts out of my head. "Caine could control you without stepping a toe inside the room."

Donovan's aggravation joined my own. "Stop. Stop talking to her."

Rosemary didn't acknowledge him. "Take what Vincent said to heart. Because if you don't do it, I'll have Caine's precious cousin and her son at the end of a gun, a knife, or a catchy spell to ensure you do what you should've done already."

I smoothed the blanket, getting dismissively comfortable. "So much bluster from a woman who didn't give a shit about her own kid until she needed a hole to hide in."

Rosemary shot to her feet, her glare caustic.

Donovan grabbed his mother's arm to stop her from going anywhere. The quick effort was so tiring he dropped his hand.

"At least I'm here, caring for my son. Where're your parents? Right. Your mommy's cowering behind her useless family and your daddy's too Blind to lift a finger."

"Stop!" Donovan yelled.

A punch of power shot into the room, too potent to ignore.

It snapped back into him.

In his sickness, Donovan's energy was useless against his mother, its presence a weak warning for Rosemary pushing things too far.

The angry black-haired beauty's gaze fell on him. "You know—"

"I know," he said with edge. "Take a walk."

"Donovan."

"I know, Mom. Please...take a walk."

Leaving at her son's request, I knew it wouldn't be the last time Rosemary lost her shit. The woman was still Tainted. The fact Vincent let her into the Prison Creation was absurd. And now Issát was here. Maybe he and Rosemary were colluding with Loring. She would love a controlling stake in the Sovereignty.

"Can you get your shit together, maybe? Just a little?" I ignored the rustle of Donovan's bedsheets. His voice was now clearer as he faced me. "I know you think you got the shit end of the stick here, but you're acting like an entitled child."

"Suck my pox, asshole."

"Let me try."

I eyeballed him for the first time in a while. Pox clustered all over his face, crowding around his left eye, nestling into his upper lip, and up around his ears.

"You're no prettier, Rumpelstiltskin," he said, hearing my inner recoil. "I could fix this easier with your help."

I rolled onto my back and put my arm over my face.

The room fell into a tense quiet while I tried to ignore his fluctuating emotions running through me.

A vibrating sensation tingled along the surface of my skin, enough to aggravate the pox and intensify their itchiness.

Donovan was now laying on his back in much the same position I was, but he wasn't resting, his brows cinched with concentration.

"Hey!" I threw a cold, wet washcloth at him. It splat against his neck.

"What the hell?" He tossed the washcloth onto the floor between our beds.

"I can feel what you're doing. Stop it."

"I'm not leaving our Soul Magic broken and with seeping sores. Bought the 'I Survived Smallpox' t-shirt. I'm done with this shit."

"Done with it? It's your fault we're dealing with it at all."

Donovan closed his eyes again, ignoring me.

He pushed his power to the surface, immediately awakening the ritual stone magic. He managed to steady both at a low hum, though my skin burned and my head swam with his attempt. The vibration increased until I thought I was going to puke and then suddenly snapped like a rubber band and flushed away.

I slumped into the thin mattress, laughing and coughing. "Fail."

Frustration sparked across the connection, worsening as I continued to laugh.

The hum of Donovan's power reformed, fueled by spite thick enough to stop me from laughing and fight to hide an uncomfortable grunt.

The pressure of the energy he expended built again, greater than his last attempt, until he lost control and it vanished.

"Learn when to give up."

He was breathing hard. "Back atcha, sweetheart."

Sweetheart? Asshole.

Proving his relentless stubbornness, Donovan kept at it for a good hour. Each time he would reach a certain point and each time it would slap him down like a pesky mosquito, leaving us nauseous and panting.

After a good fifteen minutes or so of no attempt, I thought he finally realized he was too weak to pull it off. He started his shit up once again when he noticed I was getting comfortable enough to sleep.

I huffed and dug deeper into my sheets.

The tingling energy rose to an uncomfortable vibration again, making my skin itch and my stomach swirl. When the moments dragged on, I waited for the inevitable slap on the ass, but the magic grew stronger into a multiplying pressure to a point registering far beyond discomfort and sliding into painful.

"Donovan..." I tried and failed to break his focus.

A surge in my stomach had me bearing down to stop a rush of bile threatening to shoot through my teeth again. A licking fire across every inch of my skin overshadowed the struggle.

Echoes of my screams were a beacon of alarm. People rushed into the room. Rosemary pushed Evelyn aside.

"Fix her!" My brother's demands were jumbled in the chaos, as were Denise's failed attempts to get him out of Evelyn's way.

"This is no smallpox symptom," I heard her say above a mash of competing voices.

Donovan pushed at his mother. She slapped his hand away, but he wouldn't let her interfere. Her cheeks reddened with frustration and rejection.

Dripping sweat and the ooze of split-open pox pustules along my skin and intensified with Donovan's magic. A rancid smell wafted and kept the nausea rolling and the dry heaves gripping my gut. Writhing did nothing to lessen the pain in my aching joints or the pressure in my chest and lungs, but I couldn't stop moving. Pawing for comfort and thrashing against the bed did nothing, neither did tearing at my skin with my fingernails.

The ache washed out of me on the end of a ragged moan. I

collapsed in a puddle of chilled, wet sheets, my limbs heavy with exhaustion.

Roughness dragged down my arm. I grumbled against the overwhelming fatigue, unable to buck off Evelyn running a washcloth across my skin in heavy strokes, turning my arm to do so again and again. Olive joined the others in the room. Her wide and anxious eyes peered over Evelyn's shoulder.

Olive gasped. I fought exhaustion and saw her smile light up with relief.

No more pox, no more scabs or oozing.

Olive pushed around Evelyn, grabbed my shoulder and squeezed, then kissed me on the top of the head. "He did it."

The elation in Olive's voice fueled a deep rage.

"Bastard." I would have said or did more if my jaw wasn't too sore from gritting my teeth during the onslaught.

"What'd you do?" Serena asked Donovan for an explanation while I tried to situate myself, now shivering without the fever.

Donovan rolled onto his back, hand in his hair with a palm against his galloping heart where the dull and lingering sensation of the ritual stone magic nested. "I did us a favour."

28

INHERENT CHARACTER FLAW

Vincent

Around the twelve-foot African blackwood Sovereignty boardroom table were many masks of collected fear. When my father reigned, and even with Chase, the masks were the same. While I never feared my father in a way that resulted in serving him, standing in front of his hand-picked board members wearing the same expressions directed at me, did not generate ease.

As presumed, Roger Offerman took the bait Issát set. He was now claiming to be one of the inconvenienced and ignorant, huffing on cue, and complaining of why they were convened on short notice.

To keep his comrades from knowing he was dirty up to his elbows, Offerman told everyone whatever he needed to in order to fill those chairs so late in the day. He left guilt somewhere else to shrivel and die so he could keep up his air of victimhood.

The members with passive fear cared nothing about me except for my next move and how whatever I said might impact the future they planned for themselves. If my plan fell inside appropriate parameters, they would be complacent allies. If they were in the same soul pool as Offerman, they would fight this with fervor.

"I'm not drinking that." Roger Offerman pointed at the container of soul-glow-revealing liquid Kim duplicated from my missed Alchemist friend, Moira. "It could be poison, and a quick sip will expunge us all. If you want to run the company, then fire us. Leave us with fair compensation and you won't hear another word."

"So much for loyalty," Hall called out. Every part of him was rigid with hypervigilance.

"Loyalty?" Offerman glared at me. "You have a Recondite Magic calling our loyalties into question?" He leaned forward to focus on Hall. "Don't think I'm ignorant to who you are." Offerman shifted the lapels of his suit coat to expend some impotent anger and reclined in his seat. His attempts to showcase his lack of intimidation and the thought of his reputation reaching such heights amused Hall.

"And you..." Offerman motioned towards John. "You're a little rat we should've squashed decades ago. Alasdair knew of your connection to his son and never interfered. You think you know anything of substance? You know nothing."

John remained quiet and with everyone's thoughts still closed to me, I had no avenue to verify if these words were true spite or misleading theatrics.

"What exactly do you plan to do with the company?" a usually quiet member James Kleinstead inquired. As far as members went, James represented the opposite of Offerman.

Some of these Magics worked hard, went above and beyond, and bore families depending on them. These Magics I understood. By the time they climbed the Sovereignty corporate ladder, they were captives to my father's rule, glued to their positions until they expired. Retirement was usually met with a trip somewhere their families could never find them or an untimely sickness which cut them down unexpectedly in their sleep.

"Honestly, I intended to dismantle it."

"You cannot be serious!" Offerman shouted along with another member, Ada Ghillingham, whose soul I would not be surprised to find equivalent to Offerman's.

James lifted a hand to quiet the outburst. Another board member added, "Our people need to know justice is being upheld."

"Agreed," I responded to Joanne Woytovich, a woman I highly respected for sitting at the table in more than a show of fairness to a perceived inferior sex. "Until recently, destruction was my singular plan. The world does not require an organization which prides itself in the number of Magics it captures or disappears. Our needs differ from the Blind and therefore require differing governing. They do not mean we devise those rules to do nothing but amplify our personal connections and portfolios while innocents suffer."

Richard North scoffed with an indolent chuckle and swivelled away from the table in a chair furthest from me.

"You think me wrong?" I challenged across the room.

The man remained stoic. He sat forward and clasped his hands on the table, the action bringing forth an image of my father preceding many lectures. "With Alasdair's death one of shock and upset, one where you were to blame, the fact you have the nerve to point fingers at Magics who have sat in these chairs for centuries, is appalling. How many have perished in your pursuit of your agenda?" He scoffed again. "You want change, develop it. You want to rule, enjoy your seat, son. But know no decision large or small was passed without the say of the board in its entirety."

Some gave a hearty "hear, hear" and pounded on the table in chorus, but not all shared this viewpoint.

"How many times did someone around this table challenge Alasdair's decisions?" James asked. "And how many times did the coot change his mind based on a member's opinion?"

"Many a time."

"Hogwash and you know it!" Joanne hollered back at Richard sparking a sparring match of words. A few sprung from their chairs and went at each other like howler monkeys.

When this went on longer than I cared to endure, I turned to Caine, the kid's gift an asset no one could ignore.

With an understanding nod laced with something else blooming questions for another time, Caine brought forth an energy I felt graze the skin of my cheeks.

"Stop talking." Caine barely raised his voice above a normal speaking level, and his persuasion closed the lips of the board members up tight. All of them looked to each other and then to me, eyes wide and mouths agape in stunned silence.

"Sit down," Caine commanded and waited until they did. "What now, boss?" Caine asked me while holding the members' will with less than full concentration. Perhaps I should have done this from the beginning.

"Steadfast for now," I told him and addressed those at the table. "My purpose today is to catalogue whose interests are invested in all Magics, who is too self-involved to consider anyone who does not directly affect their lives, and who is flat-out working for Tainted agendas. Every case I tried while my father held me under his thumb was a case I should have lost. One of my first acts as heir of this company will be to right those mistakes and ensure justice is upheld. Untold scores of cases mirror this corruption and have left families broken and the unjustly convicted never heard from again.

"Now, despite the fact that forcing you may seem counterproductive, no amount of reform can occur in any level of governing body until it changes at the top. This board will not be made up of aristocratic self-serving asshats any longer." I mentally thanked Sophie for the fitting asshat term. "Also, every Magic will have the opportunity to review their contracts, negotiate alterations, or leave the company all together. Internal strife will be dealt with as in any company. If behind-the-curtain colluding occurs, it will be handled swiftly by an investigative team of Magics." I motioned to Caine. "With his method or another's, I will know the truth."

Bronya, Ismail, Gregor, and Arden moved forward with liquid-filled vials to counteract the concoction the board used to hide their soul glows from Soul Seers.

Anticipating the directive, Caine said, "When the vial is handed to you, you will each drink every drop of what's inside. After you've swallowed, place the vial on the table, drop your mental barriers, and sit quietly until I say otherwise."

Good instincts.

Each of the board members drank as Caine willed them to. One by one their true soul glows were exposed to Lewis and Issát. Since Sophie's presence was impossible, her uncle volunteered to represent the Mother Coven Soul Seers. And while Lewis would perform adequately, I missed Sophie at my side.

Lewis surveyed the group in front of him. I stood in anticipation of the reveal, and he projected everything to me.

Of the twelve Sovereignty board members, a mere four Magics registered relatively clean souls. Another five were wading half in the Tainted pool, and three were nothing better than the enemies that slaughtered innocents at the safe houses or drowned them in The Chiff. Offerman being one of them.

A heaviness fell over me. I recognized the sensation of being watched. The board members wore vacant masks, unable to stare at me. The Team was focused on them in case they slipped from Caine's compulsion. With all attentions in the room elsewhere, the palpable gravity of someone's observation weighed on me.

Was my father observing me harangue his carefully groomed and cultivated staff?

"He is here," Issát said as if reading my thoughts. "Your father observes these proceeding with rapt interest in how you handle a beast you spent your life avoiding."

"He can—"

"He requests leniency for certain members, knowing some are lost causes."

So, this was a case of mediumship with demands. "Does he now?"

"He claims no ill-will for the events of his passing." Issát side-eyed the empty space where my father presumably stood. "And he states that if this is his singular interaction with you in death, he is proud you are preserving the Sovereignty in whatever form you choose." Issát paused. "This includes an extension of pity and empathy for the heft of the crown he has passed on."

Pity? The man never pitied anyone with any amount of empathy.

"If this is his only chance, he wants to warn you of foreign factions interfering in the region's more political endeavours. Mainly, threats to—" Issát stopped and squinted with concern.

"Issát..."

Issát lifted a couple of fingers to stop my father from speaking and then turned to me. "If the Mother Coven, and by extension the Sovereignty now that you have assumed leadership, cannot regain control of parties responsible for acts of unmanageable exposure of Magics to the Blind, foreign entities will do so for you. Namely, the greater European factions and ones within northern and southern American borders."

"What?" I heard a couple of the Tactical Team members mumble, unable to retain composure.

Ranlyn stepped closer to me and Issát in his shock.

The danger of such a threat hit low in my gut. I did not need them to see me rattled.

"Negotiations thus far have come to the Sovereignty and not the Mother Coven Elders?" How could we not know of this? Judging by Ranlyn's anger and Veata's confusion, this was an unanticipated threat.

Issát looked to the empty space where my father stood, listening. "The Sovereignty is responsible for the law in this region and viewed by other nations as the entity of justice. If parties were to be held responsible for such behaviours which could expose Magics and cause potential civil strife between them and the Blind, then the Sovereignty was thought to be the primary source of regulation."

"They thought they were calling in the cops, when they were

really tapping the local mafia and expecting them to do anything other than whatever's in their best interest," Caine said.

He may have been brash, but Caine's analogy was accurate. The Sovereignty would do what was best for themselves, which may not align with what benefited Magics.

Would my father have contacted the Mother Coven Elders if international factions were moving to intercede in local affairs? Or let the region be attacked and claim the violence was from others greedy attempts to takeover while burying the truth about Loring?

"He adds that tensions have already been high among the Sovereignty, the Mother Coven, the Sorrels, and others. No one wants to lose what the Sorrels provide for the region, and they are gleefully hosting Loring whose attack in Niagara Falls was highly publicized. Other incidents like the Creation takedown went unseen by the Blind and hold no risk of exposure, but do pose questions regarding those in power and their ability to police its citizens.

"Loring's disregard for discretion and plans to kidnap and release the Blind's power with help of a Soul Seer have become a great concern. Same with Gualichu, though the Architect demon's actions are passive and not of Loring's calibre when considering exposure. People have thus far assumed he is a ghost, another innocuous supernatural being, or a hoax."

"But Loring no longer has a Soul Seer to corrupt the Blind since you left. Unless you plan on returning to his side," Ranlyn said as if Issát should not be insulted by the assumption that Issát may betray the Mother Coven.

Issát shook his head. "My involvement or not won't make a difference. All my absence will have done is re-establish Loring's desire to obtain another Soul Seer."

"Sophie?" Lewis asked and Issát nodded in confirmation. "No one else in the family has her power. It may be unpracticed, but still has leagues to grow."

"And Sophie is a feather in Loring's cap if he can get to her as well as corrupt her." Issát was right with that one. He would scream it from the rooftops if it meant he had control over her and her power since he spotted her all of those months ago.

"And as a bonus he gets Donovan and a tighter connection to the Sorrels," Bronya added.

She was not incorrect. Donovan would end them both before allowing any such future with them working alongside his father and Loring to come to fruition.

Either way, Loring no longer having a Soul Seer at his whim would not convince foreign factions to remain out of current affairs if they did not hold confidence in the leader's ability to control those within their borders. If Loring continued to be an exposure risk, those factions would unseat the region's current modes of power, which was now mainly the Elders and me.

I needed to make some calls.

"This is political, Alasdair points out," Issát stated to clarify the opinion source. "He has thus far been successful in holding off an incursion, but they do already have scouts in the area compiling reports of any public Magic activity and deciding by their own scales which are acceptable and which are deemed enough to warrant a FIRC."

"I've dealt with foreign-imposed regime changes before," Hall said with a grim expression. "Usually involves a lot of spilled blood."

I nodded in thought. I, too, have been around long enough to see the results of such a revolt and whether or not the people are liberated, mass causalities are expected.

Diverting a political coup or full-on war would have to come after concluding these proceedings. The board members were still under Caine's persuasion.

"Caine," I said, covering my unease with my father's exchange, "release your hold from James, Joanne, Wilson, and Bartlett."

I watched as those members regained control of their will.

Issát made no comment on if these were the members my father vaguely mentioned should receive leniency.

"What is this?" Wilson removed his thick glasses, blinking free of Caine's hold.

"Caine's persuasion, along with the soul-revealing concoction and Lewis's Soul Seeing, has shown the four of you with acceptably clean souls. Do you wish to continue working with the Sovereignty under a new rule? Make no mistake, I am sincere when I say if you want to walk away that you are more than welcome to. You have served your people and somehow retained your honour. A full compensation package is included without fear of reprisal."

"I'll stay," Wilson answered and returned his glasses to his nose. "If you don't live up to your word, I'll disappear somewhere you'll never find me, I can assure you."

I nodded, though his threat was thin since Wilson had done nothing to oppose my father all these years.

"I'll take the compensation package," Bartlett said and fiddled with his tie. "My wife has been in Sacramento for many years. When I requested leave to be with her on a more permanent basis, Alasdair refused. I've served my time. I'm ready to move on."

I understood and heard in Bartlett's mind the truth behind every word.

"If you want to leave now that is acceptable. Any paperwork drawn will be sent to your contact information and processed without your direct presence if you so choose."

Bartlett stood, shook the hands of the board members released from Caine's will, and approached me to do the same.

I returned the gesture in a show of respect.

Bartlett's hold lingered. "I hope you realize the walls you're up against. Your father's influence reached far beyond this boardroom."

"To ones who wish to overthrow this establishment if the locals continue to act up?"

"Ugly business." Bartlett looked to the others still trapped within Caine's will. "Remove who you need to and you won't have such a fight when it comes to safeguarding the area."

They all knew about it.

Corruption was anticipated, but not selfishness to the degree of allowing your people to be forcibly taken over when they held no control over the methods to prevent such action.

Joanne and James both agreed to lend their clean souls to the restructuring of the Sovereignty, which I was truly grateful for since their experience and knowledge still held value.

"Caine..." I pointed to a reed-thin man. "Release him."

Caine removed his persuasion from Sawyer Martel and maintained hold on the others without issue. Sawyer surged to his feet. The Team twitched for action, but I hit Sawyer with enough energy to shove him backwards into his seat without injury.

"Your soul is partially Tainted. A cur as it has been described." Another thought of Sophie came to mind. "If you were allowed, would you remain a board member and assist me towards change?"

Sawyer's paranoid stare landed on his board mates who were in no position to influence his decision. "What if I refuse?"

"I will choose to believe the actions that altered your soul were done so to please my father and not an inherent character flaw. You will be allowed to leave. If you choose to stay, Issát will cleanse your soul of any evil. That part is non-negotiable."

With his thoughts open, Sawyer was a slew of insults until he collected himself enough to consider the choices I presented. He still believed leaving or disagreeing with me would end his life. The defining decision came down to him lacking other avenues of fulfillment. The Sovereignty was his family, no matter how dysfunctional. He believed he would be better off dead at his desk than without purpose in the free world.

Sawyer grabbed at his chest in obvious discomfort when Issát's power roared forward. I watched the transformation through Lewis's open thoughts. The stains of Sawyer's past drained away leaving a bright silvery thread of immortality.

Sawyer blinked in amazement. He felt different without the ability to pinpoint where the changes began or ended. And he prayed this was not some kind of spell to temporarily alter his emotional state.

I gave the four other curs the same opportunity. One chose to leave with a cleansed soul. Two others were out the door with minimal commentary aside from their resignation. And one other agreed to remain with a clean soul. A particular client shadowed her thoughts. One she refused to abandon.

"For the rest of you," I continued, "your souls are saturated with evil. Even with clean souls, you will be held to your victims. Amends are long overdue. You will remain acting members of the board to be closely monitored. If you decide against this course of action, you will be incarcerated. I am suspending all of my father's regimented punishments and you will sit in solitary. If you choose the first option and I find you or any other on this board has become re-Tainted than my next avenue will mirror your second option.

"Due to the nature of this agreement, I require your answer prior to your freedom. Your courtroom is these four walls. The Coven Elders and the Sovereignty heir are the presiding judges asking for your plea. Guilt is established down to your very souls. Your lone gift is your say in your sentencing. Far more generous than most were afforded when they faced any of you."

They all refused.

Maybe they thought I would fail to follow through. They would live to regret the choice and do so in the boredom of their cells.

The burden of being watched persisted. No matter the years I spent in this place as king of the incarcerated, my father's shadow would follow me, and I could not decide if I detested this this or found it to be my father's most fitting punishment.

I had envisioned my father dead and gone in a plethora of ways. Extracting his soul from his body was not one. And if Alasdair was earthbound, this is where he would remain, forever lending his footprints to every inch of carpet until the Sovereignty Creation was demolished.

If my mother could see me now, would she be brimming with

pride for me outliving my father and spoiling his plans? Or would she bristle at me slipping into his shoes?

Or the younger version of myself. Was he watching me take up the position I always detested? I imagined he would be distraught at the life sentence and feel abandoned.

Was I doing the right thing?

29

WITHOUT A SAFETY NET

Donovan

"Are you okay?" Rosemary's voice was low and full of genuine concern.

"Fine." I was better than an hour ago, yet still shitty. The smallpox was healed, the remnants of pus drying, but we still didn't have enough energy to move around and shower the rest away. Plus, the fix did nothing for our broken Soul Magic.

"Can I get you anything?"

"No."

If I ever prayed for an attentive mother, I had one now. I didn't need anything from her and couldn't even hold her hand due to my psychometry.

Aside from suddenly gaining a mother worth the sentiment, all I could think was, "What happens now?" Sophie and I were clear of the pox, but I overheard what Vincent and Issát said to her. About how I could heal our Soul Magic and heard every pejorative word she thought in response.

I tried to fix her once. I thought I succeeded. What if I

needed to dose her with ritual stone power daily to keep us from breaking again? I would do it, but she might not let me. And if I did do it like forcing a vitamin down her throat, did she really love me? Pathetic and desperate was not a relationship.

Vincent threatened her with Caine's persuasion. He cared about Sophie enough to do the dirty work, but shit. It wasn't Vincent's or Caine's or even Issát's responsibility. Since the damage would never pull a reversal on its own, fixing our Soul Magic fell squarely on my shoulders.

It was all I could think of while stuck in these beds ignoring each other or at least she was ignoring me and said nothing nice when she wasn't.

When Evelyn took used and crusty cloths to the laundry room and Sophie's family left her to rest with promises of chocolate milk and chicken fried rice, I saw my chance.

"Mom, would you mind grabbing me some orange juice?"

Calling Rosemary "Mom" lit up her eyes. "Are you up for some food?"

"Nah, the drink's good." I forced a smile, and Rosemary flashed her set of dimples.

Alone time with Sophie was the ultimate goal. If Rosemary knew why, she wouldn't have left.

When the door shut behind my mother, I raised enough power for a lock spell without drawing Sophie's attention. She would hopefully think I was testing my strength. Which maybe I should since a low-level spell shouldn't have my palm tingling.

Sitting on the edge of the bed, Sophie laid on her own with her back to me. I absolutely hated her blonde hair. It was another aspect of her not being herself.

I sought the ritual stone magic again and funnelled it straight into Sophie. Her shoulders flinched on impact, the stir of her immediate irritation flared in my chest.

Sophie spun around to come after me. I telekinetically forced her onto her back, holding her down on the bed. She grit out my name and tried to spin out of my hold.

With the ritual stone power awake, I closed my eyes, keeping Sophie trapped while filtering the magic into her to also block her from using her own magic.

I needed to find the broken Soul Magic.

Our ancient power pried her open to explore her essence. Sophie's outrage scratched at the energy I filtered into her, then she flailed and cursed at me. Unwilling to let go, I prodded the power along to figure out how to fix her.

Finding the break itself was harder than anticipated, not because it was buried, but because it was everywhere. A sizzling and snapping anger encircled her soul like a festering infection.

Her emotions raged on around me, attempting to overwhelm me.

Beyond her anger was something dark and toxic. Frigid shots from this darkness pierced the energy I used and then coiled away.

Afraid or hurt?

Sophie called my name again, her voice much quieter than she must have been.

I refused to let her distract me. Instead, I held tighter to my telekinetic grip to ensure she couldn't escape while the majority of my focus was elsewhere.

Whatever this darkness was inside of her, it went beyond feral, beyond lethal, beyond anything I had ever felt. Unlike the Taint of evil, this was not a stain on her soul. It was a tangible acrid-smelling despair rooting itself inside of the soul and bubbling up from the gaping injury of our broken Soul Magic to poison the rest of her. I waded through the viscous venom the brokenness released with only the ritual stone magic as protection.

The further I ventured, the more I felt trapped.

I don't know how I knew my choice of leaving was gone, but I knew turning back no longer existed. Terror momentarily panicked me because failure wasn't an option. If I fumbled this, whatever was left of Sophie wouldn't be someone I could save. Without this fixed, we would never find each other again in future lives. I was sure of it.

I continued, ignoring my fear, and pushed on without a safety net.

Something moved. Not a snake, something bigger slithering in the darkness that sighted me as prey while remaining far from my reach.

A surge of energy rushed me and clawed a slice from my back. I had no no skin in this place, but it still impacted me as if I did. Was I bleeding through my shirt? I couldn't check the damage of the bracing agony rolling through me and threatening my hold on the ritual stone magic.

I found some grit, and kept on looking for the crack in the Soul Magic.

Whatever was inside of Sophie, it wasn't a festering hatred or trauma my father created during the Conception Rituals. It was as if the fracture in our Soul Magic released a physical entity who was hiding inside of her, and the crouching evil was now swimming around and taking swipes at me as I threatened its survival.

With every inch of progress I made came another chomp, slice, or blindsided attack meant to scare me into giving up.

If it knew anything about me, it must know I was too stubborn to quit on her. And if it was coming after me, it meant I was doing something right.

"You can't have her. Whatever you are, you can't fucking have her."

It hit me again.

If I had knees to fall to, they would be bruised and bleeding.

Keep moving. Keep pushing. Find the source. I win when I fix her.

The mantra kept me focused on why I was here and not on the monster without a face to break or talons to dodge or a throat to slit. One imbedded in the coldness of her eyes staring back at me every time I searched them for a sliver of hope.

The monster's desperation to keep it's hold on her and remain free of wherever it was before the broken Soul Magic let it loose, enveloped me in a chilled bleakness.

The ritual stone magic around me was battle-worn and heavy. So heavy. I fought to keep it activated as the monster or entity continued to try to batter me off course. Straining to hold my own with the addition of Soul Magic was like carrying an electrified bolder up a sun-baked sand dune while stinging scorpions struck my ankles with every step.

Everything hurt.

A jarring smash to the jaw was a shock of new pain.

I gasped and opened my eyes from the attack that couldn't have been from the monster with no fists, seeing the makeshift medical office around me and Sophie seated on the other bed. The ritual stone magic was still active and doing its thing. I was still trapped inside of her, chained to the process. Retreating meant the end in a way I refused to accept, but the monster or entity also refused to retreat and now it was glaring at me through Sophie's eyes, the white swimming with tiny threads of blackness.

Whatever the monster did to me, it broke my telekinetic hold keeping her on the bed. She grabbed my shoulder and thrust a lightning bolt of pain through me.

I roared with the driving spike to my nerves. Just me. It didn't hurt Sophie. How was the entity saving her from feeling what I felt?

Fuck, I'm losing.

"Stop this!" Sophie shrieked with the entity coiled around her vocal cords.

I shoved her hand away and grabbed her arms in a telekinetic hold since touching her skin would blind me in a psychometric vision. A growl rumbled deep within her chest as I whipped her around and slammed her back onto the bed. I tried to crawl on top of her and caught a knee to the gut.

She sat up with a swipe of her clawed hand like the monster was defaulting to its base instincts.

Regaining a hold on her arms, I threw my weight into it and parked my ass on top of her with a sheath of magic around us to keep the entity from accessing her powers. The ritual stone magic was still doing its thing by maintaining the ground I already won inside of her, but I needed to finish this.

No going back.

Locked into position with her body squeezed between my legs, I closed my eyes to focus inward and feel for the gaping fracture inside of her.

Pressure built in my chest where I usually felt our connection. I inched the ritual stone magic forward, using it as a shield to move closer to the Soul Magic fracture. The entity taking over Sophie may be bound from using her power while I held her down, but it still fought within its own realm and was beyond playing coy.

I poured the ritual stone magic from me in all directions. My ribcage squeezed to the point of breathlessness. Was it the entity trying to drain me? Was it the ritual stone magic at the end of its well of power?

Taking in the deepest breath I could and holding onto it, I ignored the sounds of the feral beast in Sophie's voice over a dull pounding. People heard us and were trying to break the door down, but none were stronger than the ritual stone magic's lock spell.

Light-headed waves of weakness washed over me.

Fuck. I couldn't feel my body.

The energy rolling through me into Sophie vibrated so strongly nothing felt tangible. I quickly checked my hands to ensure they still held Sophie in place. They did. And I caught a glimpse of her straining to buck me off.

It's not her. It's not her.

I kept telling myself this, but my concentration was slipping. Her escape attempts caused me to lose my balance. Without sensation in my body, I positioned myself so I listed forward. If nothing else, maybe my dead weight would keep her down, even if it meant losing an ear to her gnashing teeth.

I gripped the ritual stone magic as hard as I could. It was doing its job, but I couldn't keep it together.

I slumped onto her.

No! I've got it. I've got this!

The binding power keeping her down vanished when my body flagged it. She slipped her hands between us, and shoved me off of her and onto the floor. My head bounced off of the hard surface, rocking my skull and exploding stars in front of my eyes. Balls-to-brains numbness lessened the physical pain and still made me want to curl up like the neglected baby I once was.

I couldn't shift onto my side, I couldn't kick my legs, and my arms were rubber.

Panic hit when my hold on the ritual stone magic loosened.

I concentrated with every pulse of energy inside of me on gripping the power and fighting the good fight internally. Dark tendrils the monster embedded inside of her flowed from her body with its newfound foothold. This bloated her with magic so frosty, its chill bypassed the numbness and plummeted my body temperature as it snaked its way over my internal organs.

Sophie climbed off of the bed. The entity was alive in her eyes as she stepped towards me and kicked me in the gut.

Breath huffed from my lungs and drove me into a hacking cough. I couldn't grab my stomach to soothe the cramping.

Nothing in her eyes said she cared what she was doing to me. They were as cold as the magic the entity punished me with. They were too dark, the whites now bloodshot and sickly.

This wasn't her. She's saved me too many times for me to fail her now.

I had to get up.

I tried to say her name, to connect, but nonsense fluttered off my lips. Sounds. No words.

Sophie disappeared from my eyeline. I couldn't move my head to track her.

She popped into view a few seconds later with something in her hand.

An IV pole?

She raised the metal up and swung it like a golf club. It smashed into the side of my head.

Everything spun. A sharp ringing pierced my left ear.

Fuck. I have to get up. I have to—

Blackness.

Pain.

She hit me again.

Hold your shit together, man. You've taken far worse without the lights turning off.

I blinked to clear my view. When it did, I saw Sophie twist the IV pole into two pieces and throw half aside with a muffled clang of metal on the floor.

I tried to call up some power, mine or the ritual stone magic. Nothing sparked.

Sophie lifted the IV pole again and drove it down through my stomach with such force I heard it hit the floor underneath me with a metallic ring.

The taste of blood shot up onto the back of my throat. I still couldn't feel anything, and I couldn't heal. I focused on Sophie's face. She was still gripping the pole stuck into me, her knuckles as white as her teeth the monster bared.

Blood dripped from a wound above her eye. She wasn't immune to the damage the monster inflicted on me after all. Not completely. The monster numbed her body as well while still able to control it, but it caused as much damage against me as it did to the body it piloted.

We were both dead if I didn't find a way to stop this.

Sophie wobbled to the side, unbalanced, catching herself on her forearm. Confusion coloured the monster's eyes. It saw blood seeping through her shirt exactly where she skewered me. It touched it and appeared dumbfounded at how the metal still flag-poled in my gut could have harmed her body.

A war cry sounded from somewhere far away and then an ear-splitting explosion blasted a shower of debris over the whole room.

My body swung to the side. Yelling. Dust lined my nostrils and tongue.

Voices rose...lots of them.

The others found a way inside.

"Donovan..." My mother's voice was so full of worry I almost didn't recognize it.

I opened my eyes to Rosemary leaning over me, her long, dark hair in my face.

I'm okay, I thought, unsure if I could speak, though doubly certain I was far from peachy-fucking-keen.

One second Rosemary was in anxious mom-mode, the next her expression twisted into a raging scowl, and she was scouring the room. I didn't have to ask to know what she was seeing.

She leapt over my body after Sophie. I couldn't stop her to explain why Sophie wasn't herself.

Rosemary knew she couldn't hurt Sophie without potentially harming me. Maybe that would slow her down. Maybe she didn't care if she thought I was dying anyway.

"Look at me!" Evelyn's hand hovered around the metal planted in me. Her other one grabbed my chin, trying to gain my attention.

Did I pass out?

I couldn't keep my eyes open.

An icy dip back inside me and into the entity's realm was a chilled slap to the balls.

Did I retain the connection? Or maybe the entity did? Either way, we may not have been right next to each other, but we were still locked in an internal death battle.

Blackness squeezed in around me, blinding me from the room and what was happening in it.

I could feel again.

Not my true body, it was still numb, but the part of me within this inner darkness connected to the entity in battle. My disembodied essence scrambled forward, taking advantage of the fact the monster sacrificed the integrity of its host.

A scream ripped through my lips, tearing me from the inner fight. Jared muscled the pole from my gut and the floor beneath me. Now holding it like a weapon he would turn on me if I went after him.

Damn, I sure as fuck felt that.

A fogginess still surrounded me, but the rest of my body was pain-free.

Was that a good sign?

Growls filled the room. Scrambling from boots and shoes scraped my ears. I couldn't see what was happening. Was Sophie attacking them? They didn't know about the monster possessing her. They could handle her wrath, they have before, but what would the monster do to them?

I tried to concentrate inward and found I had gained more ground than I had the whole time I faced the monster. The pain or whatever the others were doing must have distracted it too much for it to defend its internal territory.

The coldness in her persisted, grasping for me...to help it? To swallow me whole? It was my monster as much as it was Sophie's if it was a part of the Soul Magic, no?

A sudden shot of energy sliced through me, amping up the pain. Evelyn hovered over me, expression crimped with concern as she tried to heal me. Tingling spread over my torso, her healing the tunnel through my insides and sparking something deeper. The ritual stone magic gained a boost from Evelyn's power.

Yes! Something more to work with.

A punch of pain from the monster was an attack the others couldn't see with it happening inside of her against me and my tether.

We could never have anticipated dark consequences all those years ago. I didn't see any monster through the ritual stone magic vision, only love in her smile and the feeling of utter assurance that what we were doing was the most natural thing in the world.

Focus. Focus.

I squeezed my eyes shut and sensed the fracture as well as where the monster was.

Sounds in the room around me sharpened, voices of the others trying to help Sophie, my mother at my side asking if I was okay.

None of them mattered.

I opened my eyes and shot to my feet as Sophie sprung to hers, throwing off those around her. She was as focused on me as I was on her.

Sophie's eyes blackened in full. Adam and Serena backed off, Olive calling her name without a response. The same from Kim.

Sophie let rip an inhuman shriek and sprinted at me.

Ritual stone magic flooded to the surface. I telekinetically snatched hold of her. A buzz of power surrounded us in a clear barrier. Sophie tore and kicked at the empty space between us until I tossed her onto her back. She landed with a huff.

I jumped onto her, pinning her to the ground by the shoulders and gripping the entity as I had when we were still on the beds. Those on the outside of our bubble tried their own magic to beat down the barrier, probably thinking we were going to kill each other.

Sophie bit my arm. I roared in pain as a vision of burning oil splashed onto my arm and then disappeared when she ripped the chunk of skin off with her teeth and spat it onto the floor.

Blood dripped down my arm and over her chin. The monster raged on and scratched whatever part of her nails could reach me, sparking blips of visions I dodged as best as I could.

Pushing the entity towards the fracture was met with resistance. The entity really didn't want to return to the crack it escaped from.

Too fucking bad.

I pushed harder and faster, earning far more ground. So much so, warm light from the Soul Magic swamped the entity the closer I pressed the fucker towards it. The ritual stone magic found stable footing to plant itself and leaned in with everything our love created.

Tentacles thrashed from the entity, screaming to retain freedom, but losing ground. Feeling its waning strength I muscled the monster towards the precipice of the fissure and felt it panic the closer we got to her soul's warmth.

I've got this.

With a last push for our future and our promises coalesced that formed the ritual stone magic, I heaved the entity into the fracture and healed the crevice closed like a zipper, locking it away.

Nothing but Sophie's Soul Seer green and her intense white light soul glowed all around me and warmed something inside of me.

I collapsed next to Sophie with nothing left to keep me upright.

The barrier around us dropped.

No one moved or said anything.

She blinked up at the ceiling. Frazzled emotions scrambled across our fully healed connection. I nudged the tether keeping us together in silent question. Was she herself again? Did she feel any different?

She turned to me, eyes glossy, but nothing waded within except stunned panic.

Terror filled her as she curled into the fetal position in tears against my chest.

I held her tight, smoothed her hair, and kissed her crown, knowing she was one hundred percent the woman I loved, and this time for good.

For the first time since my father's cells, I was seeing the whole version of my Sophie. The woman who walked through Aunt Lacey's doors naive to her greatness, the woman who changed my life so completely I never wanted to face the mirror and see the man I had been without her.

She took in a long, heavy breath, fighting to collect herself.

We sat up in mutual shock.

A well of something gathered in my chest and bled into a

pounding in my temples. Something like dread or worry. Something unsteady and frenetic.

Sophie's brows crinkled in concern.

Someone's hand gripped my shoulder, surprising me.

Rosemary.

I jumped up and bolted through the hole in the wall in a full-out run for the elevator. My heart hammering inside of my ribcage drowned out the annoyed rubberneckers who were pushed aside when I escaped.

"Open it!" Liam the veil guard flinched as I yelled.

He stood from behind the desk. "On whose authority?"

I reached over the desk and grabbed Liam by the throat.

He grunted when I dragged him around the chunk of fancy wood and high-shined laminate.

"Hey!" I trapped his arm with mine so he couldn't go for his weapon and injected some magic of my own to stop him from raising his.

Once at the elevator, I shoved Liam into the wall. "Open it!"

I didn't let go until the elevator doors were opened, then I dropped Liam onto his ass and shot into the metal box.

It took everything in me to remain still. A thick clot of something settled in my throat, my chest filled with Sophie's mirrored confusion and worry. If I could jump through the elevator walls, I would have. No ceiling escape hatch like in the movies.

"Fuck!" I pounded my fist on the doors knowing it would do nothing.

The elevator doors finally slid open on the earthly side of the veil. I spilled out of the thing, pulling in fresh air too quickly through my nose in a stuttering gasp. It wasn't enough. I couldn't breathe.

Pressure in my lungs built until they ached. I forced my mouth open and gulped in cold winter oxygen too fast.

What the fuck was wrong with me? This should be the most exciting moment of my life. Sophie's back. She's back.

Excitement wasn't what I was feeling. Not even close.

My head spun. I groped for the cement wall and went down onto my ass. Keeled over, hugging my knees.

"Donovan?"

Thankful the voice wasn't Sophie's, I managed a, "Uh-huh," without lifting my head.

"What happened?" Vincent's voice closed in with the soft sound of his loafers.

Pulling in a deep shuddering breath I hoped wasn't so desperate-sounding, I lifted my head and dropped it back against the cement wall. Focusing on Vincent wasn't easy but I managed. The guy was squatted a few feet away, narrowing his eyes in worry, curiosity, or confusion, I couldn't tell.

Behind him was the rest of the Team and a few expensive suits. Issát followed closely.

Wait...Issát?

"Inmates or guests?" An easier question than answering Vincent.

"Inmates," he said. "Is Sophie okay?"

Of course Vincent was more concerned for Sophie's welfare than mine.

"I inquired about your welfare first," Vincent reminded me.

Guess my mental barriers dropped without me noticing.

"Tell me what happened."

The thought of repeating it all didn't cause me any dizziness, it made me full-on nauseous. Beyond reason, I wanted to pick a fight with Vincent so the guy would cold-clock me unconscious for a few hours, giving me time to recalibrate my brain to answer his questions like a person not freaking his shit right now.

"Take your time," Vincent said. "I prefer to save the cold-clocking for when you truly deserve it."

"How do you know I don't? Liam sure thinks I do." I forced myself to stand. Wobbly on my bare feet as the parking garage around me dimmed into near-black. I held the wall for support.

"Are you assaulting my employees again?" Vincent was standing now, looking like he wanted to grab me to stop me from falling, but knew I wouldn't want him sparking my psychometry.

"He wouldn't let me out."

"What were you running from?"

"Who the fuck knows," I mumbled and paced.

A breeze rushed through the garage hitting a sweat over my whole body. The chill forced me to inhale deeply, and I was able to think a bit clearer.

Shit. I was still covered in blood. My face, my stomach, my arms, and my hands from the monster scratching me and gnawing on my arm.

"Hold on." Vincent stepped closer to stop me from pacing. "I find you outside, alone in the midst of a panic attack, underdressed for the weather, and your thoughts are stuck on Sophie and a monster? Something happened. Do I need to go inside—"

"It's done."

"Done?"

"Crisis averted. All good. Super fine." I couldn't think up details to help Vincent understand the situation.

"Donovan, if I have to go in there and deal with you assaulting a guard and whatever this monster business is, I prefer to enter prepared when Edson throws a fit."

"You're not my lawyer."

"I have defended guiltier and won."

Guilty. I was guilty. This started with me. I touched her hand so long ago when I thought she was a hot new coven recruit assaulted by some asshole. I saw so much with that touch. Too much to walk away and leave her in happy trauma-bonded bliss with Caine like I should have.

Another gust of wind blew through the parking garage and reminded me of my missing winter gear or anything passing for proper clothing. I felt it more now than when I first fixed our Soul Magic. A pit stop to my cell had not been a goal in the midst of losing my mind.

Vincent took a step closer. "You fixed your Soul Magic?"

I braced my hands on my knees. Tightening in my chest re-registered enough for me to press my fist into my sternum.

"The smallpox is obviously healed, but your Soul Magic? Donovan—"

"Yes! Yes, I fixed it. All of it." My voice echoed against the garage's cement walls. "It's all fixed. It's done. She's fi—"

Nope.

I sprinted to a set of cars, braced an arm on each, and dry heaved between them. Nothing came up while the spasm rocked me, my gut bone dry. Round two hit with ferocity, an empty tank not enough to stop my stomach from cramping and bucking.

Sophie's worry doubled as she also heaved, having no clue what was wrong with me, and probably surrounded by her family wanting to know what was going on.

"Do I need to fetch Caine?" Vincent called over from where he stood. He wasn't going anywhere without the whole story.

Wiping my face of lingering sweat, I started slow and recalled the healing that felt more like a prize fight.

Vincent didn't need to point it out for me to notice the sound of complete dissociation in my tone. I was barely keeping it together and doing so without an emotional angle was pure survival. When I finished with the whole ugly brawl with the entity, Vincent fought and lost against the materialization of a wide smile, hiding it almost as fast as it escaped.

"You have no idea how happy this makes me, Donovan."

Vincent earned nothing from me but a lifted brow that said, "no kidding."

"What does not please me is seeing you struggle. You fought hard for this outcome. You rallied when many would have allowed Fate to direct the path regardless of negative consequences."

"I didn't..." I paused with no choice as Vincent's question threatened to pop my bubble of detachment making this conversation possible. I pressed my fingers into my burning eyes, opened them, and my feet started moving me again.

"Not a chance." Vincent grabbed my shoulder this time, stopping me.

I realized even if I hadn't planned it, my feet were taking me to the exit of the parking garage. Where was I trying to go?

"Anywhere but here, away from dealing with whatever is happening with you, I presume. To your home where, until now, it has been your refuge." Vincent read my mind again. "Stay. Feel as you need, but do not run."

Dread filled me up to my molars. Mine mixed with Sophie's. Through the veil, it didn't matter. Not this veil. Through Diluculo, we experienced a zombie effect that would be divine right now.

"We can investigate the differences in connection if you please. You must remain in order to do so. There is a problem here. Tell me—"

"I could have lost her!" I blurted, the statement forming and spitting through my lips.

Vincent calmly waited for more.

I looked down at my blood-covered arm where the healed chunk of skin had been missing. "I could have lost her. I could have lost myself trying. I could have lost our futures together. I could have lost everything. What if I'd lost?"

This terrified me because I realized I didn't want to die. I had contemplated death when my father sliced me up in front of the flock, beating me, shaming me. I contemplated death when I was on the run, terrified I'd be dragged back to the Sorrel Compound. I contemplated death after running through one chick after another in an alcohol-induced fog day after day. And more recently, I contemplated death when Sophie despised me and I was aching to hit the reset button onto another life so she would love me again.

All I knew was I was ecstatic we were both alive in this timeline. I didn't know how it happened, could barely articulate the jumbled mash of what my body was feeling because of it, but I was glad we were.

"Since we got out of my father's cells..." I cleared my clenching throat. "Since then, her eyes haven't been hers. They belonged to the monster or entity or dark whateverthefuck it was that escaped our Soul Magic and slowly poisoned her. I thought she hated me and hated herself and hated our love and our past selves for creating it. She was so cold and mean and I knew it must be some kind of karmic payback for years of my bullshit, and...it was none of it. Jordan! Ah, fuck." I raked my hands through my hair. "She... It wasn't her. I could've lost her. The real her. Now, she's herself again. Her true self." Saying this flushed me with adrenaline. My hands shook and my eyes burned again. "Freaked my shit...I guess."

I couldn't be subjected to those eyes. Her eyes. She was there, and I couldn't handle her looking at me and knowing that while she wasn't herself, I was still me. There was so much I should be ashamed of for thinking about her and not saving her sooner.

"I owe you both an apology which will not erase my neglect as your Overseer."

"You don't—"

"I should have insisted on a fix earlier. I put Sophie's needs ahead of your own. I knew you could handle yourself as you have for the entirety of your life, and while you could and did, you should not have had to. It was my responsibility and my failure to see the best course of action. I chose a solution I could live with instead of putting your and Sophie's needs to the forefront. We played our parts and have arrived here, not by accident, but by justified hard work in momentarily comfortable ways.

"I am bewildered but ecstatic to see you and Sophie have survived and am honoured to continue on as your Overseer if it is what you choose."

I managed a hollow laugh. "You think we had a choice?"

Vincent smirked and shrugged. "I wish I knew."

I nodded. None of us knew how this all started or how Vincent managed to follow us through time and land in this icebox of a parking lot trying to help me unravel my shit.

Fate stepped in again or did we orchestrate this in a past life?

Ugh. I didn't have the brain cells for this right now.

"I would like to check on Sophie if you are ready to return inside." Vincent's invitation was more than his curiosity about Sophie. He did want to check in, I'm sure, but he was making it about him so I wouldn't stand here longer trying to pinpoint exactly when I might be ready to face her. Inside was better than running down the highway and losing our feet to frostbite. Sophie felt the cold as I did. I may not be able to handle her as she is now, but she didn't deserve to be frozen.

Forcing myself to step inside the elevator took another few seconds. Vincent waited patiently and then stepped inside and stood with the doors open while I took far too many breaths to convince myself against the prospect of running.

Sophie's dread still settled heavy in my chest as we travelled through the veil. Not knowing why made my balls clench up into my pelvis. So much so that the courage I mustered to step my ass into the elevator had fizzled out, and as soon as the doors opened into the lobby of the Prison Creation, my feet took me straight to the cell console and into a cell.

Vincent didn't try and stop me.

30

NOTHING ELSE MATTERS

Sophie

Questions needed answering. Ones asked of me over and over. What happened? Why did my eyes turn black? Why did Donovan run? Some people asked questions out of curiosity or worry, like Olive and my brother, and some asked in a raging rant of who deserves to know what and why, like Rosemary.

Regardless of their motives, I couldn't answer any of them.

Why would I impale Donovan with a metal pole? What happened with the barrier thing around us? Why was I screaming? Why did I have blood in my mouth and bite marks on my arm? Did I bite myself? Why would I bite Donovan? Or did I?

Most of what those around me asked were simple questions, but my head was a beehive full of honeycombs of information, snapshots of fury and gore I found impossible to process.

Something was inside me. It didn't want to remain in its place. It wanted...it wanted to be seen and heard. It wanted to hurt others like it hurt. Like I hurt?

"It couldn't've been all bad," Adam said, pulling my focus. "Your soul glow is normal again."

"Really?"

I looked to Olive, her Soul Seeing gift far more practiced than my brother's. Her beaming smile confirmed my soul was back to working order without the cast of haziness.

Adam mumbled something sounding like, "Told ya."

Denise scoffed but refrained from adding her opinion to the mix. Adam's ego was fragile enough, and he half-turned to her, eyes hidden behind dark glasses.

"No reason is good enough to shove a metal pole through someone's body. As if you haven't hurt him enough." Rosemary stormed out of the room, probably on mission to find Donovan. I was surprised she hadn't already gone after him.

Her snide comment sparked memories I wished didn't exist. All the times I insulted him, yelled at him, physically hurt him, blamed him for things beyond his control.

Oh, fuck...Jordan. Naked Jordan! The recall of a skin-filled Jordan came with a blast of shame. Why would I do that? Not just to Donovan, but to myself?

Thinking back, I was one hundred percent ready to have sex with the guy. Even though I knew he was a lying, skeevy traitor who planned to send Loring after people I cared about. I would have followed through and enjoyed every minute of it. Or at least enjoyed that Donovan would hate every moment of it. Nothing else had mattered.

Gut heavy and nauseous at the thought of my time with Jordan, I tried to stand and pace, my body needing to move. I was too overwhelmed to sit still to let Evelyn check me over.

My heart pounded, my ribs ached, and my head spun with faintness. I knew this feeling. I recognized the panic rolling through my body. My panic? Donovan's? Probably the both of us and it was gaining too much control. Sweat dripped down my back. If I'd been alone, I would've ripped my shirt off. Dry heaves took over a couple of times, but I muscled down the impulse and kept pacing.

"What's the matter, Firefly?" Olive asked.

"I don't know."

"Could it be Donovan?" Serena asked.

I nodded and closed my eyes, trying to breathe through waves of dizziness.

Why wasn't he angry? With everything that happened, I would have bet he'd be steaming with rage and demanding answers. I didn't feel the metal pole in my hands when I stuck Donovan with it like a pig. Not completely, anyway. I remember wanting to kill him. Or thinking he deserved to die? It was all mashed up in my brain.

Judging by how I felt, it wasn't a long shot to assume Donovan succeeded in healing our Soul Magic, and if so, maybe for good this time. But how did he do it? I remembered being furious and in pain but everything else was in disconnected snapshots.

Evelyn muscled me to one of the beds again and put a cold cloth on my forehead. For what felt like a long time everyone stood around in the room that had a giant hole in the wall from where they broke through and talked in low voices. Some I managed to throw apologies at if they came around the bed. Nothing I said was enough. Deeper conversations were needed if I hoped to repair anything at all.

I pointed out Kim's new bracelet. "Not quite your normal style, but I like it."

She looked down at it and then fiddled with the leather strap. "Thanks. Me too."

"Whoa. Whatever caused that expression comes with a story. Share time once I get my head right long enough to absorb some of your sunshine?"

She giggled. "Sure thing."

I stayed on the bed, trying to wrestle my thoughts and memories together to find sense in it all while Kim and the others either helped with the debris or chatted about what happened.

Some discreetly stared. Probably worried I might revert to whatever state that was. Was I different now? I was cold, probably because of Donovan, but I wasn't angry. My frustrated desire for vengeance, to do something about my anger, was all-consuming with the broken Soul Magic. I had questioned my every thought and scrutinized other's motivations. My worst-case scenario suspicions always won. Even in the mess of confusion with what happened and of the emotions railing through the connection, my thoughts were far clearer by comparison. Nothing like when Nya rode my vessel, but a murkiness was lifted. Now I had visual confirmation of the things I saw instead of guessing at the shapes and intentions of what was beyond the haze.

"I told you so." Vincent leaned against the doorjamb, the smile on his face had me belly laughing until I remembered how I treated him for the last while.

That smile of his dropped and he straightened in concern.

Filled with the impulse to do so, I ran for him, and then threw my arms around his strong shoulders. "I'm so sorry. I should've never—"

"Stop, Sophie. Stop." Vincent laughed again, pulled back to look me in the eyes. "Donovan told me what happened. Your Soul Magic is repaired. Nothing else matters."

"Your Soul Magic is fixed?" Kim yelled from the other side of the room then squealed in happiness and bopped on her toes. She added a giddy punch to Serena's forearm.

My cousin flinched and punched back.

"Was that what Donovan did, Firefly?" Olive asked.

I half-shrugged, half-nodded, and couldn't help the tears blurring my vision. "If Donovan told Vincent that's what he did, then I guess that's what he did."

I swiped some fallen tears off of my cheeks.

Vincent rubbed my arm. "Nothing was your fault."

"It all feels like my fault." My voice caught.

I wanted to believe him, but no part of me did.

"Thanks for not letting me kill anyone." A memory hit of the Magic outside of the Ballard Family Estate that I attacked and turned to dust. "Well, no one I loved anyway." That heaviness in my stomach kicked up a few notches. Damn, I killed that guy like his life didn't matter.

A lot of people were due heartfelt apologies, but I couldn't help but think of Donovan and how he took off.

"You can find him in his cell. Untethered, but processing, as they say." Vincent added quietly, "It has been some time since he has seen the true you."

The true me?

I hadn't thought about it like that. Had I really been someone else? Not completely.

"I..." I looked from him to the others amid the chaos, the room still covered in medical equipment, traditional and non-traditional supplies from the smallpox treatments.

"I will provide them with an explanation. The rest is maintenance a few spells can rectify. Go to him. You have ample time to catch up."

I didn't want to add bailing on my family to the list of shit to apologise for, but let's be honest, one more thing wouldn't make a difference. I needed to check on Donovan and connect the cascade of emotions running through our connection to the man and what they meant. Until I had better understanding, I couldn't focus on which family member needed what from me.

I rushed off to the cell console, ignoring concerned stares at my dishevelled and bloodied clothing. There wasn't enough time to think of what I should say once I found him. I got tripped up by the Tactical Team who were with a small group of suits I didn't recognize. When Caine told one to take two steps forward, I understood they were not going to have the same open-cell policy as the rest of us.

Hall disappeared with one prisoner and Caine waited with the remainder.

Caine noticed me waiting in line. "This is gonna take a minute."

"No worries."

His thick brows clenched together so fast they could have caught a fly. He then scanned my blood-covered threads. "You okay?"

I laughed. "Was I that much of a raging bitch?"

"Was?"

I shrugged. "Donovan fixed the Soul Magic."

"No way!" He left his prisoners to bear hug me. "I mean, the smallpox is obviously gone, but the Soul Magic is fixed too?"

"I know. Finally. And, hey, I'm really sorry. I was horrendous, and you were truly amazing. I appreciate you letting me fall apart on you."

He shrugged one shoulder. "You've saved my ass more than once. I'd rather you not go all broken Soul Magic again, but damn. I can't believe he did it."

Hall returned from a cell. "Who did what?"

Caine updated him.

"Finally. The guy must be flying."

"Not exactly. I was trying to find him—Whoa!" I up-and-downed the guy. "Caveman... What the fuck happened to your immortality?" Seeing people's souls came with the bloodline, but yesterday I may have only tracked the change if it made an impact on my life. With the Soul Magic fixed, the difference was glaring. I should've noticed immediately.

The smirk on Caine's face told me nothing.

Caveman hooked his thumbs into his tactical vest. "Being Kim's Verndari came with some changes in the lifespan department."

"Verndari? Is that like a yoga instructor?"

Caine laughed.

Damn, something else I missed. "You know what, I promise I'll do the rounds for simultaneous updates ASAP, yeah? Oh, and thanks for playing referee. The fact you didn't kill us is a testament to your endurance."

"More like survival." He crossed his beefy arms. "You think Lewy or Rosemary would've let me take you two out? Next time, I'm ending you both."

"It happens again and you have full permission to take us out. I'll let Vincent know you get dibs."

Caveman and Caine smiled with something like sympathy in their expressions.

I itched at dried blood on my arm and pointed at the people in expensive suits waiting at the cell console clearly without their free will. "Bad guys?"

Caine wasn't even paying attention to them, and they still did what he wanted.

"Sovereignty board members who refused the deal of a lifetime." Caine stepped aside. "Go ahead of us. They can wait all day."

"Well, I can't," Caveman complained. "Need to check on Kim."

"Last I saw she was fine. None of this blood is hers, I don't think."

Caveman completely stilled, searching my face with uncomfortable intensity.

"Just go ahead," Caine waved me forward again.

While I was punching in the information for Donovan's cell, Caine was reassuring Caveman that Kim was probably fine, but he had things handled if Caveman wanted to go check on her. Caveman argued he had a job to do, but sounded like he would rather find Kim.

Damn. Kim had her hooks in the man.

Compared to the perpetually noisy lobby, silence punctuated the already mute cell. Loud breathing would have been nice, but I heard nothing when I looked across the small space at Donovan sitting on the bed with his back against the wall. From his profile, all I saw was his knees up with his hands in his hair and the drying blood of his injuries streaked down his forearms.

Now what? He was so in his head he hadn't realized I came through.

"I'm sorry," I said without sitting in case he kicked me out. It wouldn't be anything less than I deserved.

Donovan's head dropped into his arms, obscuring his profile even more, and he still didn't say anything. His emotions weren't hidden from me, but they were bouncing everywhere. Taking his lack of anger as a good sign, above the fact he wouldn't look at me, I braved a potential outburst by sitting on the bed next to him.

"I'm really, really sorry. I put you through—"

"I didn't think I'd find you again."

This tripped me up and I felt a lump in my throat. I didn't know who it belonged to. "You always promised to keep trying."

He shook his head. "I gave up many times."

"I didn't make it easy."

Quiet fell again until he finally looked at me. His dark eyes locked on mine, both of us searching for something. I remained quiet, letting him dig through whatever words he was trying to find.

"Shit," he mumbled and put his head back against the wall, pressing his fingers into his eyelids.

So much went down between us. I didn't want him to hide from me. I wound my hands around his elbow resting on his bent knee, and laid my head on his arm. He then shifted us to wrap his arm around me, pulled me in close, and kissed my crown.

Neither of us could formulate the right words so we opted out of conversation and held each other instead. This brand of communication we understood. With the tether between us, the emotions we felt swam to the surface, saying everything we couldn't form sentences for until we slid down next to each other on the small bed.

When Donovan shifted, I opened my eyes and realized we had fallen asleep.

He closed the gap between our lips. I sank into a soft kiss that held no urgency or impatience to move on to anything more naked. The sense of contentment spread and simmered between our souls in much the same way as lying next to each other all night. Or for however long we had been in this bed together.

When we ended the kiss, Donovan laughed and rubbed his eyes. "Shit."

I shifted my head on the thin pillow. "What?"

He reclosed the inch of space between us, my head now resting on his shoulder. A smooth tactic so I couldn't see his face.

"I was so scared I'd fix the Soul Magic and you'd still hate me."

"Nah, can't stay mad at those dimples for long."

A laugh rumbled through his chest and his dimples deepened.

Tense quiet bloomed. I could tell he wanted to say something, and I fought against the need to tell him to spit it out already.

"I wouldn't have been with them—"

"I know." I stopped him, understanding he was speaking about his part in the Conception Rituals. "I do remember that small win against whatever that was before shit went sideways again. I couldn't see things in full at the time, of course. Tobias forced that on you. But still, I chose to be with Jordan and would have slept with him if you hadn't busted in. Thanks for the cock-block by the way."

"Ugh, Jordan." He exhaled. "Jordan meant nothing."

Things went quiet again. Sure, Jordan was nothing to me now, but he was a symptom of something big between us.

Afraid to see his face, I kept him close as he did with me. "Can we move on from this? I don't mean pretending nothing happened, but as far as you and me... How do we move forward?"

"Call a mulligan?"

"A mulligan?"

We both laughed like we couldn't help it.

"I have zero experience at this, babe." Hearing him call me that made my heart swell. "I think we just do. We realize we were bastards to each other while we were desperate to squeeze out from under something we didn't understand. Realize that what escaped the Soul Magic fracture took over and poisoned your memories, thoughts, and actions.

"I don't understand why there's some kind of monster or entity within our Soul Magic. Whatever the reason, nothing after my father's cells was all you. You don't need to apologize for anything. You might want to say sorry to a few others who won't understand the gravity of broken Soul Magic, but you and I are good."

He kissed my forehead and relief relaxed my shoulders.

"Actually..." He kissed my forehead again. "I have something for you."

I laughed as he straddled over me to get off of the bed. "I'm sure you do."

He paused with one foot on the ground, still above me. "Keep that saucy brain of yours occupied for two seconds."

The fact my mind went there was testament to how differently I was thinking with the Soul Magic fixed.

Donovan rummaged around a backpack and pulled out a dark green velvet pouch and sat on the side of the bed. "This is for you. For us."

I sat up. "When'd you have time to shop?"

He made a throaty noise. "Never. It's from Fox. He feels indebted to me for solving his failing magic issue and has spent his time in hiding doing some metal working."

Inside of the pouch was a wooden, hand-crafted and carved, rectangular box and another smaller square one. I didn't know if the design meant something or if it was just a stylistic choice, but it was beautifully done.

"This one's for me," he said and took the smaller box with a small shake in his hand.

Borrowed anticipation tingled in my chest. "Whoa. Why are your insides buzzing? You're freaking me out."

He laughed an awkward laugh, re-enforcing my anxiousness. "I wanted to give it to you the moment he finished them, but there wasn't a good time with us.... Just open it and I'll explain."

For someone so self-assured, seeing him nervously await my reaction to whatever Fox made us was unsettling and endearing.

I lifted the lid of the hinged box and found a necklace nestled onto green velvet matching the pouch. "*Ohmyword.* It's flippin' gorgeous."

The cell's overhead lights glinted off of the silver chain and charm with what I was pretty sure was a smoky quartz gemstone in the center of a triquetra. Something was inscribed into the knotted shape of the symbol. Latin? No, the Theban alphabet. I recognized it as the same letters from Aunt Lacey's old grimoire as well as from some of her clothing when I first joined her Sect.

"Yeah, they are." He turned his open box for me to see inside.

On more soft green velvet was a leather braided bracelet with an identical triquetra symbol. Not dangling from the leather, but set onto it so it wouldn't get knocked around.

"What do they say, polyglot?"

Donovan's dimples caved with his soft smile. He traced each of the lines of the triquetra with his finger, reciting the words I couldn't begin to decipher. "Two souls travel the same path. Collide with unending love. Nothing shall come between them."

"Wow." I fought gathering tears. "Fox really is a softy for a tatted-up biker."

"That he is." The introspective way he said this and the renewed anticipation wiggling around in his gut caught my attention.

"And..." I asked.

Those dark eyes of his flipped to mine.

I raised a brow, waiting for him to say whatever he held onto.

"They *are* beautiful." He took my necklace from its resting place, clasped it around my neck, and swept my hair out of the way. His fingertips lingered on my skin.

"And..." I prompted again.

He chuckled low. Another beat passed. "Firstly, it's not just a sex thing."

"Not just a sex thing, but is still a sex thing? Does the necklace give us god-like stamina?"

"No, but without being blinded by my psychometry, I'll be able to concentrate a little better." Sensing my continued confusion, he went on. "Fox found a way to harness the concoction he created when he did our tattoos."

"In these?" I felt the raw smoky quartz under my fingers and thought about the psychometry-dampening result of the concoction all that time ago. It blocked Donovan's visions whenever he touched me for many hours after Fox did the tattoo.

He nodded slowly. "It doesn't touch our Soul Magic. Everything there remains the same. And it won't work if I have physical contact with other people or things, but I won't be blinded when I touch you anymore." He ran his fingers down my arm until he reached my fingers and intertwined them with mine. "Moot point in here since the cells dull my visions either way. The real test is out there. When I can actually hold your hand without losing you."

He lightly squeezed my fingers and lifted them to kiss my knuckles one-by-one.

I couldn't imagine keeping a permanent safe distance from the person you loved. I could do without the touchy-feeliness of some boundaryless people. To not be able to reach out and hold someone or have them hold you without consequence was isolating. Even for an introvert. Which he may have never been without his power and the way he was raised.

I helped Donovan put on his bracelet. The braided leather matched the other one he never took off and made me wonder if maybe Fox crafted that one as well.

"Do you want to try them out?" I asked him.

He groaned, grabbed a hold of me, and pulled me down on the bed to lie next to him. "I'd rather stay in bed with you for a month, but we've been off the playing field for a bit." He kissed my forehead and squeezed me tightly. He was filled with a happiness reflected in me. "Probably an update or two we've missed."

I moved up on my elbow to ran my fingers over his hair. Between Jordan's illness and the fight, his usual casual style was a greasy mess. "Can they wait until after we shower?"

"We?" He opened his eyes from soaking in the contact once he registered what I said.

"Unless you're suddenly into unwashed crevices full of dried pox-juice and blood. I don't kink shame, but it's difficult to re-invent when your in the mood for it. Pox-juice is a tad difficult to come by. Or not...if you're into it." I rolled off of the bed.

Donovan's dark stare followed as I pushed my pants and underwear over my hips and down my thighs. "Are you sure?"

"Yup." I wiggled and stepped out of my clothes. "Things are crunchy."

He smiled, yet a thread of seriousness waded within his half-caved dimples. "You know what I mean."

"Up to you." I peeled off my stained and torn shirt and tossed it into a pile with my bottoms. "Our last shower was rather aerobic. So, if your energy isn't quite up to par..."

I stepped into the cinderblock shower space and turned on the water.

Hurried rustling above the sound of water lasted a couple of seconds and then Donovan's hands were on my hips. His bare chest pressed at my shoulders. His lips on the side of my neck. I leaned back against his hardness and earned a surge of desire through the connection.

I spun, wrapped my arms around his neck, and walked us backwards under the spray.

He dipped his head to press his lips to mine, and I moved onto my toes to deepen the kiss.

We let the hot water rinse away the grime of our illness, blood of our battle, and stress of our time apart.

I knew without the influence of the broken Soul Magic that I loved him. The Soul Magic itself may still be manipulating us, but right now, being in the Prison Creation cells meant Donovan's psychometry was neutralized and we could explore a reunion without our past blinding him. And as a bonus, once we left the cells, PDA was an option without assaulting him with visions.

This was a celebration of the many things we fought for and won. I wanted us to forget all of the lingering unanswered questions, including evil awaiting us on the outside of the Prison Creation, and reconnect in a way that made sense to us in this life.

31

SHARED EXISTENCE

Sophie

My jelly-like muscles were a puddle of limbs lying in bed with Donovan where we rested after our shower. No wall clocks or phones meant time didn't exist in the cell —unless someone was brave enough to sneak a peek and try to interrupt us. If they had, we never noticed.

Issát was out there. My ancestor...well, a Ballard ancestor. In my next life, I wouldn't know him or the Ballards. And now I didn't know my previous families either. Milicent's family, or all the ones I had no names for that Vincent quickly mentioned.

I should have sought those answers out by now. Something stopped me from learning about the people I was in each of those past lives and about the people I left behind. Donovan wasn't the only one beside me, others birthed me, raised me, confided in me, trusted me with their secrets, and maybe even knew mine. Technically, if they were also a Magic, they may still be out there, alive and fondly looking back at our time together every once in a while.

"What's on your brain?" Donovan asked, eyes closed, sensing my mind turning over.

I shifted a bit more towards him, enough he opened his eyes in worry of what I might say. "If I wanted to look into our past lives, where should I start?"

He blinked a couple of times, flooded by a dash of relief surrounding the topic. "The beginning? If you want a full history lesson, it would be less confusing if you worked chronologically. We've seen where our Soul Magic started with the ritual stone magic. What comes next is a mystery."

"What if we get trapped in unending seizures? We could die and no one would know."

"You think Vincent didn't plan for an emergency? The cell would trigger an alarm and warn whoever needs to know."

"Oh. That's actually comforting."

I stared at the blank ceiling, thoughts spinning, considering, and ultimately preparing.

"You ready?" I asked him.

The slight caving of his dimples answered for him. His roiling anticipation spoke even louder.

With a flick of energy, Donovan awakened the ritual stone magic, overriding the cell's defences. We closed our eyes, and I sank into our ancient power that started it all, riding it to a different time.

An iridescent light gathered weight in my hands as I fought to embrace it, to force the Soul Magic spell to look upon Betyn and me and grant us the lives we desired at each other's side.

Betyn's efforts to soothe me with his stare and steady presence were a silent balm which granted me the confidence to complete the spell.

Pressure closed in. I knew he sensed it, his head fallen back, allowing the power I wielded to work without struggling for breath or space, trusting it was a part of the spell and would culminate in all we planned for... A future, many futures, alongside each other without the need for any other to call lover and confidant.

More light spawned and I struggled to retain a sense of my hands. They grew heavy and numbed from the immense power between them.

Sensing the end, I called without words for Betyn. He peered through the blinding light to find me. We remained in captivated synchrony as our heart ceased to beat, the light failed, and the world around us fell away.

A whirl of energy whisked me from the grove of trees and the smell of wood smoke and tangy berries. Awareness of Betyn at my side flickered, others near, grander than us, assessing. Shifts of grey and black brightened to prisms of light and colour as if they catalogued our reactions. Betyn feared this for its unknown threat, the sense around us one of caution and questioning our presence.

No skin or bones kept us up, no feet to stand on. Collections of spirit were all we were. Floating. The scrutiny of the ambient consciousness roamed over our essences with questions, finding answers within our energies where no lies could hide and no bravado could lead astray.

Do I speak? Could I speak?

Betyn nudged me as if seeking solace in proximity.

The sensation of examination rolled over what was left of me in this place. What did it seek?

When it left me, Betyn's essence stiffened as if enduring his own inspection.

When I found the spell to stitch our souls together, it did not speak of this.

Light flickered again when the oppressive being left our sides.

What now?

"We will communicate in the language of your last iteration of life for ease of process," I heard all around me in a voice which held no specific accent, tone, or identity. The sound emanated from the collection of shifting light and then was accompanied by two others as if silently called forth to join the meeting.

"Do—"

"A conclusion does not require your input," another light source stated with a warning. "We have learned all information required from the imprints of your souls, displaying the choices which brought you to this plane and how our response may carry you forth if your requests are granted."

I remained quiet, safeguarding my arguments and drive to be heard while remaining exposed to these beings' analysis. Betyn sensed the calm with which I forced over me and mirrored the stance, both awaiting what was handed down from these presences.

The spell allowed this collective, nothing more. If they determined we did not meet their unspoken expectations, we would never gain their audience again, I was certain.

A snap of power shocked our surroundings. A vacuum of darkness grew from a shadowy spot into a slithering obsidian mass off to the side of the lighted beings.

Betyn and I shrank away in a huddle of energy.

"You have been granted a shared existence. Instead of a life of trials and sequences of unchoreographed events leading to enlightenment, your paths will meet when we see fit to cross them and then you will face a crucible of instances designed to test your bond. You lose, you die, and the paths are reset. You may meet an infinite number of times and never acquire the peace you have sacrificed your destinies as individuals for."

The dark form flew at us. Not an attack, as no altercation occurred. It flinched in action, split in two, and drove into our floating forms to mix with our light essences.

The sensation was an invasion like no other. The dark soldier of these light beings stretched within us until it explored all crevices and then remained, its stain a part of us.

No, it did not split as I thought. It may have opened its arms to welcome both my and Betyn's soul, but between us was an ethereal tendril of light and dark interlaced in a perpetual handshake. As soon as the darkness and light settled in that bridge, everything Betyn felt filtered to me as if we shared one knowledge.

"You have also been granted a guide. Another to show you the way. Another with their own destiny. Once you have bested and controlled that which now resides within you and gained enlightened understanding of the true sacrifices you have both made, you will no longer need an Overseer. You will not need to fear the swift and calculated decisions of the darkness causing death and a reset in life and of knowledge. You will have earned your shared existence and can live a full life as others do."

"How will we—"

"Failure to achieve perspicacity," the one being continued to speak over me, "will grant the darkness possession of your souls. Once they belong to the dark realms, your souls will no longer be ours to provide purpose and direction."

"Fuck!" I sat up in a rush of urgency, Donovan seated beside me. He had been watching as I soul read and saw the bargain we made and the entities we made them with.

"Were they the Fates?" I said from quivering lips.

"I-I think so."

"So, then was the dark thing a demon?"

Donovan ran his fingers through his hair and leaned to the side against the wall. "Fucked if I know. If not a demon in the way we think of demons, then close to it."

"It's inside of both of us." It nearly won. I almost lost this for the both of us.

"We won!" Donovan thrust his arms up into the air and then grappled me into a hug. "We did it!" He grabbed my face and planted a big kiss on my lips. "They said we would live shitty lives until we bested the dark beastie, and we did." He laughed again and collapsed back onto his thin pillow.

He was right. The Fates, or whoever they were, laid out the rules and while we screwed the pooch in countless other lives, we figured it out in this one. With Vincent's help, we managed to get there eventually.

"Shit." I grabbed his wrist to still his hand rubbing my arm.

"What?"

I thought about the words the Fates used. "Vincent."

Donovan's brows creased trying to gain my meaning in mentioning his name.

"How do we tell Vincent that this is the last lifetime where we'll see him?"

Donovan opened his mouth to say something, but he didn't find the words. While their relationship was more contentious than Vincent's and mine, they still cared about each other. And there was a host of lives I never looked into yet that may show them during friendlier interactions.

I laid next to him with my new necklace cold against my fingers between us. He slung his arm over me, holding on with excited relief he knew I also felt, even if it was tampered by the thought of losing Vincent.

No matter if I found Vincent or not, in future lifetimes Donovan would be here next to me like this. Vincent would find solace in knowing he did a good job and fulfilled this part of his own journey. He wouldn't fault our happiness for finding each other and never having to experience the shortened lifespan ending in his own heartbreak.

After Vincent was tied to our perpetual drama, it would be good for him to live for himself, but I still felt it as a loss for future versions of me, even if she wouldn't technically need his guidance.

Of course, the Fates didn't promise us an easy life, but one where the difficult factor of our love working against us wouldn't exist.

For now, in this life, no matter how long it lasted, Donovan and I could lean on each other with our whole hearts, without worry or questioning our commitment. We earned this life and the future ones we gambled to win hundreds of years ago.

My only hope now was for us to be able to focus beyond our relationship victory and live long enough in this life to see Loring fall or personally induct him into the Prison Creation cells where he and all of his devotees deserved to rot.

Donovan sensed my mind running all over the place. He moved my hair behind my ear to gain my attention and soothe my worry to better soak in the win of our Soul Magic.

We were never ones for much luck, but after winning our shared existence, everything about our future had changed.

He pressed his lips to mine with such softness I melted into the kiss, excited and grateful to do this for countless lifetimes.

ABOUT THE AUTHOR

S.J. Cairns creates paranormal romance fantasy from her hometown in Southern Ontario, Canada. When S.J. is not plugging away at her laptop on her comfy couch, you can find her chasing around her six-year-old daughter alongside her husband of over twenty years or working in true chaos with human trafficking survivors.

Website: www.sjcairns.com
Facebook: www.facebook.com/SJCairnsauthor
TikTok: www.tiktok.com/@sjcairnsauthor
Email: samijocairns@gmail.com

www.ingramcontent.com/pod-product-compliance
Lightning Source LLC
LaVergne TN
LVHW010636110826
845149LV00014B/2852

* 9 7 8 1 9 9 8 8 7 5 0 2 3 *